WHAT SHE LOST

WHAT SHE LOST

Melissa W. Hunter

cennan

PUBLISHED BY Cennan Books
an imprint of Cynren Press
101 Lindenwood Drive, Suite 225
Malvern, PA 19355 USA
http://www.cynren.com/

Printed in the United States of America on acid-free paper

ISBN-13: 978-1-947976-15-3 (pbk)
ISBN-13: 978-1-947976-16-0 (ebk)

Library of Congress Control Number: 2019930314

This is a fictionalized account of true events. The author
has re-created events, locales, and conversations from the
narrator's memories of them, as related to the author. To
maintain their anonymity, in some instances, the author has
changed the names of individuals and places, and she may
have changed some identifying characteristics and details,
such as physical properties, occupations, and places of
residence.

COVER DESIGN BY Tim Barber

L'dor v'dor
From generation to generation

Prologue

Columbus, Ohio, September 1982

The approach to Harding Hospital, north of Columbus, Ohio, is pleasant. Just off the highway, a long stretch of tree-lined pavement leads to the institution where my grandmother now lives. Her single room is housed in a two-story clapboard building surrounded by sycamores, oaks, and evergreens. Walking paths weave through clusters of mature trees, branching off to a cafeteria, a recreation and arts center, doctors' offices, and other residential buildings. Gardens with fountains and wrought iron benches are situated just off the main path, giving the grounds a parklike setting.

I sit beside my father in the passenger seat of his Audi, the window open, my hand rising and falling on currents of crisp autumn air. My father had been an aerospace engineer. He had once explained to me about lift and thrust and the speed of a moving vehicle, using scientific terms to explain why my hand, like an airplane, glides on the air outside the open window. He tried to calm my fear of flying the way he comforted me about everything, providing rational explanations and applying logic. Now, as I glance at him, I wonder what rationalization he could give to explain my grandmother.

My mother had stayed home with my little brother Josh. He doesn't understand why my grandmother acts the way she does, and he refuses to see her. But I have other memories of my grandmother, memories from before my grandfather passed away. I remember her humming as she prepared Shabbat dinner, scolding her little poodle Heidi when she nipped at my toes. I remember the perfectly buttered grilled cheese sandwiches that she cut into triangles for me after Sunday school when I went to my grandparents' house to change into my soccer uniform. I remember her warm, plump hands, her soft fingertips tracing circles on my arm whenever I sat beside her. I remember counting her rows of perfume bottles as I sat on her vanity stool in her very pink bathroom and she braided my hair. I remember sinking into bubbles in her large pink tub surrounded by curtains, imagining I was a princess.

But everything changed after my grandfather died.

As my father shuts off the ignition, he turns to me and says, "Remember, sweetie, your grandmother might not seem happy to see us. But it will be good for her to know we are here." I nod and take the hand he offers me.

The air smells of autumn as we walk to my grandmother's room. The scent of soil, earthy and damp, combines with a hint of burning leaves. Rose bushes line the path, blossoms burgeoning in a rush of late Indian summer bloom. But the moment we step into the dim hall, I am aware of a different smell, one I would come to identify as institutional and sterile. I squint into the shadows, waiting for my eyes to adjust. My father takes my hand and we walk halfway down the hall, stopping before a faded green door with a nameplate beside it that reads "S. Werthaiser." My father knocks gently. "Mom," he says, "it's us." He doesn't wait for an answer, turning the knob as he speaks.

We step into the room, and I immediately see my grandmother sitting, motionless, on a plastic chair in the corner. She is a hollow shell of a woman. Her face, once meticulously made up with powder, blush, and lipstick, looks pale and drawn. Her cheeks are sunken, and her brown eyes appear cloudy and unfocused. I step behind my father, grasping his hand tightly as he walks to her. He gives me a reassuring squeeze.

"Mom? How are you?" he asks.

She nods vaguely, then turns her face away.

"Look, Mom. I've brought Melissa with me. We came to take you for a walk."

Again, my grandmother nods, but it is a vacant gesture. Her eyes skirt the room as though she is searching for something. My father kneels beside her, taking one of her plump hands in his. "It's a beautiful day," he says. "Why don't we get some exercise? We can go to the cafeteria, get a bite?"

"The food here is awful," she responds. Her voice comes out hoarse, her thick eastern European accent noticeably husky.

"It's not that bad," my father says in the cajoling tone he sometimes uses with my brother and me when we are being stubborn.

"I hate it here," my grandmother says in a near-whisper. I inspect the room. It is not awful, but it isn't particularly welcoming either. The walls are cement bricks painted a pale yellow. Her bed sits in a corner, covered with a thin green blanket, a pillow propped against the nondescript wooden headboard. Next to the bed is a chipped nightstand holding one of the few personal belongings in the room: a picture of my grandfather. A threadbare rug lies on the cold linoleum floor, a simple wooden dresser stands against one wall, and next to the chair where my grandmother sits is a four-paned window framed by two thin curtains. The bright autumn leaves outside her window are a stark contrast to the muted tones in the room.

"Mom," my father begins, exasperation creeping into his voice.

"What do I do?" my grandmother interrupts, looking over my father's shoulder. "Esther, what do I do?"

I frown and glance behind us at the door to the room. No one is there.

"Mom?" my dad asks, trying to meet her eye.

"Esther, I don't know what to do," she says again.

"Daddy," I whisper, "who is Esther?"

My father says with a frown, "I have no idea."

Part I
BEFORE

One

Olkusz, Poland, spring 1938

I knew all too well why my parents were dressed as they were.

My mother was wearing her best scarf. She kept the scarf carefully folded in a drawer in her bureau, only pulling it out for holidays, weddings, or the occasional funeral. The drawer was a small treasure chest, holding every cherished item in my mother's life: the cloth her own mother had embroidered that covered our Friday night *challah,* the ivory pin she had inherited from her aunt, her few mismatched pieces of china, the knitted shawl she had made from the expensive yarn my father once bought her, her single strand of pearls. Her scarf was neatly pressed and preserved in the drawer between two sheets of tissue wrapped in newspaper. My mother didn't read, and we only read Polish or Yiddish. This newspaper was in German.

It was unusual to see the scarf on my mother's head in the middle of the week. I should have known at that moment, as I watched from behind the curtain that separated my small alcove from the rest of the apartment, that this was a premonition. She was dressed in what I knew to be traveling clothes. My father, for once, was not wearing his work trousers and apron with his sleeves rolled up to his elbows. That day, he wore a pair of weathered boots and a long black coat, his beard neatly trimmed, a fur-brimmed hat covering his *kepah.*

Tears gathered in my eyes as I watched them collect their few bags. My mother's hands worked nervously as she looked around for anything she might have forgotten. Behind me, on our shared mattress, lay my sister Esther. Her face was white and her breathing labored. Over the past few weeks, her complexion had grown increasingly sallow, so that her beautiful brown eyes looked too large in her gaunt face. We had watched helplessly as her energy drained a little each day. Now she didn't even have the strength to lift her head from her pillow. She was sick, yet without the usual symptoms. She did not have a cold or cough or complain of a sore throat or upset stomach. It was a mystery to everyone. She had random aches and pains that sometimes woke her in the night, fevers that spiked at any hour, and as she had grown weaker, her appetite had waned. Every remedy my mother procured was useless.

I turned to look at her. Her eyes were closed, but sensing my gaze, she opened them and gave a faint smile. "Don't worry, Sarah. I'll be back soon," she whispered. "You should enjoy having the bed to yourself."

"No, Esther," I replied in a choked voice, moving to her side and reaching for her hand. "I won't enjoy it. Who will I talk to at night? I'll be lonely without you."

"No, you won't," she wheezed in a voice that barely escaped her dry lips. "You always complain that I kick too much."

My parents were standing behind me now. My father rested his hand on my shoulder and gave a gentle squeeze. I nodded, swallowing over the lump in my throat and moving aside as my father lifted Esther in his strong arms. I followed them into the adjoining room, where my brothers waited. They were standing in a line beside the door, their concerned expressions mirroring my own. Jacob and Sam were almost the same height, although Jacob, at seventeen, had dark hair growing along his jawline and upper lip, while Sam, at fifteen, still had the smooth face of youth. Isaac was slightly younger than me and stood just off to the side, staring down at his feet. David and Majer, the five-year-old twins, ran to my side as I joined them.

Esther was small and fragile in my father's embrace. As they passed us, I reached for her hand once more, not wanting to let go.

"We'll send word at the post office," my father said. "Jacob, you're in charge while we're gone."

Jacob nodded and stood taller. "Yes, Papa," he said.

"You'll have your meals with your aunt and uncle," my mother continued. "Aunt Leah will be here to see you off to school each day. If you need anything at all, they are just upstairs."

We all nodded silently.

"Good-bye, *meyn kinder*," my mother said, leaning to kiss each one of us on the cheek. Mr. Geller, one of our few neighbors who owned a car, had offered to drive my parents to the train station. They would continue from there to Krakow and the hospital our small town of Olkusz lacked. Our local doctor had finally admitted to my mother, after numerous visits to our home, that he was baffled by Esther's condition and had done everything he could. My parents now hoped, as we all did, that the more experienced city doctors would have the answers to help my sister.

Mr. Geller stood beside his car, cap in hand, as my parents walked to meet him. I ran out the door and onto the path, a feeling of deep panic turning my stomach. I was only twelve and still needed my parents. This was the first time I had ever been left at home without them.

My father gently set my sister in the back seat of the car, and my mother slid in beside her, resting Esther's head in her lap. My father then turned to shake Mr. Geller's hand and stepped around the car to the passenger seat. As the car pulled away, my mother looked out the window and waved at us. My brothers stood behind me and waved back, but I only stared after them, feeling an awful sadness. I didn't know if I'd see my sister again.

I'd first noticed something was wrong a few weeks earlier, when Esther was setting the table for supper. I had been sweeping the floor in the corner and jumped when I heard the crash of a plate. Both my mother and I turned in surprise. Esther was staring down at the broken fragments, her eyes wide, her hands covering her mouth. After a moment, my mother knelt before her and started to gather the pieces.

"Sarah, hand me the broom," she said. I obeyed, but I'd noticed something that my mother hadn't—Esther's hand was shaking. She gripped her left hand in her right, desperately trying to stop the movement. I could see the guilt on her face. We had so little money, and to provide enough place settings for a family of nine was not cheap. Now we would have to replace the broken plate.

"I'm sorry, Mama," she whispered, and her voice shook along with her hand. My mother was a soft-spoken woman, and while she could be strict, she knew an accident when she saw one. Instead of scolding my sister, she simply replied, "Nothing to fret over. It must have slipped from your hands." Then she glanced up. I think she was surprised that Esther still stood there instead of bending to help collect the broken pieces. My mother opened her mouth again, perhaps to ask for help, but then her eyes rested on the unmistakable trembling of Esther's hand. A little too hurriedly, my sister clasped her hands behind her back.

Another moment passed before my mother said, "Perhaps you're tired, no? Why don't you go rest a bit, and then join me before your father and brothers return home. I'll need some help peeling the potatoes."

"Yes, Mama," Esther said, backing away, the muscles in her cheeks going slack as she unclenched her jaw. She disappeared behind the curtain into our alcove. "Sarah, please finish setting the table, and then you can continue your chores," my mother said, turning to me.

I opened my mouth to argue. It wasn't fair! Now I had twice the work! But I could see my mother's brow furrow in concern as she continued to gather the shards of broken plate into the skirt of her apron. I frowned at the injustice of the situation and continued my work in sulky silence.

When I was finished, I walked into the alcove, pulling the curtain closed behind me. It was a small space my sister and I shared. There was one window high in the wall that let in the late afternoon light. At night, we would lie next to each other and look up at the stars through the thick pane of glass, gossiping or telling each other stories and laughing until our sides hurt. Our mattress was tucked into a corner, topped with a featherbed and wool blanket. Tacked to the wall above our pillows were pictures we had drawn over the years, notes our friends had written us, school notices, and the academic ribbons Esther had received for handwriting and etiquette and I had received for mathematics. A small writing desk passed down from my father's brother stood in the other corner with our schoolwork spread on top.

Esther was lying on her side, facing the wall, when I entered. My annoyance simmered and I asked, "What happened? What's wrong with you?"

She sighed and rolled over. When I saw her face, I immediately felt remorse for my harsh tone. Esther still cradled her arm against her chest, although her hand had stopped trembling. Her cheeks were pale as her bloodshot eyes fixed on my face, and she looked frightened.

"I don't know. I just—I don't feel right," Esther muttered.

"Well, what's bothering you? Are you sick?" I asked, sitting beside her. I reached for her hand. It felt cold and clammy in my palm.

"I felt tired and faint all of a sudden. I can't really explain it. My head went all fuzzy and my arms felt weak. I thought I was going to fall, and when I reached out to grab the table, I dropped the plate. My hand was shaking and I couldn't stop it. Do you think Mama noticed?"

"No," I lied, hoping to make her feel better. "Besides," I added as I lay beside her so our heads were next to each other on her pillow, "you're probably just tired. You didn't sleep well last night."

"I didn't?" she asked, glancing at me. She frowned and bit her lip.

"It's nothing," I insisted. "You were talking in your sleep again. That's all."

Esther often talked in her sleep. It was a fact I found both irritating and amusing. Some nights, I'd kick her softly to stop her murmuring, and other nights I'd prop myself on my elbow and watch her in the moonlight, her eyes closed and moving beneath the lids as she dreamed, furtively listening for whatever secrets she might reveal.

"Anyway," I said, sitting up again and reaching for my homework, "you got out of setting the table. I had to do it."

Two

A low, distant thunder pulled me from sleep a few nights after Esther dropped the plate. Rain clouds concealed the moon, so our alcove was unusually dark. I was disoriented as I lay quietly blinking at the wall. I heard a soft sigh and rolled over to glance at my sister. She was lying on her back with her arm thrown over her eyes, her chest rising and falling with even breaths. But her lips were slowly moving. Bemused, I leaned closer, trying to figure out what she was whispering. More often than not, her words were a jumble of nonsense, but tonight she kept repeating a name—Aaron. I frowned, trying to make sense of what she was saying. She gave a small laugh, said Aaron's name again, mumbled, "We'll see tomorrow," and rolled over, her back to me.

I lay back against my pillow, watching rain-drenched shadows ripple across the ceiling. The only Aaron I knew was the boy who went around town delivering groceries in his rickety wooden cart. His cap always lay askew on his head, and to me, he was gangly and awkward. I never so much as glanced at him. His fair hair curled delicately against his freckled face. His soft blue eyes were almost a dull gray in color. Because of his slight frame, he was always panting and sweaty while pushing his wagon. I wondered why Esther was dreaming about him, of all people. Then, with a start, I remembered how Esther had smiled to herself and smoothed her long skirt and dark hair when my mother had asked her to search him out in town to place an order earlier that day.

Does she like him? I thought incredulously. They were both eighteen, but he seemed much younger. Jacob sometimes mentioned that it was a shame Aaron didn't attend the *yeshiva,* the religious school for boys, because he was smart and inquisitive. But he was apprenticed to Mr. Abrams, the town grocer. Did that mean he would make a good living for himself? Would Mama and Papa think him a suitable match for Esther? Excited thoughts kept me from falling back to sleep, and I giggled into my pillow.

The notion stuck in my mind for the remainder of the week. I attempted to mention him casually to Esther when we ran errands together or hung the laundry out to dry or washed the twins in the barrel that served as our tub.

"Did you know that Mr. Abrams is selling more cabbage this year than last? That's what Mama said. It must have been a good season, and Mama's happy because she can make cabbage stew more often. In fact, I think I saw cabbage heads on Aaron's cart the other day."

I'd watch her face for the slightest change. Esther's face was smooth as silk, and her mouth could display the simplest message with a twist or a frown. Now, she smiled and gazed down at her feet, and I thought, *Ah-ha! It's true! She does like him!*

I was proud of myself for putting the pieces together, but like any pesky younger sister, I kept mentioning him, until one day, on our way home from school, she turned on me.

"Will you please stop making fun of Aaron? He's very sweet!" she said in a flash of anger, a blush coloring her cheeks. I realized that I had, in fact, been poking fun at him. I'd laughed at how he constantly had to push his sleeves up to his elbows because his arms were so slim, and how he was always blowing his hair out of his eyes. "I know you may not think so," Esther continued, "but Aaron is kind and thoughtful. He's always giving me little presents, like an extra vegetable from his cart or even, the other day, a flower." Then, stopping herself from revealing more, she said, "Now, don't go telling Mama. And quit staring at me like that, Sarah. Come on. We're going to be late."

Presents! Well, it was easy to see why Aaron was so taken with my sister. Wherever we went, whispers followed Esther. In town, she was known as the *shayna maidela,* the "pretty girl." From the time she was an infant, her raven hair and striking porcelain complexion drew attention. I had heard the stories of how strangers stopped my mother on the street to peer into Esther's baby carriage. "Such a beautiful child!" they'd exclaimed. "Look at those eyes! And skin like a doll's—flawless!" Later, as Esther grew into a toddler and skipped alongside my mother, passersby would gaze after her, enthralled. When she looked up, her eyes were pools of black, so dark the pupils were lost. Long lashes brushed her cheeks. Her lips were rosebud red and pouted naturally. "Have you ever seen such beauty?" the townspeople remarked. "Like an angel."

My mother always scowled at them and spat three times into her hand, "*pu, pu, pu,*" or muttered "*keynahora*" after such comments. They were meant as compliments, but my mother believed they brought the evil eye upon Esther. I knew my mother was superstitious. Every day she performed small rituals and strange routines that were supposed to protect us and keep us out of harm's way. She took particular care with Esther. She had tied red ribbons to Esther's baby buggy to ward off evil and later tied red ribbons to the ends of Esther's braids.

Recently, I'd noticed how the town boys stared after my sister as we walked home from school, or even changed direction to follow close behind us. Her changing body was hard to hide, despite the long skirts and shawls she wore. I no longer teased Esther or chattered idly on our walks but instead watched every move she made, finding the way her hips swayed intriguing and the way her hair flowed straight down her back enviable. I wanted her dark hair, hair so dark it was almost black. My hair was lighter, like my mother's had been, but unlike my mother's, it still had too much red in it.

I hated my red hair and freckles, especially when the boys poked fun at me. My mother often told me that it would grow into the rich auburn locks hers had once been. After marrying my father, she had cropped her hair short, as was customary, and wore her head covered beneath a kerchief. But among her possessions was a single photograph taken in her youth. She would sit me on her lap and show me the sepia-toned image of a young girl with honey-colored eyes and thick hair spilling over her shoulders. "See," she would remark, gently brushing back my unruly mane. "Your sister looks like your papa with his dark hair and eyes, but you, you look like me." I would study the beautiful girl in the photograph, hoping breathlessly one day to look like my mother, but I didn't believe her.

I was used to being Esther's shadow, used to receiving everyone's polite, remembered nods after they'd addressed her. Lovely was often the way she was described. And I? Playful, willful, precocious, pretty for a young girl. Young girl! I would fume when I heard this. I was thirteen, after all!

Quietly, I observed the exchanges that became more frequent between Esther and Aaron. I noticed how Esther began watching for him in town, stopping on the street corners that were his known route or asking after his whereabouts from Mr. Abrams. More often than not, when they saw each other, my presence was quickly forgotten.

"I wish I could go to the university in Krakow or Warsaw," Aaron told her one time, while they huddled in a narrow alley behind the town's water tower. I sat on the street corner, drawing random patterns in the dirt with a stick and listening to their every word, though I feigned indifference. "I want to see more of Poland and Europe, maybe even America. But my mother and father won't hear of it. They think I shouldn't risk a future as a grocer for something unknown. Mr. Abrams is nice and all, but I feel restless delivering onions and turnips all day."

"Why, Aaron?" Esther asked. "You'll make a good living when you take over for Mr. Abrams. It's an honor he picked you. You'll be able to support a family. I've heard my mother say you'll make a fine match for someone. Isn't that the most important thing?"

"Important for us, you mean?" Aaron whispered.

I looked up at that. Esther's face flushed a bright red as she fixed her gaze on her shuffling feet. She bit her lip and whispered, "You shouldn't say such things. It's not right."

"What's not right?" Aaron asked. "To speak about our feelings?"

Esther put her hand to her mouth, *pu, pu, pu,* in perfect imitation of our mother. Aaron reached out and took her hands in his own. In a voice I strained to hear, he whispered, "Let me say a prayer for us, Esther. God will surely grant our union if I were to ask for your hand in marriage."

I breathlessly pretended not to hear. The moment felt suspended, frozen, as they stared into each other's eyes. But then Aaron stuck out his lower lip and blew the hair from his face, and the magic of the moment was broken. He noticed me for the first time. "Ah, Sarah, let me give you something," and he pulled from his basket a ripe apple. I eagerly took it, looking at Esther. She was embarrassed as she smoothed her skirt with her hands, but she smiled and nodded.

"Thank you, Aaron," I said. My approval of him increased in that moment, until he said, "A red apple, just like your hair."

I frowned and took a large bite, chewing loudly, irritably. But he didn't notice. He had turned back to Esther and was handing her an apple as well. "And red, like your lips," he said to her. Esther took the apple and placed it in her basket. She looked away shyly and said, "Come on, Sarah. It's time to go home."

As we walked back to our house, I kept glancing behind at Aaron, who stood by his cart watching after us. "Not a word of this to Mama and Papa, Sarah, understand?" Esther whispered, looking at me out of the corner of her eye. "Do you promise?"

I nodded. "Yes, Esther," I said. "I promise."

Three

Shortly after that, I began to notice a change in my sister. She always lagged behind on our way to school, arriving at the steps with a pale, clammy face and short of breath. It was early spring, and while her cheeks were usually sun-kissed and rosy, they now appeared pallid and gray. When I asked her what was wrong, she only shrugged. While she was subdued and quiet during the day, her nights were restless. She tossed and turned until she was twisted up in the sheets, leaving me shivering on the edge of the bed. Sometimes she'd wake herself gasping for breath, and other times I'd have to shake her awake to stop from being assaulted by her flailing arms and kicking legs. She'd contemplate me with red, puzzled eyes. "Why'd you do that, Sarah?" she'd wheeze.

"It's just . . . you were . . . oh, nothing," I'd sigh. "You were dreaming again."

I was afraid to tell her how agitated she seemed because I didn't want to upset her, but I suspected something was wrong. I felt an overwhelming sense of disquiet every morning when I watched her rise painfully from bed and try to blink back the look of exhaustion that lingered in her eyes.

"Are you all right?" I'd ask.

"I'm fine."

"You don't seem fine."

"I'm fine!"

"I think I should tell Mama."

"Quit being a busybody, Sarah!"

The memory of Esther's shaking hand was still fresh in my mind. I kept my silence, but guilt weighed heavily on my conscience. I worried that if I didn't tell my mother soon, something bad was going to happen. Each night, Esther's sleep was becoming more and more troubled. She moaned as if in pain. One morning, I waited until I was alone with my mother to tell her what was happening.

"Mama?" I asked, watching as my mother boiled water on the stove for the twins' bath. I heard their laughter in the yard outside as they chased a stray tomcat who liked to come begging for scraps. "Hmm?" my mother replied distractedly, wiping a hand across her forehead. The small counter of our kitchen was already crowded with pots and pans for that evening's Sabbath meal. Chopped onions and parsley lay beside the whole chicken my mother had been plucking. Steam rose from the pot on the stove, condensation fogging the glass window that looked out to our yard. I wanted to ask if she had sensed a change in Esther, but my mouth was dry. I swallowed and shuffled my feet instead.

"What is it, Sarah?" my mother asked impatiently, turning to glance at me. When she saw the look of concern on my face, she wiped her hands on her apron and knelt beside me.

"Mama," I said again, "I think something's wrong with Esther."

"What do you mean?" she asked, frowning.

"She doesn't sleep well at night. She tosses and turns. I don't think she feels well. Have you noticed, Mama?" My mother's face grew pensive and she stared at the wall over my head. She started nodding thoughtfully, and I wondered if she was just now realizing something was amiss.

"How long has this been happening?" she asked.

"A few weeks maybe?" I said, feeling even worse for not confiding in her sooner.

Laying a hand on my cheek, my mother smiled gently and said, "Don't worry yourself, Sarah. I'll take care of it." Her soft arms came around me in a hug, and I instantly felt better. I nestled into her embrace, inhaling her familiar scent of talcum powder and lye soap, and was comforted for the moment.

Although I felt a weight had been lifted, I was still worried about my sister. My parents became watchful. My mother sent Esther on fewer errands after school, which meant I had to do more. She told Esther to rest in bed or sent her outside to soak in the sun to bring some color back to her skin. Esther complained and was irritable when my mother confined her to the house. She claimed she was fine. I knew the real reason she wanted to leave—to see Aaron. Soon, she gave up trying to persuade my mother to let her go and asked me to be her messenger instead. She told me little confessions to repeat to him, how she missed seeing him on the street and kept the bouquet of wildflowers he'd given her pressed between her schoolbooks. I felt uncomfortable telling all this to Aaron, watching him squint and wipe at the perspiration on his brow, but I knew it was the least I could do for her.

Then one evening when I entered our alcove, I found Esther frantically combing out her long hair, pulling almost ruthlessly on the brush. "What's wrong, Esther?" I cried, running to her and taking the brush from her hand. "Don't do that!" Her nose was red, and a rash of small bumps stood out near the corner of her mouth. I frowned as I gently placed the brush on the bed and sat beside her. Usually so composed, her complexion so flawless, I was shocked by her appearance. She wiped at the corner of her nose and sniffed. I noticed that her arm was covered in bruises. "What happened?" I asked, taking her arm and pushing up her sleeve to get a better look. She wrenched her arm from my grasp.

"Why don't Mama and Papa let me out?" she cried. "Are they punishing me?"

"No, Esther," I said softly. "No, they're worried. You don't . . . seem like yourself lately."

"I'm fine!" she insisted again, but her flushed face and wild expression told a different story. "Did you see Aaron today, Sarah?" she asked. "What does he say to you? What does he tell you?"

I wanted to reassure her, to describe in perfect detail how he frowned when I said our mother was keeping her home to rest, how he searched my face and listened to my every word for some sign of affection from Esther, how he told me he missed her and hoped to see her soon. But before I could open my mouth, Esther's frenzied energy faded completely, and she closed her eyes, leaning against me heavily. "I guess I do feel a little strange," she admitted.

"Rest, Esther," I said, helping her lie back against the pillows. She blinked up at me as I brushed her hair from her forehead. Her skin felt warm. "Do you want a cool washcloth?" I asked, but she didn't answer. She seemed asleep already. I changed into my nightgown, then crept under the blankets beside her. I closed my eyes and felt myself shaking. Something was definitely wrong with my sister. I'd overheard my parents say that if she did not improve by the end of the month, they'd fetch the doctor again. I silently vowed to tell my mother the following morning not to wait.

My parents, particularly my mother, did not put much faith in doctors. She had her own remedies that had been passed down to her from her mother and grandmother. The women in town exchanged their secret recipes so that the entire community tended to take care of each other. My mother had given my sister most of the food and drink our neighbors said would help restore energy and revive the blood. Esther had taken long baths surrounded by certain flower blossoms. She had drunk tea infused with medicinal spices. I, however, felt nothing was working.

As I thought of these cures, I drifted into a troubled sleep. The blankets around me became large flower petals. I was trapped in their heat and strange scent, fighting against blossoms that seemed to suffocate when, all of a sudden, I was drenched in water. Someone was watering the flower, and I was reaching out, trying to escape the petals that enfolded me, the water that doused me, crying for them to stop, to help me.

Then I heard a horrible sound. It was animal-like and guttural. I sat upright in bed, startled, roused quickly out of the nightmare. I was momentarily relieved to find that the quilt I threw from my body was not the hungry flower petals of my dream. But the sound still reached my ears. It took me a moment to realize it was coming from Esther. She was groaning, low and deep, and the sound was terrible, like it was being wrenched from her throat.

"Esther," I whispered, turning to shake her awake. "Esther!" I repeated louder as I reached for the candle and match on the bedside table. The moment I lit the wick and turned to look at her, I gasped.

She was completely drenched in sweat. Her nightgown clung to her, as did the blankets that were twisted around her thrashing legs. Her head was tossing from side to side with each moan, and beads of perspiration stood out on her cheeks and forehead. Her lips were blue.

"Esther!" I cried again, planting my hands firmly beside her. I only half acknowledged that the whole bed was wet, that my nightgown was clinging to me as it had in the dream. I placed my hand on her forehead then withdrew it in shock. She was burning up.

"Oh, God, oh, God," I murmured, trying to shake her awake. I felt her fever emanating from her so that our whole alcove was filled with heat and smelled of sickness. Then she finally opened her eyes. I couldn't tell if she saw me or not. She started crying and moaned, "My legs. Oh, my legs . . . they hurt!"

Before I could do anything else, she rolled over and vomited on the floor.

"Mama! Mama! Papa!" I cried, jumping out of bed and running to where they slept in the apartment's main room. They woke with a start, both of them blinking at me in surprise.

"It's Esther," I panted. "Come quickly!"

My father was out of bed instantly, rushing past me. My brothers had heard my cries and all but the twins had come to the door of their room to peer out at us. "What is it?" Jacob asked. "What happened?"

My mother followed my father into our alcove, the curtain swinging closed behind her. I just sat on their bed, unable to speak, unable to answer Jacob, thinking I should have done something sooner.

Four

After my parents left in a rush with Esther in their arms, I was too despondent to sleep. I curled up on their bed, hugging my mother's pillow close, staring sullenly at the curtain that led to our alcove. The idea of going back in there made my stomach churn. All I could think about was Esther trapped in feverish sleep, moaning, crying, her pain evident in every bodily twitch and shudder. I thought of my mother kneeling beside her, cleaning her face with a damp cloth, smoothing her hair back and tenderly cradling her head in her lap while my father hurried about contacting our neighbor and booking tickets for the train to Krakow. I remembered the blue tinge to Esther's lips and her shallow breathing, and how she cried as my mother sang her a lullaby.

I wanted to cry myself as I closed my eyes and inhaled the smell of rosewater that lingered on my mother's pillow. I felt alone and afraid. At one point during the night, the twins came out of their small room and crawled into bed beside me. David's tiny hand reached for my own. I put my arms around them as they snuggled against me. Majer began to snore softly with his thumb in his mouth, and David's dark curls tickled my chin as he nestled closer to my side. When the first light of dawn began to work its way under the curtain, I heard my older brothers moving about in their room. I blinked in the dim light, dazed from lack of sleep. Before I could get out of bed, Jacob stepped into the main room. He was dressed in his school clothes. We looked at each other, and I noticed the dark circles under his eyes.

"Did you sleep?" he asked. I shook my head silently, not wanting to disturb the twins.

"Let's get ready for school," he said, assuming an air of authority, but as he stood in the kitchen holding his cap in his hands, he looked helpless as a child. He peered at the empty table where breakfast usually waited and the cold stove where my mother always greeted us in the morning.

"I don't want to go to school," I muttered, lying back against the pillow.

"I think you should, Sarah," he said, coming to sit beside me. "Mama and Papa said we should."

"I don't care," I sighed, closing my eyes.

Jacob gave my shoulder a gentle nudge. I looked up at him, ready to argue, but when I saw his face, I fell silent. He was biting his lip and blinking fiercely, his large, dark eyes, so like Esther's, filling with tears. He gave a quick shake of his head, trying hard to maintain his composure. In that moment, my heart softened, and that stubborn part of me that was always ready to quarrel fell silent.

"I'm scared, Jacob," I whispered.

"I know, Sarah," he said. "I am too. But Esther is going to the big hospital. The city doctors will know what to do. And we have each other. I'll take care of you."

I looked into his eyes and said, "We'll take care of each other."

The memory of Esther's smile haunted me in the days that passed. At school, I tried to focus on my work, but I kept slipping into a daze, remembering Esther's face as she looked up at me from our bed, the painful smile on her dry lips as she tried to reassure me. The thoughts were fresh in my mind every night when I closed my eyes. Lack of sleep put me in a fog. Once, I even fell asleep at my desk. "Sarah," my cousin Gutcha hissed in my ear, waking me before our teacher noticed.

Every afternoon, Jacob ran to the post office to see if my parents had sent any news. We didn't have a phone in our home, and neither did our aunt and uncle. The closest phone was at the post office, and it was there that my parents had promised to call or send a telegram. Each evening when Jacob returned without any news, we sat silently in our living room, attempting to do homework and chores until my aunt came to collect us for dinner.

My Aunt Leah and Uncle Abraham were watchful of us and did everything to make us feel safe and loved. They lived in the apartment above ours with my cousins Gutcha and Daniel. Aunt Leah cared for the twins during the day while we attended school, but I insisted on bathing them and washing their clothes, singing to them at night and tucking them into bed with kisses on their foreheads. I wanted the normalcy of routine as much as they did, perhaps more. Keeping busy kept my mind from worrying obsessively about my sister.

On Friday evening, we gathered around my aunt's dining table as she lit the Shabbat candles. After repeating the prayers over the wine and *challah* and welcoming the Sabbath, my aunt stood with her hands over her eyes and added another prayer. "Watch over our Esther and return her to health."

"Amen," we chanted, and I stood with my eyes closed tightly, willing the prayer to rise up and up and up, higher than any other prayer, to where I imagined it would be heard.

A week after our parents' departure, Jacob burst through the door, an envelope grasped in his hand. "It's a telegram from Papa!" he exclaimed as we all turned to look at him in surprise. We gathered around him as he tore open the envelope.

"Dearest children," he began to read. "We are here in Krakow. Your sister is in the hospital. We have a room and are comfortable while we wait to see what can be done. We miss you all very much and think of you daily. Please be strong and we will see you soon."

Jacob looked up.

"What else does it say?" I asked eagerly, trying to see over his shoulder.

"That's it," he said, turning the page over in his hands. The blank side of the thin, yellow sheet of paper mocked us. What was Esther's diagnosis? How long would they be gone? Where were they staying? We were left with more questions than answers, and no way of reaching our parents. But I took some comfort in the fact that Esther was being treated by the city doctors. Surely they'd find a cure for her.

I missed my parents dreadfully and hadn't slept in my bed since they'd left. "What a silly girl," Sam said one evening, ruffling my hair teasingly. "Still need to sleep in Mama and Papa's bed? I thought you'd outgrown that."

I pushed his hand away defensively and stormed out of the room. I didn't want to tell him the truth—how every night I couldn't get the image of Esther tossing and turning out of my head, how being in our alcove only made the memories more intense, and how, more than anything, I didn't want to wake up in our bed to find Esther gone. The only time I slipped past the curtain was to change clothes or grab my schoolbooks. The twins slept with me at night in our parents' bed, abandoning their own room for my company, and I took some solace in having them near.

It was a hot evening, a sign that summer was fast approaching, when Jacob finally returned from the post office with a stricken expression on his face. I had become accustomed to seeing him shake his head as he came through the door, hang his cap on the hook, and say with a touch of resignation, "Maybe we'll hear something tomorrow. I wouldn't worry. They would have sent word if something was wrong."

I was only vaguely aware of Jacob when he first stepped into the room because Majer had just grabbed David's small wooden toy horse. "That's my horsey!" David wailed. "Mine! Gimme back!"

"Boys," I said, kneeling beside them. "You have to share. Majer, that wasn't very nice." It was then that I realized something was wrong. Majer dropped the toy without any argument and looked past me to the door. From the kitchen table where they were studying, I noticed Sam and Isaac both staring silently over my head. The whole apartment was suddenly too quiet.

Puzzled, I turned and caught my first sight of Jacob's face. His eyes were unfocused, his face white, his lips set in a grim line.

Tears fell silently down his cheeks as he twisted a piece of paper in his hands. I felt a ghostly punch to my gut as my blood turned to ice. My pulse throbbed in my ringing ears, and I suddenly felt light-headed.

"Well?" I demanded almost hysterically. "What is it? What's happened?"

When Jacob didn't answer, I glanced over at Sam and Isaac. They remained frozen in their chairs. No one spoke. I couldn't bear it. "Say something!" I screamed, getting to my feet, but some part of me knew instinctively that I wouldn't want to hear Jacob's response.

Sam finally stood and, moving to Jacob, grasped his shoulder, rousing Jacob from his stupor. He swallowed painfully and turned to Sam. Taking a deep breath, he choked, "It's over. Esther's—" Shaking his head and covering his face with his hands, he sobbed, "Esther's gone."

I don't know who made the first sound. I don't know who gasped, who cried, who started shouting loud denials. The room swam. I heard Isaac whisper, "Sh'ma Yisrael, Adonai Eloheinu, Adonai Echad." I trembled. I gathered the twins to me, squeezing them so tightly they started protesting. David looked up at me, his chubby little hands pushing against my chest. I watched as a teardrop fell onto his face. That's when I realized I was the one who had gasped, who had cried, who was saying "no, no, no" over and over and over.

That night we all wept together. We sat huddled, each of us only a child, on our parents' bed. I held Majer and David close, seeking comfort in the smell of soap in their curls, the feel of their round cheeks as they nestled against my shoulder, the tender way they reached up with their arms to be held and hugged. I don't think they understood why we were crying, but they imitated our sorrow by wiping at their own tears and asking for their mama. I was a poor substitute, and in my few moments of coherent thought, I'd whisper to them that Mama would return soon to care for them and love them as only a mother could.

We didn't light the candles when the sun set. We sat in a darkness appropriate for our grief until our aunt finally arrived. She knocked gently at the door and called, "Jacob? Sam? Sarah, dear, are you all here?"

The door opened, letting in a small amount of light from the streetlamp outside. "Tante Leah!" Majer cried, eager to have an adult in our home. He jumped off the bed and into her embrace. David followed him. My arms were suddenly empty.

"Oh, boys," she said, lifting them in her arms as she stepped inside. "What are you doing in the dark?" That's when she saw the rest of us sitting on the bed. Her face mirrored our own heartache.

"Tante Leah, Esther's dead," I said, feeling the urge to speak the words in the hope that she'd reply, "Silly girl, Esther's not dead. *Pu, pu, pu,* don't say such things! She's fine! I've just heard from your parents and guess what? They'll all be home soon!"

But Leah did not say that. She only nodded. "Abraham just received a telegram as well," she said in a whisper of a voice. "I can't believe it. I just can't believe it."

She held her hand out to me. I jumped off the bed and ran to her, burying my face against her chest and giving in to sobs that threatened to rip me apart. Her hands gently soothed my back, and I realized just how much I needed to be comforted as well.

"Come upstairs," my aunt said gently to all of us. "I don't want you children down here by yourselves tonight. In the morning, we'll prepare the house for the *shiva.* Boys, you can notify the rabbi then. Your parents will surely be exhausted after their trip, and we don't want them to worry about a thing. They should be home soon."

My heart lifted ever so slightly at these words. I was eager to see my father, to curl up in his lap and rest my head against his broad chest and inhale the sweet confectionary scent permanently ingrained in his clothes. I closed my eyes and thought of the treats he always brought home from his bakery, sticky icing and drizzles of honey melting on my fingers as I pulled freshly baked rugelach and small honey cakes out of their paper wrappings. I longed to have my mother place her soft hands on my head as she recited the Sabbath prayers, to feel the whisper of her breath against my cheek, to smell the sweet perfume of her skin. I ached so much from missing them, from missing Esther, that I felt suffocated. I wondered, as we held on to each other in grief and disbelief, if I'd ever be able to breathe again.

Five

The morning came too soon, pulling me out of dreamless sleep. I blinked in the early light, feeling confused. I was lying on a hard surface that was not my bed. Small bodies pressed against me, and I glanced down to see the twins curled up on either side of me on our mat on the floor. My cousin Gutcha slept beside me in her bed. I was in her room. That's when I remembered.

Esther. *Esther.*

I had never experienced death before, and the aching, almost manic feeling that assaulted me was both foreign and scary. I felt feverish and queasy. I couldn't think straight. I wanted to fight against the emotion, to deny it, to close my eyes and insist I was in a bad dream and would wake again in my own bed with my sister beside me. But I heard my aunt moving in the other room, talking in soft whispers to my uncle. I heard Jacob's voice then, a low murmur, saying words I couldn't make out, and I knew I wasn't dreaming.

"Sarah?" a small voice asked. I looked down at David, who was sitting up and rubbing at his eyes. "Sarah, I'm hungry."

"Where's Mama?" Majer grumbled in a tiny voice, hugging the blankets close to his little body. "I want Mama and Papa. You said they'd be home soon."

"They will, Majer," I said. "Very soon, I promise."

Gutcha began to stir in her bed. She sat up and stretched, her chestnut brown hair disheveled, her drowsy green eyes meeting mine. She hadn't spoken much since my aunt brought us upstairs the night before. She had been awkward and uncomfortable in my presence, but she had stayed by my side the entire night, even offering me her bed to sleep in, but I'd wanted to stay with the twins.

The door to the room opened and my aunt peered in. "I thought I heard voices," she said, wiping her hands on her apron. "Did you sleep at all?"

I nodded solemnly. I *had* slept. After tossing and turning and holding in sobs so as not to wake Gutcha or the twins, I had finally succumbed to my exhaustion. I wanted nothing more now than to escape into the void of sleep once more. But the twins were rising from the floor, pulling at me to get up too.

"I've made breakfast," my aunt said. "A hearty breakfast for all of us."

"I'm not too hungry," I muttered.

"I am!" David shouted, running into the kitchen ahead of us, Majer on his heels. My aunt waited for me in the doorway. She put her arm around my shoulder and guided me toward the table where my uncle Abraham, cousin Daniel, and brothers sat. "I know you might not be hungry now," she said, "but it's important that you eat. I'll need your help today. Another telegram came this morning from the post office."

I looked up. "What did it say?"

"Mama and Papa will be home tonight," Isaac answered for her, a hint of relief in his voice. "They are catching the train back from Krakow and should be home before supper."

I relaxed a little at this prospect. Part of me felt that, with the return of my parents, I could lay my sorrow aside, let them hold it for me, and tell me everything was going to be OK.

"We are going to see Rabbi Blumenfeld when we're finished," Jacob added, wiping his fingers on a napkin.

"We'll need a *minyan*," my uncle said, stroking his dark beard. My brothers nodded. Ten men were required to recite the prayers for Esther's death.

I picked at the eggs my aunt set before me while my little brothers ate heartily and talked eagerly about seeing my parents. Their sorrow from the previous evening was forgotten in their youthful excitement. They didn't understand the extent of what had happened and only focused on the good news that my parents were coming home. I wished I could be so blissfully unaware myself.

Work kept me busy that day. My emotions were in check as I helped my aunt dust, polish the surfaces of her dining table and breakfront, prepare food for the *shiva,* put out her best china, and drape the mirrors with black sheets. We were forbidden from looking at our reflections during this time of grieving; this was not a moment to be vain. I knew this, but I still caught a glimpse of myself as I helped cover the mirror by the front door. My eyes were red-rimmed and swollen, my face pale, the freckles I so detested standing out like paint splattered on a canvas. I knew it was wrong to be concerned about my appearance, but still I ran my fingers through my hair and pinched at my cheeks as I turned away from the mirror.

Sadness ebbed and flowed, punctuated by moments of denial, as the day wore on. We heard my parents before we saw them. The sound of an engine grew louder outside, followed by a horn honking and muffled voices I immediately recognized. "They're here!" I exclaimed, running to the front window and looking out at the street below. My father and Mr. Geller were lifting luggage from the trunk of Mr. Geller's car as my mother emerged from the back seat. Her head was downcast so I couldn't see her eyes beneath her kerchief, and my father's tall hat kept his face from view. I let the curtains fall back into place as I ran to the door. The twins were instantly at my side, and soon Jacob, Sam, and Isaac were there as well.

We heard footsteps on the staircase outside and stared eagerly at the door as it opened. I was prepared to run into their arms the minute they walked in, but when I saw their faces, I froze in place. Papa stood in the doorway, only it wasn't Papa—he had changed since the morning he'd carried Esther out of our lives. His eyes were surrounded by heavy wrinkles so that they appeared sunken and small. They were glazed with tears that did not fall, dark pools surrounded by withered skin. The humor that usually danced beneath their surface was gone. His shoulders sagged forward as though he could not support his own weight. But the most drastic change was to his hair—what had once been a thick, dark, full head of hair had turned white. Silver strands ran through his beard as well. He looked like he'd aged fifteen years in just over a month's time. An old man had replaced my father, sapping him of energy and humor and, as I'd later discover, his abiding conviction and belief in a benevolent God.

My mother stood slightly behind him, her face blank. She wore the same traveling clothes she had left in, her good coat, dress, and the beautiful scarf over her head, but she looked disheveled, as though she hadn't taken any time or care when dressing in the morning. Her coat wasn't buttoned properly so the hemline appeared uneven, and her long skirt was heavily creased. Her eyes were empty, lifeless, blind to her surroundings. Her movements were slow and stilted as she put down her bags.

But the twins saw the one person they had been longing for the most.

"Mama!" they cried, running to her. Something stirred in her as they wrapped their tiny arms around her waist. She looked down at them, and suddenly, she was crying, her tears falling on their heads as they reached up to be encircled in her arms.

"Oh, my babies," she sobbed. "Oh, my dears. My sweet, sweet dears."

I felt tears surface in my own eyes. I wanted to run to her too. I wanted her to comfort me as well. I wanted my father to look up and smile, to hold his arms open to me, but I stood rooted to the spot. I watched as my brothers approached my father and took his arm, leading him inside. Still, I didn't move.

My aunt and uncle were there, taking my parents' luggage, guiding them into the small living room and telling them to sit. My mother fell into a chair, the twins crawling into her lap. I glimpsed Gutcha and Daniel hiding in the shadows of their bedroom doorways.

"Is it true?" Aunt Leah asked, as though the past day was just a dream and there was still a chance this nightmare would end, still a chance Esther would walk through the door, smiling and healthy and young, ready for a long life.

My mother nodded, accepting the handkerchief my aunt offered her and dabbing at the corners of her eyes. Aunt Leah sat across from her and gently took her hand. "She is at rest now," my aunt said with comfort in her voice, but my mother began twisting the handkerchief in her hands, tears falling fast down her cheeks.

"They took her from us," my mother choked. "They took her into a room and told us to wait. She was so weak, so pale. I wanted to be with her. I wanted to go with her and hold her, but they told us we had to stay where we were. I shouldn't have listened, I shouldn't have—"

My aunt put her arm around my mother and tried to comfort her, but my mother pushed her away. "We begged them, day after day, but they wouldn't let us see her. And when they finally came out, all they said was they were sorry. She was gone. No explanation. They had taken her away. She's buried, and I don't even know where! My angel, my sweet, sweet angel." Then she fell against my aunt, sobbing uncontrollably.

We were all crying then. I had never felt a sorrow as piercing and deep as I did in that moment. It wrenched my gut and made me want to scream. I realized then that I had hoped seeing my parents would make me feel better, but instead, the finality of the situation weighed down on me, and I was forced to accept that Esther was really not coming home. Esther would no longer lie beside me at night, holding my hand as we whispered our secrets to each other. Esther's voice would no longer ring through our home, her laughter and smiles brightening our days and lifting our spirits. Her beauty would no longer charm everyone who saw her and turn heads on the street. And the idea of her in a grave in an unfamiliar city, far away from us, made me ache. I tried not to think of her alone and afraid, buried in an unknown grave, but instead imagined her running beside me after school, her face flushed and healthy, her eyes bright and her lips red, her hand forever held in mine.

Six

Olkusz, Poland, summer 1939

"Sarah, wait for me!"

I turned to see Gutcha calling to me as I walked home from town, my arms weighed down with grocery bags. It was early summer, and the air was already heavy with heat. Gutcha waved as she ran to catch up to me, her slightly plump cheeks flushed, her braids flying in the air behind her. I tried to wave as well, but the bags shifted precariously, and I caught them before they fell to the ground.

"How are you?" Gutcha asked as she took a bag from my arms and we started walking together. It was always the first thing anyone asked me: How are you? How are your parents? How is your family? It was polite conversation, but it was also a way for others to find out how we were faring after Esther's death. I always smiled and said, "We're doing well, thank you."

What I didn't share was the truth—that even after a year, my mother still cried herself to sleep at night, my father was exhausted and despondent all the time, and in general, a little of the life had gone out of our home. Over time, I had begun to feel comfortable in my alcove again, though I didn't want to admit that I still had nightmares and would reach for Esther in my sleep, only to find the space beside me empty.

"Have you heard the news?" Gutcha asked as we turned onto the path that led toward home.

"What news?"

"Papa's been talking about it all day. He says we're going to war."

My head turned. "War?" I asked. "With Germany?"

Although we didn't have a radio, gossip was a reliable source of information in our town. And each day, neighbors whispered new information between themselves. I had even overheard my father's customers talking about what was happening when I helped in the shop. Germany was under the leadership of a man named Adolf Hitler. Austria had been annexed the previous year, and now there was widespread fear that Poland would be next. My mother and aunts gathered around the kitchen table to talk about the latest rumor or guess at the future as they hung laundry to dry. My father and uncles stood outside most evenings to escape the heat, huddled in the doorway of the bakery, smoking cigarettes, heads bent in discussion.

"Have you heard what's happening to the Jews in Germany?" Gutcha asked now, lowering her voice. "I heard Mama telling Papa that her brother's business was destroyed."

"Your uncle's business?" I asked. "What happened?"

"They threw bricks through the windows and set fire to the building," Gutcha said, her eyes downcast. "Mama read the letter Uncle Shlomo sent us. It was scary."

"But that won't happen here," I said. "That couldn't happen here."

We continued walking in silence. Gutcha kicked a pebble with the toe of her boot. We watched it roll to the other side of the dirt lane and ricochet off the wooden wheel of a wagon. Glancing up, we saw Aaron pushing his cart in the opposite direction. For a moment, our eyes met. His lips turned up in a smile of greeting, and he nodded. I nodded back mutely. Then he gave his cart a shove and passed us without a word. We occasionally saw each other in town, but we never spoke about my sister. The way they felt about each other was a secret between us, and we had reached an unspoken, mutual understanding that it would remain that way. I still remembered Aaron's face when his family paid their respects at Esther's *shiva*—the haunted look in his eyes, the quiver to his lips, bright blotches of red staining his cheeks. Later, when I'd stepped outside, I'd heard him sobbing in the alley behind our home. I'd retreated silently so he wouldn't know I was there, but my heart broke a little more in that moment.

We had reached my front path. The windows were open to let in the midsummer breeze, and I heard music from inside our home. I smiled and turned to Gutcha.

"Jacob's playing for Helena again."

Gutcha grinned back at me, and we walked to the window to peer inside. Our concerns about the larger world melted away as we spied on Jacob and our next-door neighbor's daughter Helena.

I had to admire my brother as he stood in the center of the room, eyes closed, swaying slightly with his head bent over his violin. He had turned eighteen earlier in the summer and was tall and handsome and strong, resembling my father more with each passing day. But while my father used his hands to mold and sculpt dough, Jacob used his to make music.

His love of music began at an early age, when my mother took him to see a traveling klezmer band perform in the town square. According to my mother, Jacob had stood transfixed, his small hand gripping hers tightly, refusing to move as he watched them play. Once the sun was low in the sky, he began to shiver from cold, but still she had to urge him to return home. He kept turning to gaze back at the musicians, even as they were swallowed by dusk, the rise and fall of musical notes pulling at him like a magnetic force.

One of our wealthier neighbors, the Gellers, owned a radio, and one day after school, Jacob heard Franz Schubert's Symphony no. 4 in C Minor playing through their open window. He froze on the spot, listening, until Sam finally threw his cap at Jacob to get his attention. Jacob soon made a habit of walking past the Geller house each day in the hope that Radio Poland was broadcasting symphonies by Mozart, Beethoven, Bach, or one of the more contemporary composers. Mrs. Geller found him one afternoon sitting in the bushes beneath the window and invited him in to hear Władysław Szpilman play Chopin over tea.

He became fascinated with the stringed instruments, particularly the violin, and he begged for one of his own. His passion soon became obsession. My mother surprised him on his tenth birthday with a hand-me-down violin she had purchased with a little money she had saved, and he immediately began to play. Like a magician, he was able to conjure the sweetest melodies from the strings without having taken a single lesson. When he played, he appeared transported, stuck in a dreamlike daze. He swayed, lost in the music that surrounded him, turning the violin into a vessel of lyrical poetry. The Gellers invited him over whenever a symphony was broadcast, and he would come home and play by ear what he'd heard.

We all loved to hear him play, but his best audience was my mother. She asked him to play for her almost daily. She said the moment he pulled the bow over the strings, the moment the first notes rose into the air, she was hearing the voice of God. His music filled our home in the evenings. Her favorite melody to hear him play was "Kol Nidre," the solemn and reflective music of Yom Kippur.

Now, he was playing a tune that was light and happy, and Helena was watching him with large green eyes filled with adoration.

"When is the wedding?" Gutcha asked.

"They haven't set a date," I said, "but I imagine it will be soon."

"It's no wonder they both agreed to the match. Just see how they look at each other!" Gutcha sighed as we turned away from the window.

"I know," I said, recalling the afternoon when, shortly after Jacob's eighteenth birthday, my father had proudly announced that Jacob and Helena had given their consent to the proposed match. We had always known Helena's family; Helena's father, Shimon, was a reputable *czapnik*, or hatmaker, in the town. Her mother, Dina, had been my mother's childhood friend. But I was still surprised when my father made the announcement, standing proudly beside Jacob with his hand on my brother's shoulder. Jacob's face was flushed and embarrassed.

"Did you have any idea they felt that way about each other?" Gutcha asked.

"No!" I said, shaking my head. "I wonder if they even knew themselves. But ever since it was agreed upon, they haven't left each other's side."

Gutcha hugged the grocery bag close to her chest and said dreamily, "I'd like to feel that way about someone."

"I'd like someone to feel that way about me!" I exclaimed, and we giggled as we opened the door.

Jacob's wedding soon became all we talked about. With his schooling almost behind him, he worked longer hours in the bakery beside my father. We all knew he would take over the business one day. Helena's presence became commonplace in our home as well, along with her mother and older sister Malka. Malka had turned down a marriage proposal to attend college to become a teacher. She was one of the few girls in our town to go away to school, and she was now home for the summer. Together, Helena, Malka, and Dina visited often during the warm summer afternoons. They gossiped as they sat around our table, chopping vegetables or ironing linen or mending our school clothes for the coming autumn. They shopped at the market stalls for Shabbat on Friday mornings. They were showing Helena how to keep a suitable Jewish home, to become a proper *berryer,* and I was occasionally allowed to join them. I loved listening to the details of the wedding that was to take place that fall, after the High Holy Days.

One afternoon, Helena and Dina showed up on our doorstep with a box in their hands. My mother let them in, and they placed the package on the table. "Look, just look!" Dina exclaimed, her hands clasped to her chest as Helena gently raised the lid of the box. I bent over to see what was inside. Helena lifted what appeared to be a white gossamer cloud in her hands. "Isn't it beautiful?" Dina breathed, gingerly spreading out the fluid material for us to see. "It was my grandmother's veil," she said. "My mother wore it at her wedding, and I wore it for mine. And now, Helena will wear it for hers."

My mother and I moved closer for a better look. The fabric was two layers of a sheer, delicate tulle attached to a comb with small crystals sewn to the edge. Iridescent threads were woven throughout and shimmered in the light.

"Oh, Dina," my mother exhaled, "how lovely."

Dina took the comb and turned Helena around to face the mirror. We watched as she smoothed back Helena's chestnut-colored hair from her face and secured the comb to the crown of her head. The diaphanous material cascaded over Helena's shoulders, down her back, and gathered at the floor. She smiled at her reflection in the mirror, and I thought I had never seen anything so beautiful.

As we stood beaming at Helena, the door burst open. We all jumped as Sam rushed in, his face red and flustered.

"Mama, where's Papa?" he asked breathlessly.

"Samuel!" my mother exclaimed, her hand to her chest. "You gave us a scare! Papa's at the bakery like always. What's the matter?"

There was a noise behind Sam, and we heard Jacob calling my brother's name from the street. My mother and Dina snatched the veil from Helena's head and, as carefully as they could in their haste, folded it back into its box. Sam turned without answering and ran from the house, leaving the door open in his wake. I hurried to the door in time to see him sprint past Jacob, headed toward the center of town, holding his cap to his head. Jacob was standing at the foot of our walkway, staring after him. He turned then and paced up the path toward our door. I stepped back from the threshold to let him enter.

"What's the matter with your brother?" my mother asked, her voice calmer now that the veil was safely hidden. "He was in quite a state."

"Mama, listen," Jacob said softly, glancing around at each of us. "There's a rumor spreading around town, and it's serious."

"What is it?" I asked, curious, as my mother and Dina frowned and Helena stepped closer to Jacob.

"Sam overheard Mr. Geller talking to Mr. Applebaum. Mr. Geller says he heard an emergency broadcast on the radio that Germany is assembling troops and plans to invade Poland."

I turned to look at my mother. A million thoughts raced through my head—what did this mean for us? Would Poland fight back? Would there be a war, like everyone was predicting? And why was Sam so agitated?

"This can't be true," Dina gasped, her voice a whisper of disbelief. "Come, Helena. We must go find your father." She reached for her daughter's hand and pulled her toward the door. As Helena passed Jacob, she looked searchingly into his eyes but didn't say a word. Jacob stood silently in the doorway as she left, watching her go.

My mother wiped her hands on her apron and began untying it from around her waist. "I must find your father too," she said in a decided tone. "Perhaps he should hear the news from me, not Sam."

"He may know already, Mama," Jacob said. "The whole town seems to be gathering in the square."

My mother frowned as she headed out the door. Jacob turned to follow, but I reached out and grabbed his hand before he could leave as well. "Jacob," I said, "why did Sam run off? What's his rush?"

"Mama's not going to like when she hears." Jacob sighed, shaking his head. "Sam wants to join the Polish army."

Seven

The cobblestone streets in the center of town were already crowded by the time I reached them. I recognized many of our neighbors waving to one another or moving in groups to find shade under the eaves of the shops that lined the sidewalk. Voices carried on the still air like a low hum. A charged energy pulsed from the town square. I could smell the familiar odor of motor oil and horse manure mingled with the scent of salted meats hanging from hooks, fresh fish packed on ice, and fried onions from the vendors' carts. My father was standing with Sam by the door to the post office. By the looks of it, they were already in a heated discussion.

"Papa!" I called, waving to him. He gave a distracted wave in return, but I could tell from the frown on his face that he was preoccupied.

"It's going to happen, Papa," Sam was saying as I ran to join them, breathlessly blowing hair out of my eyes. "Yosef, Morty, and I have been discussing it for a long time. It's not going to be good if the Germans take over Poland. We need to fight back!"

"Leave it to the *goyim*, Sam," my father said in an exasperated tone. "We have no place in this war."

"Are we going to war, then?" I asked eagerly, but Sam's voice drowned out my question.

"How can you say that? Haven't you heard what the Germans are doing to the Jews? They've already taken over Austria. That could happen here!"

"It's out of our hands," my father said. "It does no good to worry about something that hasn't happened yet."

His face red with frustration, Sam raked his fingers through his hair, disheveling his curls. "Papa, how can you turn a blind eye to this? I don't understand!"

My mother, who had been talking to the other women nearby, broke away from the group and joined us. I noticed a nervous twitch in the corner of her eye. "Samuel," she said in a quiet but firm voice, "don't upset your father."

Sam turned to face my mother then. He took a deep breath.

"Mama," he said, his voice lower and more controlled, "look at this." He reached into a pocket and pulled out a piece of paper that had been folded into quarters. The midsection had been squeezed tightly as though by an angry fist, so the paper resembled a heavily creased hourglass. As he began to unfold it, I leaned forward to get a better look. Staring back at me from the page were four horribly deformed caricatures of men with long beards, eyes narrowed, ugly, and glaring. Their noses were unnaturally long and lumpy, and their faces were framed by a red Star of David. Flames rose in the background, and large letters stood out angrily in the foreground: DER EWIGE JUDE. The Eternal Jew.

"What does it mean?" I whispered as my mother turned my head away and my father took the paper in his hands. Once again, my question went unanswered.

"Don't you see?" Sam pleaded. "This is all over Germany. This is what they think of us."

"Where did you get this?" my father asked in a low voice.

"From Morty."

"So, this is how you spend your time?" my father replied, looking up from the page to stare Sam in the eye. "Looking at this *mishegoss*?"

"No, Papa, we spend our time debating. Planning."

"Planning for what?" my father asked. "You think you can fight the Germans if it comes to it?"

"Well, we can't just sit around and do nothing!" Sam stomped his foot angrily. I took a step back. A tone of urgency clung to his words. I could see that he was visibly upset yet strangely excited at the same time. Red blotches stood out on his cheeks, and his eyes were alive with manic energy.

"There is nothing to do," my mother said in a decided voice. "Nothing has happened yet. Don't put your cart before the horse, Samuel. This may all turn out to be nothing."

Sam let out an exasperated breath and turned away. I heard him murmur something but couldn't make out the words. Then he straightened his shoulders and said, "I'm going to find Yosef."

"Samuel," my mother called after him, but my father put his hand on her arm and said gently, "Let him go, Brocha. Give him time."

"Is it true, Papa?" I asked again. "Is there going to be a war?"

He finally looked down at me, and I saw the worry that clouded his eyes fade slightly. He smiled and gently cupped my chin, lifting my gaze to his. "My Sarah*le*," he whispered tenderly. "How can there be war when my sweet Sarah*le* is in this world?" He leaned down and kissed the crown of my head, adding, "Don't worry, little one."

I hugged him tightly, smiling against his apron as his large arms embraced me. War, angry words, and ugly, mocking pictures became a distant thought as my father gently stroked my head and tickled under my chin. Here, in my father's arms, I was safe.

A few mornings later, I woke to an argument in our small kitchen. I walked to the table in my nightdress, rubbing sleep from my eyes. Jacob and Isaac were sitting at the table across from my father, who was dressed in his work clothes, his apron folded neatly beside him. Sam was pacing behind them.

"Samuel, sit down," my father said. "You promised your mother you wouldn't say any more on the subject."

"But Papa," Sam fumed, "last night Yosef told me he was going to enlist."

I thought back to the night before as I slipped into my chair. Gutcha had rung for me after supper, pulling me eagerly onto the steps outside our building. "What's gotten into you?" I'd asked, laughing at her flushed face and glancing over her shoulder. I'd spied Sam and his closest friends, Yosef and Morty, huddled together across the street, deep in conversation. Immediately, I'd known why Gutcha was so giddy and shook my head.

Over the summer, my cousin had developed a tremendous crush on Yosef, Sam's tall, blond companion. There was no denying Sam and his friends were young and handsome—so unlike the ugly images of the men from the poster that kept materializing in my mind. Gutcha often made a habit of stopping over to watch them play soccer in the streets outside our home until long after the sun had set. We sat on the steps to cheer them on or pretended to ignore them when they showed off, competing against one another to see who could score the most goals. But lately, they had been doing more standing and whispering than shouting and chasing after the ball. And last night, when they looked up and saw us watching them, they didn't smile and wave but immediately turned and walked away.

Now I understood why they had looked so serious.

"What Yosef does or doesn't do is none of our business," my father was saying. "You and your friends spend too much time debating the affairs of the greater world when you should be focusing on your studies and your futures here, in Olkusz. All this nonsense about fighting? Hmph." His voice was calm, but I could tell from the way he clutched his mug in his hand, knuckles white, that anger was boiling beneath the surface.

"What's happening?" I asked, looking around at them. "Where's Mama?"

My father and brothers didn't answer at first. Sam turned his back on us while Jacob and Isaac sat silently eating their breakfast, heads lowered. My father sighed and said, "She left with the twins to visit your great aunt Isador."

"What?" I asked, surprised. My mother was always home in the morning. She was always the first one up, preparing breakfast, dusting, hemming and mending our clothes, sweeping, washing and hanging laundry to dry, and beginning the evening meal before we were even out the door. The kitchen counters were bare, and the stove, which usually had several pots and pans boiling and simmering by this time, was cold. My father and brothers had plates with cold slices of bread, butter, and jam before them.

"Your mother needed some air to settle her nerves," my father explained. "But there will be no more disruptions to upset her." He cast a meaningful look at Sam, who sighed and pulled out a chair, slumping in it as though defeated, and sullenly reached for a slice of bread. After a few moments of tense silence, my father wiped his mouth and set aside his napkin. "Jacob and I are headed to the bakery," he said. "Sam and Isaac, I want you both there this afternoon as well. I'm expecting a large shipment of flour and will need help stocking the storeroom."

"Yes, Papa," Isaac replied, while Sam just nodded.

"Can I come too, Papa?" I asked. I often liked to visit my father at the bakery during the summer, helping him roll out the dough or prepare the sweet icings, glazes, and fruit marmalades he spread on the pastries. I would sit on a high stool behind the counter and greet customers as they entered or wipe the display cases with a clean rag until not a smudge was seen. As a reward, my father always let me lick the spoons he used to stir melted chocolate or sugary, unbaked batter. "Not today, Sarah," my father said. "I imagine your mother will need help around here when she returns." I wanted to protest, but I knew my father was not in a mood to argue. We ate without speaking, until my father pushed his empty plate to the side and rose from the table. Jacob stood to join him.

As my father was reaching for his hat, the front door opened and my mother walked in, David and Majer at her side. She paused on the threshold. Sam kept his head lowered, refusing to meet her eyes. The twins pushed past her and ran to the table, eagerly grabbing the remaining slices of bread and thickly spreading on butter and strawberry jam, licking their sticky fingers. After a moment, my mother untied her kerchief from her head and reached for her apron.

"I'm making a pot of soup for supper tonight," she said in a business-like tone. "And the twins need to be bathed. Sarah, later you and I will go into town. I must visit the butcher, and I need to buy some more thread and needles. I'll have to patch your red dress for the holidays, Sarah. Honestly, I don't know how you ripped it. And I need to let out your pants, Jacob."

My father silently passed my mother on his way to the door, but I noticed how his hand lightly brushed the back of hers, his fingers gently caressing her skin. It was a small gesture, almost imperceptible, but she paused in listing off her chores and glanced at him. Their eyes met and held for a brief moment. A tender look softened her face, and her shoulders fell as she let out a held breath. As she turned to the stove, she started humming, the faintest of smiles on her lips.

For the moment, everything was normal once more.

True to his word, Sam said no more on the subject. His presence was silent and grim, but he didn't argue. He kept mostly to himself behind his closed bedroom door.

It was impossible to go anywhere without hearing talk of war. Rumors began to spread with ever increasing urgency. Poland was mobilizing its army. Hitler's army was advancing. War was imminent.

But in our home, we didn't speak of it. We went about our daily lives, each of us doing his or her best to ignore the feeling of anticipation that had settled over the whole of Olkusz, like the town was collectively holding its breath. Then one evening late in July, as we were sitting down to dinner, the relative peace of our home was shattered by a loud knock on the door.

"I'll get it," Isaac said, jumping out of his seat.

"Who could that be?" my mother asked with a small frown as she brought a bowl of potatoes to the table.

I turned in my chair as Isaac opened the door. The early evening light outlined the tall figure of a man who was otherwise hidden in shadow. The man extended an arm, holding out a thick envelope, and said, "I have a postal delivery for Mr. Jacob Waldman."

We all looked at Jacob. He rose from his seat. "I'm Jacob Waldman," he said, starting toward the door.

I stood and came around the table to get a better view of the stranger standing on our threshold. I recognized the man who rode his bicycle through our streets, delivering the daily mail. He was wearing his postal uniform, his bag slung over his shoulder, and his face looked red and weary, as though he had been out all day in the heat. He smiled at Jacob sympathetically, and I thought I heard him whisper "good luck" as he handed the envelope to my brother. We watched in silence as he walked back down the path to his bicycle.

The hairs on the back of my neck stood on end. Some instinct told me this couldn't be good news. I watched my parents' faces. My father looked confused as he laid down his fork and knife and stood up, but my mother had gone pale. "What is it?" she whispered. "What did he give you?"

Jacob walked back to the table and set the thick envelope down next to the plate of vegetables and broiled chicken. For a moment, nobody moved. We stared at the letter, afraid to move it, afraid to touch it, as though it were a ticking bomb about to explode. A number of official-looking stamps were pasted to the upper corner, and written across the top of the envelope were the words

Office of the Polish Armed Forces
Krakow, Poland

My mother looked faint. She reached for her chair and sat down heavily. Sam's face, however, had come alive. His eyes glinted with excitement, and he moved around the table to Jacob's side. "Open it, Jacob," he urged, reaching for the letter and handing it back to my brother. Jacob hesitantly took the envelope and tore open the seal, pulling out the crisp white sheet inside. In a quiet voice, he began to read: "To Mr. Jacob Waldman, 42 Slawkowska Street. You are hereby ordered to report for induction into the armed forces of the Polish military on August 1, 1939."

I heard a cry and looked up. My mother had pushed her chair back and was standing with her hands to her mouth, shaking her head. "I don't understand," my father whispered, reaching out and taking the paper from Jacob's hand.

"He's been drafted, Papa," Sam said. "Don't you see? I told you! I told you we were going to fight the Germans, and now Jacob has the chance to defend our homeland. If I can't fight in this war, then Jacob will. It's an order!"

Jacob's face had grown as pale as my mother's, but he didn't say a word. My eyes shifted back and forth between them, seeing the triumphant look on Sam's face, the shocked look on Jacob's, the confused look on my father's, and the horrified look on my mother's. The feeling of dread I had managed to keep at bay for the past few weeks suddenly rose up through my body, and I had to swallow down a feeling of panic. The dinner before us was forgotten.

"No!" my mother yelled suddenly, loudly, and we all looked at her. "No! They can't do this! They can't take my son! I can't lose another child!"

"Mama," Jacob whispered, blinking back his fear. "Mama, it's all right."

"No!" my mother cried again, and turning, she rushed out the door, slamming it behind her.

Eight

The morning Jacob reported for duty, I sat on the floor with the twins while my mother sobbed into a handkerchief and my father paced behind her. I knew they hadn't slept, because I had overheard them arguing the night before. I had tried unsuccessfully to block the sound of their voices with my pillow, tossing and turning in my own bed. Finally, I gave up and stared at the ceiling, letting their words wash over me.

"You have to stop this, Leibish," my mother pleaded. "He cannot go."

"I've tried, Brocha. You know I've tried. I appealed to the local government. I wrote away to the national military headquarters. The reply is always the same. He has to go. There's nothing we can do," my father whispered.

"How can you say that?" my mother cried. "He just won't go. He'll stay here. That's it."

"Then he'll be arrested. You're being unreasonable."

"They can't do that."

"Yes, they can."

There was a pause, and I imagined my parents staring at each other in anger and defeat. I knew the helplessness my mother felt, because I felt it as well. It hovered like a ghost over my bed. It ensnared me, pressing with a suffocating fist on my chest. Even as my eyelids grew heavy, I blinked back sleep, powerless as the hours ticked away, bringing the dawn and the moment my brother would have to say good-bye.

The door to my brothers' room opened and Jacob walked out, followed by Sam and Isaac. He carried his one small suitcase in hand. His hair was neatly trimmed, his face clean-shaven. He looked so different to me without his beard and long *payot*. He appeared a stranger in his uniform, the collar rigid against his exposed Adam's apple, the shape of his muscular arms, so used to lifting sacks of flour, discernable beneath the muted brown sleeves of his army jacket, the polished toes of his black boots peeking from below the cuffs of his pants. My mother had spent the day before ironing the many pieces that made up his uniform, so now the pleats were crisp and the collar stiff. Her silent tears had fallen on the fabric as she'd worked. Jacob's dark hair curled against his forehead beneath the rim of his *rogatywka* field cap. His large brown eyes, ringed with thick black lashes, stared back at us with a resigned expression. It struck me that Jacob, standing there so stoically, seemed more like a man than I'd ever seen him.

A truck was scheduled to take all the young men who had been recruited from our town to Krakow, where they would go through basic training. Jacob had received the details of his orders a week earlier and had shared the information with us in his quiet voice. Up until that moment, my mother had refused to believe the summons. "They can't make him," she kept repeating.

The only one who seemed happy was Sam. He followed my brother into the room with a proud grin. "I wish I were going too, Jacob," he said as he put an arm around Jacob's shoulders. "I wish we were fighting the Germans side by side."

My mother gave a small cry. My father glared at Sam, but he didn't notice. Jacob turned to Sam and said, "You have to stay here and keep everyone safe. Watch over Mama and Papa." Sam nodded and extended his hand. Jacob grasped it, but then pulled Sam into a long hug. Isaac, who was standing at the window, turned around and announced to the quiet room, "The truck is here."

"No," my mother moaned into her handkerchief. She was crumpled in her chair at the table.

"Mama," Jacob implored, releasing Sam and turning to her, "please don't be sad. I will be all right."

My father came to my mother's side and helped her to stand.

"Come, Brocha. It's time to say good-bye."

"No," my mother whispered again, shaking her head and leaning heavily against my father. I ran to Jacob's side and threw my arms around him. He put his hand under my chin and tilted my face up to his. I saw the glazed expression in his brown eyes. "Be good, Sarah," he said. "Help Mama with everything, OK?"

"I will," I promised, nodding. The twins were hugging him around his legs. He bent down and lifted them into his arms, tickling them until they giggled, then set them down to hug Isaac, who had come to stand at my side. My parents waited at the door. Jacob picked up his suitcase and walked with a tentative gait toward them.

"Be safe, son," my father whispered, pulling Jacob to him. It was rare for my father to show physical affection to my brothers, but now he held Jacob tightly to his chest, his strong hands on Jacob's back. "Come back home soon," he whispered in his ear. Jacob nodded. When my father finally let go, Jacob turned to my mother. Her face was lowered, hidden by her handkerchief. She was unable to look him in the eye.

"Mama?" he whispered.

She nodded, swallowing over her sobs, but still she couldn't bring herself to look at him. My father sighed and put his arm around Jacob, helping him out the door. We huddled on the doorstep, watching as Jacob walked down the path to the truck. Other young men were sitting in the back of the truck dressed in identical uniforms. They stared at their feet or gazed into the distance with vacant expressions. Jacob paused for a moment with his back to us and steeled himself before continuing forward. Suddenly, a voice cried out his name.

"Jacob! Wait!"

We turned and saw Helena running down the sidewalk. Jacob froze. Helena stopped a few feet away, panting. She looked at him and gave a small sound, a cross between a gasp and a sigh. She reached out to him, poised to run, but her feet remained planted where she stood. They gazed at each other until her arms slowly fell to her sides. They continued to stare until the driver of the truck pressed impatiently on the horn. Jacob couldn't take his eyes off Helena as he climbed into the truck bed. He was drinking her in, memorizing her every detail.

As the vehicle pulled away, taking my brother with it, I heard my mother sobbing against my father, but I could only watch Helena's face. I saw her heartache and longing. I saw the hungry look in her eyes as she ran after the truck until it turned the corner. And despite my concern for my brother, a small part of me longed to be in their shoes.

We woke to the sound of sirens.

I gasped as I bolted upright in bed. "Esther!" I cried, reaching for the empty space beside me. It took only a moment to remember that Esther wasn't there. I felt the familiar punch to the gut. Would I ever get used to the realization that Esther was gone?

I ran from my bed into the main room, my heart racing. Occasionally, the ground beneath my feet quaked, and I heard a distant boom like thunder. "Mama! Papa! What's happening?" I cried anxiously. The twins were curled up between my parents, the blankets pulled up so only their startled eyes peered out at us. I fell into their bed as well and buried my head against my mother's shoulder as another crash sounded, reverberating off the walls. The door to my brothers' room opened and Sam and Isaac rushed to join us, their faces pale in the darkness. For a moment, all other sound was drowned out by a steady rumbling from overhead that caused the bed to vibrate.

"Those are planes," Sam whispered, going to the window and parting the curtain to look out at the darkened street.

"Samuel, come away from the window!" my father hissed, but he stood up and rushed to my brother's side, gazing out as well. There was an explosion somewhere closer now, and the whole room shook, the glass of the window rattling against the pane. I jumped and buried my head under the blankets.

"Are we at war?" I whispered, terrified. My voice caught in my throat. "Are those bombs?"

My mother wrapped her arm around me tightly, clutching me closer. "Oh, Jacob," I heard her breathe into my hair. "My Jacob, please come home."

"What time is it?" Isaac whispered.

"It has to be near dawn," Sam said, pressing his palms to the glass.

"What do we do, Leibish?" my mother asked, searching my father's face. The sirens were still sounding; the rise and fall of the alarm reverberated in my ears, undulating in time to my quickened heartbeat. "Should we take shelter? Where can we go?"

My father held up his hand. "Let me think," he said from across the room, closing his eyes. Another blast right outside the window sent my father and brother running back to the bed. "Get up," my father ordered, throwing back the blankets. "Hurry! Follow me!"

We ran to the kitchen table, where my father told us to duck underneath. We crowded around each other, crouched shoulder to shoulder. My teeth chattered with each explosion, and I was sure the walls would cave in around us. I put my arms over my head and squeezed my eyes shut. The minutes passed like hours, until finally the sounds became more distant, the explosions fewer, the sirens finally falling silent. "I think we're safe," my father whispered at long last, and my whole body relaxed against my mother. My head fell on her shoulder and my fists unclenched. Still, we didn't move.

I didn't realize I had begun to doze until a soft voice said, "Come, Sarah. Let's get you back to bed."

"Don't want to sleep in my bed," I muttered as my father lifted me from the floor. I felt his cheek against mine as he carried me to their mattress and laid me upon it. I don't know how long I slept, but I woke with a start sometime later to sunshine pouring through the window. Birds chirped in the branches of the tree outside, and the clear blue sky I glimpsed through the parted curtains was in sharp contrast to the darkness and blinding explosions of the night before. Beside me, the twins were curled up, sleeping peacefully.

I frowned and got out of bed. Our front door was slightly ajar.

I heard voices on the other side. I found my parents standing on the front step with my aunt and uncle. My mother glanced at me and said, "Oh, good, you're up, Sarah. I was just about to come and wake you. Hurry up and get dressed."

"Why?" I asked, groggy and confused. Had the previous night been a dream?

"We are all going to the Gellers," my mother explained. "Radio Poland is off air, but they're trying to catch the BBC from London to hear news about last night. Everyone is going over to listen."

"Were those bombs, Mama?" I asked, my eyes scanning the street and the buildings that still stood, intact.

My mother didn't answer. She eyed Aunt Leah, who pressed her lips together. Their silence said more than words ever could.

I noticed my cousin Gutcha standing behind them and caught her eye. She quickly walked to my side. "Come on, Sarah," she said. "I'll help you get ready."

We stepped into my small alcove, letting the curtain fall closed behind us.

"Oh, Sarah," Gutcha breathed when we were alone, sitting on my bed. "I was so scared last night."

"Me too," I said. "The whole house shook."

"I know. It sounded so close. Do you think this means we are officially at war?"

I didn't answer at first. I sat beside her, looking at the window where daylight streamed in, falling across my pillow. It felt like any other morning, yet somehow I sensed it wasn't.

"I hope not," I finally answered. "Mama's so worried about Jacob. I miss him too."

"I know," Gutcha said quietly.

I looked at the pillows on the bed. Where I had spent most of the night, the pillow was concave like a deflated balloon, a few strands of my auburn hair glinting in the sunlight. The pillow beside mine was still plump, untouched, and I reached out a hand and gently stroked the cotton pillowcase. "I miss Esther, Gutcha," I whispered. "I miss her all the time. I wonder what she would think if she were still here."

Gutcha reached out and placed her hand on mine.

"And now we're so worried about Jacob," I said, the words falling out of my mouth before I could stop them. "What does he know about fighting? If we lose him too—"

"Don't say that, Sarah," Gutcha whispered.

"But what if we do, Gutcha?" I asked. "I don't think Mama could take it. And Papa's not himself anymore."

Gutcha put her arms around me. Her soft brown hair tickled my cheek and her scent reminded me of spring. It was somehow familiar and comforting. I let myself imagine a field of flowers, the sun warm overhead, the sky clear, birds circling in the treetops as my sister and I lay hidden in the tall grass, weaving dandelion stems into crowns.

"Girls!" my mother's voice called, jolting me back to reality. "*Mach shnel*! Hurry up!"

We drew apart, and I blinked. I quickly dressed, and we went out to join the rest of the family. The twins were up and getting into their jumpers, grumbling because they were hungry and still half-asleep. Sam and Isaac were standing by the door with my father, and my aunt and uncle were standing on the front steps with Daniel, my aunt tying her shawl beneath her chin. "Come, come, come," my mother said, giving us a gentle push forward. Then she grabbed both twins by their hands and ushered us all out the door.

Nine

Olkusz, Poland, September 1, 1939

By our standards, the Gellers were considered well-off. Their home was larger than our own and more richly furnished, with red silk sofas and oversized settees, a large mahogany dining room table, colorful tapestries hanging from brass rods on the walls of their formal living room, a china cabinet filled with delicate cups and saucers, and tabletop lamps sparkling with crystal droplets. They displayed their gold-dipped *menorah* and Shabbat candlesticks proudly on their breakfront, and they even had a modern stove and radio and car.

When we entered, their home was already crowded with neighbors. In the living room, Mr. Geller stood over the radio, tuning the dial in an effort to reach the right frequency. All I heard was static occasionally broken by a distant voice whispering inaudibly before being swallowed once more by white noise. Mrs. Geller carried a tray with tea and small biscuits. The twins eagerly pulled on my mother's skirt, asking for some, irritable because they'd missed breakfast.

"Yes, yes," my mother said, handing each one a biscuit and shooing them away. A couple of the younger boys from our town were sitting on the thick wool carpet playing marbles, and the twins ran to join them. I saw some of my classmates standing by a window draped in a rich burgundy velvet and waved. For all intents and purposes, the Gellers were throwing a party.

"What have you heard?" my mother asked, turning back to Mrs. Geller.

"We've been able to make out a little from London, but we're mostly just getting noise. We can't get a good signal. Radio Poland is off air for now, but I believe there's going to be a broadcast sometime today."

"So we wait?" my mother asked, and Mrs. Geller nodded.

Gutcha tapped my shoulder and nodded at our friends standing by the window. They were waving us over. We excused ourselves and made our way through the crowded room to join them.

"Sarah," my friend Rachel said, reaching for my hand, "is everyone all right?"

I nodded. "Yes, we're fine. Did you all hear the bombs last night?"

My friends nodded solemnly.

"We hid under our beds," Rachel said. "Mama was sobbing. We were so frightened!"

"We were too," Gutcha whispered.

"There doesn't seem to be any damage here, though," a girl named Hannah said. "My brothers went into town this morning and said everything was still standing."

"My Papa said Krakow was probably hit," Rachel added.

"My aunt and uncle live in Krakow," another girl, Idel, said, growing pale.

We exchanged silent looks. Then, to break the tension, Gutcha leaned forward and whispered conspiratorially, "Rachel, I heard a little something about you."

Rachel looked confused. "What do you mean?"

Gutcha raised her eyebrows and said, "A rumor reached my ears that you and Eli were seen together in the park this week."

The other girls laughed as a blush spread over Rachel's cheeks and her eyes grew wide. "Shhh!" she hissed. "My mama and papa are right over there! What would you know about that? Who said so?"

"Is it true?" Hannah asked, leaning forward.

Rachel gave a small, secretive smile and shrugged, but said nothing.

"Come on, Rachel. Tell us!" Gutcha urged.

"I hear Eli's going to study at the *yeshiva* in Warsaw," Idel said.

Rachel nodded dismissively. "Yes, he told me the same thing."

"What else did he *tell* you?" Gutcha prodded, and we laughed again.

"That's none of your business," Rachel pouted, but her voice was playful.

"Do you like him, Rachel?" I asked excitedly. For the moment, it was easy to forget why we were all there. The laughter in Gutcha's eyes, the eager expressions on my friends' faces, and Rachel's enigmatic answers transported me to the schoolyard, where we shared our most intimate secrets.

"I'll only tell if you tell who *you* like, Sarah," Rachel challenged. Everyone turned to look at me, and I felt my own face grow red.

"Yeah, how about it, Sarah? There must be a boy you've had your eye on," Hannah giggled.

"Not really," I said, feeling heat rise up my neck.

"Oh, come on," Rachel said. "I've seen the way some of the boys look at you."

My head shot up. "What do you mean?"

The girls glanced at each other and started to laugh. "Well, Sarah," Rachel began, "you've got nice—" With her hands, she imitated lifting her bosom up and down.

"Boys like that," Hannah nodded with a smirk.

I crossed my arms over my chest defensively, my mouth open. "That's crude!" I gasped, but I couldn't help smiling a little. Though I wouldn't admit it, I liked the idea of boys noticing me the way they had noticed Esther. I knew my body was changing, and I felt a surge of emotion, something I couldn't quite explain—something like power.

"So?" Gutcha asked. "Confess, Sarah. Who do you like?"

"Oh, all right," I relented with a huff. "There *is* someone."

"I knew it!" Rachel clapped her hands together excitedly. "Tell us everything!"

"Well, a couple of weeks ago I was in Papa's bakery and Chaim came in."

"Chaim?" the girls asked in unison. "Chaim Gutman?"

I nodded. Chaim attended the boys' school where my brothers studied. Even though I had known him since we were children, that day he came into the bakery, there was something different about him. For the first time, I had noticed just how green his eyes were, how the light made a halo on the crown of his head, how his hair looked like wisps of soft down, and how the corners of his eyes crinkled when he smiled.

"He is rather handsome," Idel whispered.

"I think I saw him earlier with his parents," Rachel said. Now my cheeks were so red I was sure they matched my hair.

"Don't you dare say a word!" I hissed.

"I won't if you won't say anything about Eli," Rachel shot back.

We exchanged looks for a moment, then we all burst out laughing.

The hours passed more slowly as morning turned into afternoon. Mrs. Geller and the other women prepared a simple lunch for everyone while the men stood around Mr. Geller, deep in discussion as each took a turn at the radio. Everyone strained to make out any news over the crackle of static. Mr. Geller occasionally shouted in triumph as he tweaked the knob and a distant, tinny voice sounded, and someone would yell, "Everyone, hush!" Still, we could not make out any news.

As the temperature began to climb outside, the press of bodies turned the air inside stagnant. The smell of cigarette smoke mingled with that of sweat, and it was obvious everyone was growing impatient. My friends and I ended up sitting on the front steps, enjoying the stray breeze that occasionally disturbed the treetops in the park across the street. Other than that, the streets were quiet, the park empty. It felt to me that Olkusz itself was waiting for something.

Finally, as the sun was lowering in the western sky, Rachel's mother appeared at the door. "Come quick, girls!" she exclaimed, signaling us to come inside. "Radio Poland is back on!"

We ran into the now packed living room. I looked around for

my parents and saw them standing near the window. I made my
way to them, pushing through the bodies, straining to hear the
voice issuing from the radio. Everyone stood mute as we heard
the newscaster's announcement:

> The general staff has issued the following communique,
> number one, at 6:15 P.M. On the first of September 1939,
> the Germans crossed into our territory. German air
> force and regular army unexpectedly invaded Polish
> territory without a declaration of hostilities. In the early
> morning, the German airplanes attacked a number of
> towns all over Poland.

We gasped. I clutched my mother's hand as the newscaster listed
the numerous cities hit by bombs in the early hours that morning.
So many were attacked that I soon lost track of the number. "Casualties have been reported among the civilian population. Further
bombings are taking place," the broadcast continued.

"Those monsters," my mother whispered, her face pale.

An evacuation train was hit by both bombs and machine gun
fire. A number of churches were destroyed. The capital city of
Warsaw was a target.

I felt the blood rush to my face. It flooded my ears, drowning
out the broadcaster's voice for a moment. *War. War.* We were at
war. There was no more guessing, no more wondering. Then I
heard him announce, "Fighting is going on in the frontal region.
Polish defenses are outnumbered. We are receiving reports of a
large number of Polish casualties."

My mother swooned. My father steadied her before she fell.
"Mama?" I asked, clutching at her in concern. She closed her
eyes and turned away—but not before I heard her whisper my
brother's name.

"*Jacob.*"

Ten

My mother went to the post office every day that followed to see if there was a letter from Jacob. The last letter we'd had from him was dated a week before the fighting broke out. She carried that letter with her day and night, whispering silent prayers to the paper when she thought no one was looking. The list of known casualties and deaths was posted around town. Crowds gathered to see if they recognized the names of the unfortunate.

My mother was afraid to check the lists, so Sam and I went into town daily to see for ourselves. Every time I raised my eyes to the register of names, I felt fear swell in my throat, robbing me of air. Though it took moments to scan through the names, the anticipation, the *not knowing,* made it feel like forever. When I didn't see Jacob's name, warm relief rushed through my limbs, and I let out my breath. Then I ran home to report the good news. His name was not there. He was, to our knowledge, still alive.

Almost immediately, the German presence was noticeable in town. Tanks drove through our streets. German soldiers patrolled our sidewalks, laughing and clustering in groups, their guns slung over their shoulders. I felt their eyes on me whenever I walked home from school, causing my step to quicken as I rushed by with lowered head. My friends and I stopped talking whenever we passed them, huddling closer together, avoiding their eyes. Most of the time they ignored us, but occasionally I would hear a snicker or a low, derisive whistle. Some of the German soldiers seemed no older than us.

One afternoon on my way home, I passed our neighbor Mr.

Applebaum on the sidewalk. "Good afternoon, Sarah," he said, nodding politely at me. "Any word from Jacob yet?"

"No sir," I said. "We're still waiting."

"I'm sure you'll hear something soon," Mr. Applebaum said with a reassuring smile. "And I'm sure he's just fine."

"Thank you, Mr. Applebaum." With a small wave, I began to walk away, but a loud voice snapped, "You! Come here."

I froze, hugging my schoolbooks to my chest. Slowly, I turned my head to see who had shouted. My cheeks burned. Walking toward me was a young German dressed entirely in uniform, shoulders squared and stiff. I swallowed. Had I done something wrong? I was about to obey and walk to him when I noticed Mr. Applebaum had also paused, looking at the soldier. The German approached Mr. Applebaum and stopped only when he was standing directly in front of the older man.

"Are you a Jew?" the soldier asked in a clipped voice. I flinched when I heard his question.

Mr. Applebaum looked confused. "I am," he said, nodding carefully.

"What is your name?"

"Eliezer Applebaum."

"What kind of name is that?" the soldier asked, his lip curling unpleasantly into a sneer.

"I beg your pardon?" Mr. Applebaum said politely. "I don't think I understand your question. It's my given name."

"Are you being smart with me?" the soldier snapped.

Mr. Applebaum shook his head. "No sir," he said, removing his cap and twisting it in his hands nervously.

"Do you know the consequences of speaking so insolently to a member of the Third Reich?" the soldier asked.

"I'm sorry," Mr. Applebaum said in a shaky voice, "did I do something wrong?"

The soldier eyed Mr. Applebaum for a moment in silence, then without a word, he punched Mr. Applebaum in the stomach.

Before I could stop myself, I cried out. The soldier turned to me as if realizing for the first time that I was there. "Get out of here," he said in a low, cold voice. I began to run before I could think. I ran until I turned the corner and could see the park across the street. I darted into the shade of the tall weeping willows that bordered the lake, breathing heavily as I fell against a tree. I couldn't believe what I had just witnessed. My heart thudded against my ribs like a trapped bird. Poor Mr. Applebaum. In the fleeting moments before I had fled, I saw him doubled over, gasping, his face a grimace of shock and pain. And I had run. Like a coward, I had run.

I had to tell someone what had happened. I had to find Mr. Applebaum to make sure he wasn't hurt. He and his wife lived a few houses down from our own. Their children were grown and had moved to Warsaw and Krakow. Mr. Applebaum attended *shul* regularly with my father. Mrs. Applebaum brought fresh flowers from her garden to us every spring. I had to make sure he was OK.

I was careful as I walked home to avoid any of the German soldiers. I kept my eyes on the sidewalk and my head bent over my books, hugging the shadows under the eaves of the houses I passed. As I approached my house, I saw our front door was open. Pausing on the path, I thought I heard sobbing from inside. My heart sank even further.

"Mama!" I cried, rushing across the threshold. My whole family was gathered in the center of the room, their arms thrown around each other. "What is it?" I asked desperately. "What's happened?"

"Oh, Sarah!" my mother cried, turning to me. That's when I saw Jacob standing between Sam, Isaac, and my father. David and Majer were jumping excitedly next to them.

"Jacob!" I exclaimed, dropping my books and running to my brother. He grabbed me around the waist and spun me in a circle, laughing loudly. "Sarah*le*!" he said, planting a kiss on the crown of my head. "I've missed you!"

"You're back!" I cried breathlessly, pulling away to look at him. "I can't believe it! We were so worried when we didn't hear anything from you!"

"My prayers have been answered," my mother said, still weeping into a handkerchief. I was relieved to realize they were tears of joy.

"Our unit just returned," Jacob said. "I couldn't wait to get home."

"Are you all right?" I asked, my eyes taking him in hungrily. Dark stubble grew along his jawline and chin. I noticed dirt on his uniform and several gashes in the fabric. His boots were covered in mud.

"I'm fine. I was one of the fortunate ones."

"You have to tell us all about it." Sam's voice was eager, his arm draped around Jacob's shoulders.

"Give him a moment to catch his breath," my father scolded, beaming at my brother.

"I'm going to make a big meal!" my mother said, clapping her hands together in joy. "We'll invite the whole family! We must celebrate this miracle! God has answered our prayers!"

"Mama, please don't go to any trouble." Jacob took off his hat and wiped his brow. I saw that his hair was even shorter than before, the curls that usually kissed the tips of his ears now clipped short.

"My son is home! You wouldn't deny me the pleasure of cooking a proper meal for you, now would you?" my mother asked affectionately, stepping forward and taking the battered suitcase from the floor at Jacob's feet. "And Helena and her family. We must invite them too. I'm sure you're eager to see Helena?"

My brother's face turned red, but he didn't protest.

"For now, go rest and wash up. I'm sure you must be exhausted. Sarah, go tell your aunt and uncle the wonderful news."

"Yes, Mama," I said.

Sam accompanied Jacob to their room as I ran upstairs to my aunt and uncle's apartment, all thoughts of Mr. Applebaum forgotten.

Later that evening, we all gathered around our dining room table. Wine was poured and glasses touched as a chorus of "*L'chaim!*"

echoed through the room. The laughter was contagious. Gutcha and I sat at one end of the table, giggling as we watched Uncle Abraham grow more and more inebriated. I hadn't seen my parents so happy in a long time. My mother's face glowed as she piled Jacob's plate high with roasted chicken and *tzimmes*. It felt like a holiday. I was warm and full and happy. Now that Jacob was home, I forgot all about the war.

Helena sat between her parents, stealing glances at Jacob from beneath her eyelashes when she thought no one was looking. But I noticed how they kept meeting each other's eyes, then quickly looking away. Her face was flushed, and she picked at her food, barely eating a bite.

After the meal had been served and my mother and aunt had begun to clear the table, Sam turned to Jacob. "Well? What was it like, brother? Tell us!"

We all fell silent, staring at Jacob, who shifted uncomfortably in his seat. He looked around at everyone and swallowed. A shadow darkened his face, and his eyes grew cloudy. After a moment, he said in a hushed voice, "It was hard, Sam. Hard—and frightening."

Sam's smile faded a little as he considered my brother.

"We weren't prepared," Jacob explained in a flat tone. "The Germans overwhelmed us. We really didn't stand a chance."

"But you weren't even injured, Jacob," Sam said proudly. "You must have been brave! Fearless! Shown the Germans we won't be easily intimidated."

"It wasn't like that," Jacob insisted, turning almost angrily to Sam. "Listen to what I'm saying, Sam. It was luck, pure luck, I wasn't hurt. Many of the men in my company died. Most were farmers, not soldiers. Only a few had military training. Most were drafted like me. I saw it all. Men fell at my feet. One minute they were alive, the next they weren't. The captain of our unit fought at my side and he was killed by gunfire. I was right there, next to him. The bullet could just as easily have hit me. I don't know why I'm here and he isn't!"

Jacob's voice grew in intensity and volume until his final

shouted words silenced us all. I stared at my normally gentle, soft-spoken brother and tried to imagine him amid the horror he described. I couldn't picture it. I didn't *want* to picture it. He was surprised at his own fury and shook his head, taking a deep breath. In a softer tone, he said, "I'm sorry, Sam. I know you think fighting is heroic. Little good it did us. And now the Germans have occupied Poland, and what was that loss of life for?"

Sam didn't answer. For once, he was speechless. He blinked and turned his head from Jacob's gaze, picking at the edge of the tablecloth. My father cleared his throat and said, "You're home now. That's all that matters."

Then, as though the ugliness of the situation had shaken the memory loose, I remembered Mr. Applebaum.

"Papa," I said timidly, breaking the silence. "I have something to tell you."

"What is it, Sarah?" my father asked, looking across the table at me.

"On my way home today, I met Mr. Applebaum in the street. While we were talking, a German soldier came up to us. Papa, he punched Mr. Applebaum. He asked him his name, and then he punched him in the stomach."

"Sarah!" my mother gasped, rushing to my side and taking my face in her hands. Her eyes searched mine. "Why didn't you tell us this earlier? Are you all right? Did he hurt you too?"

"No, Mama," I reassured her. "I'm fine. I—I forgot to mention it. After seeing Jacob, I just forgot."

"Poor Mr. Applebaum," my aunt murmured, shaking her head.

"I don't want you going anywhere by yourself anymore, Sarah. Do you understand?" My mother's voice was stern, her expression grim.

"It's true what Sarah says," my uncle replied, turning to my father. "I've heard other reports of things like this happening ever since the Germans showed up. They seem to be targeting Jews. I heard from Nachum that they knocked a bag of groceries from his wife's arms and laughed as she scrambled to pick it all up. I heard they painted ugly, profane words on the Levines' shop window. And I read we are to carry papers on us now. We are to register with the police."

"Yes," my father nodded. "I read that too."

"See, Papa?" Sam said, his voice returning. "I warned you this would happen, didn't I? What's happened in Germany is going to happen here now. We need to leave Olkusz."

"Leave Olkusz?" my father said, leaning back in his chair and staring over our heads thoughtfully. "And where would we go, Sam? Our home is here. My business is here. Our synagogue is here. This is where our life is. We can't just leave, can we?"

"Our families have lived here for generations," my mother added, sitting back in her seat. "There's no family anywhere else to take us in."

"So we stay and wait to see what the Germans are going to do?" Sam asked, exasperated.

"What other choice do we have?" my father said. "We stick together. We are careful about our business. We obey the law. We don't cause trouble. That way, we'll be safe until this has all settled down."

There was silence once more, then we heard Jacob whisper, "I'm just glad to be home." His eyes met Helena's again.

"Will you play for us, Jacob?" my mother asked, reaching across the table to squeeze his hand. "It's been so long since we've heard you play. We need to hear a little something beautiful right now."

Jacob nodded and retrieved his violin. He lifted it tenderly from its velvet-lined case and cradled it between his shoulder and chin. When he raised the bow and gently caressed the strings, a haunting melody filled the room. It was both stirring and mournful, somehow appropriate for the mood that had settled over us. We listened silently, transfixed. I was overwhelmed by emotion as I watched him become part of the music. Jacob closed his eyes and began to sway, subtly at first, and then in earnest, the dulcet melody sweeping him into a world where only music existed.

Later that evening, as I stood in the yard shaking out Mama's tablecloth, I heard whispers around the corner of our home. Curiously, I walked toward the sound, but when I recognized Helena's voice, I paused.

"Why, Jacob? Why should we wait? I missed you so much. It was so hard not seeing you, wondering what was happening, wondering if you were safe. All I want is for us to be together."

I froze, torn between my conscience and my curiosity. I knew I shouldn't eavesdrop, but some stronger part of me wanted to hear what they were saying. My brother sighed and spoke in a low voice. "Helena, you know how I feel about you. But there is a war on. I don't know what is going to happen. I want us to be married when our future is certain. It feels like an omen to marry now."

"I don't believe in omens," Helena insisted.

Jacob gave a soft moan. "You know I want to be with you too, Helena. I want it more than anything."

His words were followed by a silence that seemed to last too long. I shifted, wondering what was happening. My curiosity finally won out, and I tiptoed forward, peeking around the corner.

Jacob had his arms around Helena in a close embrace. Her head was lifted to his. She sighed as his mouth moved over her lips and along her jaw and down her neck. His hands ran down her back as hers entwined in his short hair. I gasped and fell back against the wall, my heart thundering in my chest. I clapped my hand over my mouth, afraid they had heard, afraid that at any moment they would turn the corner and I'd be discovered.

I couldn't believe what I'd seen. I had only ever guessed at that kind of passion, at what it felt like to surrender to such desire. I had never even seen my parents embrace like that. I had always been told it was wrong, that after a certain age, a man and a woman shouldn't touch unless they were married. I felt embarrassed and strangely exhilarated. I stood rooted to the spot, listening to the soft sounds they made, wanting to peek again but at the same time wanting to run away. Then I heard a choked cry and Helena said, "Jacob, no. We shouldn't do this. It isn't right."

I stepped away from the wall when I heard hurried footsteps approaching and began shaking out the tablecloth, pretending I hadn't seen or heard anything. Helena came around the corner. She glanced at me in her rush and tried to smile, but she couldn't hide the tears that stood out in the corners of her eyes.

Eleven

Olkusz, Poland, July 31, 1940

The knock came in the early hours of dawn. Like a rude shake, it pulled me unceremoniously from sleep. My mother's face swam before me as I blinked in the dim light. Majer was sleeping in her arms. David held on to her skirt, his thumb in his mouth. "Sarah," she said urgently. "Wake up!"

"What's happening," I murmured, looking up at her frightened face.

"Stay in here," she whispered, laying the twins in bed beside me and pulling her shawl around her shoulders. "Whatever you do, stay in here with the twins and stay quiet. Stay hidden."

David and Majer whined as they crawled into my lap. My mother quickly kissed each of our foreheads then stepped into the main room, pulling the curtains closed behind her.

"*Öffnen Sie die Tür!*" The command was shouted from outside our front door. "Open the door!"

I had just turned fifteen, and in the ten months since the Germans had occupied Olkusz, I'd witnessed their brutality and cruelty grow bolder with each passing day. Panicking, I grabbed the twins' hands and fled to a corner of the alcove, pulling them with me. They whimpered as their little arms hugged me close, curling tightly around me in fear. I tried to squeeze as much reassurance as I could muster into their trembling bodies. "It's all right," I whispered. "We just need to be quiet now, OK?"

They nodded, staring up at me with large, solemn eyes. "Good," I said. "Think of this as a game, like hide and seek." They nodded again. I heard movement in the main room and my parents' urgent whispers. The knocking became a pounding on the door. The twins jumped. Despite my better judgment, I told them to remain where they were and crawled forward to peer out into the main room, making sure to stay hidden at the same time.

My father waved my mother behind him, unlatched the chain, and opened the door a few inches. It was thrust open completely by a black boot.

"Papers," a voice barked. The soldier who filled the doorway was dark and faceless. All I could see from my corner was the sign of the swastika emblazoned on the arm of his uniform, and the letters *SS*.

"Please," my father beseeched, fumbling inside his pajama pocket for the papers he kept close at hand. *Please, please, please*—a word I would hear over and over, in prayer, in appeal. "Please, we've done nothing."

Then the butt of a gun slammed against my father's face. I felt all the air leave me and I wilted against the wall. My brothers cried out, but I waved them behind me, my finger to my lips. "Papa!" I heard a voice exclaim, and I turned back to see Jacob, Sam, and Isaac rush out of their own room. My father stood holding his bearded cheek, shocked into silence and submission. The soldier who crowded the doorway now stepped into the small room. He was tall and dressed head to toe in the SS uniform, his menacing presence pervading our crowded living room. "Papers," he said again, and this time there was no pleading or arguing. Papers were presented.

I remembered the day we went as a family and stood in a line to receive our identification papers stating that we were Jewish citizens. I remembered the day my father came home from the bakery, face white, and told us a large Jewish star had been painted across the storefront. I remembered the night last October when my father joined the other Jewish men in town to discuss the fate of the Jews who had recently arrived in Olkusz from other towns, including my father and Abraham's brother Berish and his wife, Tova. It was then that the Judenrat was created.

The soldier's eyes now scanned the room as he leafed through our identification documents. They shone like a spotlight from beneath the brim of his hat. I was sure he'd see me, peering from behind the curtain, but I was unable to turn away. "You, you, and you," he said, pointing at my brothers, who stood, frozen, against the wall in their nightclothes. "And you," he said, indicating my father. "You will come with me."

My mother threw herself at the man, only to receive a slap across her cheek from the soldier's gloved hand. He was unmoved as she stumbled backward. "Mama!" Majer cried. I hugged him against me as hard as I dared, hoping to swallow him permanently from view, hoping to stifle his cries as he struggled against me. If the man saw or heard us, he said nothing.

Jacob, Sam, and Isaac stepped forward to join our father. Dressed in nothing but pajamas, they scrambled to grab coats, caps, and shoes, but the soldier thrust them forward with brute strength. I desperately searched their faces as they were shepherded out the door—Jacob's large brown eyes were melancholy and despondent, Sam's face was defiant and angry, his hands clenched into fists at his sides, and Isaac's gray eyes darted back and forth in fear. Our father, with stooped shoulders, eyes downcast and unable to meet our mother's tear-stained face, shuffled out the door. Before I could utter a sound, before I could even think a coherent thought, the door closed behind them, shutting out the darkness of the predawn. Then, there was nothing but silence.

Once the door closed behind my father, the twins escaped my embrace and ran to our mother, who sat weeping on the floor. She wrapped them in her arms, whispering soft prayers under her breath as her lips gently kissed the crowns of their heads, her hands smoothing back the fine curls from their foreheads. I remained frozen where I'd crouched, filled with a quiet dread of the unknown. Daylight stretched outside, soft tendrils of light unfurling beneath the drawn shades as we stayed where we were, unmoving, for what seemed like hours. Finally, David looked up and said, "Mama? I'm hungry."

My mother roused herself from her trancelike state and muttered, "Yes, darling. I imagine you are." And she stood on shaky legs to prepare a meager breakfast from whatever rations were left in our cupboard.

"Mama?" I asked tentatively. "Can I help?"

She didn't answer, her back turned to me, shoulders hunched as she sliced bread at the counter. I sighed and began to set the table, but my mother whispered in a low voice, "Keep the children away from the windows. Keep them quiet. Do not open the blinds, even if they ask. Understand?" I nodded.

We sat down together around the mostly empty table. I stared at my father's seat at the head, then at my brothers' empty chairs, and my eyes finally fell on the place where Esther used to sit. A lump rose in my throat. I couldn't eat, and I kept glancing at the bolted door in the hope of a soft rap or gentle twist of the knob, a voice saying from the other side, "We're home." I prayed silently that my father and brothers would return soon, unharmed, saying it had all been a mistake. I prayed harder than I ever had before.

The day seemed to last forever. We waited throughout the morning hours with our breaths held for the slightest bit of news. The twins asked periodically where Papa had gone. I tried to think of games to play to keep them occupied, and to keep my mind from worrying and agonizing over the fate of my family.

Around midday, there was a knock on our door. I jumped, my chest constricting in both fear and hope. My mother ran to the door and called out, "Who's there?"

"Brocha, open up! It's me!" Aunt Leah's voice whispered urgently from the other side. My mother quickly pulled back the latch and let both her and Gutcha inside. Leah was breathless and pale, her shawl pulled tightly over her head to conceal her face. Her hands were shaking as she hugged my mother to her, then opened her arms to the twins and me.

"They took Abraham!" my aunt sobbed as we all embraced. "And Daniel. They took my Daniel."

"They took Leibish and the boys," my mother said. "Whatever could they be doing?"

My aunt shook her head. "We couldn't stand being alone," she murmured. "I needed to come to you, to see what's happened."

"I don't know any more than you," my mother said. "Come and sit. I'll make tea."

My mother went to the stove to boil water, but I noticed how her hands trembled as she tried to strike a match. I took the matches from her and grasped the kettle in my other hand. She nodded gratefully, leaning against me as I lit the stove.

"We didn't see a soul, not one person on the street outside," Gutcha said, standing behind her mother. "But I heard voices shouting from the center of town, and a loud sound, like a—a shot." She shook her head as her voice trailed off.

"A shot?" my mother gasped, her face draining of color. "A gunshot?"

"I don't know, Tante Brocha," Gutcha whispered. My mother stumbled to the table and fell into her chair. I joined them at the table, setting cups for each of us and slipping into the chair next to Gutcha. None of us drank. David rested his head in my mother's lap, and Majer climbed onto her knee, wrapping his arms around her. Over the past year, they had become my mother's shadow, afraid to leave her side. They were frightened of the soldiers in town and clung to my mother's skirt whenever we left the house. It hurt to see the fear in their eyes. I tried to make a face at them, to get them to smile, but they just stared back at me solemnly.

The tea sat untouched. I looked into the weak contents of my cup, unable to erase the image of a gun trained on my father or my brothers or my uncle and cousin. My stomach churned. I don't know how long we sat there before another sound caught my attention. My mother and aunt didn't hear the soft scratching coming from our window, but Gutcha and I exchanged glances. We stood up and tiptoed to the curtain, pulling it back just enough to peek outside. Helena was standing there, eyes wild and red, a frantic look on her face. She waved at the door and I nodded, then went to it and lifted the latch.

"Sarah, what are you doing?" my mother cried fearfully, turning in her chair. "Come away from there!"

But then Helena was in the room, falling back against the door, breathing heavily. "Where's Jacob?" she whispered. "Tell me Jacob's here. Please. Where is he?" She appeared half-mad, her hands twisting together as she beseeched us.

My mother hurried to her side and put an arm around her shoulders. I reached for her hand. We led her to the table and told her to sit. She was looking around wildly, whispering Jacob's name over and over.

"He's not here, Helena," my mother said softly. "Does your mother know you came here?"

Helena finally focused on my mother, blinking rapidly. She nodded and said, "She didn't want me to come, but I insisted. My sister Malka stayed with her. The soldiers came this morning and took Papa away. We didn't know what was happening. I went with Malka to the square and we saw, we saw—"

Her words fell away, and she wiped a tear from her cheek.

"What did you see, Helena?" my mother asked urgently.

Helena shook her head again and swallowed before she was able to continue. "There was a crowd in the square. The soldiers were there. So many soldiers. And the men and the boys—it looked like the whole town. I saw Eli and Wolf from next door. I looked for Papa—I couldn't find Jacob."

"What were they doing?" my mother implored, kneeling before Helena. "What were they doing with the men and the boys?"

"I couldn't tell!" Helena cried, burying her face in her hands. "They were all lying on the ground. They were facedown with their hands behind their backs. The soldiers were yelling, and their guns were out. I heard shots fired and dogs barking, but I couldn't see what was happening. Malka made me leave. I wanted to stay, to find Jacob—" Her voice trailed off as sobs overtook her.

"What do we do now?" my aunt asked, fear sharpening her voice.

"What can we do?" my mother asked, standing again and beginning to pace. "We wait. We pray."

I walked over to Helena and rested my head on her shoulder. Her desperation and pain spoke to some emotion I could only imagine was love. And I loved her for loving my brother so much. If they had married last autumn and not postponed the wedding, she would now be my sister-in-law. If Esther had lived, maybe she would be married to Aaron now. Maybe I would even have a niece or nephew. I longed to be in that happier world where my family was whole, where fear and sorrow did not overshadow our days.

I closed my eyes and tried not to picture my brothers and father lying on the cold ground, guns trained at their backs, rough German voices shouting. I was both scared and angry. And although I heard my mother whispering prayers under her breath, I doubted God was listening.

Twelve

Finally, as dusk began to fall and we had begun to give up hope, the doorknob rattled. We all jumped, turning fearfully toward the door. But to my relief, the sound I'd been waiting for all day reached my ears. "Brocha, it's us. Please let us in!"

My mother cried out and ran to the door. The moment she lifted the bolt, my father and brothers stumbled through the doorway. Their feet appeared incapable of supporting their weight. They held on to each other tightly. Their faces were pale and filthy. Their eyes were bloodshot. Leah and Gutcha eagerly ran past them, back to their own apartment. I ran to my father and threw my arms around him in relief. He remained immobile, still as a statue in my eager embrace.

"Papa?" I asked, gazing up at him. His gray beard, usually so neatly groomed and smelling of sugar and honey, was a tangled mess on his face. Rust-colored flecks clung to the bristles, and I couldn't tell if they were bits of dirt or dried-up blood. A nasty lump had swelled where he had been struck by the German soldier earlier that morning. Had it just been this morning? I wondered. It seemed like ages ago. He placed his hand on my head, but when his eyes met my mother's across the room, he broke down into sobs.

I backed away, stunned. I had never seen my father, so strong and proud, cry—not even after Esther had died. But now he stood just inside the doorway, broken, defeated. My brothers huddled behind him. Their clothes were caked with mud, their hands filthy as they clung to each other. I began to tremble. Then, my father's legs gave out. He swayed, and Sam reached for him just in time. He fell against my brother, holding on tightly, looking like he might drown if he let go.

Jacob stepped into the room and collapsed on the sofa, burying his face in his hands. His shoulders shook as sobs overtook him as well. Helena rushed to his side and hesitantly sat beside him. There was a look of conflicted yearning on her face as she watched him, her hands twisting in her lap. When she reached out gingerly and placed her hand on top of his own, he opened his eyes and turned to her as if seeing her for the first time. Then he crumpled against her, holding on to her, gripping her shoulders and weeping against her neck. It didn't matter that we were all there. It didn't matter that they weren't married. In that moment, for the two of them, the rest of the world fell away, and they existed only for each other.

"Mama," Isaac choked as he ran into my mother's outstretched arms. She rocked him like a baby as he, too, wept, smoothing back his black hair. When he had finally settled, she held him at arm's length and looked at his dirty and bruised face. A line of blood ran from his brow to his jawline. His left eyelid was purple and inflamed. "What did they do to you, those monsters?" she whispered with a rage I had never before seen.

"I want them to die," Sam said vehemently, still supporting my father. Rather than wet with tears, Sam's face was red with fury. "They deserve to die."

"I don't understand," my mother said. "Why did they do this? What have we ever done to deserve this?"

"They don't need a reason," Sam spat angrily. "They can do whatever they want. And they want to kill us, Mama. After today, I'm sure of it. They won't be satisfied with just taking away our schools or our jobs or our rights. They *like* doing this to us. If they can do this, they can just as easily kill us without a second thought."

Isaac, who had been silently holding on to my mother, gagged and ran to the sink. My mother hurried after him, rubbing his back as he vomited out his fear and shock. I felt like I had slipped into a nightmare as I watched my father and brothers. I didn't recognize them, crushed and defeated as they were, pale with shock and fear. I knew how cruel the soldiers could be. I had seen for myself the bullying and humiliation that happened daily on the streets. But I felt like an outsider, distantly removed, unable to know the extent of what they'd experienced. What could possibly have happened to make them appear so broken? I suddenly felt like I would be sick as well.

Sam eased my father into his chair as my mother led Isaac to the table. She filled a basin with water and placed it next to him, gently dipping a clean washcloth into the water and wiping my brother's face clean of blood and dirt and sick. With Helena's help, Jacob stood and joined my family at the table. I sat next to Helena, quietly feeling like I wasn't supposed to be there. But no one told me to go away. There was a sense of anticipation. We were silent as my mother cleaned first Isaac's face, then tenderly administered to Jacob, Sam, and my father.

She cautiously touched my father's cheek where the lump was dark purple beneath his gray beard. "Does it hurt?"

My father shook his head. He reached up and took my mother's hands between his large palms and kissed her knuckles. "No, Brocha," he assured her. "Now that I'm home, nothing can hurt me. We have been spared, thank the Lord."

"*Spared*," Sam muttered contemptuously under his breath. He gave a small, angry kick to a chair leg. "Sam," my mother spoke in a stern voice, "you've already said enough." She gave a meaningful glance at Isaac, who was sitting quietly, his face gray, and Sam closed his mouth. The single lit candle sent dancing shadows across the tabletop and stretched our own shadows along the wall. Jacob finally spoke for everyone, summarizing the experience in his soft voice.

"At first they marched us into the street," he said, his eyes never leaving the small, flickering flame in the center of the table. "Uncle Abraham and Daniel were there already. It was cold. We were all shivering. They had tables lined up in the center of town. We were told to put our hands up—"

"Like criminals," Sam mumbled.

"—and approach the tables in single file. They kept their guns on us the whole time. We weren't allowed to lower our arms until we reached the front of the line."

"They prodded us along, like cattle," Sam interrupted. "They jeered at us and called us 'dirty Jews.' I could have fought them." Sam's mouth twisted in a scowl.

"No," my father finally spoke up. "No, Samuel. You would have died. You saw what happened—" His voice trailed off then, and his head slumped against his chest.

"What happened?" I asked, though I was not sure I wanted to hear more.

"There were those who did fight," Jacob said after a moment. "And those who tried to escape. A lot of good it did them."

"What happened to them?" I asked again. This time, it was Isaac who spoke up.

"They were shot."

The word hung in the air. *Shot. Shot.*

I pictured Sam's frustration and anger, every fiber of his being wanting to fight back, to wrench the guns from the soldiers' hands. And then I imagined the sound of a gun going off, and my brother falling, lifeless, on the street. I couldn't stop shaking.

"What did they have you do when you reached the front of the line?" my mother asked. She was sitting beside my father now, her hand grasped in his.

"We had to present our papers. We were given these," Jacob said, lifting the sleeve of his coat and showing us his arm. A cloth band was wrapped around his upper arm, white in color with a blue Star of David stitched onto the fabric. My other brothers removed their overcoats and revealed the same band. "We are supposed to wear them whenever we go out."

"So everyone will know we are Jewish," Sam added.

"But why?" my mother asked, examining my father's armband.

"So we can't hide," Sam said.

There was a moment of silence as we exchanged looks. The candlelight flickered off my brothers' faces.

"But that couldn't have taken all day," my mother said. "Why didn't they let you come home afterward?"

Isaac began to shake again, and he looked down at his hands, which were twisting in his lap. I put my arm around him and rested my head on his shoulder. "It's all right, Isaac," I whispered. "You're home now."

"We were told to lie down," Jacob said, staring straight ahead, refusing to meet anyone's gaze. "We had to lie on our stomachs in rows. There were so many of us, we filled the market square. It was awful."

"I saw it," Helena whispered.

"What do you mean?" Jacob asked sharply, turning to face her.

"I snuck out with Malka. Mama was crying after they took Papa. We couldn't get her to stop, so we said we'd look for Papa. Malka told me to stay with Mama, but I couldn't just sit there listening to her cry. I needed to see for myself. We left around midday. We heard the shouting and the dogs barking. Malka told me to stay behind her until we reached the corner, then we saw everyone—lying there. I wanted to stay, to try to find you and Papa, but Malka made me leave. She was scared what would happen if they saw us."

"Oh, Helena, you shouldn't have come," Jacob moaned. "Your sister was right. What if you'd been caught?"

"But I wasn't, Jacob. And then Malka went home, and I came here. I'd hoped you'd be here—I couldn't bring myself to go home until I saw you."

Jacob reached up and cupped Helena's face. They stared into each other's eyes for another long moment. There was something so intimate in the gesture that I looked away. Just a few months earlier, I don't think my parents would have allowed them to touch so affectionately and so openly, especially not before marriage, but now they kept their silence.

"The worst part was that we couldn't move," Isaac said so softly I thought I was the only one who heard him. "Our faces were in the mud. They told us to keep our arms behind our backs. They laughed as we lay there. Sometimes they talked to each other as if we weren't there, and sometimes they yelled such mean things at us. Sometimes they kicked us. And if we moved even a little, if we put our arms at our sides, or turned our faces, they, they—"

Isaac swallowed over and over.

"Don't, Isaac," Sam said, reaching across the table for my brother's hand. "It's over now. You don't have to say it."

Isaac shook his head. "But after a while I had to move. I had to, to go to the bathroom. I didn't know what to do." He looked down now in total humiliation. I blinked back tears, not wanting to hear more.

"It's OK," Sam whispered. "You weren't the only one."

"I was so scared, Sam. I couldn't breathe lying like that all day."

"Me too," Sam said.

"And me," Jacob said.

My father nodded mutely but didn't raise his head to look at us.

"They killed the men who tried to escape," Sam said, "and they forced the rabbi to pray over their bodies. They beat us ruthlessly with their rifles. You did what you had to do, Isaac, to survive."

Isaac began to weep again. My mother rushed to his side and wrapped him in her arms. His tears fell on her shoulder. "It's all right, *meyn eyngl,* my sweet boy," she soothed. "You're home now. I won't ever let them hurt you again!"

Thirteen

Olkusz, Poland, autumn 1941

News came in the first few days of September. We had to move.

The twins played outside in the late summer warmth, oblivious to our situation. My father and mother stood in the kitchen, holding the sheet of paper that detailed the latest order in their hands. My father shook his head over and over, murmuring under his breath, "I don't believe it. I don't believe it."

"Where will we go, Leibish?" my mother asked. She sat down at the table, dazed. "This is our home. They can't kick us out."

Jacob, Sam, Isaac, and I were sitting at the table with our schoolbooks open before us, but no one was concentrating. Since they had closed the religious school my brothers attended and passed the law prohibiting me from attending the girls' school, there was nothing left for us to do but study at home. Jacob was now too old for school, and while he should have been working alongside my father, they had been forced to close the bakery. The doors were boarded up. After the Jewish star had been painted across the glass front, an official notice was posted on the door, indicating it was an establishment owned by a Jewish proprietor. Graffiti had appeared on the windows overnight, and more than once my father had arrived to find the glass had been shattered by thrown rocks. My father's customers stayed loyal to him for as long as they could, but he finally received the order that he had to close the shop for good. He had come home that day and sat in his chair for the longest time, silent and unmoving, looking lost and bewildered.

The math equations that always came easily to me swam before my eyes as I thought about having to leave our home. It wasn't big, but it was the only home I'd ever known, and the memories that filled it suddenly overwhelmed me: the Sabbath meals my mother made every Friday, the laughter around our kitchen table, the familiar creak in the floor when the twins jumped into my bed, the summer breeze that lifted the curtains and smelled sweetly of honeysuckle—and Esther.

Her ghost, her presence, filled every corner of our home. I could still hear the echo of her laughter, could still feel her next to me in bed at night, could still picture her out in the yard, bathing the twins in the tub or hanging laundry to dry. To leave here would be to leave her, to have to part with her, again.

"It's an order," my father said. "How can we refuse? We have to go."

"Maybe Sam was right," my mother whispered. "Maybe we should have left before now."

"No," my father asserted. "Think of the Meltzers."

We silently remembered the Meltzer family. Like some of our other neighbors, they had packed their cherished belongings and left in the middle of the night. Their home was found vacant the next day, their front door swinging open and shut in the wind. A small group had gathered on their lawn as Mr. Geller went inside, calling, "Joshua? Frayda?" He came back out a few moments later shaking his head. "They're gone."

We all wondered where they had fled. Did they have family elsewhere to take them in? Passports? Would they make it out of the country? A few days later, rumors began to circulate. Someone had seen them picked up on the road outside of town by an official-looking vehicle. The children had been clinging to Frayda's hands. Had they been shipped off, taken to the new buildings that had been built in the country? Or had they met their fate like others who were caught on the side of the road? There were reports that whole families had been shot near the river, their bodies left to float downstream on the current.

"No," my father sighed. "This is best. We'll be together. If we don't make trouble, if we go where they tell us, we'll survive, Brocha." He gripped her hands in his.

My mother shook her head and looked around her. "What are we supposed to do with all our belongings?"

My father looked at the letter again. "It says to pack only the essentials. We are allowed a cartful of belongings. The house will be here for us when we return."

"But why, Leibish?" my mother asked. "Why send us away only to have us come back one day?"

"Do they need a reason?" Sam asked in a low voice.

My mother's brow creased in confusion. "When do we have to leave?"

"In two days."

My heart sank. Two days? It was impossible to believe.

Wiping her hands on her apron and squaring her shoulders, my mother turned to us and said, "No use waiting until the last minute. Go gather what you need, children. Sarah, when you're done, you can help me with the twins. We should be ready when the time comes."

I stepped into the small space that was the only bedroom I'd ever known. I had an old, worn suitcase under my bed that my uncle had once given me. "For when you travel the world, Sarah*le,*" he'd said. I lifted it onto my bed, then simply stood in place, wondering what to take. What did I need? I had my books, my school awards, my pillow and blanket. My clothes were hung along hooks and folded in the dresser in the corner. I wanted to take my one favorite dress of pink satin that I'd worn on Purim, but I knew Mama would want me to take clothes made of sturdier stuff. I threw my shawls into the case, along with a couple of woolen dresses. I took a couple of books and my doll, Shayna, though I hadn't played with her in years. I took an extra pair of shoes, the fancier ones I wore for the holidays and Shabbat. And then I looked around again. The walls still held Esther's posters and poems, and her drawings from when she was little were still tacked next to mine. I glanced at my childish illustrations and immediately dismissed them, but when I looked at Esther's, I remembered her sitting at the kitchen table, head bent over the pages with her braids brushing the table's surface, her few colored pencils grasped in her soft hands as she deliberately drew a house, a rainbow, a sun, a family.

They're silly pictures, a voice whispered in my ear.

"No, they're not," I said. "I always loved your drawings. I wanted to make my pictures look just like yours."

You're just saying that because I'm gone.

"I wish you were here with us. I don't think I'd be as scared if I had you."

I turned to the empty space. I had spoken the words aloud, and now they echoed in the silence. Without a second thought, I gathered Esther's pictures from the walls and placed them lovingly on top of my belongings, closing the suitcase with a soft click.

At noon the following day, Mr. Geller showed up on our doorstep. He was accompanied by a German officer. Because of their wealth, the Gellers were granted certain privileges that the rest of us weren't, and Mr. Geller had been appointed head of the Judenrat, the Jewish council that enforced the laws passed by the Nazis.

"What can I do for you?" my father asked as he fixed a wary gaze onto the Nazi officer. Mr. Geller nodded to the officer, who eyed us for a moment before turning and walking down the path to the street. Mr. Geller stepped into the apartment and leaned the door closed while the officer waited outside. I breathed a sigh of relief that the German soldier didn't enter our home. We all turned to Mr. Geller as he stood awkwardly in the center of our living room, glancing at each of us. He cleared his throat and said, "I'm here on behalf of the Displacement Commission of the Judenrat to collect a fee for your new flat."

"A fee?" my father asked as Sam and Isaac stood up. Mr. Geller nodded. "Whatever you can contribute," he added. "For your new flat. Assignments for housing are based on what you can pay."

"Is that so?" my father asked, scratching his chin.

"But we have nothing!" my mother exclaimed, coming to stand next to my father.

Mr. Geller spread his hands helplessly, looking at my father. "It's out of my hands, Leibish," he said. "You know that."

My father didn't answer.

"And how much did you pay, Mr. Geller?" Sam asked bitterly. "I'm sure you paid a pretty penny to be set up in a nice new home?" Mr. Geller looked down at his feet. Sam's face was red as he spat, "Your money won't always be there to save you, you know."

My father put a hand on Sam's shoulder. "I won't have you speaking to our friend like that, Sam. The Gellers have been nothing but kind to us." Sam closed his mouth but continued to glower at Mr. Geller. My father nodded and walked to the cabinet, opening a drawer and pulling out a small coin purse hidden in back. He emptied a few złoty into his palm and handed them to Mr. Geller. "I'm afraid that's all we have to give," he said.

Mr. Geller fingered the few coins silently, then nodded. "Thank you, Leibish," he said. "I'll see what I can do."

Without meeting our eyes again, Mr. Geller walked out the door, closing it behind him.

We were up early the following morning. My mother didn't speak as she opened and closed cupboard doors, wiped the surface of our kitchen table, and checked the belongings she had packed into numerous satchels to make sure we hadn't forgotten anything. My father stood inside the doorway quietly reading out of his *siddur,* his personal prayer book. I watched as he kissed the spine of the book and touched it to the *mezuzah* posted to our doorframe.

Around noon, troops of Nazi soldiers entered the streets. We heard the commotion from blocks away as they systematically went door to door, evacuating Jewish families from their homes. I waited outside with Gutcha and Daniel. We shivered from an unseasonal chill in the air. The overcast sky was appropriate to the mood of the day. I clutched my shawl closer around me, keeping my eyes on the twins, who ran through the yard kicking a ball, unaware that this was to be their last morning in our home for a long time. I looked up at the windows of the apartment; the shades were drawn, the shutters latched. I wondered how long we would be gone—how long it would be before I looked out those windows again from the inside.

My reverie was shattered by the sound of a harsh whistle. I jumped as I looked back at the street. Two lines of Nazis were marching in orderly formation on the cobblestones, approaching our small cluster of homes. Gutcha moved closer to my side, reaching for my hand. My heart raced as I realized the finality of the moment. This was it. We were leaving. My mother came to the door to join my father. I was tempted to run back inside, to look one last time at the rooms where I had spent my childhood. The twins rushed to my mother's side and buried their faces against her skirt. They were suddenly quiet, subdued, eyes downcast. Their fear of the men who marched toward us was painfully evident.

"Everyone out! On the streets!" the soldier at the head of the line yelled as they came to a halt in the cul-de-sac. Jacob, Sam, and Isaac came around the side of the house with a large cart that was piled high with our belongings. There was commotion as everyone crowded onto the road. Helena and her family moved quickly to join us. Helena ran to stand beside Jacob. Abraham and Leah called for Gutcha and Daniel, and my father's brother Berish and his wife, Tova, pushed through the throng to be near us. The soldiers closed in around us, yelling at those who lingered too long. Some wept as we began to walk, surrounded on all sides by soldiers and guns.

Jacob and Sam pushed the cart ahead of us, while Isaac walked alongside my father. I fell into step beside my mother. We reached the corner that led to the town market, and as we turned, I glanced back over the heads of my neighbors to catch one final glimpse of the gabled roof of our home. I wanted to delay the moment, to watch the trees brush against the windowpanes in the gentle breeze, to memorize the image of our front door, our red shutters, the chimney that rose against the gray sky, the ivy that climbed to the eaves of the roof. But I was jostled by the crowd, my hand pulled by my mother. "Don't look back," she whispered, and I turned again to face forward, closing my eyes briefly, hoping to imprint the memory of our home on my mind forever.

Fourteen

Once we reached the center of town, I noticed that the sidewalks outside the stores were filling with people, other citizens of Olkusz. They stood back and watched as we were paraded through the square. Some of the townspeople looked on with ugly sneers, their eyes glinting with an almost hungry look. Still others looked appalled and turned away. I saw a few faces I recognized, loyal customers of my father's bakery who looked on unhappily, but no one said anything. No one did anything.

One face stood out from the rest. He was tall and thin, long blond bangs falling across his forehead. He followed our progress, ducking behind the crowd only to reappear again a little farther down the street. His eyes were so light I couldn't make out their color as he watched us. They reflected the sun that broke through the clouds overhead like pools of clear water. My eyes were drawn to his, but whenever we met each other's gaze, his eyes bore into mine until I grew hot and had to look down. I felt like crying. Why was he staring at me like that? Why were they *all* staring?

The crowd undulated like a wave as we marched along the street, some people jostling for a closer look while others fell away. I squeezed my mother's hand tighter. "How much longer do we have to walk?" I murmured after an hour had passed. I wasn't tired. I simply hated the feeling that I was on display. We were nearing the edge of town, drawing closer to the country-side, to the suburbs of Pareze, Slowiki, and Sikorka. The foliage around us turned from green to shades of orange and rust. As the road changed from cobblestone to dirt, the crowd of onlookers thinned, and I finally began to relax. I lifted my head, taking in my surroundings. We were walking along a road surrounded by farmland, the gentle hills of the countryside rising to become the mountains on the horizon. A few farmhouses peppered the landscape. Finally, we came to a cluster of dilapidated buildings, a small, poor, rural community on the outskirts of Olkusz that now looked deserted. We were told to find our new living quarters as detailed on our latest orders.

There was confusion as the soldiers stood back and the crowd dispersed. "Where do we go, Leibish?" my mother asked. My father consulted the paper and peered around. "This way, I think," he said. "Sikorka Street."

I followed my family down a dirt path to a dwelling no bigger than a shack. My mother took one look at our new home and her face fell. Inside the small flat was a bare floor and a single window that looked out on a back alley, one of its panes broken and boarded up so only a small draft of light entered the dilapidated room. An old, rusty stove stood in one corner, a table took up the center of the room, and a flimsy mattress lay on the floor. The room was half the size of our living room at home.

My Uncle Berish and Aunt Tova had been assigned to live with us since they had no children. "What do you see, Berish?" I heard my aunt ask as she and my uncle pushed into the already overcrowded space behind us.

"This is it?" my mother asked in despair. She turned to my father, who stood with his hands at his sides. My aunt stepped around my mother and looked as well, her eyes mirroring my mother's hopelessness.

"No, no, no," my aunt said. "There has to be some mistake."

My father looked at the sheet of paper in his hands. "There's no mistake," he murmured.

My uncle walked to the end of the room. A door stood slightly ajar next to the stove. He pushed it open and peered inside. "There's a small room here," he said.

"Two rooms?" my mother asked incredulously, an edge of hysteria rising in her voice. She looked at all of us. "Two rooms for ten of us? How are we *all* supposed to live in just *two* rooms?"

"And what about our belongings?" my aunt asked. "And the furniture? Where will we put it all?"

"We'll make it work, Brocha," my father said. "We are family. We may be crowded, but at least we are together. There's worse things in this world than not knowing where to put our belongings."

"The children," my mother whimpered, as though she couldn't imagine us all crowded together in such a confined space. Tears stood out in her eyes. I reached for her hand again and squeezed.

We heard a shout on the street. Sam and Jacob opened the door to look outside. Other people were seeing their living conditions for the first time as well and did not seem happy. I heard tones of desperation, yelling from doorways, bargaining and negotiating between neighbors. Sam pulled his cap forcefully onto his head and stepped outside.

"Where are you going?" my mother asked.

"Out," Sam muttered.

"But Sam—" my mother began, but my father silenced her. "Let him go, Brocha. Give him space."

"I'll go with him," Jacob said softly.

"Make sure he doesn't get into trouble, Jacob," my mother begged. Jacob nodded as he turned and pulled his own cap over his curls.

"And remember the curfew!" my mother called after them.

We spent the rest of the day figuring out where everyone was to sleep. It was decided that my mother and aunt would sleep in the small room in back with the twins and me, while my father and uncle would stay in the larger room with Jacob, Sam, and Isaac. Isaac, my father, and my uncle unloaded the cart, placing my parents' mattress, which we'd brought from home, onto the floor in the small room, while my father shook out the mattress in the main room. My mother and aunt investigated the old stove, wiped off the tabletop, and swept the floor and corners free of dust and cobwebs. Whoever had lived there before had left the flat in a filthy state.

Around twilight, Sam and Jacob returned with what we all agreed was a small treasure. Sam pulled three potatoes from his pocket, and Jacob unwrapped a wool blanket to reveal a cluster of turnips, a hunk of cheese, and a pack of cigarettes.

"Where in the world did you get this?" my mother asked.

"We traded for it," Jacob said. "There's already a small black market in place."

"What do you mean?" my father asked.

"The Poles know a good opportunity when they see one. There's a whole crowd bartering for whatever goods we want to trade with them. They say food won't be easy to come by."

"And what, exactly, did you trade?" my father asked skeptically.

With his eyes downcast, Jacob answered, "My violin."

My mother was beside herself.

"How could you do that?" she demanded, reaching over and immediately wrapping the food back in the blanket. "How could you trade your violin, Jacob? We are not that desperate. We still have money enough to feed our family without you having to trade away something so valuable."

"It's already done, Mama," Jacob said in a resigned voice.

"No," she shook her head, thrusting the bundle of food back into his arms. "We must still have some beauty in our lives, Jacob. Look around," she said, sweeping her arm at the small room where ten bodies crowded together. "Your music will bring us joy. We will need that in the coming days just as much as some extra potatoes. You will trade back for it. Go, go, before it's too late."

Jacob sighed and moved toward the door. I could see in his eyes a flicker of relief at the prospect of reuniting with his violin. Sam regarded my mother in disbelief for a moment then shook his head, following in Jacob's footsteps.

Shortly before nightfall, Jacob returned with his violin case in hand. He stepped silently into the room, and we all stared at him as he gently placed the violin in the corner near the mattress. My mother turned back to the stove where she was boiling water, her shoulders squared, her mouth set. Throughout our meager dinner, as we ate elbow to elbow at a table half the size of the one we'd left behind, I glanced at the violin case, wondering if a time would come when we would indeed have to make the choice between music, between beauty, and our very survival.

Fifteen

Olkusz Ghetto, outskirts of Sikorka,
late autumn 1941

It had been a month since we'd moved into our new home. I spent most of my time at my mother's side, preparing small meals from what we were rationed or could afford to buy, and keeping the twins occupied. At first, they thought of it as an adventure, all of us sleeping together crowded on the mattress on the floor. But soon they complained about Uncle Berish's snoring, a loud rumbling from the men's room that shook dust free of the rafters, and how Aunt Tova kept brushing their hair from their eyes and scolding them for being too loud.

As winter approached, the draft that penetrated the thin, bare walls made us shiver under our threadbare blankets, and we woke in the mornings to a layer of frost on our floor, our noses feeling partially frozen. The stove barely worked enough to cook our food before it sputtered and died and provided no warmth to the small flat. I went to sleep fully clothed, my gloved hands up to my nose, watching my breath form little clouds through my fingers. Soon, our meals became a repetitive mix of potatoes, watered-down soup, and bread. "Not again," the twins protested daily. "When can we have something sweet?"

Jacob, Sam, and Isaac set out each morning with my cousin Daniel. I wasn't sure where they went, but occasionally they came home with a hunk of cheese, a tin of diluted preserves, or a satchel of flour. I heard them whispering about what they could trade.

Each day they scavenged among our belongings for anything of value that wouldn't be missed. I overheard them furtively talking about their connections outside the ghetto, about the Poles they met when the guards who patrolled the outskirts of the ghetto weren't looking.

"Is it dangerous?" I asked, leaning toward them, but they pushed me aside, looking pointedly over their shoulders at my mother and aunt. "Hush, Sarah," they said, and I stomped away.

I felt sad when I remembered how we used to take everything for granted—the fruit compotes my mother made, simmering on the stove, or the bowls of soup we had every Shabbat filled with fresh vegetables and *kneidles.* My mouth watered when I thought of these meals, while I picked at the bland, meager portions we ate each day.

"Rationing is happening everywhere," my father said at our quiet evening gatherings. "We have to make do, just like everyone else."

When we could, Gutcha and I met outside, recalling our school days and missing all the little things we used to complain about. Aunt Leah, Uncle Abraham, Gutcha, and Daniel now lived a few doors down with Aunt Leah's relatives. Despite the cold autumn wind that stung our cheeks, we still preferred being outside to the crowded confines of our flats. The walls did little to keep us warm anyway.

"I would love to have homework again," Gutcha sighed one afternoon as we stood outside her doorway.

"I know," I said, rubbing my hands together. "Remember Morah Schneider? Remember how she used to scowl all the time, and hitched up the back of her skirt whenever she wrote on the chalkboard?"

"And she never heard a word we said!" Gutcha added.

"What? *What?* Speak up, you're mumbling!" I imitated our elderly teacher, turning in circles with my hand cupped to my ear. We started giggling. "I wonder what happened to her," I murmured, and our laughter died.

"Have you seen Yosef recently? Does he still hang out with

Sam?" Gutcha asked coyly. Our eyes met. A smile pulled on my lips.

"You still like him!" I exclaimed.

"Well, you like Benni now, don't you?" Gutcha asked, and I punched her gently on the arm. "How do you know that?" I whispered, and she started laughing.

"It's rather obvious, Sarah. I've seen how you look at him."

I blushed, thinking of the boy who had caught my eye over the summer. Like so many of the boys I had grown up with and ignored in my childhood, I was suddenly aware of Benni's presence, of his good looks and deep voice. Even here, in the ghetto, I couldn't help but stare at him when he passed on the street.

"Remember how Rachel used to fawn all over him?" Gutcha asked. "I mean, I can't say I blame you both for liking him, but she really did act silly whenever Benni was around."

"Shhh!" I hissed. As luck would have it, Rachel was at that moment passing our doorstep. Gutcha turned, saw her, and instantly grew red in the face.

"What are you looking at?" Rachel asked, pausing before us with a frown. "I saw you both whispering. What were you whispering about?"

"Nothing," Gutcha said quickly.

Rachel's bright blue eyes flashed at us. "I don't believe you."

"It's none of your business, Rachel," Gutcha said tersely. I looked at Gutcha in surprise. Rachel was one of her closest friends, but now something passed between them that made me wonder if they'd had a fight. Then, to my bewilderment, Rachel turned to me and accused, "You think you're so special, don't you?"

"What are you talking about?" I demanded, feeling my own face grow hot.

"Gutcha told me everything. She told me how you like Benni. She told me not to make a fool of myself in front of him because he already has his eye on you."

I turned to my cousin, feeling a mixture of excitement and betrayal.

"You think just because you have a nice figure that all the boys are going to like you?" Rachel taunted. "Don't be so vain, Sarah."

"I never said I was!" I shouted, standing up angrily.

"Well, don't worry. You can have him. I'm not interested anymore!"

"I don't want him, or anyone!" I insisted, turning on the spot to run away, my feet crunching in the dirt.

"Sarah, wait!" Gutcha called, but I didn't turn around. My mind was racing with thoughts of Benni and what Rachel had said—I had a nice figure. The boys looked at me. Before I knew it, I was wandering along the back street that bordered a series of fields at the edge of the ghetto. I paused as the sudden sensation of being watched washed over me and looked around. A tall young man was standing half-hidden in the long grass, leaning against a hoe and staring in my direction. When our eyes met, I froze. He raised his cap in greeting and I swallowed, looking away, my heart beating. The man looked familiar, but I couldn't place him. To my surprise, he laid down his hoe and began walking in my direction. I watched him nervously. As his features came into view, I realized with a start that he was the same young man who had watched me as we'd left Olkusz. I felt my throat constrict in panic. What could he want? Why was he walking my way? Was I even allowed to talk to him?

I hastily turned, preparing to run back home, when he waved his cap again and called out, "Wait!"

I looked around. To my surprise, I was alone on this stretch of road. There were no soldiers patrolling the border. The clouds overhead were heavy with rain or perhaps the first snowfall. The wind whipped against my face, turning my hands red as I clutched my shawl to keep it from flying away. I could have left then, but something held me back. I heard his footsteps as he stepped onto the road. Taking a deep breath, I turned back to face him.

He glanced at my armband, then looked back at my face. Now that we were standing so close, I could tell that his eyes were a cross between green and gray, surrounded by lashes the color of sunlight. And those eyes were looking at me intensely, causing me to blush nervously.

"What's your name?" he asked.

I hesitated, then said, "Sarah. Chaya Sarah."

"I'm Fryderyk," he said. He took a step toward me and asked, "I've seen you before, haven't I?"

I shook my head, staring at my feet. "I don't think so," I whispered.

"I have," he insisted. "That day—that day in Olkusz."

My gaze shot up and I swallowed. "So?" I asked, suddenly defensive. He regarded me silently for another moment, and I took a step backward. "Listen," he said in an undertone before I could retreat, "my grandmother owns a farm just over the hill. I work in these fields every day, usually before the sun comes up."

I didn't know how to respond, so I simply remained silent, watching him warily.

"We had a decent crop this year. We have eggs, and a little extra milk," he whispered. "If you could manage to meet me, when it's safe, I'd like to share some with you."

I took another step back. My thoughts raced. I didn't understand. Was this a trick? Why was he offering to share when food was so scarce? Why was he being so generous? And why would he risk his life to help me?

"I don't think that's a good idea," I said softly, shaking my head.

"When I saw you that day, were you walking with your family?"

I nodded.

"You have little brothers?" he asked.

"David and Majer. They're twins."

"They're very thin," Fryderyk commented.

I immediately took offense at his words. "We can take care of ourselves," I asserted.

"It's hard, though, isn't it?" he asked sympathetically. "The Germans are being ruthless, to all Poles. Many of our neighbors' farms were seized and they were forced to move. We were fortunate. I'm just trying to help. We want to help."

I swallowed and looked away. He shuffled his feet. We were

both still. Neither of us spoke. A few cows grazed in the pasture nearby. One of them gave a low moo, its tail swinging like a slow pendulum counting down the silent minutes. Finally, Fryderyk placed his cap back on his head and said, "Don't make any decisions now. Just ask your family. If you'd like, I'll be here again tomorrow at the same time. You can let me know then."

I nodded and began to turn away, but he reached out for my hand to stop me.

"I just want you to know," he said gently, his eyes on mine, "we don't all feel the same way."

Sixteen

My mother and father exchanged looks when I told them that evening. I could tell they were both eager yet wary at the prospect of Fryderyk and I meeting. I could see them mentally calculating the risk. Under normal circumstances, I knew they would never agree to such an arrangement, yet the idea of more food on our plates and in our stomachs was too enticing.

"Who is this boy?" my father asked, studying me skeptically.

I shrugged. "I don't know, Papa," I said. "But he seems kind. He doesn't agree with the Germans. He said his family wants to help."

"Why us?" my mother asked my father. They both glanced at me, then back at each other. The knowing look in their eyes communicated something silently, but what that was, I didn't know.

"Did he say anything else to you?" my father asked. "Did he ask you for anything in exchange?"

"No, Papa," I said, confused.

Again, my parents were silent as they considered this.

"Can we trust him, Leibish?" my mother asked. "Is it safe?"

"Of course it's not safe," my father said, sitting down heavily in a chair and stroking his beard as he deliberated. "I don't know," he murmured at length. "Our only daughter, risking everything for some extra bread and milk."

"I can do it, Papa," I insisted, lifting my chin.

"Some extra bread and milk will make such a difference," my mother said almost to herself. "How are we supposed to survive on what they give us? A few potatoes? And we have so little money to exchange."

As if we were all thinking the same thing, we turned to see the twins sleeping in the corner. They were growing thinner and thinner each day, even though we all sacrificed part of every meal for them.

"Let me think about it," my father said. "In the morning, I will tell you my decision." Then he opened his arms to me, and I stepped into them eagerly. "My brave girl," he whispered into my ear. "This is asking a lot of you. Please think carefully about this."

I nodded against his chest. "I will, Papa," I whispered, but in some recess of my mind, the idea of seeing Fryderyk again excited me as much as the idea of helping my family. I was not afraid.

It was Majer who ultimately decided the matter for us.

The following morning, we woke to his fitful coughing and whimpering. His arms were wrapped around his abdomen, and he was crying out in hunger. His face was blue from cold. My mother searched frantically for any extra scraps from yesterday's meager meal. She only managed to find a few crusts of bread to give Majer and David for breakfast. Tears stood out in her eyes as they eagerly devoured the dry crusts, no more than crumbs. They had stopped complaining about the monotonous meals and now ate whatever they were given silently and without protest. My father turned to me and, with both hands squeezing my shoulders, nodded.

"You must be discreet and quick."

"Yes, Papa," I said.

"Leibish?" my mother whispered. My aunt and uncle lingered in the doorway. They all turned to look at me.

"I can do this," I asserted again.

That afternoon, I walked through the streets to the road that separated the ghetto from the outlying fields. I was eager to see Fryderyk, to make arrangements. The sound of Majer's crying rang in my ears.

As I turned the corner onto the small lane, heedless of my surroundings, I almost walked headfirst into two Nazi soldiers. I jumped back quickly, opening my mouth to apologize, but when I saw their tall black boots, the medals pinned to their lapels throwing sunlight into my eyes, my voice froze in my throat. Fear paralyzed me to the spot. I felt like my reason for being there was written guiltily across my forehead.

They regarded me silently at first. One of them held a cigarette between his teeth, while the other took off his cap and scratched the top of his head. The one with the cigarette exhaled a long stream of smoke, then smiled jauntily. "*Guten Tag!*" he said in a booming voice. "Going somewhere?"

I balked. My brain worked frantically for a reason to be this far from the center of the ghetto. I remembered the previous day, when I had run away from Rachel, angry and frustrated. I had ended up on this very street, so close to the fields and farms beyond. I figured telling the truth, no matter how trivial, was the best solution.

"No, sir," I answered meekly. "My friend and I got into a fight, you see, and I just—needed to get away."

The two soldiers looked at each other and laughed. The second solider pulled his cap back on his head and murmured something I couldn't quite hear to his partner. Then he looked at me and said, "Jewish girls. They bicker and squabble like so many chickens."

His partner regarded me in silence, the smile still playing on his lips. There was something predatory about his expression. The glint in his eyes made me uncomfortable. I turned my gaze away.

"And what were you arguing about?" the second soldier asked. I thought again of Rachel, of her comments about Benni, and felt my face grow hot. Before I could answer, the soldier said, "Ah, yes, let me guess. Boys. Am I right?"

"I bet a pretty girl like you gets a lot of attention," the first soldier said, taking another long puff on his cigarette before throwing it to the ground and crushing it with his boot. He took a step forward. My heart pounded painfully in my chest.

He reached out a hand, and before I could move, he was stroking my cheek, fingering my braids. "Red hair," he murmured. "So unusual to see red hair on a Jewess."

The look in his eyes now scared me.

His partner seemed bored. "Kristoff, enough messing around," he said shortly. He eyed me as well, but his eyes were cold and flat. The soldier named Kristoff moved his hand away, but not before touching my lips.

"You'd do well to go home," the second soldier said.

I nodded. I couldn't catch my breath. I peeked over their shoulders toward the fields. In the distance, I saw a small figure pulling a cow, heading in our direction. My heart jumped into my throat. But the two soldiers were watching me carefully, so I turned around and quickly hurried back toward town. I could hear them laughing as I fled.

When I was a block from home, I ducked into an alley and leaned heavily against the wall. My mind was racing. Did I dare go back to meet Fryderyk? What if the soldiers were still there? They would instantly suspect me then. But if I returned home, I would be met with David's hollow eyes and Majer's groans of hunger. My own stomach rumbled, and I realized I hadn't eaten since the day before. I took a deep breath and stepped back onto the street. I just hoped Fryderyk would still be there.

To my great relief, I saw him in the field when I reached the edge of town once more. I hid behind an abandoned shack, checking to make sure the lane was empty before stepping onto the open road. If the two soldiers were still patrolling the border, I knew I would have no choice but to turn and run. Thankfully, the road was empty. But still I trembled as I stepped out into the open, fearing they might reappear at any moment.

Fryderyk saw me and raised his cap in greeting. As we approached each other, I noticed how his eyes crinkled in the corners when he smiled, how white his teeth were, how his hair shone like gossamer strands of fine silk in the sunlight. I wondered at the fact that my breath caught just a little, and I felt the blood rush to my cheeks.

"You came back," he stated simply when we again stood facing each other.

"Yes," I nodded, looking away from his penetrating eyes, so unusual in color.

"I'm glad. Did you think about my offer?"

I nodded again. "I talked about it with my family."

"Did they approve?"

I considered his question. "I don't know," I said honestly. "But my brother Majer was ill this morning. He looks so thin. My older brothers are trying to find work in the ghetto, but we don't get any money. And we have so little to eat."

I don't know why I revealed all this personal information. I felt suddenly vulnerable. As if he could sense my thoughts, he said softly, "I know how hard it's been. It's been hard for us too. It's just my grandmother and I now. My parents died a few years ago."

"I'm sorry," I murmured.

"They were good people. They believed in charity."

Again, I felt affronted. "We don't need charity," I insisted, even though that's exactly what I was agreeing to.

"I meant no offense," he asserted quickly. "We are friends now, yes? And friends help other friends. True?"

I swallowed. "Yes, I suppose so."

"Good," he said. "Meet me tomorrow before dawn. It's safest that way. There's a path through the field just over there," he said, pointing. "It will lead you to our farm. I will have the lantern lit by the front door. If for some reason the lantern isn't lit, it's not safe, so don't approach. Understand?"

"Yes," I repeated, nodding.

He reached out then and took my hand in his. I was startled by the contact, but some part of me was pleasantly surprised as well. He held it for a moment in silence as our eyes met.

"You are brave, Sarah," he murmured, giving my hand a squeeze before letting it fall.

I looked down, knowing full well my parents would disapprove. When Fryderyk let my hand drop, I backed away, embarrassed and uncomfortable. Yet I also felt a rush both exhilarating and enticing that I couldn't quite explain. I turned to walk home, staring at my hand the entire time, still feeling the pressure of his fingers against my own.

Seventeen

"How can you let her go?"

Jacob and Sam stood just inside the doorway, watching as my mother fussed over me. It was 4:30 in the morning. The sky outside was pitch-black. The wind hummed like breath over a reed as it lashed the side of our flat. I shivered, but I wasn't sure if it was from cold or fear. My brothers hadn't been home the day before when my father had agreed to let me go meet Fryderyk. They left every morning before we were awake. Lately they had found work laying bricks outside of Olkusz. They were marched there each morning and returned home exhausted every evening. They were paid a pittance. Now Sam took a step forward and said, "How can you do this, Mama? She's just a girl. It's too dangerous."

"I'm sixteen," I said crossly.

My mother was silent as she wrapped my shawl around my head. Her lips were set in a grim line. My father coughed on the stained mattress. The night before, he had gone to bed early, complaining of pains in his stomach. Like the twins, he was growing thinner, a shadow of who he'd been, his cheeks gaunt and his eyes sunken. I'd notice his hands shaking at times, and his breath rattled in his chest; occasionally, he would have coughing fits he couldn't control. I tried to push away my concern, but it was getting increasingly difficult to do so.

"There's still another way," Sam said, lowering his voice. "We have more to trade."

My mother had allowed them to trade a few pieces of jewelry and china, even our Sabbath candlesticks, but still she refused to part with the violin. Again, our eyes shifted to the instrument sitting silently in its case in the corner. Most nights, Jacob was too tired to play. But the nights he did, we all gathered around him. The music was something apart from the ghetto, something beautiful, something sacred. When I listened, I closed my eyes and could imagine being somewhere else—somewhere with green grass and blue skies, somewhere warm and clean, not gray and dirty and crowded. Jacob's fingers were now rough, his nails soiled with dirt and grime, but still they produced pure, sweet music. No one wanted him to trade the violin, least of all my mother.

"No," my mother said softly.

"I don't understand," Sam insisted. "I know someone outside the ghetto, Mama. We could get so much for the violin."

"No," my mother said again, slightly louder.

"You're putting Sarah in danger!" Sam exclaimed, and my mother's face turned pale.

"I want to do this, Sam," I interjected, turning on him. I *did* want to do it. The idea of seeing Fryderyk filled me with a strange sense of exhilaration and longing I didn't quite understand. The idea of helping my family gave me courage. And if I could keep the music in our life, keep some part of our old life intact, I felt I was doing something good. "I can do it, Mama," I said bravely, turning back to her.

My mother looked down at me; her eyes were an unfathomable pool of worry. "You'll be safe, won't you, Sarah?" my mother whispered, searching my face. "You'll be careful? If you see anyone, look straight ahead. Don't look away nervously. Don't do anything to rouse their suspicion. If you come across any trouble on the street, turn and come home immediately."

"Yes, Mama," I promised.

My mother lifted a corner of my wool cloak to inspect the sleeve of my shirt. The band with the Star of David was wrapped firmly around my upper arm. My eyes followed her gaze. She swallowed and pulled the cloak more securely around me, fastening it below my chin. I knew I was to hide whatever food I was given beneath the cloak, but now my mother said urgently, "Once you are outside the ghetto, make sure no one sees the star, Sarah. Do you understand?"

I nodded, my thoughts running wild. Fryderyk had told me to take the path that led to his farm. Would I pass other homes on the way? Other farmers setting out for their day's work? How would I know which farm was theirs? I hadn't thought to ask. Now I felt my stomach clench nervously. What would happen if I got caught outside the ghetto?

My mother pulled me forward into her arms. I felt her breath against my ear. I felt the warmth of her body against my own. "I love you, Sarah," she said.

I clung to her for a moment. She rarely spoke such words. Her love was always felt, always freely given, but rarely addressed. I closed my eyes and rested my head on her shoulder. I wanted desperately for that moment, when I was safe in her arms, to last forever. "I love you too, Mama," I whispered.

Crickets chirped in the tall grass on either side of me. An owl gave a loud hoot from a nearby tree. I clutched my cloak close around me, glancing in all directions as I followed the path to Fryderyk's farm. I had passed through the streets of the ghetto undisturbed. The whole ghetto was asleep. The soldiers were nowhere to be seen. Now, the full moon overhead played tricks on my senses; my shadow stretched out before me, rose onto the wall of grass on either side of me, so I felt pursued by a ghost. I swallowed. Each deliberate step I took sounded thunderous in my ears. By the time I saw the light of a lantern ahead of me, I felt I had been walking for a year.

Fryderyk's farm held a modest cottage that sat next to a weathered barn and was surrounded by a fence where cows stood sleeping. I was grateful that it was the first dwelling I passed. I didn't know how far outside the ghetto limits I was, and I let out a sigh of relief that there was no other building around for miles, except for a small chicken coop to the right of the cottage. A rooster stood on its roof, cocking its head, considering me as I approached. I left the safety of the grass and followed the little cobblestone path up to the door of the cottage. The lantern that stood on the porch beside the door dispersed a small amount of light as I lifted my hand and gave three quick knocks in succession, like we had discussed.

A moment of silence passed in which I stood breathlessly on the doorstep. I could see on the eastern horizon a crimson glow outlining the mountains. I wanted to be safely back home by the time the sun was fully up. When no one answered, I hesitated, wondering if I should knock again or turn and run. What if this was another farmhouse with a lit lantern? What if a stranger opened the door and questioned what I was doing at this early hour? What if I was found out?

Before I could move, though, I heard a latch turn and the door opened a fraction. The face of an older woman I didn't recognize regarded me curiously, and I thought, *This is it. I've been discovered.* But then a voice said, "Babcia, this is Sarah."

I looked up and saw Fryderyk standing in the shadows over the woman's shoulder. He stepped forward and smiled at me as he put a hand on his grandmother's shoulder. I let out a breath. My knees suddenly felt like they would give way beneath me. I hadn't realized how tense I had been, every muscle taut, prepared to run. I fell heavily against the door frame. Both the woman and Fryderyk instantly looked concerned.

"Come in, child, come in," the older woman said in a low, gravelly voice. She reached out a withered hand and took my own, pulling me inside. Once I stepped over the threshold, Fryderyk grasped my elbow, and together they led me to a chair. I gasped silently at his touch, feeling again the not unpleasant tremor at his proximity.

"You poor dear," the woman said, regarding me kindly as she leaned against a walking cane. "You're shaking like a leaf."

Her eyes, beneath folds of aged skin, reminded me of Fryderyk's. "I'm all right," I insisted. She tsked and shuffled to a stove in the corner, pouring a steaming liquid into a cup and returning to my side. "Drink," she said. "It's tea. It will give you strength. Rest for a moment."

"Thank you," I said gratefully as I wrapped my hands around the warmth of the mug, breathing in the steam that rose from the tea. Taking a sip, I felt the warmth spread through my body and I closed my eyes, falling against the chair.

"Did you pass anyone on your way here?" Fryderyk asked kindly, kneeling before me.

I opened my eyes and shook my head. "I don't think so," I said.

"You must be scared."

"A little," I admitted.

"You are very brave to do this for your family," Fryderyk's grandmother said, shuffling around the small kitchen where we sat. I looked around at the modest surroundings that were still richer than our own. Aged, hand-embroidered drapes were pulled across the paned windows, filling the candlelit room with a certain sense of security. I let my body relax as I watched Fryderyk's grandmother move from the stovetop to a small table, where she began to fill a satchel with bread and eggs. My mouth watered at the sight of the eggs. She continued to shake her head and mutter under her breath while Fryderyk stood watching me. I sipped my tea, avoiding Fryderyk's eyes.

"Here you are, dear," Fryderyk's grandmother said, returning to my side and placing the satchel at my feet. "Our hens gave us a good number of eggs, more than we need. And the bread is a bit stale but still good. We have our cow, so we have milk. And last spring I made a fresh batch of jams and preserves as well. I put some in for you."

My mouth salivated at the thought of something as sweet as jam, as fresh as milk. I could feel tears of gratitude welling in the corners of my eyes. "Thank you," I choked, swallowing hard. The old woman sighed and put a hand on my cheek. It was rough and calloused, but the touch was so kind that I started sobbing in earnest.

"Oh, my child," she said. "It's all right."

"I'm sorry," I gasped, mortified, trying to stop the tears. "I didn't mean—"

"Shhh," she said, patting my cheek. "It's all right to cry. There is much to cry over."

I swallowed again, wondering at her words. I wiped the tears that clung to my lashes, blurring my vision. "I should be getting home now," I whispered.

The older woman leaned against her cane and nodded. "Come back in a week's time," she said. "We'll have more for you and your family then."

"Yes, ma'am," I said, overwhelmed by their kindness.

"No need for formalities, dear. Call me Babcia." When she smiled, the fine wrinkles around her mouth creased her aged lips. The smile was beatific. Her eyes lit up beneath a fringe of gray bangs, and her pale cheeks turned an almost plum shade. "I am grandma to all who know me," she said genially. I imagined she must have been beautiful in her prime, but more than that, I recognized an inner strength, despite her now frail body.

Fryderyk walked me to the door. I paused, bracing myself for the journey back. My heart fluttered as I tucked the satchel in the crook of my arm, pulling my wool cloak securely around it. "Sarah," he whispered as I turned the knob. I looked up at him. "Be careful going home."

"I will," I said. The flutter in my chest grew stronger.

"You will come back, won't you?"

"Yes," I promised. "I'll come back."

Eighteen

My mother and aunt cried out in delight as they pulled the food from the bag. They stared, incredulous, at the spread before them. "What a treasure!" my aunt exclaimed, examining the jar of strawberry preserves. She lifted the lid and stuck a finger in the red jam, touching it to her tongue. Her eyes closed as she relished the sweetness in her mouth. Majer and David ran to her side, pulling on her skirt and asking for a taste. She laughed and handed them each a wooden spoonful of jam, which they proceeded to lick loudly, their lips quickly becoming a shade of sticky pink.

"Why would anyone do this?" my mother asked, shaking her head in disbelief as my father sat silently in a chair in the corner. "Why would they risk their lives, share so much, for complete strangers?"

Her question remained unanswered, but in bed that night, I pondered it myself. We were strangers. I had only talked to Fryderyk a few times and had just met his grandmother. So why did he seem so familiar to me? Why could I not stop thinking about him?

I kept imagining Fryderyk's face, his kind smile and gray, almost transparent eyes. I pictured his feather-soft hair that fell in blond waves to his shoulders. I felt a tightening somewhere in my lower abdomen when I thought of the freckles on his nose and the plumpness of his lips. I rolled over, hugging my knees to my chest, staring over the heads of my mother and aunt in the darkness.

The following morning, we had boiled eggs and toast. "I want

more!" David exclaimed, licking every crumb and morsel from
his fingertips and gulping milk from his tin mug. I savored the
taste of egg in my own mouth, chewing slowly before swallowing
to make each bite last longer.

"We have to ration what we have," my mother said. There
was a smile on her face—something I hadn't seen in a long time.
She busied herself in the little corner that served as our kitchen,
content to fuss over the cooking like she used to.

"They told me to come back next week." I said. "They told me
they'd have more."

Everyone turned to gape at me.

"Is this true?" my father asked in a low voice.

"Yes, Papa," I said.

"Are they rich?" my aunt exclaimed. "How can they have so
much?"

"I don't think they're rich," I said. "It's just Fryderyk and his
grandmother. Maybe they have more than they need?"

"Still," my father said, staring into the distance, "I can't imagine
why they don't keep what they have for themselves. War is hard
on everyone. Surely they must think ahead to their own future?"

I shrugged. I couldn't answer their questions, but I was happy
Fryderyk and Babcia had invited me back.

The week passed slowly as we made do with the food we were
given. The remaining half-dozen eggs were rationed to cover
each morning. We ate potatoes for lunch. For dinner, we allowed
ourselves thin slices of bread spread with jam. My mother fed
most of the milk to the twins. It made my heart soar that, by
the end of the week, I could see color returning to their cheeks.
They had more energy than before, enough that they chased each
other like they once had. This time, my mother didn't protest
when they got underfoot.

I tossed in bed the night before I was to return to Fryderyk's
farm. Part of me was nervous about setting out again, but a greater
part of me was eager to help my family, and eager to see his face.

This time, a frozen rain fell while I walked so that my boots
sank into deep mud and my breath rose on the air. I arrived on

his doorstep shivering. The lantern was lit just like before, its flame sputtering in the wind. I had barely knocked when the door opened and Fryderyk stood there smiling out at me.

"You're wet," he said, instantly concerned. "Come in!"

"Thank you," I said as I stepped over the threshold. His grandmother was standing by the table, already setting aside provisions for my bag. I saw a hunk of cheese this time as well as more eggs. I could barely look away.

"Go sit by the fire for a few minutes and warm yourself, dear," she said in her low voice. I noticed a fire burning in a grate on the far side of the room. Fryderyk indicated two chairs that stood near the fireplace, and we sat opposite each other, silent for a few moments. His grandmother hummed as she moved about the kitchen. I turned toward the fire, closing my eyes, feeling the warmth from the blaze heat my cheeks. Without realizing it, I reached out my hands to the flames.

"You're freezing," he said.

I opened my eyes and drew back my hands. I glanced at him, embarrassed. "I'm fine," I murmured. Then I saw in horror that I had tracked mud into the small parlor, noting with dismay the footprints that followed me to my chair. As though reading my mind, he said, "Don't worry about that."

"I'm so sorry," I whispered.

"It's just mud," he said. His mouth twitched into a grin.

"Can I ask you a question?" I asked hesitantly.

"Of course."

"My family and I were wondering—why are you doing this? Isn't this dangerous for you and your grandmother? You don't even know us."

Fryderyk regarded me in silence for a moment, then he nodded at the mantel above the fire. "Do you see those pictures there?" he asked. Confused, I glimpsed two black-and-white photographs of a man and woman. The man looked very much like Fryderyk, his eyes almost clear in the photo as they stared out at me. There was no denying the woman was beautiful as well. Her hair was in a bun with soft tendrils brushing the tips of her ears and forehead.

"Those are my parents," Fryderyk explained. "Those pictures were taken a few years before they died."

I didn't say anything. Fryderyk stood up and walked to the mantel. He touched the glass frame that held the two photographs. "They used to travel to Berlin a lot to visit my aunt. She lived there, in a home for others like her."

"Like her?" I asked.

Fryderyk stood with his back to me. At first he didn't answer, but then he said, "Yes, like her. She was different. She was born different. I would visit her too, on occasion. She always smiled and had candy for me. She was sweet and childlike, and I would play games with her in her room, or teach her the songs I had learned in school. We used to take her for walks in the park, and I saw how people stared at her. I remember a group of boys no older than me threw rocks at us once. When my aunt cried, I cried.

"My mother and father tried to protect me from how mean people could be. But one time after visiting my aunt, my father came home concerned. He told us stories about the new government in Germany. The Nazis had taken over the country. My grandmother begged my father to bring my aunt home. She said it wasn't safe for her there anymore, that we would take care of her. So my parents left to bring her to us. They never made it back."

Fryderyk stopped. Other than the crackling of the fire and the solemn cry of an owl, there was silence. He gazed down at the burning logs, twisting his hands behind his back as he continued. "There was an explosion in the home where my aunt lived. My parents were there when it happened."

I didn't know what to say as I listened to Fryderyk. I watched the flames dance against the dark stone of the grate, occasionally glancing up at Fryderyk, but his blond bangs hid his eyes from view.

"Not long after that, the Germans occupied Poland. I didn't truly believe my father's stories about the Nazis until I witnessed for myself how ruthless they could be, here, in my own country. They say the explosion was an accident, but I don't believe it. I've seen how they treat those who don't fit into their image of perfection. They are like those boys who threw rocks. My grand-mother lost both her son and daughter to cruelty, so she swore to put an end to it if she could—even if in a small way."

I stared at Fryderyk's back, shocked by his confession. The world he revealed to me was just as sad as the one I lived in daily. I realized that pain could happen anywhere, to anyone. He had lost so much as well. My heart beat for him, for his sorrow, and I had to swallow over a surge of emotion.

"I'm so sorry, Fryderyk," I whispered.

He turned to me with a rueful expression and sat once again in his chair. "That is why we want to help. What they're doing is wrong, Sarah. Like I told you, not everyone thinks the same way they do."

We continued to sit in silence, soaking up the warmth. I kept glancing at him through my lashes. I wanted to truly study him, but each time he shifted in his chair, I looked away, embarrassed. Another question nagged at the back of my mind. Tentatively, I whispered, "Why did you choose me?"

Fryderyk looked at me, his face serious, and I forced myself to keep his gaze. "I noticed you that day, on the street," he said. "Something about you made me watch you, follow you. And you were the only one bold enough to look up. You stared right at me. You were so angry—I couldn't help but be intrigued by you."

My face was hot, but I didn't think it was from the fire.

"Then when I saw you again on the road near the fields, I thought, it was meant to be. I was meant to help you."

We both looked down at our laps. His hands were resting on his knees. I looked at his long, slender fingers and wanted nothing more than to reach out to him.

A loud snore suddenly broke the spell that had fallen over us. We turned to see Fryderyk's grandmother asleep in a chair by the table, her head falling onto her shoulder.

"Babcia?" Fryderyk said, standing up and walking to her. I followed. "I should go," I said. He nodded, handing me the bag. His fingers lingered on mine. "Your grandmother really doesn't mind?" I asked as I tucked it beneath my cloak.

"We have enough to spare with my parents gone," he said. "I only wish we could give you more."

I shook my head. "No," I said, "you've already given us more than enough."

Nineteen

Olkusz Ghetto, outskirts of Sikorka,
winter 1941

A factory where German uniforms were made opened nearby, and my mother and aunt were ordered to report there, where they worked at the sewing machines until night had fallen. Despite their hard work, we received hardly a penny. I paced each day after my mother and brothers left, worried in their absence. I spent the day performing the tasks my mother left behind, planning the meals, cleaning, and trying to turn our small room into a home. I watched over the twins, who sat listlessly on the floor, and my father, who spent most of his waking hours in bed.

My father's cough persisted. He barely touched the additional food I brought him, and occasionally when he'd cough, his kerchief would come away spotted with blood.

"Papa?" I'd ask fearfully, but he'd just shake his head and fall back against the mattress. "I'm fine, Sarah," he'd reassure, patting my hand, closing his eyes.

I would have sunk into a deep depression if it hadn't been for Fryderyk. When I wasn't worrying about my family, my thoughts escaped to Fryderyk's small cottage. It was an oasis in my mind, a place filled with warmth and safety. I looked forward to each visit and found I lingered longer every time I went. Once, while I was helping Babcia fill the basket, dawn touched the bottom of the curtains. I looked up, startled. "I'm late!" I cried. "It'll be light by the time I get home!"

Babcia looked up as Fryderyk went to the curtains and glanced outside. I saw his face outlined by the first rays of sunlight. "Don't go," he said, turning to face me. "It's too dangerous."

"I have to!" I insisted. "My mother and father won't know what happened to me if I don't go home. They'll be so worried!"

"Go quickly then," Babcia said, thrusting the basket into my arms and pushing me toward the door. "Stay close to the trees until you reach the road. Fryderyk, go with her."

"No," I started to protest, but he grabbed my arm and pulled me out of the house.

We ran through the small forest, staying off the path now that daylight had broken. Small animals, disturbed by our footfall, dashed across the forest floor and burrowed in the underbrush. My heart raced in my ears. Fryderyk never stopped; he knew the way through the trees like the back of his hand. My lungs hurt from the cold and the panic I felt. When we reached the edge of the woods that bordered the ghetto, he pushed me against a tree with his finger to his lips. I panted as he crept forward, peering into the street on the other side of the tree line. He turned back to me and whispered, "It's safe. There's no one there."

I nodded, closing my eyes and taking a deep breath, bracing myself for the walk back through the ghetto alone.

"Sarah," he said, and I opened my eyes to find him staring down at me.

I swallowed, my chest rising and falling painfully in antici-pation. "Sarah," he breathed again, reaching up and cupping my chin in his hand. I didn't move. I didn't want to move. He bent down and touched his lips to mine. I leaned into him, pressing harder against his mouth, forgetting for the briefest moment where I was. The panic fell away. I was intoxicated by his scent, woodsy like the forest, and by the feel of his body against mine. "Sarah, don't go," he said, his breath entering my mouth. A beam of sunlight broke through the branches above our heads, warming my face, and the dangerous reality of my situation hit me once more. I pushed away, swallowing hard, backing away from him. "My family," I whispered, pleading with him to understand. "I have to." He nodded, eyes downcast. I peered out at the empty street and knew this was my only chance. "Good-bye."

The whisper of his voice followed me onto the road, gentle, beckoning.

"Come back to me soon."

By the time I reached the street that led to our door, the ghetto was beginning to stir. Young men were leaving for their day of labor. A few women were shaking laundry outside their doors. I saw children, skinny and listless, sitting in the dirty slush on the steps of their homes. I slowed my pace and stared straight ahead, hoping not to raise any suspicion. Thankfully, I didn't pass a single soldier on my way. When I opened the door, my mother was there, her eyes wild. She grabbed my arm and pulled me inside.

"Where in the world were you?" she gasped, shaking me forcefully. "You should have been home over an hour ago!"

"I'm sorry, Mama," I whispered when I could finally catch my breath. "I didn't mean to worry you."

"Didn't mean to worry me?" she demanded, exasperated. "Do you have any idea how dangerous this is, Sarah? Of *course* we were worried, you silly girl!"

Jacob, Sam, and Isaac were standing near the door, dressed to leave. I looked at them over my mother's shoulder. They stared at me with mixed expressions of relief and irritation.

"I'm sorry!" I cried again, tears coming to my eyes.

"That was too close, Sarah," my mother said, her voice lowering. "We can't risk that again. I don't want to think what would happen if you get caught. It will be the end for all of us."

"No, Mama. I have to go. The twins are getting better. Papa needs the food. Jacob, Sam, and Isaac need strength for their work. Please, Mama, don't make me stop!"

She regarded me in silence for a few moments, her brow knitting above her eyes. Then she turned to my brothers and shooed them from the house. "Go, go," she said, and they quickly grabbed their caps and moved toward the door. When they had left, my mother took my hand and led me to the mattress. She glanced first at my father, still asleep in the small room adjacent, then sat me on the mattress and searched my face for a long moment.

"Sarah," she said softly, "why is it so important for you to go?"

"What do you mean, Mama?" I asked.

"Is it that boy? Fryderyk?"

I looked down.

"Is it?" she persisted.

"He's kind, Mama," I whispered, unable to meet her eyes.

"Don't get any ideas about him, Sarah."

My gaze shot up to meet her own. In that moment, I was sure she knew. I was sure what I had done was written all over my face. I was sure my lips were red from where they had touched his. I had disgraced my parents. I had done something terribly wrong.

She regarded me for another moment before sighing. In a tired voice, she said, "Never mind. Just know that when I tell you it has to end, you have to listen to me. Is that understood?"

I nodded, drowning in guilt and desire.

The following week, when I arrived eagerly at Fryderyk's door, he answered gravely and ushered me inside. His face, which usually broke into a smile when he saw me, was distracted and somber. I didn't see his grandmother at the table where she usually waited for us, tea in hand.

"What is it?" I asked immediately. "Is Babcia all right?"

"She's fine," he said. "She's in the other room resting."

"Did something happen?" I asked nervously.

Fryderyk looked away for a moment then nodded pensively. "I have something to tell you."

I knew instantly I didn't want to hear what he had to say.

"We had a visit yesterday from a general in the Nazi party."

My heart sank. "Do they know?" I whispered fearfully.

"No," he said quickly, "I don't think so. But they are demanding we give them a portion of our crops. They say it's our duty. They say nothing belongs to the individual but to the Third Reich. If we don't want to raise suspicion, we have to agree, Sarah."

"Oh," I said quietly, looking down at my hands. The tip of his finger gently lifted my chin so we were staring each other in the eyes.

"Don't worry, Sarah," he said, running the back of his hand along my cheek. "They can't stop me from helping you."

I had grown used to the quiet on my walks home. I had even begun to enjoy the solitude, growing less cautious as I watched the stars fade in the ever-lightening sky. But now Fryderyk's words echoed in my ears. The Nazis had come to his home and would come again to collect their share of food. The danger of our situation felt all too real.

I was lost in thought as I turned a corner onto the main street that ran through the ghetto. At first, I wasn't aware of the line of vehicles driving onto the road opposite me. When I heard the loud thrum of their engines, I threw myself behind a wall, praying I hadn't been seen.

SS poured out of the trucks, pounding loudly on the doors of the neighboring dwellings. I held my breath and plastered myself to the wall, pressing my back against the cold brick. I heard shouting and sounds of struggle. Taking a deep breath, I peeked around the corner and saw men, women, and children forced from their homes onto the truck beds. My heart pounded in my chest. I stood where I was, frozen, my heart cartwheeling into my throat when the trucks sped past me on the street, engines revving, headed out of the ghetto. The silence that followed was so sudden, it pressed against my ears painfully.

I remained glued to the wall for a few moments, waiting to see if they would return. When the silence lasted, I risked looking back down the street. There was no one around. I stepped cautiously into the road and walked toward the cluster of buildings. Doors stood open on vacant rooms. That part of the ghetto was now empty.

I lifted the hem of my skirt and ran home.

When I burst through the door, my mother was leaning over my father with a cool washcloth pressed to his forehead.

"What is it?" she demanded when she saw my expression. I shook my head, staring at my father's listless body. "What's the matter with Papa?" I asked, leaning against the door.

"He's feverish," my mother said, turning back to him. "He'll be all right. He just needs to sleep." I saw how her shoulders stooped forward in exhaustion. Her words carried no conviction. I didn't want to tell her what I'd seen, but she read the terror on my face. "Something's happened. Tell me, Sarah."

The words came spilling out of my mouth.

"You can't go anymore," she stated simply when I was done.

"Mama," I began, but she interrupted me before I could say more. She fixed me with a look and said, "No, Sarah. It is getting too dangerous. We can't risk it. Remember what I said."

I thought of Fryderyk and his grandmother being visited by the Nazis. I thought of the roundup on the street I had just witnessed. I knew she was right.

"We'll find another way to make do," she said, but I knew the truth. There was no other way. And I wouldn't see Fryderyk again.

Twenty

"Where are we going?" Gutcha asked, panting, trying to keep up with me. I didn't answer. It had been a few days since the Nazis had evacuated a section of the ghetto. Everyone was on edge, whispering about what it meant. For me, those days had been one long nightmare.

Helena's family was one of many that had been taken away on the trucks. When Jacob found out, he raced to their small flat, screaming her name. Sam followed on his heels. A short time later they returned home. My brother's face was red, his eyes swollen from tears. "Is it true?" my mother asked, putting her arm around him and guiding him to a chair. When Jacob didn't speak, Sam nodded. "They're gone," he said. "There's no one left on that street." I noticed something clenched in Jacob's fist. It was a bit of ribbon, yellow like the one Helena always wore in her hair. "Helena," he whispered, bringing it to his lips, rocking back and forth.

"She'll be all right, Jacob," my mother said, kneeling beside him. But he shook his head and pushed away, walking to his violin. We watched as he contemplated the case, unopened in his hands. Carefully, he placed it back in its corner. My heart sank at this gesture. The music had left him.

Despite my brother's overwhelming sorrow, all I could think about was Fryderyk. After a week had passed, I was frantic to see him again. I begged my mother to let me return to their farm just once more, but my words fell on deaf ears. He'd said it was fate that we met, that he was meant to help me. Now it was meant to be over. But I wouldn't be able to rest unless I saw him, to explain, to tell him good-bye. I only hoped that, as I ran through the street with Gutcha at my heels, he'd be working in the fields. Would he be relieved when I told him? Would I be hurt if I saw relief in his eyes?

Gutcha didn't know about my trips outside the ghetto. Only the ten of us who lived in our small home knew my secret. As we ran onto the road that skirted the field, Gutcha paused and called out, "Sarah, stop! Are you crazy? We're not supposed to be this far away!"

My eyes scanned the expanse of farmland, frantically search-ing for Fryderyk. A crow lifted into the air, silhouetted against the gray clouds as it circled and gave a mournful *caw*. Gutcha grabbed my hand and started pulling me away. "What's wrong with you, Sarah?" she demanded, but still I didn't answer. I allowed myself to be pulled along, dejected. The fields were empty.

We turned a corner and were almost home when we heard a commotion. I stopped to look over my shoulder. Two large army vehicles had pulled onto the road behind us. From the lorries, a number of SS jumped out and started grabbing at the young men who were laying bricks in the street, forcing them from the work line and onto the truck beds, guns trained at their backs. I heard the shouting and confusion as some struggled, some tried to run. I heard gunshots and saw a young boy fall face-first into the road as he ran toward us. It was happening again, right before my eyes. My heart plummeted when I realized my brothers were in that work crew. "Jacob!" I yelled, turning to run toward the mob. "Sam! Isaac!"

"Sarah, come back!" Gutcha called after me, but I ignored her. I pushed my way into the crowd, searching desperately for my brothers. I was jostled, knocked to the ground. Something hard hit my head. My face was suddenly in the mud. I crawled for a moment to the gutter, where dirty water ran in small rivulets, then pulled myself up on shaky feet. That's when I saw Sam a few feet away, his back turned to me, hands raised, being pushed onto a lorry. "Sam!" I screamed, trying to run to him, but a hand caught my own. I turned, hoping to see Jacob or Isaac, hoping by some miracle I was mistaken and Sam was actually behind me, safe and sound, holding my hand. But it was Gutcha.

"Sarah, don't go after him!" she whispered, her eyes wide, pulling me in the opposite direction.

"He's my brother!" I cried, straining against her hold. "I've got to get him away!"

"Please!" she begged. Then another hand fell on my shoulder, pushing me through the doorway of an empty building. I looked up and saw, to my relief, Jacob and Isaac, doubled over, panting beside us. "They've taken Sam!" I wept, falling into Jacob's arms.

"I know," he whispered, holding me tightly. "I know, Sarah."

"We have to go after him!" I cried.

Jacob shook his head. "We have to get home quickly now," he said. "Isaac and I need to get off the streets."

"But Sam," I choked.

"We can't help him now, Sarah," Jacob said. "It's out of our control."

I had lost both Sam and Fryderyk. I felt myself grow numb, immune to more sorrow. My mother sobbed, frantic over Sam's whereabouts, but I felt nothing. I sat with my legs drawn to my chest against the wall. The twins came to sit next to me, asking in their tiny voices what was wrong, but I had lost my ability to speak.

"Where did they take him? Where has he gone?" my mother asked no one in particular, pacing the floor of our flat for hours. Her voice felt like arrows piercing my ears. I put my hands to my head, blocking out the sound, rocking myself to sleep.

Time no longer mattered. Days passed, slowly turning to weeks. Now that I no longer visited Fryderyk, our food supply was pitifully small. Without Sam to accompany him, Jacob no longer ventured out to trade what he could; there was nothing left for us to trade anyway. The twins grew so thin and sickly that I hardly recognized them. They barely moved, their cheeks hollow, the skin stretched over their bones like thin parchment. My father spent his days sleeping.

I had only ever witnessed a miracle once in my life, the day Jacob returned home from the army. I prayed for another miracle, for some word of my brother's whereabouts. To my amazement, my prayers were answered.

One afternoon we heard a sound at the door and turned, fearful it was the SS. To our astonishment, Sam stood in the doorway, leaning on a pair of crutches, blinking into the dim shadows.

"Sam!" Jacob cried, running to his side. My mother gasped and fell back against the wall. "It can't be," she whispered into her hands. "It can't be."

"I'm home, Mama," Sam said. His voice was dull. His eyes appeared sunken, exhausted, surrounded by dark circles. It looked like he hadn't slept in ages.

"Where have you been? What happened to you?" Jacob asked. I stared at the crutches and his leg wrapped in a soiled bandage. He attempted to move into the room but collapsed on the threshold.

"Samuel!" my mother cried as Jacob bent to lift him up.

"My leg," Sam whispered, his face pale. "Careful with my leg."

Jacob carried Sam to the mattress where my father slept and laid him down gently.

"I think it's broken," Sam whispered. A sheen of sweat stood out on his forehead.

"How did this happen?" Jacob asked, while my mother knelt beside them, staring at Sam in disbelief.

But Sam just shook his head, his eyes closing.

"Let him rest," my mother said, taking his head onto her lap. "We'll know more when he wakes."

Sam slept for hours. When my father woke and found Sam asleep beside him, he rolled toward my brother, grabbed Sam's hand, and pressed it to his lips, his tears falling on Sam's fingers. "He's home, Leibish," my mother said, still sitting with Sam's head in her lap. "God has heard our prayers."

We watched and waited until Sam began to stir. When his eyes finally opened, he was confused and agitated. He looked at us as though we were strangers.

"Sam?" my father spoke tentatively.

"Where am I?"

"You're home," my mother said.

Sam immediately broke into sobs. My mother tried to lift him in her arms, but he winced in pain. "My poor boy." She was desperate to comfort him. She smoothed back his hair, rocking him as though he were a toddler. Sam didn't protest.

"What happened to you?" Jacob asked, kneeling beside the mattress. "Where were you this whole time?"

Sam swallowed, regarding each of us before speaking. Finally, his eyes rested on my mother's, and he said, "It's no good, Mama. We have to get away. Now."

"Get away?" my father asked weakly. "It's impossible. There's nowhere to go."

"We have to try, Papa," Sam insisted. "We'll hide in the woods. We'll move at night when it's dark. If we stay here, we're doomed. Things are happening. Very bad things."

"What's happening?" my father asked. "What things?"

"I saw it all." Sam swallowed, shaking his head. "We were taken to a prison of some sort. We worked so hard, harder than here, harder than I've ever worked. We were treated like slaves, Papa. People were beaten if they weren't able to keep up with the work. We had to sleep on top of each other. People were sick. Some even died. We can't let that happen to us." His eyes fell on the twins and he began to sob again. I grasped Isaac's hand tightly.

"I heard conversations among the guards of more places like this being built all over the country. Anything is better than that fate, Papa. We can run tonight! We have to try!"

Then he turned to my mother. "Please listen to me, Mama," he begged.

"But your leg," my mother said. "We can't do anything until your leg heals, Samuel. What happened to it?"

"I was part of a group laying railroad tracks. We carried the weight of the tracks any way we could. If we dropped them, we were punished." Sam's face changed; a memory appeared to surface in his mind. His eyes became distant, angry, even scared. After a moment, he blinked and looked back at my mother. "A track fell on my leg, Mama. That's all you need to know."

"What do you mean?" Jacob asked. "How did it fall?"

"Don't ask me questions you don't want the answers to, Jacob," Sam said quietly. "The guards were allowed to do whatever they wanted to us. You really don't want to know how it happened," Sam stressed.

I wondered at what went unspoken, what Sam's words insinuated. I imagined the abuse he must have received and felt my entire body tremble. My mother's face turned pale. "Oh, Sam," she sighed, reaching for him again. My aunt and uncle hovered in the doorway to the small room. My uncle and father looked at each other.

"Sam," Jacob said finally, "I don't understand. How did you escape? How did you get home?"

"I don't understand it either," Sam admitted, turning to my brother. "I guess I was of no more use to them. Those of us in the infirmary were loaded onto trucks and sent home."

His head fell back on his pillow and his eyes began to close once more. We looked at each other silently. I saw reflected in my family's faces the fear I felt myself. I wondered if Sam was right, if there was something even worse looming on the horizon. If that was true, then perhaps it was hopeless. Perhaps we were all doomed.

Twenty-One

My mother watched over Sam vigilantly. With the help of my aunt, they tended to his leg, wrapping his knee tightly in clean bandages so his movement would be restricted. After a few weeks he attempted to stand and put pressure on it. Jacob helped him move about the small flat. To our relief, he continued to improve, walking farther distances unassisted until he was finally able to walk on his own. But he worried more than I'd ever seen him worry. The fight and righteous spirit that used to run through his blood had gone out of him, replaced by a jittery, nervous energy.

We witnessed more and more of our neighbors gathered up and sent off to the unknown, just like Sam had predicted. Each day when the trucks rolled into our streets, we hid inside, peering out cautiously from behind our closed curtains. We heard crying, yelling, angry shouts, and orders barked in crisp German almost daily. Occasionally we'd hear a gunshot. I would cry out, the twins would whimper from their spot in the corner, and my brothers would jump. We all held our breath. It felt like we were always holding our breath.

We became accustomed to silence, to moving about stealthily, to speaking in whispers if we spoke at all. Waiting. Waiting. We didn't even know what we were waiting for.

It was hardest on Jacob. He wondered daily where Helena had gone, and he once more longed to play his violin. Now that we never left our home, it was the only thing that gave him comfort. But we worried that the sound would carry and bring us unwanted attention. So he carried it with him wherever he went, cradling it in his lap, or closing his eyes and holding it to his chin, swaying to music only he heard.

It shouldn't have come as a surprise when we heard a loud knock on our door one day. We all froze. I looked to my mother and father in fear. It was palpable, the fear. It restricted my breath, sent the blood rushing to my feet so my head began to swim. My body went numb. I felt tears close to the surface. I had hoped we would be forgotten. We rarely opened our door anymore to the outside. If we forgot about the outside world, wouldn't they forget about us?

The fist banged relentlessly. "Open the door!" a voice shouted.

My father tried to stand, but he was weak and fell against the chair. My brothers ran to him.

"Papa," Jacob said, "you need to hide."

"No," my father whispered, shaking his head. I felt panic rise with bile in my throat. I remembered, not so long ago, a similar morning when a loud voice shouted for my father and brothers. I trembled at the memory, worrying that this time, if they were taken away, they wouldn't return. My father was no longer the man he once was. All his strength was gone. He had been replaced by an old man. His hands shook as he looked at my mother.

"Leibish," my mother said, running to him and grabbing his hands. "The boys are right. You must hide. What if they take you? I won't know what to do without you!"

Sam was pulling my father to his feet as the sound of something hard was thrust against the door. I jumped at the sudden, angry noise. The twins buried their faces in my skirt.

"Hurry!" Sam whispered. He and Jacob helped my father to kneel beside the table, pushing him down so he could crawl underneath. It was a feeble hiding spot.

It was Jacob who moved to open the door, his movements stiff, as though he were fighting gravity itself. Two soldiers stood there. They wore matching uniforms with tall black boots, long overcoats, rounded helmets, metal buttons, swastikas on their arms, and guns slung over their shoulders. One held a sheet of paper in his hands. They eyed Jacob silently, then glanced at the rest of us.

"We have orders for deportation," the soldier holding the paper snapped. He examined the list in his hand and then said, "Jacob Waldman. Gather what you need on your person and come with us."

I didn't hear anything else. A loud ringing had filled my ears. I felt like I was falling. *No no no no no no no no*—the word echoed in my head—*no no no no no.*

Then I became aware of screaming.

My mother had flung herself at the feet of the two Nazis. She was prostrate, her arms held out beseechingly. She was crying, lamenting. When she could utter words, she pleaded, "Not my Jacob. No! Not my Jacob! You don't need him. Not him! No! Take me!"

"Get up!" the other soldier barked. He kicked out at her, but she turned to him and began clawing at his boots.

"My son!" she cried. "Please don't take my son!"

"Jewish slut!" the man yelled, reaching down and shoving her away from him. He pulled the gun from behind his back and trained it on her where she lay, collapsed on the floor.

I couldn't breathe. When was the last time I had drawn breath? I couldn't think. I was paralyzed with fear.

"Brocha!" Tova cried out. Berish pulled her closer to him. I gripped Isaac's hand, squeezing until both our knuckles turned white. The twins whimpered behind me.

My father rushed from his hiding spot, crawling on his hands and knees to collect my mother in his arms. He stared up at the soldiers in horrified silence. Jacob blinked and turned to my parents. His face was completely white, but he swallowed and bent down so he could look them in the eye. "Mama," he whispered, putting his hand on her shoulder. "It's all right. I'll be fine."

She threw her arms around him. "Don't go, Jacob," she sobbed. "I can't lose you again!"

"Mama," he whispered again, "don't talk like that. You'll see, I'll come home again. I'm going to be working, like Samuel. Nothing more than that." His eyes met Sam's across the room. Sam's face was pale, his lips set in a tight line.

She didn't argue, but her tears fell silently onto his crown of curls.

A rough hand reached down and grasped Jacob's shoulder. "Get up," the first soldier said. "Up!" He pulled against the fabric of Jacob's shirt, bringing him to his feet.

Jacob moved through the room like a man condemned to death, throwing some clothes and shoes into a satchel. We watched in silence as he took up his violin case. "I'm ready," he said as he turned to the room at large.

The soldiers eyed the violin case. The taller soldier nodded at it and said, "You won't be needing that."

"But," Jacob began, looking down at his one prized possession. I saw the longing in his eyes. I knew he heard music in his head, music that his fingers longed to play. With reluctance, he turned to my mother and offered her the violin. "Please keep it for me, Mama," he said lovingly. "For when I return."

My mother took it in silence. With the help of my father, she stood, and they both threw their arms around Jacob. I wept silently, leaning heavily against Isaac and closing my eyes. I didn't want to see him walk out the door. I didn't want to see the soldiers with their guns. I didn't want to hear the sounds from the street as the door opened, sounds of other young men calling out to their families amid shouted German orders and barking, snarling dogs. This time, if I saw him go, I knew it would be forever.

After Jacob left, his absence was palpable. We lived in total silence, except for my mother's sobs. She held his violin to her chest, wrapping her arms around it, rocking it like a baby. It was never out of her grasp. She would run her fingers along the grain of wood and the fine strands of wire. It was a poor substitute for Jacob. The instrument was silent along with the rest of us. Only Jacob's hands could make it come to life. I watched as my mother's tears fell on the plush, royal blue velvet that lined the inside of the case whenever she placed the violin next to the bow. I clung to my mother and cried along with her.

Sleep was my only escape. I closed my eyes at night and imagined Jacob reunited with the violin. My mother and Helena sat
before him as he lifted the slender instrument to his shoulder,
raised the bow, and closed his eyes. He rose with the music, rose
to a place where he was safe and strong, a place where music
enveloped him forever.

Twenty-Two

Olkusz Ghetto, outskirts of Sikorka, 1942

They came for Sam and Isaac next.

Then they came for me.

My mother hid me behind her back. "There's no Sarah here," she insisted, huddling in the corner as I kneeled behind her. Her shawl was thrown over us both. I didn't dare move or breathe.

My father trembled near the door. My aunt and uncle stood together by the stove. The twins slept in the next room, barely moving themselves, covered in a dirty blanket. I couldn't see the soldier as I crouched behind my mother, but I heard his footfall as he paced the small room, looking in the usual hiding spots. My mother wrung her hands. "It's just us here," she said. "Us and the little ones. You don't need them. They're too small to work."

I felt my heart thunder in my chest. I was surprised the sound didn't reverberate off the walls. I could feel the soldier's presence. My knees shook. My legs cramped. I knew any minute I would have to move. I couldn't help myself—my legs wouldn't hold me.

I shifted in the most tiny, miniscule way, but the soldier saw. He walked purposefully to my mother, and the next thing I knew, she was thrown against the wall. The shawl fell away, and I was exposed, shaking in the corner.

"You thought you could hide her from me?" he asked, turning on my mother.

She fell to her knees on the floor.

"Go!" he yelled, reaching for me roughly and pushing me to the door.

I heard my mother's screams as I was thrust outside. My heart raced in my ears. I tasted the saltiness of tears in my mouth. I struggled to look back, to reach out to my mother. "Mama!" I cried. "Mama! Mama!"

I reached for my sister's hand, only to find she wasn't there. A part of me breathed a sigh of relief. She wasn't there. She didn't have to experience this. She was somewhere safe. Somewhere no one could harm her.

I heard a cry. "Sarah!" In the confusion, I turned to see Gutcha running toward me. We threw our arms around each other, holding on for dear life. Nothing would make me let go of her. Nothing. She shook against me as we both sobbed. Hands pushed us forward, onto a truck bed, but still we held on to each other. A press of bodies surrounded us—young female faces, shocked, crying, yelling as we were jostled against each other. Most of the faces I recognized. Some I didn't. Rachel was suddenly there beside us, weeping with us. I remembered fleetingly the last time I'd spoken to Rachel and the argument we'd had over a boy. All the petty concerns I'd once had seemed so foolish now. Who was prettiest? Who was smartest? Who did the boys like the best? What did it matter anymore? We were together in the same situation. I was shivering and holding on to Gutcha's hands. The door closed, surrounding us in darkness. There were screams. Only a small slit of light shone from a single window. We clung to each other as the engine roared to life and the hatch was shut with finality. A fist hit the side of the truck and a deep male voice yelled, "Go!" We lurched forward. Over the heads of those around me, through the small window, I saw the ghetto fade away. I saw men and women running after the truck, after their daughters and sisters and wives. I heard my mother's screaming in my ears. It was the last thing I would ever hear of her.

GERMAN POLICEMEN AND SS MEMBERS REGISTERING JEWS
ON "BLOODY WEDNESDAY," OLKUSZ, POLAND, JULY 3, 1940.
YAD VASHEM PHOTO ARCHIVE, JERUSALEM, 77F09.

JEWS FORCED TO LIE IN THE CITY SQUARE ON "BLOODY WEDNESDAY,"
OLKUSZ, POLAND. YAD VASHEM PHOTO ARCHIVE, JERUSALEM, 2501_11.

GERMAN POLICEMEN SUPERVISING ON "BLOODY WEDNESDAY,"
OLKUSZ, POLAND. YAD VASHEM PHOTO ARCHIVE, JERUSALEM, 1597_229.

RABBI MOSHE BEN YITSHAK HAGERMAN FORCED TO LAY
DESECRATED PHYLACTERIES ON "BLOODY WEDNESDAY,"
OLKUSZ, POLAND. YAD VASHEM PHOTO ARCHIVE, JERUSALEM, 69CO4.

GERMAN POLICEMEN SUPERVISING THE DEPORTATION
OF THE JEWISH RESIDENTS OF THE GHETTO, OLKUSZ, POLAND, 1942.
YAD VASHEM PHOTO ARCHIVE, JERUSALEM. 73D08.

DEPORTED JEWS WITH THEIR BELONGINGS, OLKUSZ, POLAND, 1942.
YAD VASHEM PHOTO ARCHIVE, JERUSALEM. 73F02.

PINKY WERTHAISER (RIGHT) WITH AN UNIDENTIFIED MAN,
BELIEVED TO BE EITHER HARRY OR THEIR OTHER BROTHER, DAVID.

HARRY'S FIRST WIFE, ESTELLA, AND THEIR SON, HIRSCH.

EARLIEST KNOWN PHOTOGRAPH OF SARAH WALDMAN,
DATE UNKNOWN.

SARAH AND HARRY WERTHAISER AT THEIR WEDDING.

SARAH (WALDMAN) AND HARRY WERTHAISER, CIRCA 1945.

SARAH IN HER PREGNANCY WITH HARRY, CIRCA 1946.

Part II
AFTER

Twenty-Three

Cincinnati, Ohio, January 1983

In my dream, my grandmother stands at an empty crossroads. Two road signs point in opposite directions. She stares to the left, down a stretch of road that leads to Cincinnati. She turns to the right and gazes at the longer road that leads to Israel. My father and uncle stand some distance down this road, silently waving her forward. She raises her foot and takes a hesitant step. She doesn't look back. I hear her whisper, "I'm coming. I'll be with you soon."

I hold my mother's hand as the airplane outside the window taxis to the end of the runway. Somewhere behind one of the small oval windows, my grandmother sits with my father. I watch as the plane begins to pick up speed, its engines growing louder, and finally its nose lifts into the air, headed for Israel. I continue to watch as it grows steadily smaller in the sky, finally swallowed by gray clouds heavy with snow. Josh's hands are eagerly pressed to the glass. He wants to stay and watch the planes, but my mother says gently, "It's getting late. It's time to go home."

"When will they be back?" I ask my mother as we walk through the airport to the parking lot.

"Your father will be home in a couple of weeks," she says. "He's going to help Bubbe get settled. I'm not sure when she'll be back."

"Will we see Bubbe again?" Josh asks as my mother buckles him into the station wagon.

"Of course."

"Will she be happier?" he asks.

My mother doesn't answer at first. Finally, she says, "I hope so."

As I sit staring out the window, I remember the many times my aunt and uncle visited this past week. I remember the conversations in Yiddish between my father and uncle. I knew they spoke Yiddish, the language of my father's childhood, when they didn't want us to know what they were saying.

"Why did she go?" I ask, watching my mother's face in the rearview mirror. She meets my eye. She concentrates on her answer. "Sometimes people need to go somewhere new, to start fresh," she explains. "We all think this is best for her, Melissa. Even her doctors think so."

"But why Israel?" I ask, thinking about the country I'd only read about in Sunday school. I pictured the map on my classroom wall. It conjured images of deserts and camels and biblical characters. To me, it was so far away and foreign.

My mother pulls the car onto the highway. The airport terminal fades from view as we drive home. Some small part of me feels we are leaving my grandmother behind. But my mother looks at me again and says, "Your grandmother has family in Israel, family she hasn't seen in such a long time. They can help her better than we can. They understand what she's been through. They can help her heal."

I consider this as I stare out the window. What had my grandmother been through? I wonder. Who is the family she is going to meet, family I didn't know existed? And will my grandmother ever be happy again?

Twenty-Four

Peterswaldau, subcamp of Gross Rosen,
Lower Silesia, May 1945

The day dawned the same as any other: dull, gray, as colorless as an undeveloped strip of film. Yesterday I had seen purple wildflowers growing along the fence and thought, *It must be spring.* But the color had felt like an intrusion, an unwelcome interruption to the somber hues of the camp, of the barracks that we ate in, slept in, worked in. I blinked and rolled my head. The faces that stirred in the bunks around me were skeletal and pale, lips dried and cracked, shaved heads exposed or wrapped in dirtied kerchiefs. Our feet were bare and caked with mud. Our clothing was little more than rags.

But through my tired fog I noticed that something was different on this morning.

There was silence.

I sat up stiffly, puzzled. Gutcha stirred beside me, her thin limbs collecting together as she struggled to sit up as well. "What time is it?" she whispered. I shrugged and peered over the side of the plank we slept on at the girls in the lower bunk. Five or six bodies lay tangled together on the hard wood, strangers embracing each other for warmth. One of the young girls separated herself from her bedmates and looked up at us with sunken eyes. "What's happening?" she whispered. We all gazed at the grimy windows that lined one wall of our barracks. Through the dirt, pale sunlight streamed in, falling weakly on the muddy floor and on the few faces that now stood up to look outside.

"What do you see?"

"Is it morning?"

"Where is the *Aufseherin*?"

I finally threw my legs over the edge and dropped to the floor. The motion each morning made the teeth in my mouth clatter together and the limbs of my body ache from stiffness and fatigue. It was hard to sleep surrounded by so many stinking bodies, the sounds of moans and sobs and dry, hacking coughs waking me every few hours. But living on a short amount of sleep was one of the many things to which I had become accustomed.

Confusion and panic surrounded me. I reached for Gutcha's hand and pulled her with me to the window. "What's happening?" she asked, her fingers clutching my own. "I don't know," I said, pushing a few girls aside to peer out into the yard.

Before dawn each morning, we were awakened by the sound of sirens and the loud shouting of our *Aufseherin* strolling between our bunks, striking her club against our bed frames and the unlucky girls who didn't stir fast enough. We were forced to line up in the rain, or under the baking sun of summer, with barely any food in our stomachs to give us strength for roll call before a breakfast of bread soaked in murky water. If we were lucky, we had a bit of boiled potato to sustain us for the day. But now, I had the sense it was later in the morning than usual and preternaturally quiet. Standing on my toes, I gazed outside.

At first, I didn't register what I was seeing. The muddy ground outside our barracks, usually patrolled by female guards, stood vacant. The only signs of life were the few blackbirds that pecked at the ground or fluttered to the trees in the distance, beyond the barbwire fence. The fence itself reached silently toward a cruel sky, unguarded by the uniformed soldiers—an undefended sentinel.

I gasped. Someone beside me said, "There's no one there!"

As fast as the feeble bodies around me could, everyone pressed in closer to peer outside. Soon, the windows were surrounded, faces looking this way and that for any sign of life. Voices murmured, "Where did everyone go? What does this mean? What's going to happen?"

Some prayers were uttered, both in thanks and in fear. The girl standing to my right, a young brunette who had arrived just the week before, slid down the wall and began to cry hysterically. "This is it! They're going to kill us! They're going to kill us!" she chanted. Her cries hurt my ears.

"Will someone shut her up?" another girl asked angrily.

I threw my arms around Gutcha and felt her heart flutter beneath her bony rib cage. I was afraid to breathe, to hope, to think. The minutes ticked away like hours as we held each other, dropping to the floor when we became too weak to stand. Gutcha curled her body next to mine and whispered, "Whatever happens, Sarah, we must stay together." I nodded and rested my head against hers, feeling the soft stubble that grew there rubbing my cheek.

The longer the morning stretched, the more we allowed ourselves to wonder and hope, but also to fear. No one was brave enough to step foot outside. Silence fell as others joined us on the ground, huddling below the windows, waiting and wondering. Finally, a sound reached us. Low at first, it built in volume and urgency, a vibrating rattle that was both scary and yet familiar. Some of the girls crawled to the farthest corners of the barrack, squeezing together in fear. A few of the inmates continued to look outside, though, and an older girl finally shouted, "It's a truck!"

"German?" someone whispered.

The girl at the window stretched her neck to get a better view. "No. I don't think so," she said. "No, no, no—it's not German. There's a line of them. Look!"

I rose on my haunches to look outside while Gutcha knelt beside me. My stomach growled. I hadn't eaten since the night before, and that had been a third of a piece of bread. But I ignored the feeling and rubbed away a patch of filth. Trucks were pouring into the camp, along with large, lumbering tanks. Soldiers sat behind the wheels and in the truck beds, and an unfamiliar red flag waved from the foremost vehicle. I held my breath. My legs trembled. "What do you see?" Gutcha asked. I ducked reflexively as the trucks pulled alongside our barrack but then stood once they'd passed. I was close enough to see the details of the men's faces now. Their expressions as they slowly drove through the yard were cautious and grim. Some of the girls behind me whimpered. Some cried outright, in anticipation or distress.

Finally, the closest vehicle pulled to a stop. My heart raced as I watched the soldiers jump to the ground. One took off his hat and wiped his forehead with a handkerchief, while another shook his head as his eyes took in the line of gray buildings. I realized that none of the other girls in the other barracks had left the safety of their bunks either. I imagined the anxious faces peering out at the soldiers and wondered how long we would have remained like that if they hadn't arrived.

The first soldier turned to gaze in our direction. He said something to the soldier beside him. The second soldier saluted and went to the nearest lorry, returning with a megaphone that he handed to the first soldier. The silence was shattered as he began to speak, but the words meant nothing to us. It wasn't German or Polish, French or Danish. We glanced at each other. "What is he saying?" the newly arrived brunette asked, chewing nervously on her dirty fingernails. Her tears had left dark stains on her cheeks. A woman pushed her way forward. "Russian!" she exclaimed. "That's Russian!"

We let her pass to the window, where she stood looking out at the men. They congregated into a group as we watched. They didn't look unkind, only confused and curious. Finally, the first soldier spoke again, and we all turned our eyes to the woman.

"Do you understand what he's saying?" someone asked.

"Shhh!" the woman hissed. She listened as the soldier spoke into the megaphone, then turned to us, her eyes wide. "He says, do not be afraid. We mean no harm. The Germans have gone. Please come out."

I didn't believe my ears at first. "Can this be true?" someone asked. Gutcha and I looked at each other, a spark of hope igniting between us. As much as we wanted to believe his words, no one moved toward the door. We all shared a sense of apathy and a general lack of trust. The men continued to watch us warily from the other side of the glass until they all turned as one to face the neighboring barrack. We craned our necks to see a frail girl standing on the dirt path leading to the center of the yard where we lined up daily. She was alone, her threadbare, striped prisoner's gown whipping against her bony knees, her head wrapped in a soiled kerchief. She said something we couldn't hear, then collapsed to the ground. One of the soldiers rushed to the young woman's side, lifting her in his arms. As we watched, the women from the other bunk ran into the yard, surrounding the soldier, reaching for him with emaciated arms.

Before I could think to move, the bodies around me pressed forward, rushing at the door to our bunk and throwing it open. A chill wind washed over us. I was pushed forward with the rest, gripping Gutcha's hand in my own. "Don't let go!" I yelled as we were surrounded by yelling, screaming girls, voices merging incoherently.

The yard was chaos. Someone behind me fell to her knees as we were shoved and jostled, grabbing at my hem to steady herself. I jerked backward, landing beside the girl, mud splattering my bare legs and soaking through my gown. Gutcha yanked the material out of the girl's fist and I heard it rip. She pulled me up, wrapping her arm around my shoulder and guiding me through the melee. I heard someone yell, "Give us food!"

Gutcha pulled me toward one of the soldiers, a young man with dark curls flattened to his forehead and a sprinkle of freckles on his nose. His eyes were wide as he backed away from us, striking out at the hands that reached for his uniform as though shooing away pesky flies. He pulled a rifle from his back and trained it on us with shaking hands, yelling, "*Nyet! Nyet!*" I clutched Gutcha tighter, staring at the butt of the rifle only a few feet away. I felt my feet sink into muck and remembered it had rained the day before. A voice, louder than the others, began barking orders in Russian. The soldier turned in the direction of the voice and reluctantly lowered his weapon, cursing under his breath.

A tall man with graying hair beneath his fur *ushanka* and deep, heavily lidded eyes stepped forward, reaching for the megaphone. In a commanding voice that reverberated through the yard, he yelled, "Stop!" We all froze in place. A blackbird circled overhead, its singular cry echoing in the sudden silence. My heart thundered in my chest as I wondered what would happen next. Some of the soldiers huddled together, turning their backs on us as they whispered to each other. The gray-haired soldier removed his *ushanka* and ran a hand through his silver curls before speaking into the megaphone again. "I am Lieutenant Kramarov of the Soviet Red Army," he said in fluent German. "The war is over. The Germans have fled. You are all free to go."

He lowered the megaphone and looked around the now-still yard. No one reacted. I glanced at Gutcha, breathless. While his words were clear as a bell, I couldn't wrap my mind around their meaning. How was it possible, after all this time? The war was over? What war? In the struggle to survive each day, the warfront, the actual fighting, had become meaningless. A few of the girls surrounding me looked at each other with similarly confused expressions. A low hum filled the camp yard.

The lieutenant frowned at us. "Did you hear what I said?" he asked. "You are free to go."

"Free?" someone yelled in a hoarse voice. An older woman in the back of the crowd limped forward. A young girl, no older than ten or eleven, supported her as she shuffled toward the lieutenant. "What do you mean, free? We have nowhere to go."

The lieutenant's eyes moved over us as we stared back at him. Many of the women around me were coughing and shaking in the cold morning air. In contrast, the soldiers wore uniforms of long wool coats cinched at the waist with black belts and trousers of coarse fabric that the wind couldn't penetrate. The lieutenant's uniform was different from those of the other soldiers. His lapels were lined with fur, and a half-dozen medals were pinned to his chest, glinting in the pale sun. I realized suddenly how cold and wet I was and began to shiver. Another woman started to step forward but began to fall. The soldier closest to her reached out and caught her, holding her up by her arms. "Please," I heard her whisper. "We are hungry."

Abruptly, the women surged forward once more, voices rising as one. I was pushed by the crowd, still grasping Gutcha's hand for dear life. The emptiness in my own stomach, while now familiar, was no less painful. My vision swam and I blinked many times, praying I wouldn't fall and be trampled by the crowd. The soldiers formed a wall with their bodies as we pleaded with them. I watched as the lieutenant waved a few of his men to the corner of our barracks. Heads bent, he consulted with them and pointed to the trucks. They saluted and returned to the vehicles, speaking into radio transmitters. I kept my eyes on the lieutenant as he walked back to the wall of soldiers, placing his hand on two of their shoulders so that they parted for him. He held up his hand and addressed us in a firm voice.

"We must have order! Form two groups. Those of you who need medical assistance, over here. Those who don't, over here. We have called for provisions."

Despite feeling weak and cold and tired and starved, my cousin and I were better off than many of those around us. We followed the group of women who moved to the far end of the yard near the barbwire fence, huddling together for warmth. The sun was now higher in the sky, but the weak rays did little to dispel the early spring cold. I watched as the lieutenant moved between the soldiers, barking orders and gesturing with animated hands. Half of his men began setting up cots near the trucks for those too weak to stand or sit in the yard. I noticed a few of the Russian soldiers were medics, passing between the weak and sick, carrying black cases and listening to the girls' chests with stethoscopes.

By midday, the rest of us were sitting in groups, blankets thrown over our shoulders and heads, holding tin mugs of warm tea and nibbling small, dry biscuits. The tea was the best thing I had tasted in such a long time. The heat spread through my body, warming my aching limbs, but the food did little to alleviate my hunger. The dry, crumbling bread felt like a lead weight in my stomach. I watched a group of women crowd around the trucks, begging for more food. The soldiers shook their heads and pointed for them to return to the yard. A partition was set up so we could no longer see the patients lying on the cots.

"What does all this mean?" I whispered to Gutcha as she nibbled her small biscuit. She shrugged, head lowered, eyes on the ground. "Can it really be over?" I asked, looking around the yard where just the day before we had witnessed a girl whipped to death. "Yes," Gutcha nodded weakly. "When the marches began, they must have known."

I thought silently about the roundups that had been taking place almost daily. Large numbers of women had been marched out of the camp gates to some unknown location. We had whispered and speculated about their departure, wondering where they were sent, fearing it couldn't be a good sign. Somehow, Gutcha and I hadn't been separated. We had been put to work until the day before.

I expected to feel relief, hope, or joy at the idea that it was over—anything but the emptiness that filled me. When I tried to think ahead to the future, it was like stumbling into a brick wall. There was nothing there but the unknowable, a barrier stretching as tall and as far as my inner eye could see. Everything I had once thought or wished for was gone.

The gray-haired lieutenant moved among the groups of women, drawing closer to where we sat. He continued to hand out blankets that had arrived with two other trucks, bringing additional supplies. I noticed up close that the skin of his face was red and weathered like old leather and that white hair sprouted in tufts from his ears. He knelt beside each group, talking quietly to the female prisoners. His face reflected genuine concern.

He stopped before us and tipped his hat. "Hello," he said in German with a strong Russian accent. "Are you comfortable? Do you need another blanket?"

I shook my head, but Gutcha shivered and the lieutenant wrapped a second blanket around her shoulders. "Can you tell me your names?" he asked.

"I'm Sarah," I said, my voice hoarse. "This is my cousin Gutcha," I said when Gutcha didn't answer.

"Can you tell me where you are from?" he asked kindly, kneeling so he was level with our eyes.

"Olkusz," I answered obediently.

"I have not heard of Olkusz," he said, frowning. "It is German?"

"It's in Poland," I told him. He nodded and bit his lip. "And how long have you been here?" he asked. Gutcha and I exchanged a look. I had no idea how long we had been in the camp. Time meant nothing to me anymore.

He sighed and shook his head. "Poor girls," he murmured under his breath. "I can't imagine what you've been through." His bright blue eyes regarded us sympathetically before he stood again and wiped his hands on his trousers. "You will be all right," he reassured us before moving to the next group. "We will take care of you."

At nightfall, more food was distributed. This time we received a hot plate of stew along with our tea and bread. My mouth watered as I took my first bite. The flavors that met my tongue were so unexpected and delicious that I devoured the meal in seconds. Gutcha sopped up the gravy with the last of her bread and raised the bowl to her lips to lick up whatever remained. My stomach finally felt full after what had seemed a lifetime of starvation. We were sitting near the fence, and I closed my eyes and leaned back against the rusty links, exhausted, my limbs suddenly heavy. I heard drunken laughter from the soldiers who patrolled the camp grounds as they passed around canteens and sang songs in deep Russian baritones. Bonfires were lit throughout the camp. No one was barking orders at us to line up for roll call or report to our jobs. For the briefest moment, I allowed myself to relax.

Then, the full, satisfied feeling in my stomach turned into something uncomfortable, twisting painfully. I gasped and leaned forward, pressing my hands to my stomach. "What's wrong?" Gutcha asked, looking at me. Before I could answer, my stomach cramped painfully, and I gagged and turned away, vomiting everything I had eaten onto the ground beside me. I fell back against the fence, wiping my face with the back of my hand, clammy and trembling. Gutcha crawled to my side and put her arm around me. "Are you all right?" she asked faintly. A sheen of sweat glistened on her own face. I looked at her and said, "I'm better now, but you don't look well." She moaned and murmured, "I don't feel so well."

Around us, many of the women were stirring and groaning. Several girls doubled over, sick to their stomachs as well. Alerted by the sound, the lieutenant moved into the yard, followed by the army medics. One of them knelt at my side and shone a light into my face. I blinked against the brightness and tried to shoo him away. "I'm fine," I murmured. "Just so tired. Let me sleep." Then he turned to Gutcha. When I looked at my cousin, I saw her body convulsing on the ground. "Gutcha!" I screamed, crawling to her. The medic pushed me back as he knelt over her, pulling back her eyelids and rolling her onto her side. He waved for another soldier to come hold her down as her spasms subsided and she fell unconscious. As the two medics lifted her onto a gurney, I panicked. "Where are you taking her?" I cried, grabbing the hem of the soldier's pants. "What's wrong with her?"

"It's all right." The lieutenant was suddenly there, kneeling at my side and putting an arm around me reassuringly. "She needs medical help. We are going to take her to see the camp doctor."

"Take me with you," I sobbed, terrified of being separated from my cousin. I reached up to clutch her limp, cold hand in my own.

"We only have so many beds," one of the soldiers started to protest, but I interrupted. "I don't need to sleep. I'll sleep on the ground. Please, I can't leave her!"

The lieutenant nodded and helped me to my feet. I leaned against him as we followed the men carrying Gutcha behind the partition. A makeshift hospital had been set up on the other side under a massive tent. Cots were lined up in rows. The girls who lay on them were mostly unmoving in varying stages of consciousness. The trucks that had entered the camp throughout the day had brought medical equipment—medicine and bandages and bedpans—as well as an official doctor. He looked harried as he leaned over his patients with a variety of instruments. The medics helped transport and clean up the sick, changing bedding and emptying bedpans behind the barracks. I noticed as we moved down a row that some of the bodies lying on nearby cots were completely covered, faces hidden beneath a white sheet. I swallowed, not allowing myself to think what that meant.

Gutcha was placed on a cot at the end of a row. The lieutenant looked at me and said, "I wish I could give you a bed or even a chair to sit on. I'm sorry we aren't more prepared." I wanted to cry from his kindness. No one had spoken to me with such compassion in a long time, caring for my comfort. I shook my head, collapsing to my knees on the ground beside Gutcha, watching her chest, willing it to continue to rise and fall.

"Will she be OK?" I asked.

"We will do everything we can for her," the lieutenant answered. I felt my eyes closing. "Thank you," I whispered. My stomach now felt hollow and sore, but I didn't think I would be sick anymore. In fact, I was hungry again. But I also felt weaker than before and just wanted to sleep. And I couldn't stop shaking. I rested my head on the edge of Gutcha's cot. Blackness surrounded me, and I fell into fitful dreams.

Twenty-Five

I was standing in a large, cold room. The concrete walls were streaked with grime, the windows barred. Bare light bulbs flickered from the ceiling overhead. I glanced at my feet on the dirty floor and realized I was naked. I tried to cover my exposed breasts and private parts with my hands and arms, but a loud voice was shouting at us to stand up straight, arms at our sides. I blinked back tears as I looked around. Gutcha was beside me, trembling, and when her eyes met mine, they mirrored my own fear. Everywhere I looked were women of all ages and sizes, standing in the nude, trying desperately to cover themselves. We were lined up in rows, facing a wall where a large, masculine-looking woman was pacing back and forth, holding a clipboard.

A man in a white coat entered from a side door and began to walk between the rows of women. I blushed fiercely at his presence, feeling at once violated and vulnerable. As he approached me, I tried to step back, but he reached out and grabbed me roughly. He lifted my chin, examining my face; he squeezed my cheeks, forcing my lips open so he could inspect the inside of my mouth. He began to pat down my bare arms and legs, his hands moving up to my exposed chest. I started to cry, but he ignored my tears. He gave a nod to the woman with the clipboard, and she barked an order for me to move through a door in the opposite wall. Her large palms pushed against my back, and I stumbled forward on legs so weak I was afraid I would fall.

In the next room, I was forced onto a hard bench. Unseen hands grabbed at my long tresses, pulling ruthlessly. Locks of hair fell at my feet, a dull razor painfully shearing my head. Tears fell with

the curls, mingling onto a floor littered with blonde, brunette, and
auburn tendrils. I heard sobbing all around me.
  I heard a scream.

  I bolted upright, suddenly awake. At first, I was confused.
There was a dull ache in my stomach, and I clutched my middle
as I looked around. My vision swam, and I couldn't make sense
of what I was seeing. I was sitting level with a metal bed frame;
all around me were thin, cold steel legs supporting army-issued
cots. My cheek felt cold, and when I touched it, my hand came
away muddy. I realized I had been lying on the hard ground,
and my joints ached as I stretched. My feet were covered in
dirt; pebbles stuck to my arms, and I wiped them away irritably.
Blinking in the dim light, I saw the roof of the tent overhead.
Despite being dirty, at least I was dry. Then I remembered the
night before and scrambled to my knees to lean over Gutcha's
frail body. To my relief, she was breathing, her head supported
by a small, rolled pillow. I couldn't remember the last time I'd
slept with a pillow.
  "Gutcha?" I whispered, but she didn't respond. I grasped her
hand and felt her pulse, faint but steady, through the parchment
skin of her palm. I frowned as I heard a commotion outside the
tent flaps. Something had jolted me from sleep—and then I
remembered the scream.
  Gently placing Gutcha's hand at her side, I stood on unsteady
legs and stepped outside. The sky above me was the dull, nondescript shade that comes before dawn. Glancing around, I saw a
young woman run into the yard from behind one of the bunks.
She was crying and gasping, holding torn shreds of her dirtied
gown to her body. In the waning moonlight, she appeared almost
feral. A few of the women prisoners reached out to her, but she
backed away from them, shaking her head, hissing like a cornered
animal. At that moment, a shot rang out, and I jumped. Everyone froze, immobilized. The girl yelped and fell to the ground,
curling into a fetal position. My heart thundered in my chest.
Had she been shot, like a sick animal put down to rest? To my

relief, she wrapped her arms over her head, her shoulders shaking, still very much alive.

The lieutenant marched into the center of the camp, dragging a soldier behind him. The soldier was half dressed, his shirt unbuttoned, the zipper of his pants unfastened. He struggled to free himself from the lieutenant's grasp, twisting and kicking out with his feet, but the lieutenant was larger and stronger. He forced the soldier to the center of the yard and threw him to his knees, standing over him with a formidable expression. It seemed the whole camp was awake now, watching and waiting.

The lieutenant raised his gun and aimed it at the soldier. In a loud, commanding voice, he spoke so everyone could hear. "I discovered this man performing a criminal act that cannot go unpunished. He was molesting one of these poor girls who has neither the strength nor the energy to fight back." He paused, his gray eyes sweeping the camp, finally landing on the other soldiers, his face livid. "Let this be known here and now. I do not tolerate such behavior in my company. These girls need our protection. If you choose to act like animals, I suggest you leave, because you are no better than a coward and deserter. This is not what we trained for. If any one of you harms one of these girls again, there will be no warning. It is in my power to execute you on the spot." He then turned to the offending soldier and kicked him in the side. The soldier grunted and fell forward. "You are under arrest and will be detained until further notice," the lieutenant said, grabbing the soldier by the collar and dragging him to his feet. The soldier hung his head indignantly, hiding his eyes behind a fringe of greasy bangs as the lieutenant marched him away by gunpoint. The moment they were out of sight, I ran to the few women who had rushed to the girl's side.

She was shaking and bruised but no longer fought against the hands that reached out to her. One of the older women knelt beside her and gently tried to pry her arms from her head. "Shhh, there now," she said in a soothing voice. "You don't have to be frightened." The girl looked up, and I recognized her immediately. Her name was Chana. She was a quiet young woman from Hungary who had come to the camp alone and kept to herself. Despite the fact that her hair was growing from her head in short clumps and her cheeks were hollow, it was easy to see she had once been beautiful. Her large green eyes were framed by long black lashes, and her skin hadn't lost its olive tone. But as we helped her to stand, her eyes darted wildly, and she clutched her arms to her chest. I noticed blood running down her legs.

"She should see a doctor," I said. "There's one in the tent."

Another woman wrapped her in a blanket and said, "Yes, let's get you cleaned up and taken to the doctor." As she guided Chana toward the tent, the blanket slipped from Chana's hunched shoulders. I saw angry marks on her shoulders and neck from hands that had held her down. My stomach clenched. Beside me, a woman muttered, "How could they? Vile brute! I thought they were here to help us."

I glanced over my shoulder at the soldiers still gathered around the fence. The butts of their cigarettes glowed and sputtered like dying fireflies. A few spit on the ground or took swigs from their canteens. Most had their backs turned to us. "Will we ever be safe?" I whispered. Although they wore different uniforms and spoke with a different accent, I suddenly felt the Russians were no better than the Germans.

When I returned to Gutcha's side, I was relieved to see her eyes were open and staring up at the roof of the tent. "Gutcha!" I cried. "You're awake!"

She turned her head weakly to look at me. "Where am I?" she whispered.

"In the hospital."

"Hospital?"

"They set up an infirmary. A doctor arrived last night. You were sick. I was so worried."

Gutcha closed her eyes wearily. I pulled back the blanket that covered her body and crawled onto the cot beside her, wrapping her in my arms. Her body was so thin. I rested my head on her chest, feeling her rib cage against my cheek. I was relieved to hear her steady heartbeat.

"How do you feel?" I whispered.

"Exhausted," she breathed.

"Me too," I said. She rolled onto her side so we were face-to-face. I saw with dismay her hollow cheeks and sunken eyes, trying to remember her face from *before*. Fleeting memories of our child-hood intruded on my thoughts—Gutcha and I whispering behind our teacher's back in class, or hiding behind the trees that bordered the field as we spied on the boys who played ball after school, or sneaking into her room to look at the movie magazines we borrowed from our classmates. I had always envied that she only lived with her mother, father, and brother in the apartment above ours and had a room all her own, while I had to share my home with my sister and five brothers. What I wouldn't give to be back in that crowded, loud, loving home. I blinked back tears. Gutcha noticed and reached up to wipe them from my cheek.

"What are you thinking?" she asked.

I shook my head, struggling to speak. "I was so worried about you," I choked. "I can't lose you, Gutcha." She was my lifeline, my anchor to the past, and I feared she was slipping out of my grasp.

"I'm here," she reassured me. "I'm not going anywhere."

We drifted in and out of sleep, lying head to head on the cot. Sometime later, I heard her murmur, "I'm so hungry." I sat up, fighting the exhaustion that weighed on me like gravity. "Let me try to find something to eat," I said, slipping out from beneath the blanket. Noticing her teeth chattering, I tucked it around her then walked down the aisle, looking for someone to ask about food. My own stomach was aching with hunger pains. A medic stood over an empty cot at the end of the row, stripping a sheet from its corner. I noticed a stain on the crumpled blanket at his feet, and the strong stench of vomit assaulted my nose.

"Excuse me," I said as I approached him. He looked up, and I saw the look of disgust on his face. I swallowed and said, "I was just wondering, is it possible to have something to eat?"

He glowered. His nose crinkled, and he lifted a hand to his mouth as though afraid to breathe the air between us. I blinked when he remained unresponsive. "Would it be possible to get some food?" I asked again. "My cousin is over there, and she's very hungry."

The soldier shook his head and said something in Russian. I realized he didn't understand my Yiddish. "Food," I said, bringing my hands to my lips. "*Esnvarg.*" Then I said in German, "*Essen.*" As I tried in vain to make him understand, a firm hand closed on my shoulder, and I jumped.

"You are hungry," a deep voice stated matter-of-factly. I turned to see the lieutenant standing behind me and took a step backward. He regarded me silently for a moment, then asked, "How are you feeling this morning? How is your cousin?"

I looked at the lieutenant in surprise. He was speaking Yiddish. "She's awake," I said.

"That's good," he said. "I'm pleased to hear that."

"You speak Yiddish?" I asked. He nodded and said, "Quite fluently, actually."

As I continued to gape at him, he turned his attention to the medic and snapped something in Russian. The medic saluted and marched out of the tent. I stood awkwardly in front of the lieutenant. He was not wearing his *ushanka,* and his gray curls were a disheveled mop on the crown of his head. He glanced around at the sick in their beds. "I had no idea," he murmured more to himself than to me. "How could we have known? My men aren't prepared for this."

After a few moments, the medic returned with a bowl in his hands. He avoided my eyes as he passed me the bowl then quickly snatched his hand back to his side. I tried not to notice how he wiped his palm on his pant leg. The lieutenant barked something again in Russian. I saw him scowl as he ordered the medic back to work. When he returned his attention to me, his eyes softened.

"Take this to your cousin. Tell her to rest. You both must regain your strength."

I nodded and backed away. When I returned to Gutcha's side, her shaking was noticeably stronger. I sat on the edge of the bed and put a hand to her forehead. "You're warm," I said in alarm. "You must have a fever." Her eyes stared at the bowl in my lap, but her hands were too weak to reach for it. I held the bowl to her lips and told her to drink slowly. She took small, eager sips, her eyes closed, as I encouraged her. My stomach growled, and she looked up at me. "Drink some," she said in a hoarse voice, but I shook my head.

"You need to get better," I said. "I'll be fine."

I sat by Gutcha's side all day, wiping sweat from her forehead and brushing back damp wisps of newly grown hair. I knew that beneath my own kerchief, my hair was growing back as well. My head often itched so much that I drew blood as I scratched at scabs that never healed.

As night fell, Gutcha's fever broke. Her shaking ceased, and her eyes lost their glossy, faraway look. I cried with relief as she smiled up at me.

"You're cool," I said, placing my hand on her forehead.

"I told you I wasn't going anywhere."

I crawled into the bed beside her, wrapping her in my arms. "We have to stick together, no matter what happens, no matter where we go from here."

"No matter what," she agreed.

Twenty-Six

News of the rape spread through the camp. Gutcha spent the next few days in the infirmary, a few beds away from Chana. As I nursed my cousin back to health, I watched as some of the women occasionally entered the tent to check on Chana. Every morning and evening when I lined up with the other women to receive the rations the soldiers passed out to us, I heard their whispers. "She's gone mad," some said. Or, "She refuses to be touched. She's a breath away from death."

On Gutcha's third night in the infirmary, I returned to find her sitting up in bed, holding a tin bowl and wooden spoon in her lap. "How are you feeling?" I asked, relieved to see some color had returned to her cheeks.

"Better," she said in a hoarse voice. "They won't give me anything but this soup. The doctor came earlier and said I should be discharged by tomorrow."

"That's good news," I said, sitting beside her. We heard a commotion a few beds over and turned to see Chana lashing out at the army doctor as he tried to examine her. Throwing up his hands in exasperation, he stormed away, shaking his head and cursing under his breath. Chana turned onto her side and cowered beneath the blanket.

"She won't talk to anyone," Gutcha said.

"Did you hear what happened to her?" I asked.

Gutcha nodded. "She's not eating either. She just lies there in bed, or rocks back and forth, or thrashes like a wild animal."

"It's horrible," I muttered, shaking my head.

I saw the lieutenant walking along the row of beds behind

Gutcha's. He consulted with the doctor, his forehead furrowed.

"He seems decent, though," I said, nodding in his direction. "Good."

"Do you think so?" Gutcha asked skeptically. Her lack of trust, cultivated by years in the camps, was apparent in her expression. She crossed her arms over her chest as she regarded him.

"I do," I said. I remembered his kindness and concern when Gutcha fell ill. There was something in his demeanor that I trusted, something familiar in the way he stroked his chin as he spoke softly to the doctor. An image rushed into my mind, a memory that hurt too much to hold on to for long—my father at the dinner table, smiling as he stroked his beard and watched me set the table and chat idly about my day. The scene unfolded, and I was helpless to stop it. My father laughed and lifted me onto his lap. I lay my head on his broad chest. He pulled a *pączek* from his pocket and placed it in my palm. I squealed in delight at the small Polish donut. He put a finger to his lips and said, "Shhh, our little secret. Don't tell your mama or she'll have my head." His face came into focus in my mind for one glorious moment—kind brown eyes, wizened forehead, thick beard—then faded into shadow. I swallowed hard and locked the memory away, a practice I had perfected over the years. I stared down at my hands, at my dirtied, broken nails, and forced my mind back to the present.

"Has anyone left the camp?" Gutcha asked. I blinked and looked up.

"I don't think so," I said, shaking my head. Aside from the lieutenant, the doctor, and a few higher-ranking officials, most of the soldiers remained outside the camp grounds. They paced and radioed for supplies and sat around smoking, drinking from flasks, or playing cards.

"Are we prisoners then?" Gutcha wondered bitterly.

"That's not it," I argued. "They don't know what to do with us."

"They could at least give us better food than this," Gutcha said, lifting the bowl from her lap with a scowl.

"You're in a mood," I said with a small laugh. "That must mean you are feeling more yourself. The doctor explained that we got sick because we ate more than our stomachs could handle at first."

Gutcha scoffed and tried to lift the spoon to her mouth, but she was still so weak that most of the broth spilled back into the bowl. I took the spoon from her hand and helped feed her the clear soup. Despite her disdain for her meal, she drank eagerly until her eyes began to close. As she fell back against her pillow; I set the bowl aside and leaned over to kiss her forehead. "Sleep now," I said. "I'll see you in the morning."

But the following morning, when I tried to enter the tent, a soldier blocked me. I attempted to move past him, but he pushed me aside, and I stumbled backward. "You cannot enter," he said forcefully in German, repositioning his rifle across his chest. I stared at him in shock and disbelief.

"Why?"

"The infirmary is under quarantine," he said. "No one is allowed in or out."

My legs grew weak, and I was sure I was about to fall. "But why?" I asked again.

"There has been an outbreak of typhus."

"Typhus?" I whispered. I felt a vise close around my chest, and I couldn't catch my breath. "My cousin," I said weakly. "She's in there."

The soldier regarded me impassively.

"Please," I begged, "I need to see her. I need to know if she's all right."

The soldier only watched me warily.

"She was going to be released today."

Still he said nothing. Before I realized what I was doing, I charged past the soldier toward the tent flap, not caring about the consequences. I knew with conviction that if something happened to Gutcha, I would die as well. I would *want* to die.

Strong arms encircled my waist and threw me to the ground. The air rushed from my lungs, but I clambered onto my knees and frantically tried to crawl forward. A black boot planted itself in front of me, blocking my path.

"Are you crazy?" the soldier spat angrily, and I thought perhaps I was. I looked up and saw his gun trained on me. The adrenaline drained from my body, and I collapsed on the cold ground, sobbing. "Please," I begged, "I need to see her! Please!"

"What's happening here?" a voice shouted. The lieutenant was marching across the grounds toward us. The soldier's heels came together as he snapped to attention. I remained frozen, kneeling in supplication. "I asked you a question," the lieutenant demanded as he reached our side.

"Sir, this, *girl,* insists on entering the tent."

I sat back on my heels, staring up at them as silent tears fell down my cheeks. The lieutenant looked from me to the soldier, then knelt at my side and offered me a hand. I looked at my palms planted in the mud and quickly scrambled to my feet without his assistance.

"I keep telling her no one is allowed in or out," the soldier continued, shaking his head. "Is she daft?"

The lieutenant ignored him and turned to me. Again, I saw nothing but sympathy reflected in his eyes. I wanted more than anything to throw my arms around him and beg him to allow me to see Gutcha, but I no longer had the strength. I began to fall. The lieutenant reached out and caught me as my vision swam. "Gutcha," I whispered as he carried me away. I wanted to protest, to break out of his arms and run back to the tent, to beat my chest and scream Gutcha's name until I no longer had a voice, but all I could do was lie weakly in the lieutenant's embrace.

He placed me gently on a bench outside one of the barracks and told me not to move. I obeyed, bending forward, head in my hands. The lieutenant sat beside me in silence for a moment before saying in Yiddish, "This is for your own good."

I blinked up at him through my tears, once more startled by his use of the language. What was a Russian soldier who also spoke German doing speaking Yiddish?

"Those who are healthy have to stay away from the hospital for now," he explained. "We can't risk an outbreak of typhus. Do you understand?"

I understood, but I didn't care. I didn't care about anything anymore.

"I know you're worried about your cousin," he continued, "but she's stronger now. I believe she will make it through."

"Do you mean it?" I choked. He nodded solemnly. "If I might say a prayer for her?" he asked gently, reaching for my hands. I didn't pull away. His rough, calloused fingers closed over my thin knuckles; his skin felt like old, dry leather, but his hands were warm and comforting and familiar. "*Mi sheberach,*" he began, reciting the Hebrew prayer for healing that I had heard in my youth. I stared at him as he held my hands, his eyes closed, rocking slightly as he prayed.

"May He hasten to send her from heaven a complete recovery to all her bodily parts and veins, among the other sick people of Israel, a healing of spirit and a healing of body, and let us say, Amen."

He opened his eyes and looked into mine. Silent understanding passed between us. I knew.

"Amen," I whispered.

The lieutenant left me with a bowl of mush, but I was too anxious to eat. I paced outside the tent most of the morning, paralyzed with anxiety every time the tent flap moved aside and the army medics walked out. They wore masks over their mouths and carried stretchers between them. I feared Gutcha might be one of the lifeless bodies under the sheets, and that fear held me in place, wide eyed and trembling, watching helplessly as the bodies were disposed of behind the nearest barracks.

The day grew warm as the sun continued to climb in a cloudless sky, but I didn't seek out any shade. I didn't want to leave the tent, knowing Gutcha was just on the other side. A stench of rot and sickness assaulted my nose. When I thought I might faint from heat and thirst, I saw the flap part once more. I held my breath, expecting to see more soldiers carrying away the dead. Instead, a thin hand held back the flap as an emaciated body dressed in soiled rags slipped out into the yard. I gasped, afraid my eyes were playing tricks on me. My cousin stood on unstable feet, blinking in the bright sun. "Gutcha!" I exclaimed, running to her and throwing my arms around her. The relief I felt threatened to drown me. We fell against each other, our knees buckling as we sank to the ground. I held on to her with all my remaining strength.

"You're alive," I sobbed against her. "They let you out."

She didn't answer but clutched me around my waist. The rest of the world faded away. All that mattered in that moment was that we were together, and only death could separate us.

Twenty-Seven

We remained in the camp another week. We were fed slightly larger portions of bland rations and told to exercise in small doses. Most of the time, we slept. I was aware for the first time how sore my body was from years of starvation combined with manual labor. Sleep came easily, and after that first night, my sleep was dreamless and deep. By the end of the first week, I felt some strength, however minimal, return to my limbs. Gutcha was also growing stronger. We began walking the perimeter of the fence twice each day—once in the morning, once at night.

I started to notice my surroundings as if seeing them for the first time. The camp was bordered in the distance by a thicket of trees. Their leaves were starting to bud in shades of white and palest pink. Beyond those, a vast mountain range rose toward the sky, the gentle rolling foothills blanketed in forest evergreens, while shadows of clouds danced over the higher jagged peaks. In the field closer to the fence, clusters of purple wildflowers and dandelions sprouted among the grass. Beauty had been so foreign to me that I allowed myself to become mesmerized by the simplest acts of nature—bees pollinating flowers, soft, feathery clouds in a cerulean blue sky. I stood at the fence one stormy afternoon with my eyes closed and my head raised to the rain. It soaked my face and drenched my hair, but I didn't care. I stood like that until a noise startled me from my reverie. and I turned to see the lieutenant standing behind me, rain dripping from the brim of his cap.

"Are you all right?" he asked, regarding me with a confused expression.

I nodded. He swam in my eyesight and I wiped the moisture from my eyes. To my surprise, I tasted salt on my lips and realized I had been crying. I ducked my head so he wouldn't notice.

"Here," he said, wrapping a rough wool blanket around my shoulders. "You'll catch your death standing out here like this." He took my arm gently and led me away from the fence. As we walked, he watched me. I kept my eyes averted toward my feet. One of the buildings that had served as offices for the Germans had now become a sort of gathering spot for the lieutenant and his men. The Germans had left in such haste that papers were strewn across most of the floors and large piles of ash were heaped in the fireplaces. Many of the rooms were stripped of furniture, or desks and chairs had been overturned, but the offices were still cleaner and more comfortable than our hard, bare, pest-infested bunks. The lieutenant led me there now.

As we stepped under the eaves of one of the buildings, he turned to me and asked gently, "How old are you?"

I balked at the question. To my surprise, I didn't know how to answer. At first I had tried to keep track of the days, but eventually the days, weeks, years, had run into each other. I knew my birthday was in the warmer months, when the leaves outside the camps were in full bloom and the flowers blossomed on the other side of the fence, but I couldn't remember how many summers I had been imprisoned.

He looked at me sadly when I didn't answer. I thought back to my first moments in the camps, remembering the fear, the indignity, the abuse I had suffered. As the memories threatened to resurface, I felt light-headed and reached out to steady myself. Sixteen. I had been sixteen and naive when I was taken away. That much I knew. But time had ceased to exist once I entered the camps. How many camps had I been to? How many years had passed, how many birthdays had come and gone?

"Do you know how old you are?" the lieutenant asked again, softly.

I shook my head, refusing to meet his eyes. His finger reached out to lift my chin. I jerked away without thinking. I remembered other hands reaching out to touch me, and I shivered. The lieutenant took a step back and held up both hands. "I'm sorry," he said in his soft voice. "I meant no harm." I felt suddenly embarrassed, remembering that I trusted him, that I *wanted* to trust him. That we shared a bond.

"What you girls have been through," he said now, looking past me, shaking his head, "it's unspeakable. Unthinkable. I imagine you were just a child when—" His voice trailed off.

"I was sixteen." I said quietly. "Almost seventeen."

"Sixteen?" he asked. "And do you know what year that was?"

"It was 1942, I think," I whispered.

"It's now 1945," he said. "Did you know that?"

I shook my head—1945? The date meant little to me. So, three years had passed since I'd first entered the camps? Since I'd last seen my mother or father? Since I'd last played with my little brothers? Since I'd last heard Jacob play the violin? Did it feel longer than that, or shorter? I wondered. What difference did it make when every day ran into the next?

"You are still so young," he said. "You have your whole life ahead of you."

I looked away again, staring out at the rain-sodden yard, rivers of mud flowing between the buildings.

"Go inside now," he said kindly. "Get out of the rain, before you catch cold."

I nodded and turned to enter the dim building, shivering slightly, thinking about his words. My whole life was still ahead of me. The thought was terrifying.

A few days later, we were told to gather in the yard outside the main gate. The lieutenant stood before the entrance to the camp, before the large, ornate iron doors that had always been locked to us. I watched him as I entered the yard with Gutcha at my side. He held a megaphone in his hand and gazed at us steadily beneath his heavy brow as we entered. A few soldiers stood at attention at his side. I swallowed, knowing something was about to happen. My hands felt clammy and my forehead burned in the strong morning sunlight. The cold, rainy spring days would change overnight to warm, summer-like weather. I held my hand up to shield my eyes from the sun as I stopped a few yards from where the lieutenant stood. The yard was silent.

He stopped pacing and turned to face us, raising the megaphone. "My children," he spoke in clear, concise German, the one language we had all come to understand. "Today you are free to leave the camp and begin your life anew."

My heart beat faster at his words—words I'd longed to hear for so long, words I'd believed I'd never hear. I should have been happy, excited, relieved, but to my surprise, I was panicked and anxious. I saw my own feelings reflected in the faces of my campmates. As though he could sense our unease, the lieutenant's brow wrinkled, and he said, "Don't you understand what this means? You are free."

"But where do we go?" someone asked behind me. Without warning, I was engulfed in a din of voices, all shouting the same thing.

"Where do we go?"

"What are we supposed to do?"

"We have nothing!"

"I don't know where we are! I don't know how to get back home!"

"Ladies," the lieutenant shouted, his hands in the air. "Ladies, quiet, please!"

He lowered his megaphone and pinched the bridge of his nose, waving one of his soldiers to his side. We watched as they spoke in whispers, consulting a map and gesturing to each other rather heatedly. Finally, the lieutenant nodded and turned to us once more.

"We have sent scouts out and have been told of a town not far from here that can offer you shelter as you decide where to go from there."

"A town?" someone near me said in an unsure voice.

"It's called Reichenbach," the lieutenant said. We repeated the name so it echoed in the air, testing the sound of it on our lips.

Images flashed in my mind of my own town of Olkusz, the town square where we played hopscotch on the cobblestone streets, the flowers in the park in summer, the open door of my father's bakery, the smell of fresh bread filling the afternoon air, the sound of the violin drifting out of the windows of our home as twilight fell.

"My intelligence tells me the town is mostly evacuated. Some of my men have gone ahead to prepare lodging and other accommodations for your arrival. Stay together, my children, for your own safety. There are many soldiers here who have been at war a long time and are starved for the affections of women. Be vigilant on your journey."

I clutched Gutcha's hand tightly at his words. "Will you not go with us?" one woman asked desperately, fear written on her face.

"Our orders have us heading north, I'm afraid. But I send you to your lives with this prayer. May God watch over you all and keep you safe."

We stood back as two of the soldiers pulled open the heavy gates. I tried to meet the lieutenant's eyes, but he was blocked from view. For a moment, no one moved. Then we surged forward like a solid wave, spilling past the gates, stepping, for the first time in almost four years, onto soil as free women.

Twenty-Eight

The walk to Reichenbach took the better part of two days. We were silent as we walked, eyes exploring our surroundings in both curiosity and fear. The road that spread out from the arched main gate of Peterswaldau was paved, and we followed the line of tire tracks on the asphalt, staying close to the apron of the road, where shrubs and weeds grew. The sky overhead felt like an enormous roof over a rolling landscape of hills; white buds sprouted from tree branches, and clusters of pollen, like wisps of cotton, floated in the air. My eyes, thirsty for this evidence of life, drank in all in, yet a part of me felt exposed and vulnerable. Every time a small animal scurried in the brush or a bird took flight, I jumped, squeezing Gutcha's hand tighter.

By midday, our steps had slowed, our energy drained as the sun rose higher and hotter in the sky. It was unseasonably warm, and soon I found I was sweating through my rags.

"I need water," I said, stopping to sit on a rock by the side of the road.

"Get up, Sarah. We don't want to fall behind," Gutcha said nervously. She was still pale and weak from her bout of sickness. As the other women slogged past us, I could tell she wanted to stop as well.

"How will we make it without food and water?" I asked. "I'm so thirsty."

A woman named Erna turned when she heard me. She was large-boned and tall, and despite the conditions we had lived in, she had never lost a sense of authority that commanded attention. When she had first arrived at the camp, no one spoke to her. The scowl on her face had intimidated me, so I'd kept my distance as well.

But then I remembered Fanny, a young French girl who had arrived on Erna's transport. One night she woke us all up with loud, piercing cries.

"Shush!" someone hissed as she continued to cry out in her bed.

"Stop it," a second voice demanded.

But Erna's dark shadow moved across the room to the bunk where Fanny lay. I heard her ask in a low voice, "Is the baby coming?"

I sat up when I heard those words. So did many of the other girls.

"A baby?" someone whispered.

We were all thinking the same thing—how was she pregnant? She didn't appear large enough to have a baby in her belly.

Fanny lay on her side, clutching her abdomen with each contraction, moaning loudly.

"Quiet her or the *Aufseherin* will come!" a voice urged in a strained hush.

I threw my legs over the edge of my bunk and jumped to the floor. A few other women were standing beside Fanny's bedside now, pleading with her to keep quiet. Someone found a piece of wood and put it between Fanny's teeth, while another woman wiped sweat from her brow with an old rag. Erna stood over them all, her large body the size of two women, taking control.

"This won't be easy," she said in a rough whisper. "And you have to keep quiet. But we will help you."

"My baby," Fanny wailed. "What about my baby? It's too soon. How will she survive?"

"We'll worry about that later," Erna said in a matter-of-fact tone. "Right now, you need to open your legs."

Fanny twisted, caught in a throe of pain, while Erna tried to push her legs apart. A puddle of fluid stained the soiled wood beneath her. "You have to make room for the baby, Fanny," Erna commanded in a determined voice. "She's coming fast."

I watched as Fanny bit down on the wood to keep from screaming, her back arching with pain as she pushed. The woman wiping her forehead spoke soft words of encouragement. "That's it, Fanny. Push. It's almost over. Keep pushing."

But when the baby came, there was nothing but silence.

"My daughter," Fanny gasped, pale in the moonlight, a sheen of sweat on her brow. "Please give me my daughter."

We all looked at Erna, who held the bundle of blue limbs in her arms. "It's a boy," Erna said, deadpan.

"A son?" Fanny asked, lifting her head just enough to look at Erna.

"I'm sorry," Erna said, handing the stillborn baby to Fanny, who didn't seem to understand.

"He's not breathing," she said softly, then her voice began to rise. "He's not breathing! Why isn't he breathing?"

We backed away. Part of me was relieved. A healthy baby, crying and hungry, would never have gone unnoticed. Now the poor child didn't have to suffer the same fate as the rest of us, didn't have to face a future of starvation in unsanitary conditions. I doubted Fanny would be able to produce enough milk to keep him alive for the first few months. But Fanny was almost hysterical, crying over her lifeless son. Erna shooed us all away and knelt beside Fanny. "Enough," she said in her gruff voice. "You have to stop crying or you'll be found out. This is life. This happens."

I was shocked at her harsh, unfeeling words, but when Fanny looked up at Erna with a desperate expression, Erna surprised me again by taking her in her enormous embrace and rocking her like she'd rock a child. We all went silently back to our bunks, leaving them to mourn as the night brightened.

In the morning, the baby was wrapped in rags that Erna hid beneath her shapeless gown. Sometime during the day, she took the baby to the pit where many other bodies were discarded. No one ever spoke of it again. Fanny faded, performing her jobs mechanically, receiving shouts from the guards without flinching, barely eating her daily rations, until she was nothing but skin and bones. Occasionally I would wake at night to find Fanny curled against Erna's immense frame on a lower bunk. Whenever whispers spread about who the father was and how it had happened, Erna's glare was enough to silence any speculation.

Fanny died a few months later.

Now, Erna turned her scowl on me. I recoiled under her glare as she stood before us with hands on hips.

"So, you want to stop here, in the middle of nowhere, while we leave you behind?"

"I, I didn't say that," I stammered. "But I'm hungry and thirsty. Aren't you thirsty?"

"You think this is the first time I've been thirsty?" she said. "There's nothing to drink here, so there's no use wishing otherwise."

Some of the other girls had turned and were watching us. I frowned and stood up. "Fine," I muttered, falling into step with the others again. My face burned as much from anger as from the warm sunlight. Some of the other girls began to fall behind as well, near to fainting, leaning on each other for support. The words of the lieutenant rang in our ears—there were soldiers patrolling the countryside, hungry for women. Despite our exhaustion, no one wanted to be left behind.

I was grateful when the sun began to set. The hills around us had been growing steadily larger, and I could see mountain peaks in the distance. As night approached, we looked for signs of the town, but only road stretched ahead. Our feet dragged along the pavement, barely moving us forward. A few women dropped to the ground.

"We have to stop for the night," someone said. "We need to sleep."

My knees buckled and I fell with Gutcha, exhausted. Dusk threw shadows along the road, and I fought to keep my eyes open, afraid at any moment a soldier would emerge from the bushes. "All right," Erna said, moving into the center of our group. "We need to rest. But we can't be out in the open like this."

"Where do we go then?" someone asked. Erna turned to the side of the road and began to climb over a ditch. She waved us over. I struggled back to my feet. And that's when I heard a low rumbling sound growing steadily louder. We paused, turning in the direction of the sound, peering into the darkness of the road ahead. I felt the ground vibrate beneath me.

"Hurry!" Erna said urgently. "Someone's coming!"

My heart began to pound in fear. I tried to run with Gutcha up the embankment on the side of the road. There was a line of boulders where we could hide out of sight, but they were impossibly far away. The women around me scrambled to gain purchase of the embankment, pulling at each other as they tried to reach the safety of the boulders. Someone grabbed my kerchief and used my head to boost herself up. My face was pushed into the dirt, and I spit pebbles from my mouth.

Erna had reached the jagged line of rocks. "Hurry!" she hissed again, reaching out to pull everyone into their shadow where we could hide. I grasped her hand and was yanked forward and thrown to the ground. I crouched next to Gutcha with my back to a boulder, feeling the coolness of the rock face through the sheer fabric of my prisoner's uniform, my chest heaving as I caught my breath.

The sound reached a crescendo, and suddenly we saw the glare of headlights as a squadron drove over the stretch of road where we had been standing only moments earlier. It didn't matter if they were enemies or allies. They were men. I squeezed my eyes closed, feeling the boulder shake against my back, hugging Gutcha closer. After a few minutes that felt like hours, the line of military vehicles passed. The sound of their engines and the crunch of gravel faded away, and we heard crickets chirping in the clumps of grass that grew up the hillside.

"Are we safe?" Gutcha whispered.

"I think so," I breathed.

No one moved.

Gutcha's head rested on mine, and we both gave in to sleep.

The ache in my back brought me out of restless dreams. I blinked in the morning sunlight and tried to move my head, but my bent neck throbbed in pain. I reached up to rub at the kink, at first confused by my surroundings. Then I remembered the night before.

Around me, the other women began to stir. We were lethargic and weak from thirst. My mouth was parched and my lips were cracked; I tried swallowing, but my throat felt like it was closing around sandpaper. Erna stood up stiffly and glanced out from behind the rocks. "The road is clear," she said. "We should get moving."

"We could stay here and rest, then move at night?" someone suggested.

"No, we need to get to that town. We need to get to water before nightfall."

Silently, we moved out from behind the rocks. I noticed that not everyone joined us. An older woman was lying on her back in the dirt, her eyes open, unmoving. One of the women bent over and closed her eyelids. Another woman was leaning against the rock, her breathing shallow, her eyes closed. "I . . . can't," she wheezed. Her companion looked up at us and said, "Go on. We'll join you when we can." I knew as we left them behind that we would never see them again.

We started down the stretch of road. Thankfully, the day was overcast and not as warm as the previous day. But still my limbs screamed from dehydration. I felt each step might be my last. I prayed that the clouds would release the rain from their dark bellies, but only a few raindrops fell. When I couldn't take the thirst any longer, I cried, "How could they send us away without water?"

"When we get to the town, how will we find food?" someone else panted.

Erna, who had been walking behind us like a shepherd following her flock, stopped suddenly. "We'll find out soon enough," she said, pointing. Ahead of us, a steeple rose against the gray sky. The silhouette of a cluster of buildings was half-hidden beyond a bend in the road.

Crossing her arms, Erna said, "That must be Reichenbach."

Twenty-Nine

Reichenbach, Germany, May 1945

The first thing I noticed was the quiet. It was like we had entered a ghost town, everything hushed and unmoving. The air itself had grown still. We matched the silence as we walked, first onto residential streets lined with small cottages and two-story apartment buildings, then onto the cobblestone streets that led to the center of town. Reichenbach seemed spared from the constant bombings by the Allied forces. Many of the homes were intact, the taller buildings toward the city center still standing, a church steeple, crowned with a cross, rising against the darkening sky. But the streets were empty and silent. The shutters of the homes were all closed against the windows. Many of the storefronts we passed had been boarded up, closed signs hanging from the windows.

"Where do we go?" Gutcha asked, glancing around.

"Look!" someone shouted. In the middle of a small square was a well with a pump. Without thinking, we ran to it, fighting our way forward. Someone grabbed my arm to pull me back, but I pushed her hard, guided by thirst. When I was finally at the front of the line, I eagerly pumped the handle, ducking my head under the flow of water so it washed over my face and mouth. The water felt marvelous on my lips, in my mouth, on my burning skin. The water we had been given in the camps was enough to slake our thirst so we could work, but it was often murky, unclean, and more often than not made us sick. This water was fresh and cold, perhaps from a spring that ran through the mountains that bordered the town.

I could have stayed there forever, bathing in the cool stream of water, but I was pushed aside roughly. Stumbling, I looked around for Gutcha. I needed to make sure she had reached the well. I found her leaning against a nearby wall, her eyes closed.

"Did you drink?" I asked, going up to her. She nodded, her eyes still closed. "Are you all right?" I asked, and she finally opened her eyes and looked at me. "Is it really over?" she whispered tremulously, and I swallowed and nodded.

The women began to disperse, some heading toward the center of town, some retracing our steps and heading back toward the homes near the outskirts of Reichenbach. Blindly, Gutcha and I followed a few women down an alley to our right and came out onto Kopernika Street. Ahead of us, hanging above an ornate wooden door, was a sign that read "Kaiserhof Hotel."

"Is it locked?" Gutcha asked as I reached out to test the knob. It turned easily in my hand, and the door opened with a low groan. We huddled in the doorway, gawking into the ornate lobby. It was dim inside, but a smell of lilacs lingered in the air, as well as an underlying scent of cigar smoke and fried onions. My mouth watered. Erna, who was part of our little group, tried a switch on the wall, and suddenly the lights over a large front desk came to life.

We entered the room hesitantly. The hairs on the back of my neck stood on end as I looked around the richly appointed room, afraid that at any moment someone would come and throw us out or report us or arrest us. I still trembled at the idea of being seen outside the camp. I didn't believe I belonged anywhere but inside the barbwire fences—certainly not in a richly furnished room such as this one.

Gutcha approached the front desk, where vases of fresh lilacs and violets bloomed in crystal vases. She fingered them gently then turned and said, "Whoever was here must have left recently."

I ran my hand along the richly upholstered arm of a chair. I wanted nothing more than to sink into the soft, plump seat and close my eyes. That's when I noticed a glass sitting on the small table beside the chair, half filled with an amber liquid, and a half-smoked cigar lying in an ashtray by its side. I leaned forward, and the pungent odor of the cigar assaulted my nose.

"Look at this," I said. "Someone left this here not too long ago. I still smell the cigar. The ashes are fresh."

"Hello?" Erna called in her loud voice, walking to a swinging door beside the front desk. "Shhh!" I hissed. I was so used to *not* drawing attention to myself that I worried what would happen if someone answered her call. But no one did.

She disappeared into the room behind the swinging door. When she didn't return, we followed her into a lavishly appointed dining room with tables covered in crisp white linen, red velvet chairs, and crystal chandeliers hanging from the ceiling. I gasped as I looked around. But then Gutcha ran past me and I blinked, turning to see why she was in such a rush. Erna had just come back into the room from another set of doors at the far end of the dining room, her arms filled with loaves of bread and apples.

Before I knew it, the rest of us were running into the kitchen, hardly paying attention to the stainless steel cooking surfaces and large ovens and porcelain sinks. We silently jostled each other to grab what we could from the stocked fridge and pantry, struggling like we had at the well to slake our hunger. I fought my way to the large refrigerator and reached blindly for the produce that hung in baskets over the kitchen island. With my arms full, I knelt on the floor with the ripe peaches, hard-boiled eggs, and slices of cold roast beef I had found. Roast beef! I hadn't had meat in so many years that I nearly gagged as I ate it hungrily. Unlike the rations the Russians had given us from cans and tins, this food burst with flavor and texture. I was eating not only for necessity but for pure enjoyment.

When I was done, wiping my mouth with the back of my hand, I came back to myself. I realized with a start that I was alone, stooping on the floor over scraps of food like a wild animal. Blinking, I stood up, my pulse racing. I was suddenly afraid. I couldn't remember how I came to be by myself. The sudden silence in the kitchen sent me into a panic. "Gutcha?" I called out desperately. "Where are you?"

I heard a muffled response. "I'm here!" Gutcha pushed open the door of the kitchen and rushed to my side.

"You left me," I accused, trying to calm my racing heart. "Please don't leave me again."

"I didn't leave you," she said, pulling me into a hug. "I was just on the other side of the door, exploring the dining room. I would never leave you." I nodded, but my heart still pounded in my ears. She took my hand and led me through the dining room back into the lobby. Erna was standing at the base of a large staircase. "Let's make sure we're alone," she said, starting up the steps. Silently, my cousin and I followed her to the second floor of the hotel. I knew from the way our footsteps echoed in the silence of the upstairs corridor that it was deserted too.

We had the hotel to ourselves.

I pushed open the first door I came to and saw two beds made up in crisp, clean sheets, draped in gold curtains, with red velvet blankets folded at their feet. Blackout shades were pulled across the window, which looked out onto the alley. I forgot all about the other women from the camp. I didn't wonder where they were or if they had found lodging. All I knew was that there was a bed, and my cousin was with me, and for the moment, we were safe.

Someone was sobbing.

I tried to ignore it. It was muffled and sporadic, as though the person crying was trying to swallow the sound. I also heard the rough scrape of peelers against potatoes. The *Aufseherin* strolled back and forth in front of the tables where we worked, watching for the slightest infraction, trailing her whip along a floor littered with potato peels. I tried not to glance at the switch, slithering on the floor like a snake ready to strike. I heard the sobbing again and thought, *Shut up. Don't you know what will happen if you keep crying?*

"You!" the *Aufseherin* yelled so loudly I jumped. I glanced up, my heart in my throat. Was she yelling at me? Had I done something wrong? But to my relief, the *Aufseherin* was pointing the end of the whip at a girl to my right, who suddenly dropped her dull peeler and backed away from the long table. The *Aufseherin* faced her, staring at her with a cold smirk. "Pull back your sleeve," the *Aufseherin* commanded in a clipped voice.

"Wh-What?" the girl stuttered, hunching her thin shoulders instinctively.

"Your sleeve," the *Aufseherin* shouted again, pointing at the girl's arm.

I kept my head low, methodically peeling the rotting potato in my hands, refusing to look up.

"Wh-Wh-Why?" the girl stuttered again. She was younger than I and still had flesh on her cheeks. I guessed she had arrived at Klettendorf recently. I wanted to tell her not to question the *Aufseherin*. I wanted to warn her how brutal the older woman could be. But I remained silent.

I heard the whip come down on the girl's arm. I heard the girl's shout of pain and surprise. Something fell to the floor and rolled toward the *Aufseherin*'s foot. With downcast eyes, I saw it was an unpeeled potato. The *Aufseherin* kicked it to a corner of the room, at the same time grabbing the girl and dragging her in front of the table.

"You thought you could hide it from me? I saw you try to slip that potato up your sleeve, you dirty Jewish thief," the *Aufseherin* said in a low, menacing voice. "You'll soon learn there is no stealing!" She threw the girl to the floor and raised the whip.

No! I wanted to yell. My ears filled with blood, the drumming sound so loud it almost cut off the sound of the girl's screams. *No! No!*

"No!"

"Sarah, wake up!"

I blinked against sudden brightness. Gutcha was standing over me, shaking me awake. I saw her short-cropped hair, her sunken cheeks, the dark circles under her eyes. "You were dreaming again," she said, sitting down beside me. I sat up sluggishly, glancing around. I was in a beautifully appointed room, surrounded by riches I couldn't even imagine. How had I gotten here? A fog settled over my thoughts. The screams were still ringing in my ears, but as I looked around, the girl and the *Aufseherin* slipped away. In their place were memories of the night before, finding the hotel, the food in the kitchen, climbing the stairs to the guest rooms. This was more like a dream than the one I had just left.

"Where is everyone?" I asked as Gutcha walked to the window. She parted the drapes to look down on the street below. I walked to her stiffly and looked over her shoulder at the empty alley. "It's like everyone disappeared," I whispered. A bird landed on the drainpipe outside the window, gave a quick chirp, and then took flight into a blue, cloudless sky. My stomach grumbled as I turned back to glance around the room again. "I'm hungry," I said.

"Me too," Gutcha said. Our eyes met, wondering what to do next. We realized this was our first morning of freedom in almost four years. With no roll call, no orders to report to work, not even the Russians there to tell us what to do, we were helpless on our own.

We wandered aimlessly into the upstairs hallway. As we walked to the stairs, we passed a large mirror in an ornate gold frame that had been obscured by darkness the night before. I froze when I saw my reflection. The person who stared back at me was a stranger, a girl so thin she looked like she would break in half. I raised trembling hands to my mostly bald head, touching patches of dull hair growing in clumps across my scalp. My cheekbones were so prominent they protruded from paper-thin flesh. I blinked a few times, watching as the girl in the mirror blinked. It was like looking at a ghost—there was a remnant of the girl I had been before, somewhere in the brown eyes that gazed back at me, but she had been replaced by a skeleton encased in gray skin. I felt faint as I turned away.

Gutcha reached for my hand and led me away from the mirror. "Let's find food," she said softly. I noticed tears on her cheeks and wondered if she had glimpsed her own reflection.

As we entered the kitchen, we saw Erna and another woman standing at a counter, silently eating slices of cheese and bread. We joined them; without asking, we reached for the food spread on the counter and began to eat as well.

"It will run out soon, you know," Erna said over a mouthful of food.

Gutcha grunted as she stuffed a baguette in her mouth. Again, the intoxication of fresh food was enough to put us all in a stupor.

"I just don't understand," I said finally, after I felt my hunger replaced by an uncomfortable weight in my stomach. "Who was here before? Why did they leave everything in such a rush?"

"It could only have been the Germans," Erna said. "I imagine it was expensive to stay here. Who else could afford such a place?"

"So they just left?" Gutcha asked.

"Think about it," Erna said. "They must have known the end was near. Maybe they got scared and ran, just like the guards at the camp. Maybe they were evacuated."

"Maybe," I muttered. Again, we looked at each other, unsure what to do. Leaving the kitchen, we ventured out into the town square. The air was fresh and clean, the sun gilding the caps of the surrounding mountains, the sky a pure blue. We wandered through the streets, occasionally glimpsing other women from the camp who looked as lost and confused as we were.

"Look. There's a shop," Gutcha pointed as we reached a corner. Across the street we saw a small mob gathered around the door of a store. As we approached, I noticed the women in front were trying in vain to pull the door open, but it was securely locked in place. I looked through the windows and saw mannequins dressed in fine women's clothing. "Stand back," someone yelled, and a rock was thrown against the glass, shattering it into a million pieces. We joined the throng now pressing through the entrance. I glanced around the dim space, taking in the racks of silk and satin dresses, finely embroidered blouses, fur stoles, jewelry dripping in colorful gems, scarves, hats, and gloves decoratively laid out in display cases. I had never seen so much finery.

I stood frozen as everyone else ran to gather whatever they could lay their hands on. "Come on, Sarah," Gutcha said, clutching my hand and pulling me forward. "Get the clothes."

We rushed toward a rack of summer dresses in yellow polka dots and brown plaids. I paid no attention to what I grabbed. Size didn't matter; I doubted even the smallest size would fit my gaunt frame. Blindly, I piled clothes into my arms until I could hold no more. Some of the women started bickering near the jewelry. They fought, tearing articles of clothing and jewelry from each other's arms, possessive and fierce.

"Let's go," I urged, and we quickly pushed our way out onto the street once more.

As we walked back toward the hotel, I noticed a new wave of people entering the town square. They looked like us—dressed in rags, skin clinging to flesh, with vacant, almost feral expressions. There were men as well as women, and I stopped as they passed.

"Are they from another camp?" I whispered.

"Must be," Gutcha said.

I swallowed. A group of women about our age slowly walked toward us, shuffling their bare feet along the rough cobblestones. I noticed blood on the stones. I looked at my feet and saw my toes sticking out where I had cut away the tips of my stolen shoes, my heels exposed where the soles had separated. I remembered the day I had pulled the shoes off a lifeless body before anyone else could. Although they were worn and ill-fitting, at least they offered some protection.

Suddenly, one of the young women dropped to the ground and didn't move.

"Anna!" another woman cried, kneeling painfully beside her. "Anna, get up!"

We ran forward and knelt over the unmoving girl.

"Is she breathing?" I whispered. Her face was a sickly yellow. Her eyes rolled back in her head.

"Anna, don't give up now. Please. Open your eyes!"

We waited, holding our breath, watching as the girl's chest slowly rose and fell and finally stopped moving altogether.

"Anna!" the other woman cried, throwing herself on the girl's unmoving body. "No! Anna! No!"

We tried to help her stand. A few more women joined us, hoping to guide the bereaved woman away. But she fought to stay with the dead girl. I turned away, feeling sick.

"Let's go," Gutcha said. "There's nothing we can do for her."

I walked away as if in a trance. I had seen so much death already that I felt immune to the crying and suffering behind me. I wanted to get back to the hotel, to the bed I had slept in the night before. I didn't care about anything but the bed and the blankets that would hide me from the rest of the world. I felt dead inside. I wanted to drown out the crying I heard, the despair that followed us down the street. But then, through the wails, I heard my name.

"Sarah!"

I turned. I recognized the voice.

"Sarah, is that you?"

I saw a girl standing behind me. Despite her withered frame and bald head, I recognized her immediately. I knew her. I'd have known those brown eyes anywhere.

"My God," I whispered. "Helena?"

Thirty

We reached for each other, hugging fiercely, afraid to let go. "It's you," Helena whispered. "It's really you!"

"Helena!" I cried. "I can't believe it!"

She pulled back and cupped my face in her hands. We stared at each other hungrily. I noticed how much older she appeared. Her once youthful, beautiful face was now gaunt and heavily lined, dark circles under her eyes, a fine fuzz of hair growing where thick hair had once crowned her head. I touched her hollow cheeks and remembered how Jacob had touched her in the alley behind our home as they stole furtive kisses when they thought they were alone. I reached for her again, allowing myself a moment of hope.

"Which camp were you in?" Helena asked when we finally parted, grasping my hand and walking with me to the corner where Gutcha stood waiting.

"We were in Peterswaldau, a satellite of Gross-Rosen very near here," I said. "I worked in a weaving mill."

"We just arrived yesterday," Gutcha added, embracing Helena.

"I was in Auschwitz," Helena said softly. "We have been walking for days. I had begun to wonder if there was anything left of the country."

"What happened?" I asked. "How did you end up here?"

"The Germans forced us to leave the camp, to march without food day and night. If anyone stopped, they were beaten and left for dead. After a few days, they stopped us and told us to stand in a line. We were in the woods just off the road and they—they began to shoot us. I ran, Sarah. So many of us did. We ran and didn't stop. This is the first town I've seen. I'm so tired, Sarah."

"Come with us," I said, putting my arm around her, supporting her. She leaned into me. "We are staying at the nearby hotel. There is food. And Helena, there are beds, real beds! You can stay with us."

"It's amazing," Helena said, shaking her head as we walked, Gutcha on her other side, helping her stay on her feet. "The town appears untouched. So many of the homes and villages I passed were nothing but rubble from the bombings. Some people stopped to scavenge in the ruins, but I didn't dare."

"You're safe now," I said, wanting to believe it.

"I just heard someone say they found a synagogue, and it's still standing," Gutcha said.

"A synagogue?"

"Yes," Gutcha nodded. "Not far from here."

I shook my head. "How is that possible?" The question remained unanswered as we made our way slowly along the sidewalk. Helena turned to me after a few moments and asked softly, "The rest of your family, Sarah. Do you know what became of them?"

I swallowed and looked down, shaking my head. I knew what she was really asking. What had become of Jacob? I glanced at her profile and wondered what she had experienced in the years since we'd last seen each other. Did she still love my brother?

As we turned a corner and saw the hotel ahead of us, we noticed a line of parked vehicles that hadn't been there before. The front door was open, and a small crowd was assembled in the lobby as we pushed our way in.

"What's happening?" Gutcha asked a woman standing near the door.

"It's the Russians," she said in a whisper. "They just arrived."

"The Russians?" I asked. We looked cautiously at the soldiers standing near the front desk, sorting through drawers and shelves and cubbies where keys were kept. My stomach dropped a little, and I wondered if we would be kicked out of the hotel. I looked for the familiar, friendly face of the lieutenant, but these were new faces, a new unit that had moved in.

"Let's get Helena upstairs," I whispered to Gutcha, eager to get back to the relative safety of the room we had claimed as our own. The Russians were absorbed in their work as we skirted the crowd in the lobby and made our way up the steps, still supporting Helena. Once in the room, I locked and chained the door. I hadn't realized I was holding my breath, but when I heard the lock click into place, I exhaled long and loud. I guided Helena to my bed and helped her to lie down. She closed her eyes as her head rested against the pillow and let out a long sigh. I glanced at her bare feet and saw how bloodied they were. Her flesh was shredded. I swallowed and reached for a clean sheet to wrap around them. She flinched and gave a small cry, but when I looked back at her face, she was already asleep.

Gutcha and I perched on the edge of the neighboring bed. "It's a wonder she survived," I whispered, watching Helena sleep.

"It's a wonder anyone survived," Gutcha said.

"I have to get her food and water."

"I hope there's still some in the kitchen now that the Russians are here."

"I'll go look," I said, standing up.

"I'll go with you," Gutcha said.

"No," I said, shaking my head. "Stay with Helena."

I made my way back downstairs, sticking close to the walls, hoping not to be seen. In the short time we had been gone, the Russians had set up a command center in the lobby. A number of lower-ranking officers stood behind the front desk, speaking into radio receivers and barking commands at each other. The small sitting area near the door had been reconfigured to accommodate two senior officers, who sat in the large armchairs, working at portable desks. Papers and maps were spread on most surfaces. Some of the surviving men and women stood in the doorway, looking lost, waiting to be told what to do.

I ducked behind a pillar and tiptoed into the dining room. Thanking my luck, I saw that the room was empty. A small draft caused the crystals on the overhead chandeliers to tinkle as I dashed into the kitchen. Crumbs dirtied the large island in its center, and the baskets of bread, fruits, and vegetables had been picked over. I grabbed what I could carry and crept back through the lobby to the stairs with my head down. No one stopped me. When I reached the top of the stairs, I ran back to our room.

"It's me, Gutcha," I whispered through the crack between the door and its frame. "Let me in." Gutcha opened the door, and I slipped inside, spilling the pile of food onto our bed. "Quick, lock the door again."

"What did you see downstairs?"

"I think the Russians are busy setting up offices in the lobby. I'm not sure what they're doing, but it doesn't look like they're leaving anytime soon."

"Will we be allowed to stay here?"

"I don't know," I said. "Where else do we have to go?"

"Sarah," Gutcha asked softly, "do you want to go home?"

"Home?" I repeated, the word lingering like a bitter taste in my mouth. I wondered if I even had a home anymore. Was Olkusz still home? Was there anything to return to? My memories of walking through the streets to the ghetto, of the jeering faces and shouted taunts, came back to haunt me. But then I remembered my parents' faces, heard the echo of the twins' laughter as they chased after a ball in our yard. Suddenly dizzy, I reached out to steady myself.

"Are you all right?" Gutcha asked.

I nodded, although I wasn't sure if I *was* all right. "I want to find my family first," I said. "Then I'll think about home."

Over the next few days, the occupying Russians established bases of operations at the Kaiserhof Hotel and at the neighboring post office and local civic center. The kitchen was no longer ours to raid. We were told to register at the front desk and provide our names and the cities we had called home. We were issued ration cards and told when to report to the dining room for meals. For the most part, the Russians kept to themselves, but I was still wary of their presence. No one told us to leave, so we remained in the upstairs room, which became our own private sanctuary.

I stayed by Helena's side, nursing her back to health. I slept next to her, wrapping my arms around her and feeling the fuzz on her head tickle my lips and cheeks. Each morning I woke disoriented and surprisingly sore. My body wasn't used to the softness of the mattress after sleeping for so long on hard planks of wood. To our delight, the bathroom in the hall had running water. The first time I sat in the bathtub, letting dirt and grime and memories wash off me, I thought only of the sensations. Warmth. Comfort. Things I hadn't experienced in many lifetimes, or so it seemed.

When Gutcha and I joined the long line to add our names to the growing census of survivors, I studied the faces around me. I heard a mix of languages: Hungarian, French, German, Polish, Yiddish. Those around me shared the same look: a marriage of anxiety, exhaustion, disbelief, and hope. A committee of former prisoners assisted the Russians with the registry. They spoke kindly to those whose names they took, unlike some of the Russian officers, who sounded short-tempered and overworked. When I reached the front of the line, the Russian officer behind the desk didn't even look up.

"Name?" he barked in a crisp voice.

"Sarah Chaya Waldman."

"What city and country are you from?"

"Olkusz, Poland."

"Another Pole," I heard him murmur under his breath, shaking his head.

"Can you tell me, has anyone else registered with the name Waldman?" I asked breathlessly, almost afraid to hear the answer.

"I can't tell you that," he said, looking up for the first time. "The lists will be posted. You can see for yourself then."

In the quiet moments while Helena slept, I watched her, remembering the affectionate way she and Jacob had looked at each other, remembering the stolen, private moments I had witnessed. Against my will, my thoughts turned to Otto, the boy I had met in Klettendorf. I saw again behind my closed lids his green eyes, heard his soft voice. I recalled the way he made me feel, even in the ugliness of the camps. And I silently cried.

Thirty-One

Klettendorf Labor Camp, East Prussia,
November 1942

Otto and I met for the first time when I passed him his morning ration of watered-down soup in the food line. I worked in the kitchen, preparing the morning meal and serving the other prisoners. Most mornings, I barely glanced at their gaunt, tired faces, but something in his expression as I handed him the tin bowl caused me to pause and stare after him as he continued down the line. "Oy!" the prisoner behind him huffed, bringing me back to myself. "Hurry up!"

The next morning, I watched for him. He entered with the other inmates from his bunk, boys as young as thirteen to men as old as fifty. When he was standing before me again, he raised his eyes and met mine. Our eyes locked for a long moment before I ladled the soup into his bowl. The tips of our fingers touched as I passed the bowl to him. We didn't exchange words, but as he moved away, he glanced at me over his shoulder.

That was the only time during the day that I saw him. For months, we didn't speak as I handed him his bowl; we only stared at each other for prolonged moments, allowing our fingers to touch for longer stretches of time. I lay in my bunk at night and imagined his face. I couldn't understand why he occupied so much of my thoughts. I didn't even know his name.

One wet and cold evening before curfew, I slipped outside the bunk, driven by thirst and hunger. This was a regular practice, to search for food scraps or barter with other women for this or that: a scrap of bread for a pilfered sewing needle, a piece of cloth for a bit of salvaged wire to make a comb. The women's bunks were separated from the men's by a high barbwire fence. A spotlight washed over the grounds from the high tower where the Nazis patrolled day and night. Sometimes I witnessed men and women meeting furtively at the fence, whispering through the wires before being caught in the spotlight.

I wandered closer to the fence, throwing my head back and opening my mouth to drink in the clean rain that fell from the sky. Despite the piercing cold, I let the rain wash over me, my feet sinking into icy mud. I saw a rat scurry along the base of the fence and took a step back.

"You'll get sick," I heard someone whisper.

I quickly lowered my head and glanced at the fence. That's when I saw him, huddled on the other side, peering at me. "You're shivering," he said. "You want to get out of the rain. It's going to be a hard winter if this weather keeps up. Don't catch a cold or pneumonia if you want to survive."

I nodded hesitantly but didn't move.

"My name's Otto," he said, moving a little closer to the fence.

"I'm Sarah," I said.

"I've noticed you," he said. "Every morning."

"I work in the kitchens," I said, although that was obvious. "I've noticed you too."

"Where are you from?"

"Poland. And you?"

"France."

The spotlight caught us, moved over our bodies. Despite the brightness, I felt even colder, exposed. I froze, looking away, terrified of what might happen. Some of the guards didn't care if the men and women conversed, knowing the fence would keep them apart. Still others barked orders from their stations in the high towers, demanding that the couples separate or else. I'd seen a couple shot at the fence, their bodies falling toward each other, their fingers leaving a trail of blood along the chain link.

The spotlight moved away, leaving us in darkness. "Here," he said, crouching in the dirt and opening his hand. I noticed a half-eaten potato in his fist. I knelt in the shadow, and he slipped it through the fence into my hand.

"Thank you," I whispered, feeling my stomach growl, backing away quickly.

"Come back tomorrow night," he said. "I want to see you again."

I nodded as I walked away quickly, concealing the potato in my own fist. "I'll be here," I called over my shoulder.

Otto and I met every night at the fence. We chose a corner where the fence met the wall that enclosed the camp, kneeling in the snow, our feet freezing. We tracked the spotlight, knowing when to move away and when it was safe to be together.

He shared stories with me about his life in Paris. His family wasn't as religious as mine. Not only did they live in the heart of the city but his father was a successful doctor and his mother, he said, was a well-known artist. His older sister had been a dancer, performing in the major capitals of Europe, and like his father, he had studied medicine at the university.

"One day when this is all over, Sarah, I'll take you to Paris," he told me one evening. "You'll see the Eiffel Tower at night. There is no sight more beautiful. Except, perhaps, your face."

I blushed and looked down. In those moments, I wanted to forget where I was. I wanted to see the sights he described in so much detail—to walk beneath the glow of gas lamps along the Seine at twilight, to see the elaborate carvings of the Arc de Triomphe, and to stroll on the Avenue des Champs-Élysées in the spring. I knew nothing of the metropolitan world he described. It sounded like a fairy tale, so different from the small town of my childhood. And when he told me I was beautiful, I wanted to believe him. I raised my hand self-consciously to my head, to the kerchief tied around my mostly bald scalp, wondering what he saw when he looked at me.

Our fingers entwined through the fence whenever the spotlight moved away. We were never together longer than a few moments, but in that time, I clung to his every word, falling into eyes darker than any I'd ever seen. He began to grow dark stubble along his olive-colored jawline. He absently stroked it when he talked about his family and his studies, a life he mentioned as though he were only temporarily removed from it.

"Do you think we'll get out of here?" I asked one night, my breath rising in a cloud.

"Of course," he said, caressing the top of my fingers. His touch was like electricity, sparking feelings I had only experienced once before, with Fryderyk. I felt weak and excited and filled with a sense of longing I didn't understand. These moments were the only time I felt real or even human. They were the only moments of happiness I knew in the camp. They sustained me through the day and gave me something to look forward to. Otto leaned forward and whispered, "When we are free, I want to marry you, Sarah."

My pulse raced as I watched his lips form the words. *Marry me,* I thought. *He wants to marry me.*

"I know this isn't the right time to say something like this, but I can't imagine my life without you," he said. And despite the cold, my heart melted.

Thirty-Two

Reichenbach, Germany, late May 1945

The lists were soon posted on the walls outside the hotel. Crowds of survivors flocked to Kopernika Street to scan them, looking for loved ones who might have survived. Reichenbach was no longer the deserted town we had first stumbled upon; survivors of the majority of camps in Lower Silesia had made their way to Reichenbach. A Jewish community began to flourish, strengthened by a sense of shared experience and suffering.

The lacerations on Helena's feet became infected, pus oozing from the wounds, and we took turns washing away the discharge and wrapping the inflamed skin in clean towels from the hotel linen closet. When she no longer flinched and the wounds began to heal, Gutcha and I helped her down the stairs to search for our families' names on the lists. I studied every face in the crowd, hope fluttering almost painfully in my chest like a living thing trying to escape as I looked for my parents or brothers. I wondered what my parents looked like now, or if I'd recognize the twins. I ran my finger down the lists of names, which had been broken down alphabetically by country of origin, looking for Waldman. My heart sank each time I came to the end.

"Don't worry," Gutcha said, wrapping us in a hug. "People are still arriving. You see the long lines of people still registering? There is still a chance."

We held on to that hope. *There is still a chance.* The words echoed in my mind every night when I lay down, and every morning when I stepped outside to check the lists and search the faces.

We learned that the town of Reichenbach had been a center of operations for the Nazis. They had built a line of defense both in town and in the mountains to protect their headquarters, which was why the town remained mostly intact and even flourished under the Nazi regime. Some of the evacuated German residents moved back into town to reclaim their property and reopen their businesses. As we walked past small storefronts and local shops, they eyed us cautiously. The proprietor of the store we had looted our first day stood in the town square, yelling "Animals! Thieves!" at everyone who passed. When Gutcha and I passed an older man sweeping his front step, he froze and spit at our heels. "You're not welcome here," he shouted, waving his broom at us. I lowered my head and quickened my pace, grabbing Gutcha's hand to hurry her across the street. My face grew hot as I felt the man's gaze follow us down the road.

"Will we ever belong anywhere?" I whispered to Gutcha as we climbed the steps to our room, the only place I truly felt safe. We had passed through a new wave of refugees entering the town, and my eyes were sore from searching their faces.

"I don't know," she said, her voice nearly breaking as she fell on the bed. "I just want to find my mama and papa and Daniel."

"I want to find my family too," I said. Like a dam breaking open, memories rushed in, my mother screaming, running after the truck that took us away. The twins, clutching her skirt and crying. My father, frail, unable even to stand. I thought I would suffocate. I choked on a sob and felt tears falling down my cheeks. I gave in to a grief unlike any I had ever known. I rocked back and forth on the bed, wanting nothing more than to feel my mother's arms around me. I didn't want to think—*couldn't* think—that I might never see her again. Where were they? What had happened to them? The unanswered questions resounded in my head, each breath the stab of a knife in my chest. And then I saw the store-keeper spitting at us, his eyes filled with hatred, and I gasped.

"Sarah!" Gutcha cried, kneeling before me. "Sarah, stop!"

I was struggling for air. My throat was closing. I didn't know what was happening. I reached for her. "I can't," I choked.

Faintly, I heard Gutcha call for Helena. She was at my side in an instant, wrapping her arms around me.

"What's wrong with her?" Gutcha asked.

"Sarah," I heard Helena whisper. "Sarah, you need to calm down."

I shook my head, gulping violently.

"It will be all right, Sarah," Helena said, stroking my hair. "Just breathe."

"I . . . want . . . my . . . mother," I choked, falling against her.

"I know, Sarah," Helena said. "I know."

Slowly, as Helena held me, I felt the constriction in my chest ease as my sobbing turned to silent tears. I finally glanced up at Gutcha and Helena and saw that they too were crying. Drawing a shuddering breath, I wiped my eyes on my sleeve. "I'm sorry," I muttered.

"Are you all right?" Gutcha asked, sitting on my other side and handing me a glass of water. I sipped and nodded. "I'm sorry," I whispered again. "I don't know what happened."

"You scared us."

I shook my head to clear it, suddenly exhausted. "I think I need to lie down for a little while," I said.

"I'll stay with her," Helena volunteered. I lay back against the pillows and shut my eyes, my chest sore and my breathing ragged. I only wanted to sleep. Helena moved across the room to pull the curtains closed against the late afternoon sunlight, then I felt the bed sink under me as she lay down beside me, reaching for my hand.

"Do you feel any better?" she asked.

"I think so," I whispered.

"Don't despair yet, Sarah," she said after a moment. "We can't give up hope. We found each other. We'll find our families again too."

"Helena?" I asked quietly after a moment, floating somewhere between wakefulness and sleep. "If we find Jacob, will you marry him?"

Helena didn't answer at first. I opened my eyes to look at her.

She was staring at the ceiling thoughtfully. Finally, she turned her head to me and said, "I cared about your brother so much, Sarah. He was—*is*—kind and gentle. He'll make a good husband. I felt like the luckiest girl in the world when my parents and your parents arranged the marriage. But I'm a different person now. Everything is different now. I don't know what to think anymore."

"Did you love him?"

"I thought I did. But I was so young, how could I know for sure?"

"Helena," I asked after a moment, "did you ever meet anyone else? In the camps, I mean?"

She lifted up on an elbow and eyed me then, eyebrow raised. "No," she said. "Did you, Sarah?"

I nodded, my thoughts returning to Otto. "In Klettendorf," I said. I rolled to face Helena, lowering my voice as I said, "I think I loved him too."

Thirty-Three

Klettendorf Labor Camp, East Prussia,
January 1943

"Look, Sarah, I have something to tell you."

I didn't like the tone of Otto's voice or the eager glint in his eye as we walked along the fence in the bitterly cold, early twilight. "What is it?" I asked cautiously, turning and gripping the fence. My limbs ached from carrying heavy iron all day, and I longed for the days when I worked in the kitchen. The icy coating on the wire cut into my chapped fingers, but I ignored the pain. Otto leaned closer, placing his hand on mine, and whispered, "A few of us have been watching the guards at night. We know their routine. It's too cold and dark for them to pay us much attention. They are more concerned with staying warm in their little watchtowers. Chaim thinks he can escape. He has a plan."

I suddenly felt breathless and dizzy. My stomach dropped. "What do you mean?" I asked. "No one can escape, Otto."

"That's not true," he said. "We've given this a lot of thought. We plan to help him. If he succeeds, Sarah, you and I can escape next."

"B-But," I stammered, shaking my head. "But what if you get caught?"

"We won't."

I backed away a step, our fingers parting. I looked at him incredulously. The spotlight was sweeping the far corner of the fence, inching its way in our direction. I heard a small commotion on the men's side of the fence and turned to look. The *Blockführer* was walking along one of the barracks, holding a loaf of bread. He was dressed in a long wool coat and tall boots while the rest of us shivered in our rags. He began tearing small pieces from the end of the loaf and throwing them on the ground as though feeding chickens in a coop. The men nearest him crawled on hands and knees in the snow, grabbing ferociously at the bits of bread soaking up mud and slush, fighting with each other for the smallest of morsels. The *Blockführer* laughed at their efforts, kicking those who got too close to his boot. I turned away, a sick feeling in my stomach.

"Go back, Sarah," Otto said. "I'll meet you here tomorrow."

I wanted to grab his hand and not let go, to look up into his dark eyes. I fought the urge, glancing anxiously at the *Blockführer* as he drew closer to where we stood. I knew it was a matter of time before we were discovered. I held Otto's gaze for another moment, then turned to leave, but not before pleading in a frightened whisper, "Just don't do anything foolish."

A loud siren woke us a few nights later. I moaned and stirred, the cold burrowing into my limbs as I blinked in the darkness, confused.

"Get up!" the *Kapo* shouted at the door to our barrack.

I shivered as I pushed against the bodies of the other girls huddled next to me. Some slept on, despite the siren. "Move," I hissed, trying to jump from the upper bunk. I knew the punishment for not obeying the *Kapo* in a timely fashion. I didn't know what was happening as I joined the line of girls by the door. Was it morning yet? It was still so dark and cold. And the siren was causing my head to throb.

We rushed into the yard outside. The *Kapo* barked at us to line up for roll call. A thin crust of ice splintered under our bare feet as we ran to our places. Dark, heavy clouds obscured the moon overhead, and large flakes of snow fell onto our shoulders and caught in my eyelashes. My body ached with exhaustion. My feet turned numb from the cold. Across the yard, we saw the men lining up outside their own bunks. Guards patrolled both sides of the fence; the sound of their whistles and the barking of dogs added to the commotion and terror I felt in every part of my body.

"What happened?" the girl next to me whispered fearfully.

"I don't know," I said, but an ominous feeling raised the flesh of my arms. The *Kapo* strode before us, counting our numbers, wearing a scarf and gloves while our necks and hands were bare. We shivered before her. I noticed a platform the size of a small bench erected on the men's side of the fence beneath a large tree, and my heart stopped. Three nooses hung from the bare branches, swinging in the cold wind.

The *Kapo* approached the fence and spoke to one of the male guards on the other side. He nodded and marched to the center of the fence, where both the women and the men could see him, lifting a megaphone to his lips. "There has been an attempted escape tonight," he shouted in a voice that set my teeth on edge. I was breathing fast, my breath rising in white clouds. I scanned the rows of men for Otto's face.

"The criminal has been shot, but this act cannot go without further punishment," he said, emotionless, as he marched casually between us. He relished taking his time as he wiped snow from his brow and kicked it from his boots. We shivered as we waited, terrified.

"You are here to work for the welfare of the Third Reich. It is important that you understand there is no hope for escape," he said. "We believe this treasonous act was not orchestrated by just one individual. Our intelligence has provided us with the names of others who helped plan this crime. To set an example to you all, these perpetrators shall be punished as well."

I panicked then, my hands clenching into fists. The girl next to me was watching me intently, but I ignored her. I wanted to scream Otto's name. I wanted to run to the fence to search for him, but fear held me in place.

The guards began moving toward the men, rifles aimed at the line of shivering bodies. I watched them grab a few of the men roughly from the line and herd them by gunpoint onto the platform. I immediately recognized Otto with a gun in his back, head bent so the dark hair of his neck was exposed, his shoulders hunched. My legs went weak as they turned him to face the yard. He was searching wildly in my direction. Our eyes finally locked. His face was pale, his dark eyes wide. I felt like I was going to fall as the guards placed the nooses around the men's necks. Otto reached up and grabbed the blue and white cap from his head. He waved it in my direction. "Look away!" he yelled to the yard, but I knew the words were meant for me. I felt tears on my cheeks.

"Shut up," one of the guards said, hitting Otto in the stomach with the butt of his gun. I gasped, falling against the girl next to me. She held me upright as I clung to her. Otto doubled over from the blow but quickly straightened again to meet my gaze across the expanse of the yard. "Don't watch!" he yelled. "I love you—"

The guards kicked the platform from under their feet.

I finally looked away.

Thirty-Four

Reichenbach, Germany, late May 1945

It had been nearly a month since we'd arrived in Reichenbach. Gutcha, Helena, and I spent every moment together. Our days became a routine of checking lists, waiting in ration lines for food and other basic necessities, and looking for a way to make money. I was growing stronger. I could feel the waistband of my skirt growing tighter against my middle, and there was finally enough hair growing on my head to brush. Each morning, I tied a large red ribbon in place as a headband to make my hair look fuller. I remembered my mother tying red ribbons around our home to ward off the evil eye and wondered now if my ribbon would protect me against an uncertain future.

Once, I saw an older woman shuffling through the street with slumped shoulders. Something about her posture was familiar, and I was overwhelmed by a feeling of hope. "Mama!" I cried, running to her and throwing my arms around her. She didn't speak a word as I held her, but I noticed how still and unmoving she was in my embrace. When I pulled away, I realized my mistake. It wasn't my mother. The woman stared at me with a dead look in her eyes. "I'm sorry," I muttered as I turned away.

I had shut out my memories for so long, living day to day just to survive. Now that there were moments of quiet and time to fill, I couldn't stop my mind from remembering. Like a floodgate had opened, the memories of my family rushed back, drowning me. It was worse at night, when I lay awake in the stillness. I couldn't stop the tears from escaping my closed lids so that I finally fell asleep on a damp pillow each night. Some mornings, I lay curled beneath the blankets, unable even to get up. Despite the constant companionship and concern my cousin and Helena showed, I felt more alone than ever.

I heard the stories of the other camps, the death camps. At one point in my life, I wouldn't have believed the accounts, thinking them too horrible to be true. But now I knew better. I had witnessed too much. I searched each day for the names of my family on the lists of survivors, but there was still no word of them. It was like they had never existed, like they were no more tangible than the wisps of fog that burned off by midmorning and were forgotten by afternoon. My eyes were ever watchful, scouring every face I passed, blurring from the effort of trying to find someone familiar.

The first time I saw a clock on the mantel in the hotel lobby, I was mesmerized by the turning of the gears, the slow progression of the hands around the ornate face. I had forgotten about time altogether. It had blurred like an insubstantial thing in the camps. Days, weeks, months, had meant nothing to me. But now time spread before me like a void, each moment an eternity as I learned how to live again.

The synagogue in town became a center of activity for the Jewish population. We walked there regularly to take part in conversation, hear the latest news, and look for work. A Jewish committee, headed by a man named Jakob Egit, had formed in the hope of creating a Jewish settlement in Reichenbach. The synagogue became their headquarters.

The first time I saw the two-story building with the large Star of David etched on the window pane above the entrance, I stared in awe. I walked slowly up the path that led to the main door, gazing at the arched windows of the first floor, then up at the towering windows of the second. Two pillars rose to the sky on each side of the square building, topped with ornate metal Jewish stars. The building was imposing, much larger than the small synagogue in Olkusz that my father had attended almost daily, taller than the trees that grew in the yard and garden that surrounded it. I was amazed that, after all the devastation that had destroyed so many places of worship, this building should still stand.

When I passed through the doors, a sort of peace settled over me, like I had come home. I walked down the main aisle of the two-story sanctuary, staring up at the impossibly high ceiling overhead, sunlight streaming through the engraved star in the round glass window above the altar. The wooden banisters of the second-story balcony were intact, as were the pillars that supported it. The room had been stripped of furniture, so the space was wide open and waiting.

I was drawn to the synagogue, enjoying the activity, laughter, and even arguments that broke out among the men and women who came daily to gossip or exchange news. The feeling of community was warm and familiar and reminded me of my youth. Unlike the temple in Olkusz, men and women worked together to restore the benches, the floors, the pillars, the windows—though men were the only ones allowed to clean the ark that had once housed the Torah scrolls.

Every day, Jacob Egit argued for the need to build a Jewish community in Reichenbach. Meetings were held to discuss the future of the town and its new citizens.

"We can have a life here," he said to the room at large as we gathered one day in the synagogue. "We can create a community together. We can open schools and hospitals and businesses. We each have something to offer. We carry with us the lessons of the past. Together, we can build a strong foundation for the future. Isn't that what we all want?"

"What about returning to our homes?" someone asked.

"Do you really want to go back?" Mr. Egit countered. "Is there anything to go back to? If you do, then I wish you luck. But if you don't, start a new life here, with us."

I glanced at those nearest me. Each day, this question nagged at me. Do I stay or make my way back to Olkusz? A part of me never wanted to see Olkusz again, yet I wondered endlessly if my family might have returned, waiting for me. The door suddenly opened with a groan, and we turned to see an old man step into the cavernous room. He was stooped and leaned heavily on a cane. He regarded us silently, motionless, as we stared back at him. The room grew quiet.

"Can I help you?" Mr. Egit asked. The man looked at Jacob where he sat behind a table near the door. He shuffled forward, reached out his arm, and held open his hand. A key was nestled in his palm. "I have finished my task," he said quietly. "Now the synagogue is returned to you."

Mr. Egit stood and took the key from the man. "Who are you?" he asked.

"My name is Konrad Springer. I was the caretaker of this synagogue before the war."

"How did you end up in possession of the key?" Mr. Egit asked, coming around the table and facing the old man. The man, Konrad, looked uncomfortable. He glanced at his sudden audience awkwardly. I could tell he didn't like us staring at him. "I purchased the building with the help of the . . . past members of the synagogue," he said. "They entrusted it to my care. They gave me money to buy it back from the Germans."

We listened to him in silence as he looked at us through heavy-lidded eyes. "I'm sorry to say, it served for a time as head-quarters for the Hitler Youth in town."

"But it survived," Mr. Egit said, "and for that we are thankful."

Konrad simply nodded and turned to leave.

"Wait," Mr. Egit said. "We don't have any money to reimburse you."

Konrad waved a hand irritably as though shooing away a fly. "I don't need money," he said. "It's rightfully yours."

We watched as he walked past us to the doors. Mr. Egit raised his arms and said, "This is truly a miracle! A blessing, my friends! A cause for celebration. Soon, the site where we stand will be restored to a true place of worship for the new Jewish community here in Reichenbach!"

Applause broke out around me. I frowned and backed away from the crowd. I wanted to share in their enthusiasm, their desire to reclaim the freedom to worship and pray, but all I felt was apathy. I glanced at the doors where the old man had disappeared, shocked by the humble kindness he had shown. As I stared, Helena rushed in and waved me over.

"What is it?" I asked, walking to join her.

"There's another group entering town," she said, grabbing my hand. "I've just seen them. I have water and bread. Let's go."

Helena and I had volunteered to help with each new wave of arrivals, passing out rations and directing them to the synagogue or hotel or community center where they could rest until their strength returned. It also gave us a chance to greet each survivor in the hope of recognizing someone we loved. I grabbed the basket of bread she held out to me, and together we rushed to the center of town. As we entered Rynek Street, we saw them staggering across the cobblestones. I felt the familiar catch in my throat.

They were all young men, still wearing their striped prisoner uniforms. Helena and I moved among them, she dipping fresh water into a large ladle and holding it to their lips, I offering hunks of bread from the basket. I studied every haggard face. They were too exhausted to speak. Many dropped to the street to eat, hunched and silent over their food. "Eat slowly," I encouraged, pressing bread into their outstretched palms. Tears were always close to the surface.

As I turned, I saw a young man shuffling toward me. On his back he carried another young man who was too weak and frail to walk. I rushed to them, holding out my basket. "Here," I said. "Please eat. Get your strength back."

The man nodded gratefully. "Thank you," he whispered, breathless from the weight of the body he carried. "Where are we?"

"This is Reichenbach," I said. "There is a synagogue down the street where you can go to rest. There are people there who can help you." I glanced at the man on his back. He was unresponsive, his head drooping against the first man's neck, his arms draped lifelessly over the man's shoulders. "Is he . . . alive?" I asked.

The man nodded. "Just barely," he said, "but he's my friend. I can't let him die."

"Here," I said, handing a second piece of bread to him. "Take this for when he wakes. He must get stronger."

I turned to walk away, but a small voice said my name. I froze. I recognized the sound of the voice, even though it was faint. Slowly, disbelievingly, I turned my head.

The lifeless body had raised its head, bald and covered in patches of scabs and dried blood, the face so emaciated it resembled a skull. But the eyes gazing back at me were still alive. They were eyes I'd stared into so many times before.

They were my Sam's eyes.

Thirty-Five

My brother was alive! Sam was alive!

Without thinking, I dropped the bread basket and ran to him, arms outstretched. "Sarah," he murmured again. His head fell back on the shoulders of the man who carried him, but he reached out for me weakly. I grasped his hand, refusing to let go, holding it to my face, kissing the dirty knuckles and fingertips. I sobbed uncontrollably as I cried, "Sam! I can't believe it! You're alive!"

The man who was carrying Sam regarded us in disbelief.

"This is my brother," I gasped when I was finally able to speak again. The word *brother* was like sugar on my tongue. *This is my brother. This is my family. This is my life.* "Thank you! Thank you for saving him." I noticed how the man sagged under Sam's weight. "Let me help you," I said, but the man held up his hand. "I have him. You said it's just a little farther to the synagogue?"

"Let me take you to my room," I said quickly. "It's just around the corner."

He followed me back to the hotel, each step a laborious effort. I thanked him over and over. Sam moaned softly, his hand still reaching for mine. "I'm here," I kept repeating. "I'm here, Sam."

When we finally reached my room, the man laid Sam carefully onto my bed and collapsed to the floor. I crouched next to him. "Are you all right?" I asked. His face was gray and the lids of his dark eyes were heavy. "I just need to rest," he panted.

"There's another bed," I offered, but he shook his head. "I'm fine. Just need to sleep." His head fell to the side as his eyes closed. I stood and rushed to Sam, sitting beside him and reaching for his hand once more. His eyelids fluttered open, and I could see him trying to focus on me. "I'm here," I said again.

"Sarah," he whispered. I noticed a tear in the corner of his eye pool and then fall down his sunken cheek. I reached out and wiped it away, smiling gently, even though tears fell from my own eyes. "You're alive," I whispered. "I can't tell you how long I've prayed for this."

"Is it really you?" he whispered.

"Yes," I said. "It's Sarah. It's your sister."

"I've missed you so much," he said, his voice barely escaping his lips.

"Shhh," I said, stroking his cheek. "Sleep now. I won't leave your side."

I spent the rest of the day beside him, taking in his face, crying helplessly in both shock and relief. Helena came home to find me there. "Where did you go?" she asked as she came through the door, then froze when she saw Sam. "Is that—?"

"Sam," I said, laughing and sobbing at the same time. "He's alive."

I saw her eyes glance at the stranger sleeping on the floor in the hope, perhaps, that it was Jacob. Her eyes were a well of emotion. I simply shook my head. I was happy enough to be reunited with one brother. I would think about the rest of my family later.

Helena sat beside me, disbelief on her face. "I can't believe it," she whispered. I heard movement in the hall outside the door and Gutcha entered. "There's another group in town," she started, but then her hands flew to her mouth. She ran to our side, staring down at Sam. Under her breath, she whispered, *"Danken Gott."*

"Who is that?" Helena asked, nodding at the man sleeping on the floor.

"I don't know," I said. "He was carrying Sam on his back. Sam is so weak he can barely move."

"They came from Birkenau," Gutcha said, sitting on my other side on the bed. "It was a death camp, Sarah. They've been walking for weeks through the countryside. Everyone is saying how horrible it was. That's all anyone is talking about in town."

I swallowed. Holding Sam's hand was like holding dry twigs that could snap at any moment. He looked like a corpse. I tried to imagine the boy I had known before the war. I tried to picture his tanned face and dark locks of hair, his big eyes that made the other girls in town swoon. He had been athletic and strong. I remembered his spirit, the fire that burned in him, his desire to fight against injustice. Even after he had been sent to the labor camp and returned home with a broken leg, he hadn't looked as broken as he did now, lying motionless in my large bed. I forced back more tears. "You've fought for so long," I whispered, curling up next to him. Helena and Gutcha left the room as I fell asleep at his side.

Both men slept through the rest of the afternoon and the night. Helena and Gutcha shared the other bed. We threw a blanket over the sleeping stranger, careful not to disturb him. I lay next to Sam, my head resting gently against his bony shoulder. Whenever he stirred, I bolted upright to see if he was awake, but his eyes remained closed, his breath rattling in his chest. Part of me was frantic that he would stop breathing, that he would succumb to death the way so many had. I watched his chest rise and fall throughout the night, fighting the urge to sleep. I thought if I could stay awake and watch over him, he would survive.

In the morning, the man on the floor began to stir. I sat up groggily and looked down at him. He blinked in the dim light, a confused look on his face. He tried to sit up but winced with the effort.

"Here," I whispered, moving to his side and offering him a hand. I helped him to sit up against the bed for support, then went to pour a glass of water from the pitcher sitting on the bureau. I handed it to him, guiding it to his mouth. He drank carefully but desperately. When he was finished, he closed his eyes and leaned his head back against the mattress. "Thank you," he said softly.

"How do you feel?" I asked.

"I don't know how to answer that," he said, turning to look at me. "Are we really free?"

"Yes," I said softly, nodding. I understood his disbelief. I remembered feeling it myself. I still had to remind myself each morning that I was no longer in the camps, that life had moved on, and that I had to move on as well.

"Then I'm happy?" His answer was a question. We shared a silent moment. I nodded.

"I'm Sarah."

"Michal."

"Thank you for saving my brother, Michal."

"We are friends, Sam and I," Michal answered. "We look out for each other."

"Where are you from?" I asked.

"Warsaw," he said. "Sam told me a little about the town you're from. It's small, isn't it?"

"Yes," I nodded.

"Will you go back?"

"I don't know. I'm not sure what's left for me to go back to. Now that I have Sam, we can decide together." It was a relief saying those words. I didn't have to face the future alone anymore. I had Gutcha and Helena, but a part of me knew we wouldn't be together forever.

Michal and I sat silently for a long time as the room slowly brightened around us. I heard Sam moan and rushed to his side. In the morning light, he looked worse than he had the day before. His face had a sickly yellow tinge, and his mouth was so dry I could see every line etched in his lips. Dark shadows framed his hollow eye sockets. I wet a cloth with water and ran it over his lips and across his forehead.

"Will he survive?" I whispered fearfully, more to myself than to Michal. Michal rose painfully from the floor and stood next to me, looking at Sam over my shoulder. He nodded and said, "He's stronger than he looks."

"I hope you're right."

I remembered the anger simmering Sam's blood after he was forced to lie on the ground in the center of Olkusz, beaten and tortured for a whole day alongside my father and brothers. I remembered the resignation on his face when he returned home from the labor camp after breaking his leg. I remembered him begging my parents to leave, saying over and over, "It's no good. We have to get out now while we can." At the time, we couldn't have guessed at our future, but he had already glimpsed the horror to come. And now he had survived unthinkable suffering, worse than anything we could have ever imagined. I wondered as I looked at him if he would ever be the same again.

"Sarah?" I heard him say softly.

"Sam," I whispered, "I'm here."

He opened his eyes for the first time since the previous day and stared up at my face. I smiled down at him gently. He gave a small sigh and asked, "Am I dreaming?"

"No, Sam. You're safe. You're with me. It's over now." And as I gazed down at him, he dissolved into sobs that racked his frail body. "Oh, Sam," I choked, reaching for him. His arms came up weakly and he clutched me as tightly as he could. We held each other, letting the rest of the world fall away.

Thirty-Six

Sam drifted in and out of sleep throughout the day. When he was awake, I gave him small portions of food, warning him not to eat too quickly or too much, even though he begged for more. He shivered uncontrollably. I wrapped him in all the blankets I could find. While he slept, I washed his hands and feet, his face and head.

Michal stayed with me throughout the day. He was stronger than Sam and was able to walk about the room. He was also able to stomach more food than Sam, who gagged after I fed him only a few bites. Although we spoke few words, we tended to Sam in companionable silence. At one point, I noticed sweat on Sam's brow. When I felt his forehead, it was burning up. I recoiled from the heat. "I think he has a fever," I said, remembering with dismay how sick Gutcha had been, and how worried I had been that I was going to lose her.

Michal frowned as he came to stand next to me.

"Should I be worried?" I asked him, wetting a washcloth and placing it gently on Sam's forehead. "I've heard there is a Russian doctor in town. Maybe I should call for him?"

"If it's just a fever, hopefully it will break," Michal said. "I've seen much worse. If it's typhus or dysentery, then—"

I turned worried eyes to Michal. "Then what?"

Michal sat beside me. "Don't worry, Sarah. I'll watch out for him."

I frowned. "What can you do?"

"I am—*was*—studying to be a doctor before the war broke out."

"You were?" I asked, surprised.

He nodded. "I was at the university in Warsaw. I had almost graduated. I worked at the hospital." The rest remained unspoken. I turned back to Sam, watching as he tossed his head fitfully in his sleep.

"He can't die," I murmured. Leaning over Sam, I whispered, "Please, Sam. Don't die now. I need you."

To my surprise, Michal reached out and took my hand. I jumped but didn't pull away. I turned to look at him, startled. He was suddenly embarrassed, dropping my hand and clumsily standing up. "He won't die, Sarah," Michal insisted as he turned away, walking to the window with his back to me.

I wanted more than anything to believe him.

By evening, Sam was asking to sit up. I was thrilled that he was more alert. When I felt his forehead, it was clammy but cooler than before. His eyes had lost their unfocused gaze. I cried tears of relief.

The following day, he ate a little more, and color returned to his cheeks. His temperature had returned to normal, but his body was skeletal, and he had a hard time moving. Every bone jutted from his pale skin. I was able to count every rib on his chest. His eyes were sunken and his cheekbones and jaw protruded disturbingly. He had little energy to stay awake and slept most of the time. I was never away from him for longer than a few minutes, watching over him protectively.

By the end of the week, he was able to get out of bed for the first time, though he was still weak and needed help to walk. Michal and I accompanied him outside. "Fresh air will do you good," I said as we carried him carefully down the stairs to the lobby. He didn't answer. His feet barely touched the ground. We led him to the shade beneath a large tree that grew in the yard outside the hotel, its leafy branches casting dappled shadows over us. I watched Sam, studying the way he stood with his eyes closed and his head raised to the sun, leaning heavily on Michal, still and solemn. I felt like I had been holding my breath for days and was finally able to exhale. For the first time, I believed Sam would be all right, that his body would heal—but about his spirit, I wasn't as certain.

I found clothes for Sam and Michal. They didn't fit, but they were so much better than the rough, threadbare, filthy prisoner uniforms they had worn. I threw their old clothes in the fire that burned in the hearth of the hotel kitchen, watching the coarse fabric curl and blacken against the flames.

Once I knew Sam was out of danger, I joined Helena and Gutcha in town, helping in the effort to rebuild the community. When I returned to the hotel one afternoon, Sam was sitting in a large chair by the window of our room, a blanket thrown over his shoulders, staring outside at the alley and the Piława River beyond, his face void of expression. I went to sit beside him. We were silent for a moment. There were so many things I wanted to ask him—about our family, about his experiences, about the future. But the words were buried somewhere in the silence. He finally turned to me and gave a small smile.

"Where were you?" he asked.

"At the synagogue. I've been helping to restore it. They're forming a new council under Jacob Egit. He wants to start a Jewish settlement here. This could be home, he says. Reichenbach could be home."

Sam nodded thoughtfully, his eyes searching my face.

"You look well, Sarah," he said. "Working, being part of the community, is good for you."

"I need to do something, Sam," I admitted. "I need to keep busy."

He nodded again and looked down. I glanced out the window, watching the brown water of the river flow past the hotel. I could feel Sam's eyes on my face. "I'm not used to seeing you like this, all grown up," he said, interrupting my thoughts.

I glanced back at him. "I'm not sixteen anymore," I said.

"I know."

"Sam," I finally dared to ask, "do you know what happened to the others, to Jacob and Isaac?"

His smile faded and he looked away. I waited, watching his face grow blank as he stared at the yard outside. His eyes, which used to burn with passion, were hollow and empty. He swallowed before saying, "I was with Isaac at first. We were sent to Jawischowitz, where we worked throughout the winter. I tried to look out for him, Sarah. I tried to protect him. But I think he just gave up. He got sick, You know how he was."

Helena and Gutcha entered the room silently as Sam spoke. They stood behind us, listening apprehensively.

"I worked underground in one of the nearby mines, while he was assigned work in one of the camp storerooms. I was relieved he didn't have to do the hard physical labor; I thought that would keep him safe. I came back one evening and waited for him like I always did, but—" Sam's voice trailed off, and he turned to look at me. There was desperation in his eyes. "I know what you want to hear, Sarah," he said somberly, shaking his head. "I'm sorry. I'm so sorry. I wish I knew what happened to him, to our little brother. But I—I never saw him again."

When I woke each morning, I vowed no longer to cry. I wanted to believe I was empty of tears, that the pain would become a numbness I would eventually no longer feel. But upon hearing these words, I realized I was crying again, silently, effortlessly, the salt of the tears bitter on my lips. I wiped them away.

"And Jacob?" Helena asked breathlessly, kneeling in front of Sam. He gazed at her, shaking his head. "I never saw him. Our paths never crossed. But I met Moses Glaser. Remember him? From our town? He was taken at the same time as Jacob. He—" Again Sam swallowed, his eyes dropping to his lap where his hands absently toyed with the fringe of the chair. "He told me Jacob was taken into the showers when they first arrived. But they weren't showers," Sam whispered. "They weren't showers. Those who went in never came out."

Thirty-Seven

Reichenbach, Germany, June 17, 1945

Michal and Sam moved into a room down the hall from ours. Now that both of them were stronger, it was appropriate that they should have their own space. I was thrilled when Sam continued to gain weight, and I began to see a hint of the brother I used to know. I had found work on one of the new communal farms just outside Reichenbach. I spent the summer days with the other women, collecting crops from the field, milking the cows, and gathering eggs from the henhouse, while the men tilled the land and planted seeds for the fall harvest. Most days when I returned home, I ran to Sam's room, eager to spend time with my brother, but more often than not, he wasn't there. It was Michal I ended up sitting with and talking to, and soon my thoughts turned to him when we weren't together. I looked forward to our regular conversations, even though I worried where Sam was and what he was doing. In the weeks since his recovery, my brother had become reclusive, disappearing for long hours and returning to the hotel late at night. When I questioned him, his answers were vague.

One evening, as I approached their room, anxious because I hadn't seen Sam all day, I overheard voices beyond their partially closed door. "Sarah's worried about you," Michal said softly. "She asks all day if I've seen you. You have to give her some peace of mind. Tell her what you've been doing."

I pressed against the wall.

"Soon," Sam said. "She doesn't need to concern herself with my affairs. I took care of myself in the camps. I can handle myself now."

"That's not the point," Michal said. "She wants to spend time with you. I can tell she is disappointed when you aren't here. You are her only living relative. Don't shut her out."

I turned from the door so they wouldn't notice my presence, my thoughts racing. What was Sam doing? Did Michal know where he disappeared to each day? What were they hiding?

The following day, Michal came to my room holding a beautifully wrapped gift box, topped with a red bow. "This is for you, Sarah," he said, placing the box in my hands. I looked at him quizzically, noticing how his clean cotton shirt slipped from his slender shoulders so I saw the slightly sunburned skin of his collarbone. I noticed how the tan on his face made his eyes even darker. "What is it?" I asked.

"Open it," he insisted with a smile.

I tore through the gold wrapping paper and lifted the lid of the box. Resting on white tissue paper was a white silk dress with large red polka dots, shiny black buttons running the length of the front, and a red velour collar and cuffs. I lifted the dress from the tissue paper, feeling the way the material slid like fluid through my fingers. "It's beautiful," I breathed, blushing. I stood up and held it to me, twirling in a small circle so the skirt caught the air and billowed against my legs.

"I saw it in town and thought of you," Michal said softly. "I thought, perhaps, you could wear it tonight and accompany me to the celebration?"

Earlier that day, there had been an assembly in town; representatives from the emerging Jewish communities in the surrounding areas had come to Reichenbach to officially elect a Provincial Jewish Committee to serve as the local branch of the Central Jewish Committee of Poland. Jakob Egit was named the provincial committee's chairman, and headquarters were moved from the synagogue to 23 Krasickiego Street. There was a feeling of triumph and excitement in the streets, a sense of community and rebirth. It was rumored that almost six thousand Jews were now living in and around Reichenbach.

To celebrate, a festival was planned for the evening. Gutcha,

Helena, and I had planned to go together. I felt Michal's eyes on me as I walked to the mirror and looked at my reflection. My weight was slowly returning, and I noticed curves in my hips and bosom where, until recently, I'd had none. My hair now reached just below my ears and had grown in a fuller chestnut color instead of the bright red I used to detest. I had learned to style it in the pin curls that were so popular. The freckles that once dotted my nose had faded into an overall tanned glow from the summer sun. I no longer avoided looking in the mirror. In fact, I liked what I saw.

I was about to answer Michal when I noticed Sam standing in the doorway, his eyes shifting back and forth between us. He frowned when he saw the dress I held against me. "Where did you get that?" he asked. I looked at Michal, who turned to face him and said, "I bought it for her. I thought she deserved something beautiful. Don't you agree?"

Sam didn't answer as he stared at me.

"Are you going to the festival, Sam?" I asked casually to break the sudden tension. "The girls and I are all going. Why don't you and Michal come with us?"

Michal quickly nodded. "Yes," he said, "we should all enjoy tonight together."

Sam frowned. "I've been talking to Rubin and he thinks we should be cautious."

"Rubin?" I asked, carefully setting the dress back in its box and facing my brother. "Tell me what you're doing, Sam, please? Who is Rubin?"

Sam's face finally softened, and he walked across the room to take my hand in his. "Come with me," he said. He led me back to their room and approached a large trunk sitting in a corner, covered by a thick woolen blanket. He lifted the blanket and removed a chain from his neck. I noticed for the first time the key that dangled from the end of the chain. He told me to close the door, and only then did he turn the key in the padlock that secured the lid of the trunk. Lifting it, he waved me over. I stood over him, peering into the depths of the trunk.

Lining its bottom were rows of guns and rifles, ammunition and bullets. I gasped and backed away. Sam looked at me soberly as he closed the lid again. "This is what I've been doing, Sarah."

"But why, Sam?"

Sam stood and walked to the window that looked out at the garden behind the hotel. His hair had started to grow in as well, dark like my father's had been, the scabs he had picked raw from lice finally beginning to heal.

"I won't be caught off-guard again," he said with his back to me. "Rubin is a Russian general stationed with one of the units in town. He is helping some of us to form our own police corps so we can defend ourselves if we need to."

"How did you get the weapons?"

"Rubin and some of the other Russians provide them for us."

"Are you still fighting, Sam?" I asked, walking to him and gently placing my hand on his shoulder. I felt it stiffen, his body going rigid at my touch. "The war is over."

"You're a fool if you believe that," Sam said abruptly, turning on me. I looked down, stung by his tone. I heard him take a deep breath, and his finger lifted my chin so we were gazing into each other's eyes. "I'm sorry, Sarah," he whispered. "I didn't mean that. I just want to be prepared."

"For what?" I asked, still confused and hurt.

"For the future," he said. "Do you think the Poles will stay out of Reichenbach? They were displaced as well. This was their home before the Germans took over. The factories and farms—it was all their property. If they come back, we may have to defend what we've taken as our own. We won't be welcome here forever."

I swallowed, considering his words. "You were always the one who said we should leave," I said, the words aching as they came out of my mouth. "You begged Mama and Papa. You knew what was going to happen. If we'd only listened to you."

"Don't think that way, Sarah," he said. "I didn't know what was going to happen. But I won't let it happen again."

At dusk, we walked to the center of town. The streets were already crowded with people. Helena and I linked arms as Gutcha walked ahead of us. We had spent the last couple of hours styling our hair, applying powder and lipstick, and penciling lines on our legs to make it appear we were wearing stockings. I was fascinated with the fashion trends and styles some of the women from larger cities described. I enjoyed looking at the fashion magazines that advertised clothes "Straight from Paris" or "The Finest in London Fashion." I remembered how my mother used to dress, in long skirts and modest blouses and shawls, her head always covered, her face free of makeup. I felt a mixture of shame and delight at my new appearance. She wouldn't have permitted me to leave the house dressed as I was. But I liked how I looked, even if it was considered indecent.

When we met Sam and Michal in the hall, I noticed how Sam studied me reproachfully. I had worn the dress Michal gave me despite Sam's silent objections, and it hugged my figure in a flattering way. Michal's eyes also centered on me, but his look was one of appreciation. I felt reckless and momentarily carefree under Michal's gaze. I wouldn't let Sam's disapproval ruin my night.

The gas lamps were lit, and the setting sun cast a rose-colored hue over the rooftops, chimneys, and steeples of the town. I heard music and recognized a strain of song from my childhood.

In the center of town, a stage had been erected, and a small klezmer band played. The lively melody from the upright bass, accordion, fiddle, and clarinet swelled around us. Helena pulled me forward so we were standing in front of the musicians with a large crowd, swept up in the music. The pulsing rhythm was contagious; soon we were clapping in unison, watching as both men and women danced together in the square. This, too, would not have been permitted in my childhood community. Men and women were kept separate not only during worship but also at celebrations, never touching in public. I was mesmerized by the abandon with which the dancers moved, the almost rapturous way their bodies glided over the cobblestones, a smell of summer honeysuckle and sweat strong on the humid night air.

"This is wonderful!" Helena said. I smiled and nodded as the music washed over me. The song turned seamlessly into "Hava Negila," and I was reminded of the weddings I'd been allowed to attend as a child in Olkusz. Suddenly, Michal was next to me. He held out his hand and said, "Dance with me, Sarah." I didn't have time to think as I placed my hand in his and was pulled into the circle. I closed my eyes and laughed at the feeling of almost flying, my feet barely touching the cobblestones. Delight surged through my limbs, and for the first time in a lifetime, I felt happy.

But suddenly a hand closed on my wrist, and I was dragged from the circle. I almost tripped as I stumbled backward. Sam was leading me away from the dancers. "What do you think you are doing?" he demanded as he pulled me beneath a tree on the outskirts of the crowd.

"What do you mean?" I panted. "I was just dancing, Sam."

He shook his head as he looked at me. "You were acting like a common whore."

Again, I was struck dumb by his hurtful words. I stared at him open-mouthed. The joy I'd felt only moments ago immediately vanished, leaving me weak and dizzy. I put out a hand to steady myself against the tree. "Why do you say such things?" I asked in a whisper. "Am I not allowed to enjoy myself even a little? Everyone else was dancing too, Sam. It was just a dance."

Sam's breathing was rapid, his face contorted with an anger I didn't understand. I noticed how tense his shoulders were, and I wanted to reach out to him, but something held me back. "I want to be happy, Sam," I said softly. "Don't you want to be happy again too?"

He looked back toward the street, where more dancers had joined the circle. "I only want to protect you, Sarah," he said, not looking me in the eye. "But I don't know how to."

"You don't have to protect me, Sam."

"How did you survive?" he asked abruptly, turning to look at me. "What did you do in the camps?" He watched my reaction carefully.

"What do you mean?" I whispered. The word *whore* echoed in my ears. I swallowed and shook my head as a memory tried to surface. I fought to push it to the back of my mind. "I don't want to talk about this now," I said, suddenly queasy. "I need to sit down." I turned from Sam and fell against the tree, closing my eyes.

"Is everything all right?" a voice asked. I looked up to see Michal walking toward us.

"Yes," Sam said in a tight voice. "Sarah needed some air."

Michal looked at me closely. "Do you feel ill?"

"I'll be fine," I said, taking a deep breath. I suddenly wanted to be away from both of them. "I'm going to take a walk," I said, and before either of them could object, I turned and walked down the street.

On the corner, I saw Erna towering over a group of women. She caught my eye, and we nodded at each other. I briefly remembered the night we'd met in the filthy outhouse outside our barracks in Blechhammer. I had crept out of the bunk and into the cold to go to the bathroom, thinking I was alone in the dark until I heard a shuffling sound beside me. I'd jumped and gasped and heard a similar sound somewhere to my left. "Hello?" I'd whispered, and a voice had whispered back, "Hello? Sarah, is that you?"

"Erna?" I had asked, standing up from my crouched position and feeling along the wall to touch her arm.

"It's me," she said. "Nothing like a pee in the middle of the night," she added, and we both laughed, despite the fact that our feet were freezing in the dirt and we had nothing to clean ourselves with.

The music in the town marketplace had stopped, and the sound of applause cut through the night air. I wandered back to the square in time to see a woman in her late thirties, dark hair piled on the crown of her head and almond-shaped eyes beneath heavy brows, climb the steps to the stage to address the crowd.

"Ladies and gentlemen," she announced. "My name is Ruth Taru-Kowalska. I was an actress before the war, performing on many stages across Europe. It is a happy occasion that brings us together this evening to celebrate the revival of our art and music, our rich culture."

Murmurs and cheers passed throughout the crowd. The actress beamed at the large gathering and clasped her hands between her breasts. She invited a number of men and women to the stage, survivors like myself, to perform readings of works by Sholem Aleichem and I. L. Peretz. I stood off to the side, scanning the crowd for Helena and Gutcha. I wanted nothing more than to be away from the men, in the company of women. On stage, a man stepped forward and bowed to the audience. At first I didn't pay much attention to his performance as I pushed my way through the crowd, looking for my cousin. But I paused when I heard the man's deep voice recite:

> And in the heart's interior,
> A secret hand is fashioning . . .
> New music's born,
> New hopes are spun . . .
> O weave yourself, Desire, weave!

I was drawn toward the stage by his words, by the idea of new hope, new music. But as I watched, another performer stepped onto the stage, raising his arms as he spoke:

> All's vanity . . .
> Live
> All you can,
> Wander
> All you want:
> You'll see nothing new
> Beneath the sun!
> What was is what will be.

I turned away, the queasy feeling in my stomach again. My mind fought with itself, wanting with such desperation to be happy while another part stirred up memories I wanted to lock away for good. I retreated, running down the quiet backstreets, leaving the crowd and the noise and the words and the music behind, hoping my memories would stay behind as well. Without looking where I was going, I bumped hard into someone and stumbled backward. "I'm sorry," I gasped. "I didn't mean—"

"Sarah?"

I looked up and saw I had collided with Helena. She was flustered as she smoothed down her skirt and tucked her dark hair behind her ears. She glanced over her shoulder, and I realized she was not alone. A young man was standing behind her, also slightly embarrassed.

"Oh," I said, startled. "I didn't mean to disturb you."

"Sarah, this is Wolf," Helena said, smiling awkwardly and nodding to the stranger standing behind her.

"Hello," I said softly, nodding back.

"Hello, Sarah," Wolf said. "I've heard a lot about you."

I raised my eyebrows, surprised. Helena had never mentioned his name to me before. Helena's hair was tousled, and her bright red lipstick was smudged. I remembered the time long ago when I had stumbled on Helena and Jacob, and I felt my face grow hot. Helena glanced between the two of us, then stepped toward me. "Where are you headed in such a rush?"

"I wasn't feeling well," I said. "I was just on my way home."

"You shouldn't walk alone if you're unwell," Helena said. "Let me walk with you."

"That's all right," I said, but she took my hand in hers and led me back onto the street. I noticed how Helena and Wolf glanced at each other furtively as we passed him, their faces illuminated in the moonlight. When we were some distance away, Helena turned to me and said, "Sarah, I've been meaning to tell you something."

"What is it?" I asked. When Helena didn't answer right away, I looked at her. She was biting her lip, and I knew without having to be told. "It's Wolf, isn't it?" I asked.

"Yes," Helena breathed, pausing to look at me. She reached for my hands. "We've been spending a lot of time together lately," she said. "He works in town, in the post office. That's how we met. He doesn't talk much, but he's sensible and kindhearted. He's a hard worker too."

I watched her silently, waiting for her to continue.

"Sarah," she said in a whisper, "he's asked me to marry him."

I inhaled sharply. "What?" I gasped.

"He wants to marry me." She looked down, as though afraid to look me in the eye. "And I think he could make me happy."

When she looked up, I saw the pleading expression in her eyes. I knew what she was asking. She wanted my permission, my forgiveness. Part of me was happy for her, but another part of me ached.

"Do you remember when I said we shouldn't give up hope, that our families might still be alive?" she asked. I nodded silently. "I don't want to give up hope that I might be reunited with my family, but I also want to move on with my life. Don't you?" she asked imploringly. I swallowed and nodded, knowing full well that moving on meant letting go.

"Do you forgive me, Sarah?" she whispered, squeezing my hands.

"Yes, Helena," I whispered back. "Of course. I forgive you."

Thirty-Eight

I tossed in bed that night, unable to sleep. The news Helena had shared with me left me feeling empty, despondent. I knew I should feel glad for her, but a small part of me felt betrayed. And Sam's voice rang in my head as I closed my eyes. I kept hearing him shout the word *whore*. The insult burned in my heart and evoked memories I could no longer ignore. The image of the *Oberfeldwebel*'s face swam before me, the kindness he had shown turning to something darker in my memory, something sinister. I felt his hand on my arm as he whispered, "You're just a child, aren't you? So young and innocent. You must be scared. I'll watch out for you, you pretty thing. Don't worry, you'll do fine here."

In my mind I saw the walls of his office, heard the static of the radio on his desk and the tapping of his pen against his chin as he stared at me. I shivered as I remembered standing before him, my knees weak from anxiety and fear. I buried my head under my pillow, trying in vain to forget, but the memories followed me into ugly dreams.

The following morning, when I went to find Michal, he was gone. Instead, I found Sam sitting on his unmade bed, head in his hands; Michal's bed appeared untouched. I stood in the doorway, looking silently around the room. Sam raised his eyes to mine and met my silence with his own.

"Where's Michal?" I asked finally. Sam sighed and ran his hand through the curls that were starting to grow back. Stubble grew on his cheeks and neck. He stood up and walked to the window, drawing the shade across the glass.

"Where's Michal?" I asked again, stepping into the room. "I want to talk to him. I want to apologize."

"For what?" Sam asked as he walked to the trunk he had shown me the other day.

"For how I acted last night. I shouldn't have run away like that."

Sam didn't answer as I watched him. He took the key from the chain around his neck and opened the trunk. He then pulled a satchel from the small cupboard in the corner and knelt before the trunk. "What are you doing?" I asked.

"Transporting these," he said as he reached into the trunk and pulled out the guns and ammunition I had seen yesterday.

"Will you get in trouble if you're caught?" I asked, sitting on the edge of the bed.

"Don't worry about me," he said.

"How can I not, Sam?" I sighed, watching my brother. He continued his work in determined silence. I noticed that the nightstand where Michal kept his belongings was bare. I frowned and walked to the bureau where Michal stored his few articles of clothing and shoes. When I opened it, it was empty. I turned to Sam and saw that he was watching me.

"Where is Michal?" I demanded now, my voice rising slightly. Sam stood up and zipped the satchel closed, throwing it over his shoulder. He turned to face me and said, "He's gone, Sarah."

I felt my breath catch in my throat. "What do you mean?" I asked. "Where did he go?"

"He left," Sam said simply. "He decided to move on."

"No," I whispered, beginning to pace. "You're lying. He wouldn't leave without saying good-bye."

"Why do you care so much?" Sam demanded.

"What did you say to him?" I accused suddenly, turning on my brother. "Did you tell him to leave?"

Sam didn't answer, but I thought I saw a hint of guilt in his eyes. "He was your friend!" I cried. "He saved your life! Why would you do that?" I turned on my heels and stormed from the room.

"Where are you going?" Sam called after me.

"Don't worry about me!" I yelled over my shoulder, throwing his own words back at him.

I ran through the streets looking for Michal, but he had vanished without a trace. While many survivors were settling in Reichenbach and the surrounding countryside, still more were deciding to leave Poland for good. As I checked for him at the synagogue and the committee headquarters, running to the fields where the farmers were already busy with the day's work, I feared that's what he had decided for himself, slipping away in the middle of the night without so much as a farewell.

When I returned to the hotel at the end of the day, feeling forlorn, Sam was waiting for me in the lobby. I was angry and didn't want to talk to him, but as I stalked past, he stood up and grabbed my hand. "Sarah, come sit," he said. "I have something to tell you."

I allowed him to lead me to a chair, where I sat with my arms crossed over my chest, staring into the empty grate of the lobby fireplace.

"You didn't find him, did you?" Sam asked softly.

I shook my head.

"Sarah, I'm sorry. I should have told you before now. I could tell how you felt about him."

My face grew hot. "What are you talking about, Sam?" I whispered, stubbornly avoiding his eyes. He leaned forward and said, "Sarah, Michal had a wife. Before the war."

Now my eyes turned to my brother, searching his face. Sam nodded, leaning back in his chair. "He told me about her while we were in the camps together. Returning to her was the one thing that kept him strong, kept him going every day."

Sam's words hurt, but I didn't want him to know how deeply they cut to my heart. "We decided last night it was time for him to find her," Sam continued.

"We?" I interrupted. Sam looked away.

"He is well enough now to travel. He didn't want to hurt you,

Sarah, but he couldn't rest until he knew for sure what happened to his wife."

I accepted what he said, but I didn't feel any better. I could tell there was something Sam wasn't telling me, some hidden meaning beneath his words. "But why like this, Sam?" I asked. "Why didn't he tell me this for himself? Why didn't he wait until morning? Why didn't he at least say good-bye?"

When we were younger and Sam came home past curfew or got into a scuffle with some of the other boys and wanted to keep it from my parents, he would bite his lip or shuffle his left foot back and forth. I saw him do that now as he shrugged, looking away. And I knew Sam wasn't telling me the whole story. Though I didn't know what had happened between Sam and Michal, I felt sure I was one of the reasons they had parted ways.

Thirty-Nine

Reichenbach, Germany, late June 1945

A crowd was gathered in the lobby of the hotel. I saw Helena talking to a few other women and walked to her. "What's happening?" I asked as I joined them.

"Someone bought the hotel," she said. "The Russians sold it to a Polish innkeeper this morning. They just informed us."

"What does that mean?" I asked, glancing at the anxious faces around me. "Does that mean we'll have to leave?"

"I believe so," Helena nodded. "I suppose we knew this wasn't going to be our home forever."

"Sarah," Sam called, pushing his way through the crowd. Some of the women in our small group looked at him and blushed. His health had returned, and with it the same good looks that once drew the girls' attention back in Olkusz. His shoulders and arms had filled out, and his hair was now mostly grown in, thick locks of auburn that brushed the tops of his ears. His face was no longer emaciated by hunger, but a dark shadow still haunted his large round eyes. He ignored the women and took my arm, pulling me aside.

"What is it, Sam?" I asked as he led me outside, where the air was heavy with the promise of a summer storm. Dark rain clouds kissed the peaks of the mountains in the distance. There was a low rumble of thunder, and the wind caught my skirt and lashed it against my legs.

"I knew something like this would happen sooner or later," Sam said as he guided me under the eaves of the hotel. "That's why I wanted to be prepared. Helping start a Jewish police force isn't the only thing I've been doing with my Russian friend."

"Then what have you been doing?" I demanded. He looked at me sadly, almost guiltily. "I know you're angry with me, Sarah," he said, and I didn't deny it. I *was* angry with him. I'd been angry ever since Michal had left, feeling Sam was somehow responsible for driving him away. I had been short-tempered and irritable with him in Michal's absence. "All I want to do is take care of you," he said. "That's why I've been working with Rubin. He has found us a private home that we can move into. We will be sharing the house with two brothers who already live there. I can pay our way with my new job, so it will be ours. No one can make us move out."

The first raindrops fell, hitting my face and running down my cheek. I saw the townspeople running for cover under the awnings of the local shops. "What about Gutcha?" I asked. "She can come too, yes?"

Sam was silent.

"Sam?" I prodded.

"Go find Gutcha," he said. "I've already talked to her. She's waiting upstairs."

"Sam, what is it?"

"I promised I'd let her tell you."

With a feeling of foreboding, I backed away, a tightness in my chest. Rain dripped onto my face from the detailed stonework over the windows of the hotel. Overhead, the stone statues and gargoyles that perched near the hotel's roof watched me mutely as I entered the building, leaving Sam alone in the rain.

I found Gutcha sitting on her bed, staring down at her hands. Her clothes were spread out on the mattress beside her. When she heard me enter, she looked up and tried to smile, but I saw tears in her eyes.

"Did you hear about the hotel?" I asked. "But don't worry," I comforted her. "Sam has found a place for us to live."

She shook her head gently. "No, Sarah," she said. "I'm not coming with you."

"What?" I gasped. I couldn't believe my ears. "Of course you are."

"No," she said again. "You and Sam have found each other. You are starting your lives together. I must do the same. Daniel is gone."

"You don't know that."

"And Mama and Papa are gone. I'm so happy you have Sam, Sarah, but seeing you both together—sometimes, it just reminds me that I don't have anyone." Tears pooled in her eyes, ran down her cheeks. I reached to embrace her. "You have us!" I exclaimed. "We have each other!"

She cried on my shoulder, and I felt the heaviness of our history, the breadth of our experiences together. I remembered our happy years as children in Olkusz. I remembered the desperation with which we clung to each other in the camps. And now she was leaving? I wouldn't allow it!

"I need to move on," she whispered. "I need to start over somewhere new. The memories are still too fresh here, too painful."

"Where will you go?" I whispered against her shoulder.

"Palestine," she said, her arms tight around me.

"*Palestine*," I whispered, pushing her away to look into her face. "That's so far."

"There's an organization in town called Bricha that helps find passage for those wishing to start a life there. I'm going to join them."

"I'll go with you."

"No, Sarah. You and Sam must stick together. He will take care of you."

I pulled Gutcha into my arms again. My cousin, who had been by my side, who had kept me alive, was leaving for good. How could I ever let her go?

Forty

Villa in the foothills of the Owl Mountains,
Reichenbach, Germany, July 1945

Rubin opened the door and pulled my brother into a hug. "Sam!"
he exclaimed in a booming voice. "Come in, come in! And this
must be Sarah?"

I looked up at the large Russian who had befriended my brother.
He was handsome in a burly sort of way: large and muscular, with
a full beard and mustache and animated green eyes. His hands
swallowed mine when he reached out to shake them.

"Hello," I said shyly as I followed my brother into the house.
I noticed two men standing behind Rubin in a doorway. Both
were fair and looked older than Sam and I. One was taller and
more slender than the other, but they both had pale blue eyes
that regarded us with curiosity. Rubin laid his heavy arms across
our shoulders and ushered us into the foyer, closing the door
behind him.

"Harry, Pinky, this is Sam and Sarah Waldman," Rubin introduced us to the two silent men. "They are the brother and sister
I told you about. They need a place to stay now that the hotel is
under new ownership." We stared at each other for a moment
before the taller man, Harry, stepped forward and said in a low
voice, "You are most welcome here."

"Thank you," Sam said, nodding at the two men.

"Come into the kitchen," the smaller man said. "Let's have a
drink."

Rubin gave a hearty laugh and said, "Yes. A drink would be nice. Just so happens I brought a bottle with me."

Sam and I followed the men into a large kitchen, where a wooden table and eight chairs stood at its center. Pots and pans hung from hooks above a cast iron stove, and mostly bare shelves lined one wall. There was a wood-burning fireplace in one corner, the bricks around the mouth darkened from years of soot, and a large kettle hung over charred logs. A window over a deep sink looked out on the mountains and the rooftops of Reichenbach in the distance. Our entire home in Olkusz would have fit in this one room.

Rubin placed a bottle of vodka on the wooden surface of the table, polished from long use. Harry walked to a shelf and pulled down five mismatched glasses. I noticed how his arms and legs stuck out of the ill-fitting clothes he wore as he reached up for them. As he paced back to the table, he caught me watching him. I turned my eyes away.

Rubin poured the clear liquid into the glasses and passed them around, one to each of us. Sam glanced at me as I took my glass. I had never had alcohol before, except for an occasional sip of the sweet wine we'd had at our family seders. Sam looked like he was about to say something to me, but Rubin raised his glass and proclaimed, "A toast to your good health!" He then drained his glass in one swallow; the two brothers did the same. I raised my glass to my lips and took a small sip. The liquid stung as it slid down my throat. I cringed.

"Sarah," Sam whispered, a look of disapproval on his face. He reached out and took the glass from my hand. I frowned, turning red when I realized they were all looking at me. "What?" I asked Sam defiantly, squaring my shoulders, suddenly embarrassed.

"Don't you think that's a bit strong?" he asked under his breath.

In answer to his question, I took the glass from his hand and drank the rest of the liquid in one swallow, feeling a slow burn spread through my chest. I tried to hide the cough that followed.

Harry walked to the counter and poured a fresh glass of water from a pitcher sitting beside the sink. "Here," he said as he set it down before me. I glanced up to an amused expression on his face. "Thank you," I said meekly. I didn't dare look at Sam.

"How did you two meet Rubin?" Sam asked the brothers. I knew he was trying to steer their attention away from me and could recognize the forced tone of interest in his voice.

"That's quite a story," Pinky said as he pulled out one of the wooden chairs. "Please," he said, motioning to the others, "have a seat. Make yourselves comfortable."

I sat gingerly on the edge of one of the chairs next to Sam.

"Ah, yes," Rubin said, straddling a chair at the head of the table, "tell them the story, Harry."

I glanced at Harry again, noticing how blue his eyes were in his angular face. He sat down next to his brother and folded his hands on the table. "My brother and I escaped shortly after the Germans fled our camp," Harry said. "We spent many nights in the woods. Before leaving the camp, though, we stole what we could. I found a perfectly good German uniform that I knew would keep me warm, so I wore it out of the camp."

"My unit was the one who found them," Rubin said, with a glint of humor in his eye. "We were scouring the woods for the Nazis, rounding them up. It was a good thing I spotted him before some of my comrades did. They were shooting anyone in a Nazi uniform, you see."

Harry nodded and said, "I could feel his gun in my back. I didn't speak a word of Russian and had no way of telling him I wasn't a Nazi."

"You must have been terrified," Sam said.

Harry nodded. "I had my hands up and was shaking my head and kept saying '*Nein! Nein!*'"

"And I took one look at the way his clothes fit and knew he was no dirty Nazi."

The men laughed, but I just gaped at them, speechless. I couldn't imagine what about that situation was funny.

"I made sure Harry and Pinky found new clothes straight away," Rubin said with a chuckle.

"And we burned the SS uniform," Harry finished with a

satisfied nod. They continued to smile as though recounting fond memories. Rubin poured another round of drinks, but Sam put his hand over my glass. I didn't argue. The heat from the vodka still burned uncomfortably in my throat.

"So," Rubin said in his loud voice, wiping his mouth with the back of his hand. "It's time I was on my way. I'll leave you both to get settled," he finished, turning to Sam and me. Sam stood and reached across the table to shake his hand. "Thank you," he said. Rubin nodded and replied, "I'll see you soon, comrade!"

"Let me walk you to the door." Pinky rose, leading Rubin back into the hallway. As they left the room, Harry, Sam, and I stood in silence, exchanging awkward glances. Harry regarded us for a moment before stepping toward another set of doors. "I can show you to your rooms, if you like," he offered.

"Thank you," Sam said again, reaching for my arm.

"Do you have any belongings?" Harry asked.

"Just what we have on us," Sam replied, indicating the satchel he carried with our few articles of clothing and the small purse I clutched to my side. Harry nodded and led us into the hallway. Doors opened on either side of the corridor. "This is my room," he said, pointing to a door on his left, "and this is my brother's. This room is empty," he said, opening the door to the room adjacent to his own. Over his shoulder, I saw a tall mahogany head and footboard centered between two large stained glass windows. Two chairs upholstered in rich velvet stood beside a window that looked out at a small garden. Gold-leaf sconces lined the walls, and a plush Oriental rug with gold fringe sat in the center of the room. I caught my breath. I was amazed at the wealth that had been spent to decorate this room.

"It is a rather fine room," Harry said, noticing my reaction. "This house belonged to one of the wealthier Nazi officers. Perhaps you would be comfortable here?" he asked, looking at me. Before I could answer, Sam squeezed my elbow and said, "I think maybe I'll take this room."

Harry glanced at Sam and shrugged. "There is another room down the hall. It is a bit smaller, but pleasant as well." He led us to a door at the very end of the hallway and opened it. The room inside was decorated in shades of white and cream, with lace hanging from the windows and draped over a small mattress. I stepped forward and said, "This is lovely." Sam followed me into the room. Harry stood in the doorway for a moment. "We hope you'll make yourselves at home," he said after an uncomfortable silence and then left us alone.

I put my purse on the bed and turned to see Sam closing the door and bending to look at the knob.

"What are you doing?" I asked.

"Looking for a lock," he said. He turned a small key in the keyhole and withdrew it, testing to make sure the door was secure before handing me the key. "I want you to make sure you lock this door every time you enter the room."

"Why are you being like this?" I asked, frowning.

Sam sat in a chair beside the door and looked at me. "Being here might not be such a good idea after all," he said softly.

"Why?" I asked again, sitting on the bed. The mattress sank under my weight.

"You are the only girl in a house of men, Sarah," Sam said. "I noticed the way he looked at you."

I felt heat rise up my neck. "I can take care of myself, Sam," I said. He sighed and said, "Just promise me you'll be discreet, Sarah. You need to be careful."

I lay in bed that night, acutely aware that I was alone in a strange room. When sleep continued to elude me, I threw back the blanket and padded down the hall to my brother's room. I pressed an ear to the door, listening for any movement. Turning the knob gently, I peered into his room and saw him lying on top of the bed quilt, unmoving, arms folded behind his head, staring at the ceiling. He turned his head as I entered, and I saw moonlight from the window reflect in the dark pools of his eyes.

"Can I come in?" I whispered.

He sat up slowly and nodded. "Why are you awake?" he asked.

"I can't sleep," I said, as I sat down beside him.

"Neither can I."

We were silent, listening to the foreign sounds of the house settling around us. A wind swept down from the Owl Mountains, stirring the branches outside Sam's window so I was reminded of fingers scraping against glass. I shivered. The night was darker and emptier there than in Reichenbach. I leaned against Sam, resting my head on his shoulder. His arm came around me, and for the moment, I felt safe. We sat like that for a short while as my eyes grew heavy and began to close.

"You're falling asleep," he said softly. "Let me walk you back to your room." He took my hand and pulled me gently to my feet. We padded to my room, and as I settled back against the mattress, he moved to the door to check the lock as he had done earlier.

"Don't go," I said, suddenly awake again, reaching for him.

"Sarah," he said, walking back to me. "What's the matter? Are you frightened of something?"

"I don't know," I admitted, feeling foolish. "It's just—it's too dark in here. Will you sit with me some more? Please?" I begged. He walked to my window and parted the curtains to let in the moonlight, then lifted the window from the sill to let in the cool, damp summer air. "There," he said as he took my hand and sat on the edge of the bed. "Better?"

I nodded, but I clutched his hand firmly in mine as I lay back against the pillows. Even in the darkness, I could tell he was troubled as well. We were strangers in unfamiliar rooms. In the hotel, Gutcha, Helena, and I had shared a room. In the camps, we had all been together, bodies stacked on other bodies. Now, I felt like a small boat in the ocean that was my bed. "Sam," I said, "do you think about Esther at all?" The words surprised me even as I spoke them. I hadn't thought about my sister in a long while, but now I felt her presence around me. Sam blinked and looked down at me. I noticed how his brow furrowed as he studied my face.

"Do you remember how we shared a bed in that little alcove?" I asked, feeling a drowsiness settle over me again. "We used to braid each other's hair when we couldn't sleep, and sometimes we talked until morning. It was nice, knowing I wasn't alone."

"You're not alone. You'll never be alone again." Sam's hand gently brushed my hair back from my forehead, and for a moment I felt like the young girl I had been, lying beside my sister, feeling her warmth next to me.

Forty-One

The following morning, I woke to a quiet house. I sat up in bed, confused at first by my surroundings. A breeze lifted lace curtains gently from a multipaned window where sunlight filtered onto a bare wooden floor. I blinked, listening to the silence, as I remembered the night before. Throwing back the blankets, I walked to my door, eager to find my brother. But as I stood in the stillness of the hallway and glanced toward the kitchen, I sensed I was the only one in the house.

I knocked on my brother's door. "Sam?" I called, but there was no answer. I pushed the door open a crack and looked inside. The quilt on top of his bed was a rumpled mess, as though he had tossed fitfully all night long. But his room was empty. I passed closed doors to rooms I had yet to explore. I peered into a large parlor and my breath caught at the sight of the rich antique furnishings and Oriental rugs. A huge marble fireplace dominated one end of the room, and silk screens depicting pastoral scenes hung from the walls in shades of palest rose, auburn, and gold. Slowly closing the door, I moved on to the next room. Inside, shelves crowded with books and expensive bric-a-brac lined the walls. A large mahogany desk stood in the center of the floor. I ran my hand over the desk's surface, dust coating the tips of my fingers. A map of Europe was spread across the desktop, and I noticed the strategic markings that had been outlined around Germany and the surrounding countries. I glanced at the books on the shelves and noticed that they all had German titles. One book was set apart from the others and propped against an ornate stand. I read the title, *Mein Kampf,* and quickly turned away. I knew this had been the officer's library, and a tendril of fear crept up my spine. I felt his presence acutely, as though he was still standing in the room, watching me. I hurried to the door and closed it behind me, leaning against it and breathing hard.

Back in the kitchen, I sat in a chair at the table and put my head in my hands. At least in this room, filled with ordinary objects and the smell of burned wood and spices, I felt more at home. I noticed a piece of paper wedged beneath a pitcher and recognized Sam's handwriting. "Sarah, went to town. Be back soon." What was Sam doing? I wondered. I worried about him when he left each day. I worried about his volatile nature and quick temper. Was he getting into trouble? Was he staying safe? There was a thriving black market in town, an exchange of banned goods and services, but those who got caught trading were quickly sent to jail. Sam may have made friends with Rubin, but would that be enough to keep him from being arrested if he was doing something illegal? I thought again of the guns he had kept hidden.

Unable to sit still, I paced the length of the kitchen. The silence in the house caused the hair on the back of my neck to stand on end. Looking around, I saw a door that led out to the garden—through its window, I spied a well with a pump. Taking a bucket from the hearth, I turned the door's knob and stepped onto a path that wove through Siberian irises, globeflower, and corn poppy, gathering baby's breath as I made my way to the pump. A small greenhouse stood at the far end of the garden near a dilapidated wall, and I noticed pots where herbs were growing wildly. I pumped the handle of the well, filling the bucket and splashing cool water onto my face. I walked to the row of pots outside the greenhouse, fingering untamed leaves of basil and lavender and sage, feeling soil dampened by morning dew, when I was startled by a noise behind me. I jumped and turned. Harry stood on the path near the door to the kitchen, watching me. I blushed, aware I was still dressed in my nightclothes, and began to back away self-consciously.

"I'm sorry," he said, raising his hand in a conciliatory gesture. "I didn't mean to frighten you."

"I . . . I . . . ," I stuttered as my back pressed against the greenhouse wall, "I didn't hear you."

"My brother and I learned quite effectively how to move without making a sound when we were in hiding. I guess it's a hard habit to break." His voice reminded me of honey—smooth and sweet. A wry smile twisted his lips as he reached into his coat pocket. "Cigarette?" he offered, holding a pack out to me. I hesitated. For a brief moment I remembered the first cigarette I had ever tried with Gutcha in Tarnoviche, the labor camp near Tarnosky Gura. The memory was fleeting but left me feeling weak. I frowned at Harry and asked, "How did you get those?"

"I have my connections," he said casually.

"The black market?" I asked breathlessly. When he just shrugged, I asked, "Isn't that dangerous?"

Instead of answering, he took a tentative step toward me, pulling a cigarette from the pack and holding it out to me. I met him halfway along the path, taking the cigarette and putting it to my lips. He struck a match and held the flame to the end of the cigarette. I inhaled deeply, then blew a tendril of smoke into the space between us.

Harry laughed, raising an eyebrow. "Where did you learn to smoke?"

"Why?" I asked, looking into his blue eyes through the haze.

He shrugged again and said, "I didn't expect a girl like you to know how, is all."

"A girl like me?"

He considered me for a second and said, "Didn't you come from a rather observant home? I imagine you had a sheltered upbringing."

I frowned. "Who told you that?"

"My brother and I wanted to know more about you and Sam before agreeing to have you live with us."

I blinked and looked away, not sure how I felt about him prying into my past—a past that belonged to someone else, a past I wasn't sure I wanted to remember. "Then why did you offer me the cigarette?"

"Curiosity?" he answered, grinning, and I couldn't help but smile back.

We walked to the brick wall and sat beside each other, both of us silently dragging on our cigarettes. The slow inhalation and exhalation calmed my nerves, and despite Harry's proximity, I began to relax. He asked me again how I'd learned to smoke, and my thoughts returned to the boy my cousin and I had met. Though I could still picture his face, I had long since forgotten his name.

"It was in Tarnoviche," I said, remembering my brief time in the second camp I had been taken to after Klettendorf. When we had arrived, the camp was still being built, so we slept on straw in structures that were only half-erected. Exposure to the wind and bitter winter cold had made me long for the dirty bunks we'd had in Klettendorf. "There was little order in the camp, since it wasn't finished," I told Harry. "Men had to work laying bricks and hauling steel beams and pouring concrete to finish the barracks and buildings. It was so hard. But at night, we often met them outside before curfew. One of the prisoners had a pack of cigarettes. He taught us how."

The first time my lungs had filled with smoke, I had coughed violently. The man had showed us how to take the smoke into our mouths, gently inhale, hold the smoke in our lungs, and then exhale slowly. After a few attempts, I found I enjoyed the rhythmic, deliberate movement of breath, the controlled rise and fall of my chest, and the sight of smoke curling from my lips.

For some reason, I found it easy to share this memory with Harry. He watched me intently as I spoke. I glanced at him, captivated by the blue shade of his eyes. They were the color of the sky. His face was thin and angular with a high forehead and cheekbones. Everything about him was long and lean.

"What's troubling you?" he asked, and I realized I was staring at him too closely. I blushed. He chuckled. "Is there something you want to ask?"

"No," I said, shaking my head. "It's just—you're very blond."

Harry laughed again. "Blond hair and blue eyes," he nodded.

"I suppose I should thank those for keeping me alive. We were in hiding most of the war, surviving how we could. Looking Aryan helped."

"Who were you with?"

"My brothers. Pinky and Joseph. Were you with anyone?"

"My cousin Gutcha."

He took another long drag on the cigarette before crushing it against the stone wall. "Can I ask what happened to her?"

"She's still here in Reichenbach," I said, my chest growing tight. "She lived with me in the hotel."

He regarded me curiously. "Where is she now, then?"

I swallowed. "She's leaving. She's decided to go to Palestine."

I could tell in the silence that followed that Harry was watching me, but I couldn't lift my eyes to his. I watched an ant crawling along the wall, feeling the warmth of the sun on the crown of my head, missing Gutcha already.

Gutcha arrived on our doorstep a few days later holding a small valise and dressed in travel clothes. "I've come to say good-bye," she said when I opened the door. "We're leaving today."

"What?" I gasped, rushing forward to hug her close in disbelief. Sam stood behind me, and Harry and Pinky lingered just inside the foyer, watching silently. "You're leaving already?"

She nodded. "There's a whole group of us who are leaving together. They are very nice, Sarah. I like them. We plan to settle on a kibbutz in Palestine. It will be like working on the farms here."

Sam stepped closer and put a hand on my shoulder, but I didn't let go of my cousin. "How can I say good-bye?" I whispered, my voice trembling. I felt Gutcha's cheek wet against my own. We hugged in silence for the longest time, unable to let go. When we finally pulled apart, Gutcha turned and strode with purpose down the front walk, shoulders squared, only turning when she reached the gate that led out to the road. She raised her hand in a silent farewell. I did the same, trying to memorize every detail of her face, her expression. I continued to wave, standing on the front step, until she turned a bend in the road and I could no longer see her, long after Sam and Harry and Pinky had gone back inside.

I wondered if I would ever see my cousin again.

Forty-Two

Harry found me in the dark, quiet kitchen sometime in the early hours of morning. Sleep continued to elude me. I knew as I stood barefoot in the middle of my room that getting in bed would be a waste, that I would only lie awake thinking of Gutcha, all too aware of the emptiness that tugged at my heart, so I wandered into the kitchen like a sleepwalker.

"Sarah?" I heard Harry say from the doorway. I shifted slightly in my chair but didn't answer. I felt him move into the dark room. In the periphery of my vision, a spark ignited, and I blinked. He walked to the table with a lit candle and sat down across from me. For a few moments, we didn't speak. Then he leaned forward and said in a gentle voice, "You miss your cousin."

It was a statement, not a question, but still I nodded. "I don't think I would have survived without her," I murmured into the darkness.

"I know what it's like to lose everything too," Harry said. Something in his tone roused me from my stupor. I looked across the table at him. The shadows of the flame danced over his face and reflected in his large eyes. As he gazed back at me, I noticed for the first time a vulnerability that hadn't been there before.

"If I hadn't been with Pinky, I wouldn't have survived either," he said. "He saved my life in more ways than one."

"How?" I asked softly.

Harry stood up and walked to the shelves above the sink. When he came back to the table, he was holding a bottle filled with an amber liquid. He held it out to me and said, "Scotch. A gift left for us from our German friend." To my blank look, he explained, "I found it, along with a bottle of cognac, a '27 Merlot, and a decanter of fine port, in the German officer's library."

He held it out to me again. I could smell the rich aroma, but then I remembered the taste of the vodka and shook my head. Harry shrugged and took a drink directly from the bottle. Eyes closed, he sat back down. I noticed that his hand trembled slightly as he set the bottle on the table.

"You see, before the war, I was married. I had a wife."

I leaned back against my chair, staring at him. A wife, I thought. Like Michal, he'd had a wife. He'd been married. When he opened his eyes and fixed his gaze on me, I could see the pain there even in the darkness. "Harry," I started, "you don't have to—"

"Her name was Estella," Harry interrupted. "She was beautiful. Her hair was thick and dark, almost your color, Sarah. And her complexion was so fair, her skin so soft. I loved her dearly." He paused for a moment, his mouth open as though he was about to say more, but then he lifted the bottle to his lips and took another long drink. Wiping his mouth with the back of his hand, he said in a softer voice, "We had a son, the most beautiful boy in the world."

His voice trailed off, and finally his eyes dropped from mine. I swallowed as his words rang in my ears. Part of me longed to escape the kitchen, frightened by the feelings his words caused in me. I was all too aware of his hand resting close to mine on the table. But another part of me ached when I saw the emotion, raw and exposed, in his eyes. I wanted to take his sadness away. "I'm so sorry, Harry," I whispered, shaking my head.

"I haven't wanted to talk about this before, Sarah. But for some reason when I'm with you, I feel like I could tell you anything. I *want* to tell you."

My heartbeat quickened at these words. I felt another surge of emotion as I watched his eyes glaze with tears. He blinked several times and took a third swig from the bottle. The smell of alcohol was strong in the space between us. "My boy, my little Hirsch, had dark eyes just like his mother's. And he was so smart.

He was curious about everything. He used to crawl onto my lap and ask me how plants grew and why trees were so tall and why there were so many stars in the sky. He loved nature and animals. He said he wanted to be an explorer when he grew up and travel to other countries. He always carried a book of maps tucked under his arm."

"How old was he?" I asked hesitantly.

"Five," Harry said, glancing at me. "He was only five. Every evening when I came home from work, he met me at the door. But one night I came home to an empty house. When I called for them, there was no answer."

Harry stopped talking and closed his eyes. I thought perhaps that was all he was going to say, and I didn't want to pry. But then he ran his hand through his hair and continued with his eyes still closed. "I searched every room. I ran to my neighbors' homes, knocking on doors. No one answered. I saw Agna, the woman who lived across the street, look out from behind the curtain of her upstairs window. I'll never forget it, Sarah. She looked right at me, then quickly hid behind the curtain again, pulling it closed. Only Hermann, the old man who lived next door, opened the door for me."

"Did he know what had happened to them?" I asked breathlessly. I realized I was leaning forward, sitting on the edge of my seat.

"At first he said, 'I can't help you. You have to go. I don't want any trouble.' But I didn't move from his doorstep. 'Have you seen my wife and son?' I demanded.

"'They were taken away this morning,' he told me. His voice was flat. He showed no emotion. 'They were loaded into a truck and taken to the station. I'm sorry I can't tell you more.' And then he closed the door in my face. I remember growing cold, so cold, like my blood had turned to ice. I ran back to my house, to our room, to Hirsch's room, tearing through the bureaus and chests. I don't know what I was looking for, but I was frantic. That's when Pinky found me. 'They came for Rachel and the girls too,' Pinky said."

I must have gasped, because Harry finally opened his eyes and looked at me. "Yes," he said, "my brother was married as well, with two daughters. He grabbed my hand and pulled me from the house. 'We have to get out of here. They'll come for us next,' he said. And that's when we ran."

Harry stopped then, and the silence that settled over us was thick and oppressive. He still held the bottle of Scotch in one hand, absently swirling the contents so it coated the sides of the glass and glinted in the candlelight. In a voice that was almost a whisper, he said, "The Nazis came back that night to round up those they'd missed earlier in the day. If Pinky hadn't come for me, I would have been captured too."

"Where did you go?" I asked breathlessly.

"We hid in the woods. We had a few friends, associates who were willing to smuggle us food and pass along supplies and information. If we thought there was a chance we'd be captured, we ran."

I shook my head, amazed. I had so many questions for him, but the most pressing one made its way to my lips. "Did you ever find out what happened to your family?" I asked hesitantly, timidly, almost afraid to hear the answer.

Still swirling the Scotch in the bottle, he said, "After they rounded up all the Jews from Katowice, the city I'm from, they were forced onto train cars, shoved in, trampled, too many bodies crushed into too small a space. I was told my little boy suffocated." Harry's voice broke. "When Pinky and I were finally captured, our fate caught up to us. We were taken to Auschwitz. There, I saw an old neighbor who had been working at the camp where all the Jews from Katowice were deported. He saw Hirsch—my Hirsch—trampled on the floor of the boxcar, lying beside Estella."

My hands flew to my mouth as I gasped. Harry swallowed hard and lifted his head to the ceiling, blinking back tears. I didn't know what to say to comfort him, so I sat shaking my head in shocked silence.

"I try to think that was better than if he had survived. At least that way he died in his mother's arms."

As the candle between us sputtered and flared, our hands inched ever closer. When he finally reached across the table and took my hand in his, his fingers entwining around mine, I didn't pull away. I knew in that moment that I would never let him go.

Forty-Three

Villa in the foothills of the Owl Mountains,
Reichenbach, Germany, July 1945

I felt Sam slipping away. He disappeared all day, sometimes
not returning home until after dark. I continued to earn my
wages working on the local farm and pooled my money with
Sam's. When he was there, he talked of the day when we would
have enough to buy our own home. I didn't ask how he made
his money, and he didn't tell me. In Sam's absence, Harry and
I became closer. He often accompanied me into town when I
shopped for groceries or traded in the market. I fell into the
role of caretaker, cooking meals for the men, cleaning the large,
empty rooms, attending to the herb garden in back. I never felt
at ease in the richness of my surroundings. Harry sometimes sat
in the kitchen while I chopped vegetables or scrubbed the pots
or boiled water for soup. He shared with me bits and pieces of
his life before the war.

He had five brothers and three sisters. He spoke often of his
sister Rachel, his oldest sibling. "She had a brilliant mind and
was the one who ran the family business," he told me one time
in a wistful tone as I prepared a hearty stew for supper. "She was
known as the Feather Queen. Everyone respected her."

I grew quiet when I listened to him talk. He was an animated
storyteller, gesturing with his long fingers, his face expressive, so
that I hung on his every word, enthralled. His upbringing had
been very different from my own. His family had lived a secular

lifestyle in Katowice, a larger, more metropolitan city than Olkusz. His father had been an educated man, and the family had owned a business buying and selling goose down and furs. "Pinky and I plan to start up the business again," he told me one day as we walked past sun-dappled fields on the way to the marketplace in Reichenbach. "We still have associates and vendors in Katowice," he said.

"You want to return to Katowice?" I asked. I found it impossible to believe he'd want to return to the city where he had lost his wife and child. Yet he believed his siblings were still alive, and he was determined to find them. "Don't you want to go back to Olkusz? Don't you want to see if your family is there?" he asked me, and I grew quiet, pondering the question that continued to haunt me. Did I want to go back? What would I find if I did? Would the memories be too painful?

Pinky sometimes joined us in town. Like Harry, he had a jovial personality and a quick smile. One morning I led them into the booksellers where Erna now worked. I liked to browse among the racks or flip through the magazines, and sometimes Erna would slip one into my bag and wave me out the door before I could pay. When we entered the dusty little store, the bells above the door chimed, and Erna looked up from behind the counter. Pinky, who had been talking, stopped midsentence when he saw her, his round face growing red. To my amazement, when I introduced the brothers to Erna, Pinky couldn't take his eyes off her. They began to spend time together. She would come to our home in the evenings, and the four of us would sit around the table, smoking and drinking. I found them to be an odd couple—Erna was so tall and large with a face that could only be described as handsome and an overbearing presence, while Pinky was shorter and portly and had a sweeter, quieter nature. Despite their differences, it was easy to see their growing affection for one another.

When Harry and I were alone, I found out about his younger brother Joseph, who had been with him until the very end, when they were separated in Auschwitz. I found out about his older brother David, who had been married to a woman named Dora and had a son named Arthur. He told me about the family that had agreed to hide Arthur when David and Dora feared they would be taken away. He had a sister named Esther as well, and I soon told him about my sister, describing her beauty in great detail. He put a hand out and tucked a wisp of hair behind my ear as I spoke, and I froze, all too aware of the small distance that separated us. "I can't believe her beauty could rival yours," he whispered in a low voice, and I blushed furiously, turning away from him and hurrying down the path.

He left his first letter to me a few mornings later. He had slipped it underneath my door sometime during the night, so that when I woke, I noticed it lying conspicuously on the floor. I picked it up, turning it over to read:

> My dearest Sarah,
>   You are like a ray of light that has entered my life. I ran for the longest time, living moment to moment, afraid to stop because stopping meant remembering. I didn't think I'd ever feel happy again, but now, when I'm with you, I see a chance for a new future. Thank you for listening to me. Thank you for your kindness. Thank you for making me feel alive again. Remembering my past doesn't hurt as much as when I can share it with you. Your beauty is unmatched and your innocence is endearing.
>
> > Your constant admirer,
> > *H*

My heart raced as I leaned against the door, clutching the letter to my chest. When I closed my eyes, all I could picture were Harry's face and eyes, the fair, wispy hair that brushed his forehead and tips of his ears like soft feathers, his slender physique and elegant hands. I had felt a comfortable companionship and fondness for Michal, but this was something more, something overwhelming and almost scary. Harry left me breathless.

I kept the letters he wrote hidden underneath my mattress. I never spoke of them, never acknowledged them aloud, but I couldn't stop the heat that rose in my cheeks when he was near me. I felt his eyes watching me whenever we were in the same room. Sometimes I would catch a private smile or glance from him that turned my stomach not unpleasantly. Every morning a new letter would appear underneath my door. Each subsequent letter grew longer and more intimate. At night when I couldn't sleep, I sat by the window and read the letters, memorizing each word.

If Sam suspected, he never said a thing.

Harry was waiting for me one day as I left the farm. He sat on the fence that bordered the fields, smoking a cigarette and shading his eyes from the sun as he watched me walk up to meet him. He lifted his hand in a wave, and I smiled. As I approached, a mother passed on the road, holding two young boys by the hands. I stopped as I watched them, my throat suddenly constricting. "Sarah?" Harry called, jumping the fence and walking in my direction. "Are you all right?" I took a deep breath and squared my shoulders as he reached my side. "I'm fine," I said with a forced smile.

The woman had stopped a few yards away to bend down and wipe something from one of the boy's cheeks. His giggle floated in the air like effervescent bubbles. I felt suddenly weak. I tried to keep my eyes from staring at them, but I couldn't help but watch as the mother lifted the other boy and swung him around so he, too, laughed.

"Do you know them?" Harry asked softly as they continued down the road, away from us. For a moment, all I saw was the back of my mother's head, her round hips and the curve of her neck beneath her kerchief. I saw David's round cheeks and soft, pudgy hands and Majer's auburn curls radiant in the sunlight.

And suddenly I began to weep.

"What's the matter?" Harry asked, stepping in front of me and lifting my chin so I had to look up into his blue eyes.

"It's nothing," I said, blinking back the tears. "I just, just thought—"

"What?"

And I told him about my mother and father, finally allowing the memories to wash over me. I told him about the twins. "They were so young, Harry. I loved them like they were my own children. They withered before our eyes, and we couldn't do anything to stop it. They were cringing on the floor when I was taken away, holding on to each other as my mother screamed. I can't get the memory out of my head. Oh, God, I can't stop seeing it!" I sobbed. I thought enough time had passed that the memories wouldn't be raw, wouldn't hurt. But my heart still bled.

Harry drew me into his arms, and I leaned against him heavily. I didn't think to be embarrassed or uncomfortable. "They're gone, Harry," I whispered against his shoulder.

"You don't know that."

I nodded, swallowing, the taste of salt on my tongue as I wiped at my eyes. "I do. I do, Harry. There's no way they could have survived. My parents were so broken. They never recovered after Esther died. They just accepted everything that happened to us. I did too. I was weak. I let them take me away. I should have fought, like Sam."

"You were a child, Sarah," Harry said firmly, but I continued as though I hadn't heard him.

"And the twins were so fragile. They needed their mother. I was a poor substitute, I couldn't protect them. We saw the smoke from the camps with our own eyes, in the ghetto. I should have known. How could I have left them?"

"You couldn't have known."

"I won't see them again—"

Without a word, Harry lifted me in his arms and carried me back home. I continued to gasp, to fight the racking sobs that threatened to overwhelm me, but his smell and his touch were like a tonic to my senses. I buried my face against his shoulder, inhaling deeply, and slowly, I was able to breathe again.

Outside the front door, Harry set me on my feet and turned me toward him. "Sarah," he said, his voice gruff with emotion. I blinked up at him through my tears. "Sarah," he said again, "we've both lost so much. But when I'm with you, I'm happy. And I want to make you happy. Will you let me try?"

The breathless feeling returned, but this time it wasn't unpleasant. I nodded silently, caught in the intensity of his gaze. "I love you, Sarah," he whispered. He lowered his head and, still holding my eyes, touched his lips to mine.

I fell into him, surrendering to a feeling that eradicated all other thought. I felt his hands pull me closer so our bodies touched. My heartbeat quickened.

"Sarah!"

A loud voice jarred me back to myself, and I jumped, pulling away from Harry quickly. Turning to the front door, I saw Sam glaring at us both. "Sam!" I gasped as he grabbed my hand and pulled me inside, slamming the door in Harry's face. He dragged me through the hall to my room, where he shut and locked the door and turned to face me. His cheeks were red with rage.

"This is just like you, Sarah," he fumed, pacing the length of the room while my eyes followed him incredulously.

"What are you talking about?" I demanded.

"You've always been too eager for the attention of men," he spat. "Even when you were a child, you liked to flirt. It's not appropriate."

Heat rushed into my own cheeks. I stood rooted to the spot, trembling in anger and indignation. Sam's eyes were narrow slits, cutting at me viciously. For a moment, he looked like a stranger.

"You weren't raised like that, Sarah. Mama and Papa would be appalled."

My fists clenched at my sides. The memories of my parents were still so fresh in my mind that this idea was like throwing salt on an open wound.

"How can you say that?" I yelled. "I haven't done anything wrong! Harry's a good man, Sam. He loves me. He wants to take care of me. Helena found someone to love. Erna and Pinky are growing closer. I want to feel love too. I'm not a child anymore!"

Sam stopped pacing and stared at me. I took a step closer to him and said, "The life we had with Mama and Papa—that life is gone, Sam."

"It doesn't have to be," he said in a low voice.

"Yes, Sam," I said in a moment of defiance. "It does."

"He's so much older than you, Sarah," he said, his voice suddenly void of emotion. "He's more . . . *experienced* than you. I don't trust him."

"I do," I said simply.

He regarded me silently, and I was reminded of the night he'd called me a whore. An ugly, sick feeling rose in my throat. The look of suspicion and judgment in his eyes bore through me, and I was sure he knew. *He knew.*

"You are naive, then," he said, and he stormed from the room.

Forty-Four

Blechhammer, subcamp of Auschwitz,
Upper Silesia, February 1944

We sat at long tables, our fingers sore from the repetitive motion of building small gauges and compasses for German planes. I was lucky I had found a pair of worn gloves that warmed at least part of my hands. Most of the girls around me had to suffer the bitter winter draft in the small shed where we worked, fumbling with the minute parts as they shivered, their fingers purple from cold.

I had been in Blechhammer for almost six months. I had befriended three girls from Czechoslovakia: blonde-haired sisters Sophia and Risa and a beautiful girl named Lotte whose family had owned a jewelry store. She spoke often of how her mother's diamond necklace was torn from her throat by a female guard when they'd first arrived at the camp, and how her own ruby ring had been forced from her finger by other prisoners as they were sorted into lines. Lotte and her mother, Miriam, had managed to stay together. Miriam had to report to the kitchen when we were sent to build parts for the planes, and every evening when we returned to the barracks, Lotte cried with relief when she saw her. Miriam became a surrogate mother to us all, wrapping her arms around us at night and singing soft lullabies in Czech that made me long for home.

I felt the eyes of the *Oberfeldwebel* on us as we worked in silence. Lotte sat beside me, and I couldn't help but notice how she kept dropping small bolts and screws onto the floor. Her cheeks were chapped and red, and her hands were so unsteady she kept rubbing them together and clutching them to her chest.

"Here," I whispered, pulling off one of my gloves and handing it to her.

She took it gratefully, but immediately stiffened as the *Oberfeld-webel* walked behind us. Two male guards supervised us each day. We had nicknamed one of them the "Khazer," the Pig, because of the rolls of skin that strained his uniform and his snout-like nose. The other we nicknamed the "Fux," the Fox, because he was silent and sly and would lash out unexpectedly. Though the Pig was the larger of the two men, we feared the Fox the most.

"Keep working," I muttered under my breath as the Fox paced toward the other side of the room. Lotte nodded, but I heard her whisper, "Mama, help me. I don't feel so good."

My stomach clenched into a knot. So many were falling sick as the winter wore on. I wanted to reassure Lotte, to put my hands on hers and stop their trembling, but I continued to work methodically, concentrating on my own work, afraid to draw attention to myself.

At some point in the day, the Pig came to relieve the Fox of his duties. I felt my body relax slightly as the Fox spoke to the Pig in clipped words, then saluted and walked out the door. Out of the corner of my eye, I saw the Pig wipe his forehead, covered in perspiration despite the cold, and take off his hat as he settled into a chair in the corner. I glanced at Lotte to silently assure her the rest of the day would be easier, but her face had turned a sickly gray.

"Are you all right?" I whispered.

She shook her head but couldn't speak. Then she fell off her stool and crumpled to the floor.

I instantly knelt beside her, trying to gather her in my arms. "Lotte!" I cried. "Lotte, wake up!" Her eyes were closed and her skin felt clammy. I realized too late that the room had fallen silent. I glanced up and saw the girls at the table staring down at us. I swallowed as the Pig stood up and walked to my side, frowning as he grimaced down at us.

"What happened here?" he asked.

"I, I'm sorry, Herr Oberfeldwebel," I stammered as sweat broke out on my own forehead. "She fainted."

I waited for the blow that would surely come, but the Pig considered us for a moment before smiling. It was a small, thin smile, but not unfriendly. He shook his head and said in a sympathetic tone, "They work you girls too hard, and in such conditions. Help her to the infirmary, then report back to me." He held out a hand, and I hesitated, unsure whether to take it. I was still waiting for him to beat us or, worse yet, shoot us. But he nodded encouragingly and helped me to my feet. Lotte blinked as I dragged her up, her eyes glazed. "Mama?" she whispered, her stale breath against my cheek.

"Let's go, Lotte," I whispered back, my heart racing.

Out in the cold yard, I trudged through the mud, half-carrying Lotte against my side. "Can you walk?" I asked, shivering as my feet sank in filth. The sky overhead was a cold steel gray, threatening more snow. Clouds of black rose from smokestacks in the distance. Lotte's head rolled back, and her feet dragged in the dirty slush. I felt my back bend beneath her weight, and it was a miracle I made it to the infirmary without both of us falling into the muck. The tired-looking prisoners who worked in the infirmary took her from me.

"What will happen to her?" I asked, glancing around at the patients lying on the cots. A smell of urine and feces permeated the air. A thin layer of ice spread over the cement floor, and sheets of plastic flapped against the open windows, offering little protection from the cold. The only light in the room came from a few spare bulbs that hung from the ceiling on frayed cords.

"We'll find her a bed," one of the prisoners who worked in the infirmary said. "The camp doctor will see her."

"Can I go with her?" I asked uncertainly.

"You don't want to be here," another prisoner said. "Everyone dies here."

I balked and took a step backward. The prisoner turned from me and began to walk away. "Wait!" I cried, taking off my other glove and handing it to him. "Take this to her. Tell her that her mother will be here shortly."

I ran back into the yard, breathing heavily, my lungs constricting from the cold. The sun was setting low in the gray sky, and the wind howled like a mad animal, blowing dead branches and dried leaves across the camp yard. I entered the work shed just as the siren announced the end of the workday. I moved to my empty stool to clean my workspace, careful to avoid the Pig's eyes. But he noticed me and stood, stretching and rubbing his gloved hands together, walking to my side as the other girls lined up by the door.

"Your friend," he said. "How is she?"

I shrugged as I gathered the small arrows for the compasses into a leather pouch, worried because I hadn't met the day's quota. The Pig made a small tsking sound with his tongue. I felt his eyes on me, but I couldn't bring myself to look at him. I heard him sigh as he turned and dismissed the girls waiting by the door. I quickly turned to leave as well, but he put out a hand and said, "Wait just a moment."

My stomach dropped. I don't know how I managed to remain standing. Fear held me in a vise-like grip. I was sure I was about to be punished. I closed my eyes, waiting as I held my breath. But once we were alone, he turned back to me and said, "You're shaking."

I swallowed and said, "It's very cold."

He took a step toward me and bent so I was forced to look him in the eye. His cheeks were puffy, his bulbous nose red. "You're scared," he said in a matter-of-fact tone. "Don't be scared. I mean you no harm."

I blinked, unsure what to do or say. He smiled again and said, "It is wrong, how they treat you girls. I have a daughter too, you know? About your age. I can't imagine her living in conditions such as these."

I remained silent, waiting. He pulled at the bottom of his uniform jacket to straighten it over the bulge of his stomach. I saw how the buttons strained against his bulk. He regarded me for another moment and said, "If my daughter were here, I'd want someone to take care of her. Perhaps, I can take care of you?"

I didn't know what he meant. He moved toward the door, then glanced over his shoulder at me. "Please," he said softly, "follow me."

Every instinct told me to run, but I knew better than to disobey. I followed him across the yard. Night had fallen so completely that the spotlights from the high watchtowers swept over the grounds, illuminating the exhausted prisoners who trudged back to their barracks. The Pig was headed toward the cluster of buildings that housed the SS offices. As he climbed the stairs, I hesitated. I had never been in these buildings. The Pig turned when he reached the top of the steps and smiled. "Come," he said, and I silently followed.

Once inside, I felt immediate relief from the cold. A long hallway stretched down the main part of the building with doors opening on either side. Small lamps were lit along the walls, creating circles of light on the tiled floor. I followed the Pig to one of the doors, the sharp staccato of his footsteps echoing in the passage. He opened it and stepped aside, ushering me in.

His office was basic but clean and neatly appointed with a desk, bookshelf, rug, two armchairs, and, most importantly, a fireplace. I sighed, eyeing the flames hungrily. He smiled gently and said, "Your clothes are so thin, you must be frozen. Go warm yourself by the fire."

This time I didn't hesitate. I moved to the hearth and put my hands toward the flames, feeling the heat from the fire work its way up my arms to warm the rest of my body. I sighed contentedly. The Pig was standing behind me, but I almost forgot his presence as my body began to relax. I jumped when I heard a scraping sound and saw that he had moved a chair closer to the fireplace. "Have a seat," he said, gesturing to the chair. I wanted to say thank you, but my mouth was dry and my heart was fluttering nervously. Instead I nodded and sat gingerly on the edge of the chair, my whole body leaning toward the fire. Just then, my stomach growled loudly.

"You are hungry," he said, moving to his desk and reaching for a glass bowl that held chocolates wrapped in gold foil. I began to salivate, imagining the taste of the chocolate on my tongue. He smiled knowingly. "Please, take as many as you like," he said, offering me the bowl. I reached out and hungrily grabbed one, closing my eyes in delight as I bit into the chocolate and a burst of cream filled my mouth. The taste was so foreign and unexpectedly sweet that I couldn't help but shove the entire chocolate into my mouth, impulsively grabbing more from the bowl in my lap.

"You are a very pretty girl," the Pig said, leaning against his desk and watching as I greedily licked chocolate from my fingertips. "What is your name?"

"Sarah," I said softly, lowering my hand to my lap.

"A lovely name," he mused. "Sarah, I usually take my tea at this time of night. It's a tradition I picked up from my travels to London in my youth." He pressed an intercom on his desk, and a tinny voice said, "Yes, Herr Köhler?"

"Bring me my tray," he replied, then dragged the other chair across the floor to face mine and sat down. A moment later, the door opened, and a young SS officer who appeared no older than me came in carrying a domed tray. He started walking toward the center of the room but stopped when he saw me. The Pig snapped his fingers, and the young man stood taller, marched to the desk beside us, and placed the tray on its surface. "Heil Hitler," he saluted with his hand in the air. The Pig dismissed the boy with a small wave. I saw the young officer glance at me with a confused look as he stepped into the hall and closed the door behind him.

I kept my head low, my eyes on my lap, as the Pig lifted the sterling silver tray cover. He leaned down and inhaled deeply. "Ahhh," he breathed, "nothing better than a cup of tea on a cold day." He began to pour a steaming liquid from a teapot into a delicate cup. To my surprise, he walked around his desk and handed it to me. Again, I wasn't sure whether to take it.

"Go on," he urged. "Drink up."

Gingerly, I reached out and took the cup into my hands. The steam warmed my face. I noticed the Pig arranging small biscuits and sliced fruit onto a plate, slathering thick butter onto the biscuits and pouring cream onto the fruit. Fresh fruit! My stomach clenched at the sight. The Pig handed me the plate with a gentle, almost loving smile. "Please take this," he said in a soft voice. "I hate to see someone as young as you suffering so much." I couldn't believe my eyes as I stared at the food before me.

The Pig walked to the fireplace, silently considering the flames with his back to me as I bit eagerly into one of the biscuits. "I'd like to help you," the Pig said in a low, soft voice, his gaze still trained on the fire. "I know you are hungry and frightened. While you starve, we have so much. It's not right. I could give you some food to take back with you to your barracks. I'm sure the other girls, like your friend earlier, would benefit from something more than the rations they give you each day, no?"

I couldn't believe what he was saying. He turned from the fireplace and walked toward me, his footsteps muffled by the thick carpet. "If you come visit me every evening, I'll make sure you are accompanied safely back to your barracks. You don't need to starve."

He was standing right behind me. Before I could move, his hands closed on my shoulders, gently rubbing them. I froze. His hands inched down my arms. I felt his stale breath on my neck. He was breathing rapidly. I couldn't move. I felt his palms move up to my breasts, cupping them, massaging them. I tasted bile in the back of my throat. But I didn't stop him. I thought of Sophia and Risa, Lotte and Miriam. I thought of what he was offering. And I closed my eyes.

Forty-Five

Villa in the foothills of the Owl Mountains,
Reichenbach, Germany, July 1945

I woke in a cold, trembling sweat. I could still feel the Pig's
hands on my body, feel his weight pressing me to the floor as he
lay on top of me. I ran from the room, barely making it to the
bathroom, where I was sick, clinging weakly to the toilet. When
I was finished, I lay shivering on the cold tile floor. That's where
Harry found me.

"What happened, Sarah?" he asked, rushing to kneel at my side
and putting his hand on my clammy forehead. "Are you sick?"

I shook my head. "I'm fine," I whispered. My throat was raw.
He took my elbow and helped me to stand, leading me to the
kitchen and pushing me gently into a chair. He fetched a warm
blanket, which he threw over my shoulders, then handed me a
glass of water. As I sipped gingerly, he knelt in front of me again,
trying to meet my eyes. "Is it Sam?" he asked gently. "Did he
upset you earlier?"

Again I shook my head. Harry reached for my hand, but I
flinched and drew away. I felt dirty. I hated the way he regarded
me with concern. I felt undeserving of his kindness. My whole
body was filled with shame. Sam's words from earlier that evening
still echoed in my ears. *You liked to flirt. You've always been too
eager for the attention of men.* And then I remembered the angry
look on his face as he'd said, "You were acting like a common
whore." I thought again of the Pig, and tremors overtook me.

"Please, tell me what's wrong," Harry begged.

"I, I can't," I said, afraid of how Harry would look at me if he knew. And I suspected Sam knew already. I recalled his eyes, watching me when I was with Michal, with Harry, accusing me as if I'd spoken my secrets aloud.

What had I done?

"Should I get Sam?" Harry asked.

"No!" I cried.

Harry nodded and reached again for my hands. "Sarah," Harry said gently, "whatever it is, you can tell me."

I wanted so much to confess, to rid myself of my guilt and humiliation. But if I told Harry, I would risk losing him. He would never look at me the same way again. When I remained silent, he moved closer and whispered, "If you won't speak, then I will. I have something I've been meaning to ask you."

"Please don't," I said, knowing already what he wanted to ask. I knew now I could never be the wife he wanted. I was unclean. I wasn't as innocent as he thought. How could I ever replace his first wife?

Before he could say another word, I told him everything. The words came out in a rush before I could stop myself. I told him about the afternoons I spent in the Pig's office, silently enduring his touch. I told him how I tried to block out the Pig's whispered words of kindness and affection as he moved on top of me, thinking only of the food he gave me when it was over. I needed to get the words out, to purge my body of them.

"Just forget about me, Harry," I said, afraid to look him in the eyes, afraid to see the disappointment and disgust I knew must be there. "I don't deserve your love."

I buried my face in my hands. Harry was so still; all I heard were the crickets chirping outside the kitchen window. I wanted to drown in self-pity, imagining him standing up and turning his back on me, walking out of the room and out of my life. But then he reached out and pulled my hands from my face. He cupped my chin. He leaned in and whispered, "Be my wife, Sarah. I will take care of you. You don't need to feel ashamed."

I fell into the safe cocoon of his arms, stunned by his unwavering acceptance. "Do you mean it?" I whispered incredulously, feeling his chest rise and fall against my cheek, breathing in the scent of him. His lips touched the top of my head.

"We all did what we had to do. I have my own secrets, Sarah. I love you. Nothing will change that."

I looked up at him, hoping, finally, to put my past behind me. He wiped the tears tenderly from my cheeks. When his lips met mine, I believed for the first time it was possible.

I told Sam the next day.

I paced the front path, waiting for him to come home, twisting my hands nervously. Harry had asked if I wanted him to be there, but I told him no.

"Are you sure?" he'd asked, holding me close.

"Yes," I'd said. "This is something I need to do myself." After a moment, I'd whispered, "What if he doesn't approve?"

"You don't need your brother's approval."

"But he's the only connection I have left to my family. How can I leave him?"

"He'll never see you as anything but a child," Harry said. "You are not a child anymore."

When the sun was low in the evening sky, I finally saw Sam walking toward home, his shadow stretching on the path before him, the limp he sometimes endured from his broken leg noticeable. I felt a lump rise in my throat. Despite what Harry had said, I knew I needed Sam's blessing.

Sam walked slowly, his head down, lost in thought. He only looked up when he was a few feet away and paused when he saw me, his brow furrowing. When he was at my side, our eyes met for a time in uncomfortable silence. Finally, Sam said, "Sarah, I'm sorry for yesterday. I shouldn't have spoken like that."

"It's all right," I said.

"No, it's not."

I searched Sam's eyes, wondering how to make things right

between us. I considered telling Sam what I had told Harry the night before, but I didn't want to see the rage and disappointment in his eyes. I didn't know how to make him understand what I had done. I just wanted his love and approval. I wanted him to look at me like he had when we were children.

"Sam," I said softly, "Harry asked me to marry him."

His body stiffened and he looked away into the distance, over my shoulder. "What did you tell him?"

"I said yes," I whispered.

Sam swallowed and bit his lip, still avoiding my eyes. "You've only known each other a short time, Sarah," he warned.

"But I love him, Sam."

At last, Sam looked back at me. "How do you know what love is?"

I thought about Harry, feeling a wonderful combination of anticipation, longing, and contentment. I shook my head. "I don't know, Sam. I just know that when I'm with him, I'm happy. I feel safe. When we're not together, time drags. I can't stop thinking about him. And I don't ever want to be too far away from him." I snapped my mouth closed, embarrassed that I had confessed these feelings to my brother.

As the sun set behind Sam's back, throwing his face into shadow, I witnessed a war of emotions take hold of my brother. His hands twisted and his mouth contorted into a scowl. He breathed heavily, shaking his head, murmuring under his breath. Finally, he sighed. "If you're going to marry, Sarah, then I am too."

I gaped at him, shocked. "What?" I asked, dumbfounded. "Who?"

"Her name is Sophie," Sam said, watching my face carefully. "We met in town. We've been seeing each other for a little while."

"Why didn't you tell me?" I asked.

"I don't know," he said, running his hand through his hair. "I've been wanting to ask her to marry me, but I was afraid of upsetting you."

"Upsetting me?"

"With Helena married, and Gutcha gone, how could I do that

to you? Sometimes, I don't know what's right and what's wrong anymore. But all I've ever wanted to do is protect you, Sarah."

"I know, Sam," I said, gripping his hands in mine. "I'm happy for you. Truly happy. This is what Mama and Papa would want for both of us, don't you think?"

He put his hand on my cheek, and for the first time I saw something soften behind his eyes. And I knew I had his blessing.

Forty-Six

Reichenbach, Germany, August 1945

Harry and I were married on August 17, 1945. I wore a dress made of soft lace, and Helena gave me the ruffled veil she'd worn at her own wedding. As she stood behind me and placed it on my head, I remembered as though from another lifetime her lifting her mother's veil from a box in our kitchen, the veil she was going to wear when she married Jacob. "You look beautiful, Sarah," she said as she spread the material around my shoulders. I reached up and squeezed her hand. "Thank you, Helena," I whispered. I missed Gutcha, but I was grateful that Helena and her new husband had decided to settle in Reichenbach.

Harry's borrowed suit was too large for his slender frame, but to me he was the most handsome man I had ever seen. We stood under the homemade *chupa,* surrounded by Sam and his new fiancée, Sophie, her sister Ruth, Pinky and Erna, and Helena and her husband, Wolf. Rubin and a large number of his Russian comrades were present as well. He beamed like a proud matchmaker, telling anyone who would listen that he was the reason we had met.

As was tradition, I circled Harry seven times, and after we both drank from the *kiddush* cup, Harry stomped on the glass to a chorus of "*mazel tov!*" Unlike the weddings I had attended in my youth, where the bride and groom didn't touch until their wedding night, Harry took me in his arms in front of everyone and kissed me full on the lips. I melted into him, losing myself in his embrace. When we pulled apart, my eyes locked on his, blue and deep, and my pulse raced.

We had a celebratory dinner in the courtyard of a tavern in town. The air was humid and clung to us like an outer garment, but we didn't care. A small klezmer band played while we danced on the cobblestones. Fireflies lit the branches of the trees like strung lights. I became drunk on wine and the obligatory vodka the Russians provided. Around midnight, a summer rain shower fell on us as we danced so that our hair and clothes were plastered to our bodies. Before parting, the Russian soldiers lifted their rifles in the air and fired in unison. The sound reverberated in the small courtyard, and I jumped with a squeal. Harry caught me round the waist and spun me in a circle.

I had never been happier.

Harry took my hand and led me to the bed. I regarded it with a mixture of excitement and trepidation. Before the war, I wouldn't have known what was expected of a woman on her wedding night, but now I knew. Memories surfaced of the Pig's office, and I fought to push them away. I didn't want to desecrate the evening with such ugliness.

Harry gently sat, and I sat beside him. Raindrops still clung to my hair and dripped down my face. I clutched my hands tightly in my lap, my knuckles white. Harry lifted my hands to his mouth, kissing my fingers softly with his lips. "Sarah," he breathed in a husky voice.

Without looking at him, I said, "I'm scared."

He turned my face to his so he could gaze at me with his blue eyes. "There's nothing to be scared of, Sarah," he said. "I would never do anything to hurt you."

I nodded. With gentleness and care, he bent his head to mine, and our lips touched. His breath tasted of vodka. My pulse quickened as his fingers entangled themselves in my hair. His body was strong and solid against mine. He tenderly pressed me to the bed, his mouth moving to my neck, his tongue moving in circles against my collarbone. I sighed at the sensation, and I could tell he knew what he was doing. His hands moved down my arms to my stomach, then lower, and I suddenly grew tense as more uninvited thoughts rushed into my mind. I was at war with myself.

"Harry," I gasped. "Harry . . . stop."

He lifted up on an elbow, staring down at me. I blinked, trying to relax, but every fiber of my body was taut with anxiety. "I'm sorry," I whispered, turning my face away. He rolled off me, gathering me in his arms so that my back was pressed to his chest. "It's all right, Sarah," he said softly in my ear. "We'll just lie here for a bit."

I drifted in and out of sleep, feeling the warmth of Harry's body against mine, feeling his heart beating steadily against my back. The clock on the mantel chimed the hour of one o'clock, and I heard Harry's low snoring. I turned to face him, drinking in his countenance in sleep. His soft, pale skin glowed in the moonlight from the window. His long blond lashes touched his cheeks, and the damp hair plastered to his forehead smelled of summer rain. I reached up and placed my palm on his warm face, my thumb tracing small circles over his cheekbones. All thought left me, except for a sudden longing, a tightening in the pit of my stomach. I leaned forward and pressed my lips to his. His eyes fluttered open, and he gazed at me in silence in the moonlight. I moved closer to him, opening my legs to him. And when we came together slowly, gently, I knew what it meant to feel true desire.

I was eager to leave the large home that had once belonged to a Nazi general, so we rented a small apartment in Reichenbach over a tailor's shop. Sam and Sophie moved above the general store next door. Sophie had worked in her parents' own store before the war, so she and Sam took over the small shop and reopened its doors to the public. I went over daily to help her stock the shelves, clean the counters, sweep the floor, and check the inventory in the storeroom. I had brief memories of my father's bakery and remembered how often I had begged to help out there, just like my brothers. I would stop occasionally and glance at the counter and thought I saw the ghost of my father, talking to a customer or kneading dough or folding pastry, his head bent over his work. When I blinked, he was gone.

Sophie's sister Ruth worked as a secretary at the local police station. She would come to the store after her shift, and together, Ruth, Sophie, and I would lean against the counter and gossip about the latest activity in town or flip through fashion magazines, studying the current hair and clothing trends. Sophie always gave me bags of goods or food in exchange for my help.

One day Helena ran into the store waving a letter in her hands. "Sarah," she exclaimed. "Sarah, look! Wolf just gave this to me! It's from Gutcha."

"Gutcha?" I asked, hurrying to her side and taking the letter in my hands. I saw my name written across the envelope in my cousin's handwriting. Eagerly, I tore it open and read:

> My dearest Sarah,
>
> I hope this finds you well. I have settled on a kibbutz near the city of Netanya. Cousin, I have never been anywhere so beautiful. The sea is the deepest shade of blue with beaches that stretch for miles. There is so much green as well, in the trees, in the gardens. We work hard, but we also find time for leisure activities. There is music and laughter and singing every day. The people are all very nice, and we work together as one community. I can't explain the feeling of kinship that exists here. I met a man named Boris. He is a good man, Sarah. He was born here and he takes me on trips to Jerusalem and Tel Aviv, sharing the history he grew up with. I hope you are happy. I hope you have found peace. I will see you again soon, my dearest Sarah.
>
> Love,
> *Gutcha*

I cried, hugging the letter to my chest. Helena looked at me with a concerned expression, but I handed her the letter so she could read it for herself. "She's happy, Helena," I said over my tears. "My cousin is happy."

Harry and Pinky began building their own feather and down business. They left each morning to meet with local farmers to examine their ducks and geese and establish working relationships. More Poles moved into the area, and I overheard Sam mention that the city was now being called by the Polish name Rychbach. Some evenings, Harry, Pinky, and Sam attended meetings led by the Rychbach Jewish committee to discuss the future of Jews in Europe. They came home and sat around the table, drinking and smoking and deliberating the growing conflict between the local Zionist movement, which argued for a Jewish future in Palestine, and the Communist and Bund parties.

I sometimes listened in on the conversations, but I was more comfortable with domestic life, turning our small apartment into a home. I was more at ease in the small, simple rooms of our apartment than I had ever been in the large villa. I sewed curtains for the windows and arranged fresh-cut flowers from the small garden outside in vases and mason jars. I tacked clippings from magazines onto the walls of all the new appliances and art and furniture and jewelry I hoped one day to own.

I waited impatiently for the moment each evening when Harry would come home and take me into his arms. We spent many nights lost in each other, not sleeping, coming together with a sense of abandon.

When we weren't exploring each other's bodies, we lay naked beside each other on the mattress, sharing stories of our time in the camps. I told him about Otto. I told him about the female guard who would pick a random number and have us count off by that number at roll call, sending those who landed on that number to Auschwitz. Harry told me about how he and Pinky had stolen a loaf of bread to save their brother Joseph when he fell ill. He told me about the job he was assigned throwing the dead bodies of young girls who died from typhus into pits and setting fire to their emaciated corpses. As we shared each horrid detail, we felt lighter, as though the memories were forever being expelled from our souls. The curve of his arm around me became so familiar that I felt I was always meant to lie against him, my hand resting on his bare chest and touching the fine hair that grew there. I began to see a life, a real life, with Harry.

Forty-Seven

Reichenbach, Germany/Rychbach, Poland,
late November 1945

As fall turned to winter, I began to suspect there was something
wrong with me. One afternoon when I was stocking the shelves
in the general store, the room began to spin, and I closed my eyes,
leaning heavily against the counter. Sophie came into the room
and saw me swaying on my feet.

"Sarah, what's the matter?" she asked, leading me to a chair
in the back room.

"It's nothing," I said. "Just a moment of dizziness. I think I
might be coming down with something."

"You look very pale. Why don't you rest for a few minutes?"

I nodded, accepting the glass of water she handed to me. Before
I knew it, my eyes were closing, and I fell asleep in my chair. The
ringing of the bell above the door in the shop woke me some
time later. As I carefully stood up, I recognized Harry's and Sam's
voices. I pushed through the swinging doors that separated the
back room from the main shop and saw them deep in conversation with Sophie.

"What's wrong?" Harry asked, immediately turning to me with
a look of concern. "Sophie said you're not feeling well."

"I'm fine, Harry," I reassured him. "I'm just very tired."

"Let's get you to bed, then," he said, walking to my side and
taking my hand. I nodded good-bye to Sam and Sophie as Harry
led me to our apartment next door. Once inside, I dropped onto

the feather mattress and again felt my eyes closing. "Let me rest just a short while more and then I'll start supper," I said in a groggy voice. Harry sat beside me, stroking my hair to fall behind my ears. "Don't worry about supper," he said. "Just sleep."

I nodded, already surrendering to exhaustion.

The following morning, I awoke sick to my stomach. I felt weak but not unwell afterward, and walked into the kitchen to find it empty. Harry had already left for the day. I washed and dressed, and by the time I entered the store, my energy had returned.

"You look better," Sophie said, glancing up as I came around the counter and tied an apron around my waist. I noticed that it felt slightly more snug than usual, but I dismissed the thought as I said, "I feel much better." I was grateful that whatever virus I had contracted was short-lived. The next morning, however, the same sudden wave of nausea turned my stomach so that I ran to the sink. I wiped my mouth afterward, frowning, trying to remember if I had eaten anything that might have spoiled. By the end of the week, as the symptoms persisted, I'd become truly concerned.

I stood in front of the mirror, my brown eyes wide with worry, even with panic. What if something was really wrong? What if this was more than just a virus? Should I tell Harry? Should I see a doctor? But then, suddenly, my breath quickened as a new thought replaced the others. I stared at my reflection, my hands folding over my stomach. It had been at least a month, I realized, since I'd had my monthly bleeding. Maybe more. I had received enough of an education in the camps to know what pregnancy looked like, and a feeling of pure joy burst in my chest, eradicating all concern. Could I be pregnant? Could this be morning sickness? Could a new life be growing in me?

I walked into the kitchen in a daze, my hands caressing my stomach. I remembered my own mother, who had been bedridden when she was pregnant with the twins. I remembered her growing belly and the way she looked uncomfortable and pale but so very happy. I remembered holding the twins after they were born, their little fists latching onto my fingers, their faces red as they wailed. I remembered the feeling of delight as I rocked them, overwhelmed by an immediate, unconditional love. Now perhaps I would have my own child to love. *Harry's* child. I realized with a start that I wanted nothing more in the world than for that to be true.

For the rest of the day I wandered the apartment aimlessly, elated, unable to keep from smiling at the idea. I was eager to share the news with Harry, but I wanted to be sure first. A small, nagging part of me also worried about how he would react. He'd had a son. Would he want to be a father again? Would he be happy? I decided to wait a little longer before telling him.

During the month that followed, I woke up with no appetite and on the verge of being sick. Some mornings were better than others. Harry looked at me once across the kitchen table and noticed me picking at my food. "You're not eating, Sarah. Is anything the matter?" I smiled and set my fork down, reaching across the table to squeeze his hand. "I'm just not hungry, that's all. Nothing to worry about."

My suspicions were confirmed as the morning sickness began to ebb and I still hadn't bled. My clothes began to grow tighter around my waist, so I had to let them out. I began to have strange cravings for foods I normally disliked. Each new sign was like an unexpected gift, but I still hadn't told Harry. I lay awake, planning the perfect way to share the news. One day, as I was preparing breakfast, I knew I couldn't keep it from him any longer. I could see in my own reflection that my body was changing. Surely he would soon notice as well.

I set the table, putting a cluster of dried baby's breath on his plate, finding the name of the flower poetic. But before he could join me, there was a knock on our door. I wiped my hands on my apron and opened it to see Rubin and a few of his soldier friends standing on the threshold, grinning at me.

"Sarah!" Rubin exclaimed, pulling me into a hug. "Just who I was looking for!"

"Rubin," I laughed, pushing him away. "What are you doing here so early?"

"We have something for you!" Rubin said, and I could smell alcohol on his breath.

"For me?" I asked, confused, as Harry came out of the bedroom, buttoning his shirt. Rubin waved him over and threw an arm around Harry's shoulder.

"What's all this about?" Harry asked. Rubin passed him a flask, and Harry paused for a moment before taking a long swig.

"Come with us!" Rubin beamed. "We have something to show you!"

Together, we descended the steps to the small garden that grew along the back of the building. In winter, the small patch of land was brown, the trees barren. At the bottom of the steps, I froze. A small calf the color of rich coffee was tied to the fence. She regarded us with large brown eyes, then bent her head to chew at the dead grass growing in tufts around a fence post.

Harry turned to Rubin with a confused expression.

"It's for Sarah!" Rubin exclaimed proudly. When Harry continued to stare at him, Rubin laughed and said, "We never got you a wedding present, you see?"

"So you got us a cow?" Harry asked in disbelief.

"Yes!" Rubin said. "A cow! For Sarah!"

I laughed at Rubin and walked to the calf, putting a hand on her soft, leathery hide. Her ear twitched, and when she looked up at me with her milky brown eyes, I smiled.

"You're drunk, Rubin," Harry said.

"But of course I am."

"What are we going to do with a cow?" I asked. She stretched her nose forward to nuzzle my palm, her tail swishing lazily. She had a white crescent around her left eye, reminding me of the moon.

"You can find a stable for her, and have all the milk you desire," Rubin said. "Or, if you'd like, you can sell her. She'll bring you a healthy sum."

"No," I shook my head. "I want to keep her."

Rubin slapped Harry on the back. "There. You see? She wants to keep her."

Bemused, Harry shook his head and, grabbing the flask from Rubin's grip, took another long drink.

"You must give her a name, then," Rubin said, turning to me. "Then she is truly yours."

I considered the cow for a moment. "How do you say 'moon' in Russian?" I asked.

"Луна," Rubin said.

"Luna," I repeated, nodding. "That's a perfect name for her."

I never had a chance to tell Harry about the baby before he left for work. We invited Rubin upstairs for breakfast, and when we'd finished, he and Harry left the apartment together. I suspected both were drunk as they descended the steps, arms around each other's shoulders. I decided to tell Harry when he came home. I would have supper laid out and candles lit. I would put his hand on my stomach and tell him, "I have a secret to share." He would take me in his arms and kiss me and whisper, "Thank you, Sarah, for making me so happy!" I moved about the apartment like a sleepwalker, happily anticipating the moment he would walk through the door. So when there was a loud knock, I opened the door without thinking, hoping to throw myself into Harry's arms. Instead, two strange men dressed in unfamiliar uniforms stood on the other side, their expressions cold. I immediately took a step back.

A feeling of apprehension settled over me. "Yes?" I whispered cautiously, holding the knob of the door tightly in my fist.

"Are you Sarah Werthaiser?" one of the men asked in a brisk voice.

"Yes," I said softly, my eyes moving between him and his partner.

"You must come with us," he said, stepping forward.

"What?" I gasped, instinctively attempting to close the door in his face. To my horror, he pushed the door open so that I was thrown backward, tumbling against the table. Both men walked into the apartment uninvited. I backed away, my heart racing. I noticed the guns holstered at their waists and a memory returned of another time, long ago, when men with guns forced their way into my home. "My husband will be home shortly," I said in as brave a voice as I could muster, my arms out, hoping to stop them. I glanced behind them, frantically trying to calculate if I could run past them and out the door, but cold fear rose through me like icy tendrils, and my feet were frozen in place. The man who had yet to speak walked behind me, and before I could turn, he yanked my arms back. I felt pain in my shoulders. I felt something cold circle my wrists, and I struggled when I realized I couldn't move them forward. Panic shot through me like an electric shock.

"*What's happening?*" I cried as the man behind me pushed me toward the door.

"You are under arrest for stealing," the first man said.

"Stealing?" I breathed. "I don't know what you're talking about!"

"We received a call that a cow has been stolen from a local dairy. They gave us your name."

"But I didn't steal her!" I cried. "She was a gift!"

The men didn't answer as they forced me out the door and down the stairs. My feet fumbled beneath me, and I worried I would fall on the slippery steps. My thoughts instantly turned to the baby in my belly, and I tried desperately to keep my footing, leaning away from the men, supporting myself against the railing, terrified of hurting my unborn child. When we reached the bottom of the staircase, I craned my neck to see Luna, hoping to explain the situation. "She's there," I said, trying to nod in the direction of the garden. "If there's been some mistake, please take her. I didn't steal her!"

They ignored me, thrusting me to the front of the building where a car waited, its engine running. My knees went weak. If I got in the car, where would they take me? And would I ever return? Would I ever see Harry again? I heard screams in my ears. *Don't take my daughter!* I started to cry. *Mama! Mama! Mama!* With a burst of adrenaline, I struggled, kicking and screaming, dragging my feet across the sidewalk, trying everything in my power to get away from my captors. But they were too strong.

"Please," I whimpered as they ruthlessly shoved me into the back seat, my wrists still handcuffed behind my back. "Harry!" I cried in vain as they slammed the door shut. Condensation ran down the glass of the foggy window like tears. The two men climbed into the front seat and drove away from my apartment, from my garden with Luna still tied to the fence post, with me trapped in back.

Forty-Eight

The doors of the prison cell closed behind me with finality. I barely stood on trembling legs, peering around the dirty cell through watery eyes. A single cot sat in the corner, along with a thin blanket and dirty, flat pillow. A bowl and bedpan sat on the floor, and near the ceiling was a long, thin, barred window.

"Why are you doing this?" I gasped, turning and gripping the cell bars until my knuckles turned white. "I haven't stolen anything!"

The two officers ignored me. The uniforms they wore were different from the Russian police officers', and when they spoke to each other, it was in Polish. I had grown leery of the Poles in town and tried to keep my distance, but their population continued to grow. Tears fell from my eyes onto the cell floor, and I shook uncontrollably.

"Where is Ruth Kohn?" I asked nervously. "I need to speak to her."

"Who?" one of the officers asked, looking at me at last.

"Ruth Kohn," I said again. "She works with the Russians in the local police offices."

The men regarded each other for a moment before answering, "They are not in charge here anymore."

My knees went weak, and I fell to the floor. Bile rose in my throat as my heart raced. "My husband," I begged weakly. "At least inform him I'm here. Please. He'll come for me."

The men had turned their backs on me once more, sorting through papers on the desk by the door and talking to each other in low tones. It was like I had ceased to exist. Despair washed over me as I pushed in desperation against the solid bars. One of the men glanced at me over his shoulder and laughed at my pathetic attempt, then they gathered a pile of folders and left the room together.

I crawled to the corner and hugged my knees to my chest, rocking back and forth. The sudden silence in the room only heightened my panic. Even in the camps, I had never been alone. I leaned against the wall, my hands shaking as I stared at them. I tried to calm my breathing, to think rationally, but a now-familiar and overwhelming panic gripped me. Would the officers send word to Harry? If not, how would he know I was here? How long would I be by myself with my tortured thoughts?

The hours dragged, and the feeling of isolation, of being totally and utterly alone, became unbearable. I was suffocating. The silence in the small room was so complete that I heard the sound of my pounding heart. I felt my pulse in my ears. Despite the cold in the cell, sweat ran down my face and dampened my hair. I was thirsty, my throat so dry that I swallowed compulsively.

When I closed my eyes, I was transported to the camps. I remembered how Gutcha and I had clung to each other as we were loaded onto trains outside Olkusz. I remembered the darkness that surrounded us when the doors were shut and locked. I remembered the cries, whimpers, and muttered prayers as I held on to my cousin for dear life. I remembered being packed body to body, sleeping standing up, leaning against each other, as small vermin ran over our feet. I remembered the stench in the car and the hunger that gnawed at my stomach and the ache in every limb as we were transported to our fate.

My eyes flew open and I gasped, shaking my head. "*No, no, no, no, no,*" I moaned as the emptiness around me, so different from the crowded train cars, yet just as frightening, threatened to pull my sanity under like quicksand. When I thought I would finally go mad, the door across the room opened, and a familiar face peered in.

"Ruth!" I cried, crawling to the bars again and reaching out for her.

"Sarah!" she exclaimed, rushing to the cell and kneeling before me, taking my outstretched hand in hers. "What happened?"

"I don't know!" I sobbed. "These men came to the door and told me I was being arrested. They said I stole Luna. I didn't, Ruth! She was a gift! But they wouldn't listen to me! I don't understand!"

Ruth looked at me, anxiously shaking her head. "There is much debate right now about who is in charge," she said quietly. "The office is in a state of chaos. The Russians are transitioning authority to the Poles, but it's messy, and there's been little to no record keeping. And the Poles want people arrested for taking property they think belongs to them."

"But I didn't steal Luna!" I insisted.

"I know, Sarah." She sighed, biting her lip. "There's no order anymore. I want to help, but I'm just a secretary. What can I do?"

"Can you let Harry know?" I implored. "Can you tell him where I am? He'll know what to do."

Ruth nodded and squeezed my hand reassuringly. "We'll get you out," she whispered back. "Don't worry."

At one point, a Polish officer came back holding a tray. I was lying on the cot, staring at the ceiling, trying in vain to calm my nerves. Waves of nausea rolled over me. Shadows were growing in the corners of the room as evening approached, and I dreaded when night would come and I'd be alone in the dark. If that happened, I thought I'd surely lose my mind. I raised my head slightly when I heard the door open and glanced at the officer. He walked to the cell, pulled out a set of keys, and unlocked the door. He slid the tray onto the floor before quickly closing and locking the door again. He wouldn't meet my eyes.

I didn't move from the cot. After he left, I spared a look at the tray, at the tin cup that held water and the hunk of stale bread and congealed stew and felt my stomach churn. I rolled onto my side to stare at the wall. I pictured Harry's face and cried silently, longing for the protection of his strong arms, drowning in my misery. Suddenly, I felt a small movement in the pit of my stomach, a tiny, indistinct flutter. I sat up, crossing my hands over my abdomen. Like being thrown a life buoy, I realized with a growing sense of awe that I wasn't alone. I had the small life growing inside me. I stared at my lap, wondering if I had imagined the little somersault in my stomach. "Do it again," I whispered into the dark. I began to hum a remembered lullaby from my childhood, closing my eyes and massaging my middle, feeling the small bump hidden beneath my clothes. A certain calm settled over me, and I held on to the fact that I wasn't alone, that I would never be alone again, as I fell into an exhausted sleep.

A sound woke me sometime later. I blinked in the darkness, unsure at first where I was. Then the memory of what had happened returned, and I sat up, fear gripping me once more. At first all I saw were the silhouettes of two or three people standing on the other side of the bars. I crept to the far corner of the cot, trembling. Someone struck a match, and then I saw Harry's face in the light of a candle.

Relief washed over me. "Harry!" I sobbed, too weak to move.

His face was angrier than I had ever seen it, and for a moment I worried he was mad at me. But then it softened into a look of pure tenderness, and he whispered, "Oh, Sarah, I've been so worried!" He ran to the door of the cell and began to shake it with a terrible ferocity.

"Shhh!" a voice huffed, and I saw Rubin step forward. Beside Rubin, I saw Ruth, her face pale even in the darkness. Rubin took the candle from Harry and shielded the flame with his hand. "We don't want to be found out," he hissed. Harry reached out a hand to Ruth, and she nodded and placed something shiny in his palm. He thrust the key into the lock, throwing open the door to my cell.

"Come quick, Sarah!" he whispered urgently, and I didn't need to be told twice.

I ran into his waiting arms.

Forty-Nine

We moved cautiously through the empty main office of the police station to the front door. Harry kept his arm around me the entire time. I wondered how late it was. I was unnerved by the silence and emptiness of the large room, weaving through a maze of desks and chairs. Closed doors led off the office to other rooms with cells, and I kept expecting a guard or officer to walk through and catch us. Surely they didn't leave prisoners alone at night? Had I been the only prisoner?

Once outside, we ran through the cold, dark city streets, sticking to the alleys, avoiding the main roads where streetlamps shone in the early-morning darkness. Snow fell silently from heavy clouds, blanketing our heads and shoulders and concealing our footsteps. We parted ways with Ruth just outside our home. "Stay with Sam and Sophie," Rubin told her. "Do not come into work tomorrow. Understand?"

She nodded and ran to Sam's door. I saw a light on beneath their drawn window shade. I wanted to see Sam, but Rubin urged us up the stairs to our own apartment. I wasn't able fully to catch my breath until we were safely inside. "Lock the door behind me, Harry," Rubin said in a low, serious tone. "Whatever you do, don't leave the house. And don't open the door for anyone. Not for Sam or Sophie or Ruth or Erna or Pinky. I will be back tonight. You'll know it's me by my knock."

Harry nodded. "Be safe, Rubin," he said, extending a hand to his friend while hugging me close to his side with his other arm. Rubin stepped forward and wrapped us both in his large embrace.

"Remember what I said," Rubin whispered as he stepped outside our door, turning up the collar of his coat and pulling his hat low on his head. Harry nodded and closed the door, turning the lock securely in place and pulling the chain across.

Once we were alone, I collapsed onto our bed and began to sob. Harry sat beside me, holding me, his emotions raging. He swore under his breath and ran his hand over his face. His cheeks were bright red from cold and anger, his eyes bloodshot. "I'm sorry, Harry," I whispered, trying to stop my tears. "Don't be mad."

"When I came home and you weren't here," he started, but then his jaw clenched and he stopped. I lifted my chin and saw the fear in his eyes. I reached up and ran my hand along the stubble of his jaw, wanting to wipe the grim expression from his face. "I'm all right," I whispered.

"I called for you over and over," he said, "and when you didn't answer, I didn't know what to do. It was just like with . . . like with Estella."

I let out a breath, realizing then what he had been through as well. I wrapped my arms around him and whispered, "I'm so sorry, Harry. I didn't mean to frighten you." He laid his head on mine and breathed softly into my hair, "I'm just so relieved you're home."

"How did you know where I was?"

"Ruth found me. She came to the apartment shortly after I got home and found me frantic. She told me what had happened. I was ready to march down to the jail and demand they release you, but Ruth stopped me. She told me that they would never listen to me and that she had stolen a key to both the main office and your prison cell before she left the police station. She knew we had to go back for you once everyone had left. I didn't know what to do with myself in the hours until then. I couldn't imagine what you were going through."

"Ruth did that for me? Isn't that dangerous?"

When Harry didn't answer, I knew the answer was yes. I shook my head in disbelief. "Oh, Ruth," I whispered. "So that's why Rubin didn't want her to go to work today?" Harry nodded, his lips stretched in a grim line.

"I always knew you would come," I said. "That kept me strong." He pulled away and looked at me somberly. Then he leaned forward and kissed my forehead. "I won't lose you too, Sarah," he whispered, his arms tight around me. Together, we lay on the bed fully clothed, falling asleep in each other's embrace as the sun began to rise.

We spent the day barricaded inside. Harry paced the rooms, peeking furtively through the drawn curtains every hour to glance at the street outside.

"Why can't we leave?" I asked. "Isn't it over?"

"No," Harry said firmly. "When they discover you've escaped, Sarah, they'll come back for you. It's a matter of time."

I felt the blood drain from my limbs and I grasped a chair to keep from falling. "I can't go back to jail," I whispered, and Harry rushed to my side. "You won't, Sarah. I won't let them take you. I didn't mean to frighten you. I'll never let anyone hurt you again."

He spoke the words so forcefully that I wanted to believe him. Every time the floorboards creaked or the wind rattled the windows, I jumped. Every vehicle that drove past on the street outside caused my chest to tighten in panic. We barely ate. We barely spoke. I was sure that at any moment, another angry knock would shake our door.

As the day turned to evening, the apartment grew dark, but we didn't dare turn on any lights. Harry moved to the window again and looked outside at the street below. "It's empty," he said, his shoulders relaxing slightly. "I think we're safe for the night."

I slumped in my seat at the kitchen table. "You look so tired, darling," he said, coming to my side and putting a hand to my cheek. "I know this has been an ordeal. Go rest and get your strength back. When Rubin returns tonight, we'll know more."

I let him lead me back to bed without a word. I was exhausted, but part of me knew it wasn't just because of what I'd been through. I longed to go back to the day before, when I had almost told him about the baby. I wanted to see his face light up with the news, with the promise of a child he could love as much as the one he had lost. I wanted to give him that joy, that gift.

"Harry," I said softly as he propped a pillow behind my head and sat beside me, holding my hand. "I have something to tell you."

"What is it, my love?" His brow knit in concern, but I smiled and put my hand on his cheek.

"I've known for a little while now, but I wanted to be sure."

"Be sure of what?"

"Harry, I'm going to have a baby."

For a moment, Harry stared at me blankly. Then his eyes widened in astonishment. His mouth opened, but the words were frozen in his throat. I nodded, reaching for his hand and placing it on my belly. "We are going to have a baby. I want to give you a son, Harry. A beautiful baby boy. I want that more than anything."

His hand lovingly stroked my stomach, wordless. Then he leaned forward and laid his head on my middle, kissing the small bump. My fingers entwined themselves in his blond hair. When he looked up at me, tears rimmed his eyes.

"Really?" he whispered.

I nodded again. "I want to name him after my father," I said, imagining the baby boy I was now certain would enter our lives. "And after your son."

"After Hirsch," Harry whispered, nodding, resting his head on my stomach once more and holding me close. We lay like that for a few wonderful moments, and I thought I felt again the small flutter deep inside.

"Are you happy?" I asked, wanting to be sure. He sat up and cupped my face in his hands. When he spoke, his words were choked with emotion. "You've made me happier than I can ever say. Thank you, Sarah. I love you. I love you more than anything."

He bent his head to mine, and our lips touched, softly at first, then more passionately. For the moment, we forgot everything else, all the terror of the past two days and all the uncertainty of what was to come. We fell into each other once more, losing ourselves in one another.

Rubin returned that evening. He gave three short knocks in succession, followed by a fourth knock. Harry moved to the door and quickly let him in. I was immediately concerned by the look on his usually jovial face. His lips were turned down in a frown, and he had dark circles under his eyes. He was dressed in dark clothes and tall black boots. He began to unwrap a scarf from his neck, snow falling into a low mound at his feet.

"I tried everything in my power," he said, "but it's no good."

"What do you mean?" Harry asked as I handed Rubin a glass of warm tea.

"You don't happen to have anything stronger?" he half-joked, and Harry went to pour him a shot of whiskey. We moved into the small living room, where the curtains were still drawn over the windows.

"They are looking to make examples out of people," Rubin said once Harry and I had settled onto the sofa, our hands clasped. "There is a lot of unrest since the Poles have taken over power. The town is now under their jurisdiction. My superiors are helping aid the transition. And some of those in authority aren't happy to find that . . ." His voice trailed off, his face growing red.

"To find that the Jews have moved in," Harry said bitterly.

Rubin ran a hand through his hair, an apologetic look in his eyes. "I don't agree with it, Harry, but, yes. You're correct."

"Do we not have a right to try to get back what *we* lost as well?" Harry demanded. "To try to make a future for ourselves?"

I squeezed his hand, hoping to calm him. I could see the rage on his face.

"Yes, of course you do," Rubin said. "But, Harry, I don't think this is where you'll find that future."

"What do you mean?"

"Look," Rubin said, straddling a chair and regarding us soberly. "This is my fault. I wanted to give you both a gift, so I purchased the calf from a Polish farmer. I should have suspected his intentions were less than honorable. He asked why I wanted the cow as I'm a soldier, after all, and I told him about you, Sarah. How I wanted to give you a wedding gift since you'd both lost so much." Rubin glanced at me with eyes that begged forgiveness. "After we made the purchase, he went to the Polish police and reported the cow stolen. I've tried to explain that this farmer is the real criminal, that he took my money in exchange for the cow, that you are innocent, but they won't listen. They just won't listen. This is not an isolated episode. There was even an incident at the local Jewish committee office by a number of returning Poles."

"Sam was right," I said softly, staring down at my hands and shaking my head in disbelief. "He always knew this was going to happen. He said we needed to protect ourselves."

We sat in silence for a moment before Rubin turned to Harry and said, "I have received intelligence that the Russians and Americans are in talks over control of Europe. This part of Poland, now that it is Polish again, will most certainly fall under the Communist regime. It may not be easy for many going forward." Again, he looked at us imploringly, the unspoken words hanging in the air—it may not be easy for *Jews*. "Already they are putting up blocks, preventing people from moving easily across borders. Once the borders are closed, it might be impossible to leave."

Rubin knelt before us. "You must go tonight." It wasn't a suggestion. "They will be back for Sarah by morning. This time the charges will be more severe since she escaped. We cannot delay."

My heart thudded in my chest, and I wrapped my arms around my stomach protectively. Harry sat beside me, lost in thought. Part of me wanted to scream, "Yes, Harry! We must go!" But I couldn't find my voice.

"Where will we go?" Harry finally asked.

"I need to get you to the American side of Germany," Rubin said. "It's the least I can do for getting you into this situation. I was drunk and stupid. Now let me help you. I have a contact at a displaced persons camp in Nuremberg—"

"A *camp*?" I whispered. The word sent a chill up my spine. I looked around the small apartment I had so painstakingly turned into a home for Harry and me—the home where our child was conceived. I remembered, as though it were another lifetime, leaving my family's home in Olkusz, holding my mother's hand as she told me not to look back. I wondered if we would ever stop running.

"I know the idea of starting over is hard, but it's safer for you there," Rubin said sympathetically. "I don't know what's going to happen, but Poland is not your home."

"What about Pinky and the business?" Harry muttered under his breath.

"I will help them cross the border as well," Rubin pledged. "You will be together in Nuremberg."

"And Sam?" I pleaded.

"I'll do everything I can."

"What about Ruth?" I asked, remembering her pale face in the darkness as she handed Harry the key she had stolen.

Rubin looked at me with a sad expression. "She's already been relocated. When they realized you were missing, they turned their attention first to who might have helped you. In their eyes, that's the greater crime. Once they realized the keys were stolen, it wasn't hard for them to figure out who was responsible."

Rubin's words left me cold. I couldn't fathom Ruth's bravery. "She risked her job and her safety for me?" I asked incredulously, feeling so helpless and unworthy. "Why would she do that? We owe her so much," I whispered. "How can we ever repay her?"

"How do you know all this?" Harry asked Rubin.

Rubin downed the rest of his whiskey before answering, "I have my ways."

We were silent, the gravity of the situation weighing heavily on us all. Harry glanced at me, and I saw how pale he looked. I squeezed his hand. "Please, Harry," I said, "I think we should listen to him. Wherever we go, at least we'll be together." I placed his hand on my stomach and he met my eyes. Then he nodded thoughtfully.

"Yes," he said finally. "We'll go with you, Rubin."

Fifty

Polish–German border, late January 1946

We left in the middle of the night, crossing the border to the American side of Germany in a gray predawn. Harry sat behind Rubin on the motorbike, and I sat in the small attached sidecar, surrounded by our few bags and belongings. I wrapped my arms around my stomach, hugging my most precious cargo close. The moon was obscured behind thick, dark clouds, and snow fell silently on our shoulders, filling the tracks made by the tires. I shivered in my seat, terrified that at any minute, we would be stopped, and I would be arrested and taken back to jail.

When we reached the border, Rubin quietly communicated with the guards, showing them papers and gesturing to us as we watched. Tendrils of our breath rose into the cold night air. I took in the red, white, and blue flags posted on either side of the border gate, watching them ripple in the cold wind. Their white stars shone brighter than those in the sky. The guards at the border watched Harry and I as they spoke to Rubin, and I was sure they would turn us away. But as we were waved across and Rubin revved the engine, I closed my eyes and relaxed against the seat. I pictured my child, growing up safe and sound, apart from the horrors we had witnessed, on soil untainted by hate and persecution. Maybe soon—maybe *now*—we would find home.

Epilogue

Cincinnati, Ohio, 2000

I visit my grandmother often. She is a bit of a hoarder; every tabletop, shelf, nightstand, and counter is covered with souvenirs and trinkets she's collected over her lifetime. A picture of the Rebbe sits on her nightstand next to a photograph of my grandpa Harry. I check on her condo when she's gone for half the year in Israel, spending time on the sunny beaches of Netanya with her cousins and their families. It was there, in Israel, that she came back to life after my grandfather died. It was there, with her cousin Gutcha, that she found happiness again. The day she came home from Israel for the first time, after a year's absence, I hadn't immediately recognized her. She'd waved at us as she walked down the Jetway, her neck adorned in colorful, flowy scarves and her hair dyed a bright red.

"Who is that?" my brother had asked, and I'd blinked and said, "That's Bubbe!"

Gone was the sad, dejected woman I'd remembered; in her place was a giddy, excited woman who hugged me tightly and exclaimed, "Look at you! What a *shayna punim*! My, you have grown!" She had smelled of perfume, and her lipstick left stains on my cheeks. As my mother and I had helped her unpack, she'd moved around the room like a bird in flight, saying over and over, "You should have seen me! Everyone loved me there!"

In the years since, she has settled into her independence, enjoying traveling, shopping, and cooking. We spend a lot of time together. Since she doesn't drive (she told me once that she'd only had her license for a short time—my grandfather had insisted she not drive, that it was too dangerous), I pick her up once a week to take her grocery shopping and out to brunch. Sometimes we come back and watch movies together in her crowded living room. Our favorites are *Crossing Delancey* and *Fiddler on the Roof.* She hosts Shabbat dinners for our family, making matzo balls only she knows how to make, hard as rocks and requiring a fork and knife to cut through—a family favorite.

At my wedding shower, guests were asked to bring a cooking-themed gift accompanied by a favorite recipe. The box my grandmother placed in my hands was large and wrapped in shiny pink paper with white ribbon. I unwrapped a soup pot and ladle and found a VHS tape nestled in tissue paper. As I held it up, my aunt explained that she and my brother had filmed my grandmother making her famous matzo ball soup—she was never strong at writing in English. We played the video and laughed as we watched my grandmother move about her kitchen, talking with her back to the camera, her apron tied around her waist, explaining how she didn't have an actual recipe—it was her mother's soup. She added a pinch of this and a dash of that. And my brother and aunt followed behind her, asking, "What did you just add there, Bubbe? How much salt did you put in? Do you use parsley and carrots? How much oil? And how long do you let the matzo balls sit?" When the tape ended, we all applauded, and my grandmother glowed.

This is the Bubbe I will always remember—the happy, flirty Bubbe. The Bubbe who loves clothes and jewelry and perfume and took me shopping when I was twelve and bought me a leopard print mini-skirt that made my mother gasp. The Bubbe who gossiped about this neighbor or that family member. The Bubbe who spoke of characters from her favorite soap operas as if they were real, living beings and read the *Star* or *National Enquirer*.

One day when I visit, I stop and look at the photographs framed on her wall. I gaze at the images, the pictures of myself as a child, my brother and cousin, photographs taken at family gatherings and holidays, and, most recent of all, my wedding portrait. I smile at my favorite picture of my grandmother and grandfather kissing in their backyard, their arms thrown around each other, framed by a dense woods. But mixed with these are faded black-and-white photos of family members I don't know.

I had learned over the years how my grandmother had lost most of her family in the war, all but her brother Sam, who now lived with his family in Kansas. But I never knew the details. A memory surfaces as I survey the pictures, and I turn to my grandmother curiously. "Bubbe," I say, sitting beside her on her plush sofa and sinking into the soft cushions. "You once mentioned the name Esther. Who is she?"

My grandmother grows pensive, and I see a flash of something in her dark brown eyes before she glances down at her lap. "I'm sorry," I say quickly. I know enough of her past to know she's experienced things I could never imagine. I know she is still haunted by these memories, these ghosts. I remember all too well the depression she suffered after my grandfather died. I didn't want to bring her more sadness or remind her of that time.

But she looks at me and smiles and settles against the sofa herself. She puts her arm around me and I lean against her soft body, so like a warm pillow. "Let me tell you about my sister," she says in the thick accent that I love. And she draws my hand into hers and begins to tell me her story.

Author's Note

When I think of my grandmother, I think of her hands. They were always soft and smooth, the tips of her fingers plump as miniature pillows. My grandmother took pride in her hands. She scheduled weekly trips to the manicurist, so her nails were always buffed and polished to perfection. When she washed dishes, she wore yellow rubber gloves. I had never seen anyone wear gloves except in Palmolive commercials. Lotions and creams lined her bathroom counter and bedside table. Large rings adorned her fingers in shades of turquoise and opal white, emerald and ruby red. On the many occasions when we sat and talked, she would take my arm, draw it across her lap, and run her fingertips along the soft inside of my arm, wrist to elbow. And she would hum a quiet tune, perhaps from her childhood.

Then the words would come. She enjoyed words, even though she rarely read and spent most of her time watching television. She often gossiped about this neighbor or that family member. She always reported something she'd seen on the evening news or the morning talk shows. She even spoke of characters from her favorite soap operas as if they were real, living beings. She would argue stories she'd read from the *Star* or *National Enquirer*. She was not cultured or educated, but occasionally, her words were heavy with history. To me, she spoke of a world long forgotten: she spoke of war and loss and family members whose ghosts still lurked in the shadows and dark corners of her home. When I looked into her brown eyes, I saw in their reflection the small apartment where she'd lived with her family, in the Polish *shtetl* where she grew to be a young woman.

Before taking the name of Sala in a crowded immigration office on Ellis Island, she was known as Chaya Sarah—or more affectionately by her family as Vilda Chaya, the "Wild One." To me, she was Grandma Sala, or Bubbe. And on one of those afternoons, I sat down beside my grandmother with a small camcorder in hand and asked her to tell me the story of her life.

It is this interview, almost two hours in length, that I used as inspiration for *What She Lost.* I attempted to stay as true to my grandmother's experiences as possible, filling in the gaps with research and adding my own memories here and there. I hope that this story honors the memory not only of those in my family who perished but of the countless others who lost their lives in the Holocaust. Your lives had meaning. You are not forgotten.

Acknowledgments

I couldn't have written *What She Lost* without help from many individuals. I thank Rachel, my editor, for her wonderful feedback and advice and all my beta readers for their encouragement and keen eyes. And the fellow pea in my pod—you know who you are!

Thanks to my publisher, Holly, and all those at Cynren Press for treating my manuscript with such love and care. I'm proud to be part of the Cynren family.

I have to say a special and heartfelt thank-you to my two wonderful grandmothers—one whose story of hardship and perseverance always inspired me, and one whose generosity of love and spirit always nourished me. I'm blessed to have you both in my life to this day.

Deepest thanks to my mom and dad, whose unconditional, selfless love has been a lifelong gift. They always allowed me to follow my dreams and believe that anything is possible.

And of course, to Stefan, Alexis, and Rebecca, thanks for blessing my life. You have my heart always and forever!

CPSIA information can be obtained
at www.ICGtesting.com
Printed in the USA
FSHW020013210919
62218FS